HARLEQUIN®
Ginger Blossom™

harlequin pink:

A Prince Needs a Princess

written by **Barbara McMahon**   art by **Reiko Kishida**

HARLEQUIN®

TORONTO • NEW YORK • LONDON
AMSTERDAM • PARIS • SYDNEY • HAMBURG
STOCKHOLM • ATHENS • TOKYO • MILAN • MADRID
PRAGUE • WARSAW • BUDAPEST • AUCKLAND

GN
McM
V. 3

Translation by: Ikoi Hiroe

Lettering by: Michael David Thomas

ISBN-13: 978-0-373-18002-8
ISBN-10:   0-373-18002-0

HARLEQUIN PINK: A PRINCE NEEDS A PRINCESS

Harlequin Pink: A Prince Needs a Princess © MMVI by Harlequin Enterprises
Limited. First published in Japan by Ohzora Publishing Co., by arrangement
with Harlequin K.K. under the title *The Tycoon Prince.* Copyright © MMV by
Reiko Kishida. Adapted from the original novel *The Tycoon Prince,* published
by Harlequin Enterprises Limited by arrangement with Harlequin Books S.A.
Copyright © MMIII by Barbara McMahon.

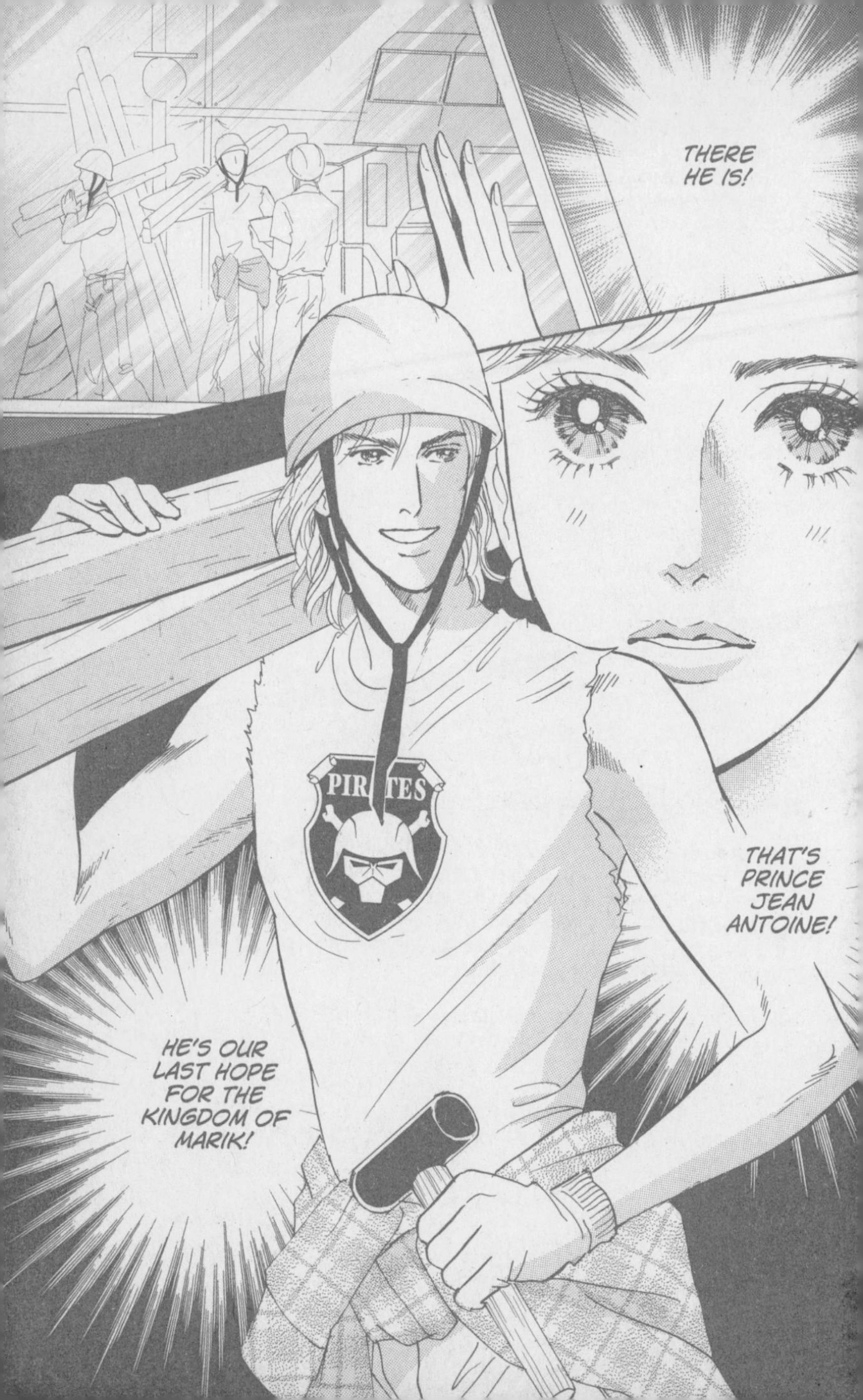
THERE HE IS!
THAT'S PRINCE JEAN ANTOINE!
HE'S OUR LAST HOPE FOR THE KINGDOM OF MARIK!

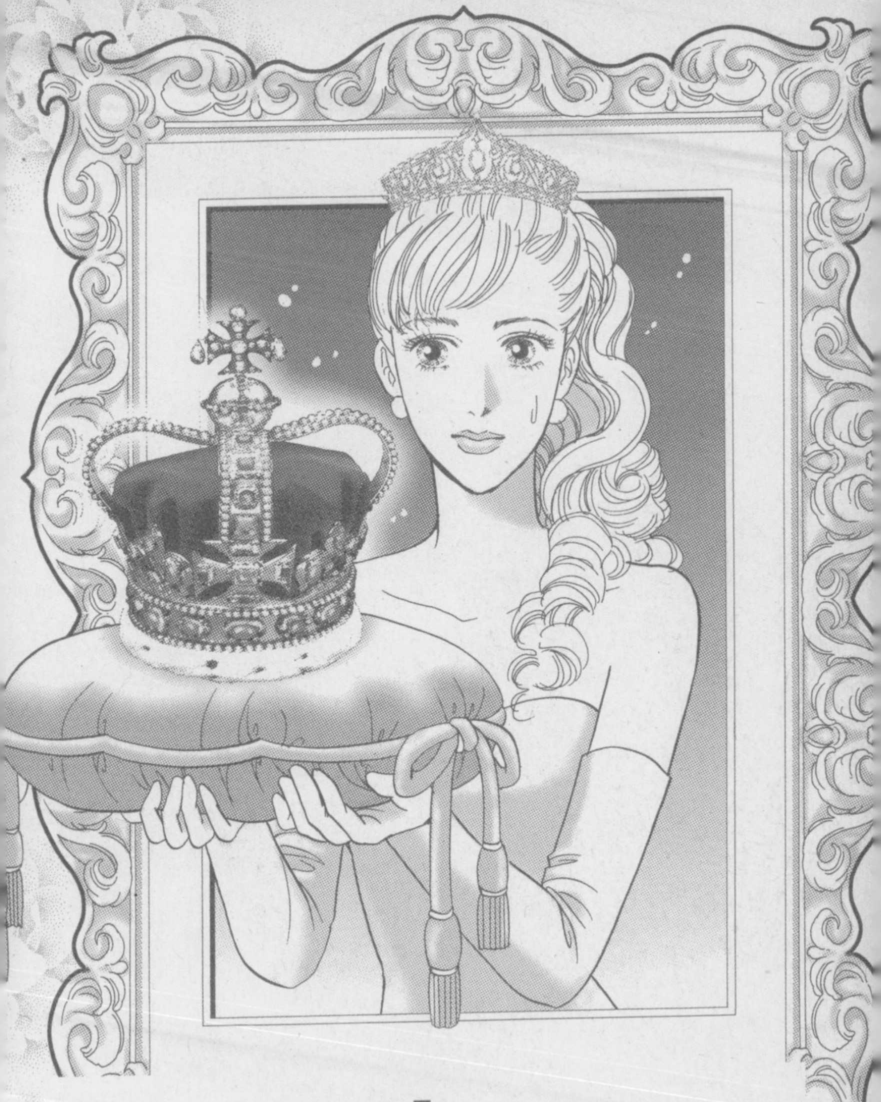

harlequin pink:
A PRINCE NEEDS A PRINCESS

Adapted from the original novel by Barbara McMahon

Art by Reiko Kishida

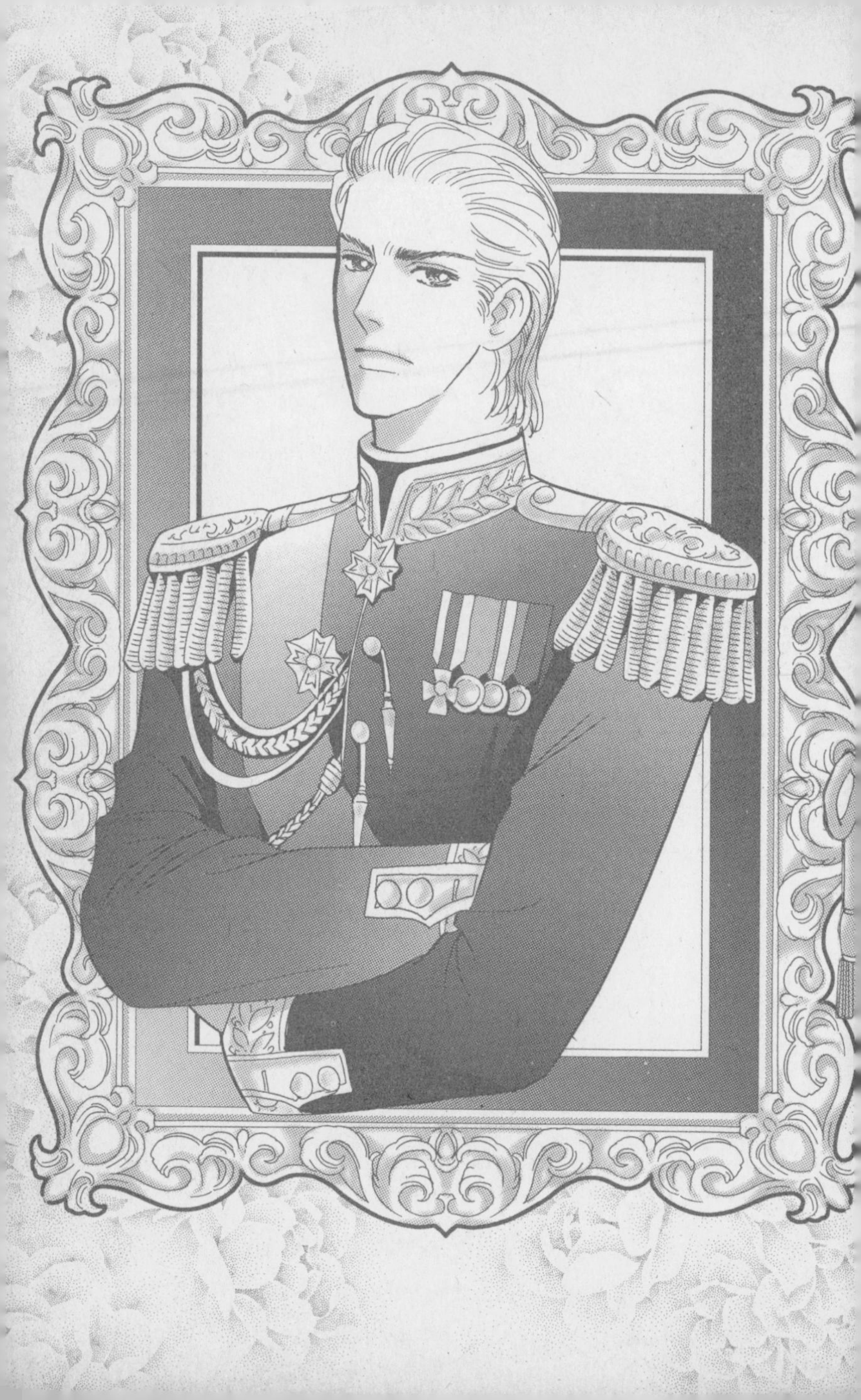

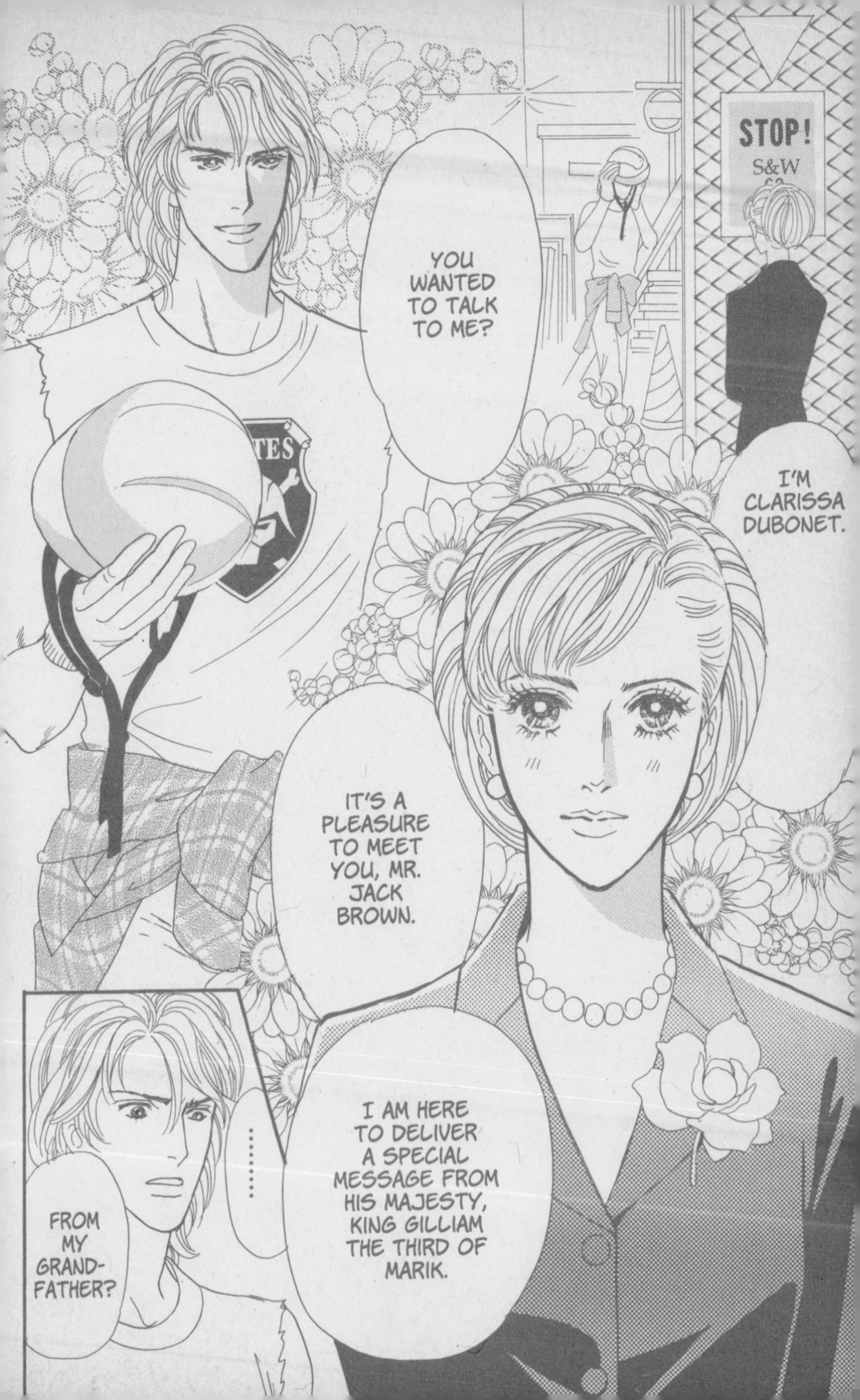
STOP!
S&W
YOU WANTED TO TALK TO ME?
I'M CLARISSA DUBONET.
IT'S A PLEASURE TO MEET YOU, MR. JACK BROWN.
I AM HERE TO DELIVER A SPECIAL MESSAGE FROM HIS MAJESTY, KING GILLIAM THE THIRD OF MARIK.
......
FROM MY GRAND-FATHER?

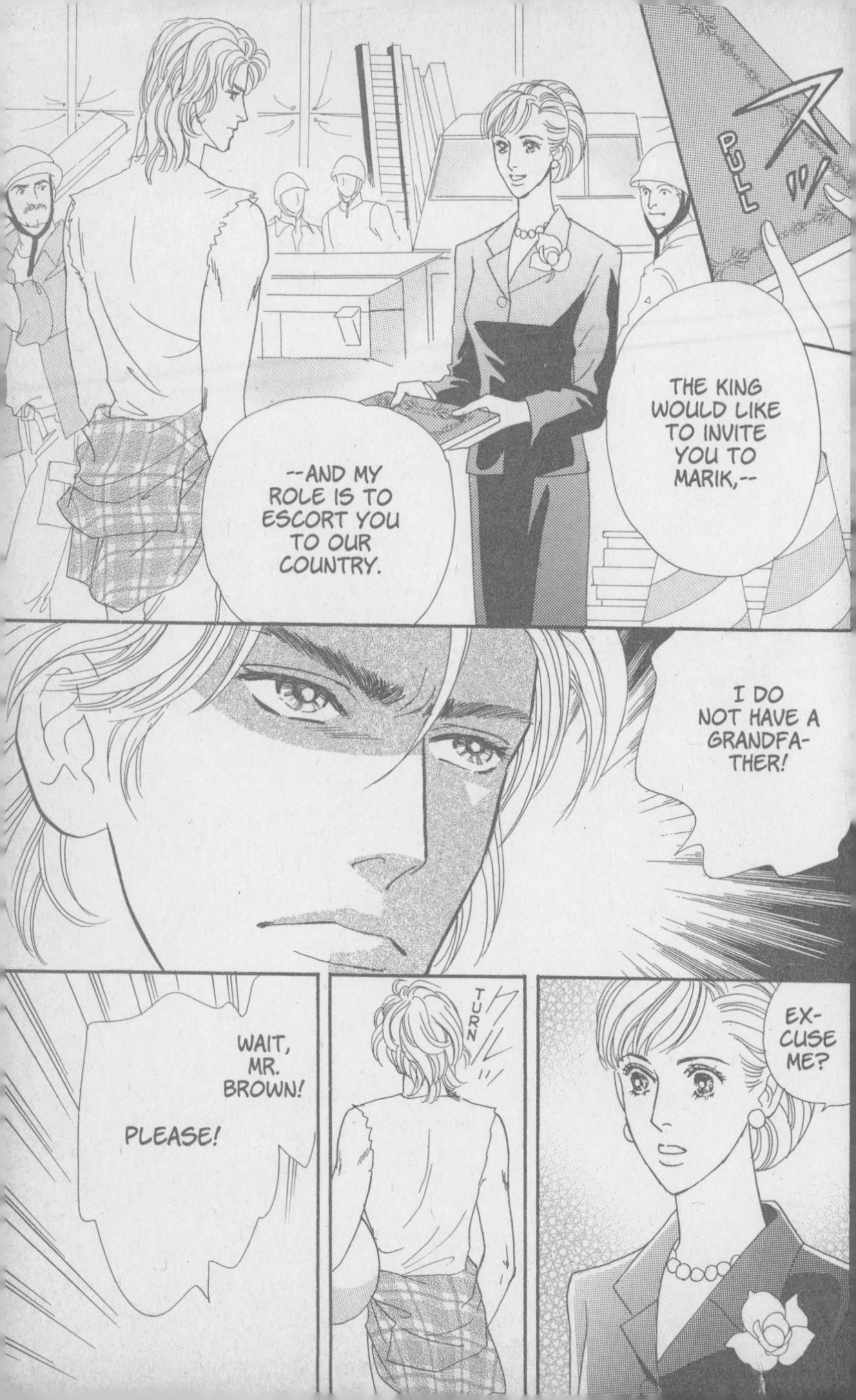
PULL
THE KING WOULD LIKE TO INVITE YOU TO MARIK,--
--AND MY ROLE IS TO ESCORT YOU TO OUR COUNTRY.
I DO NOT HAVE A GRANDFATHER!
EXCUSE ME?
TURN
WAIT, MR. BROWN!
PLEASE!

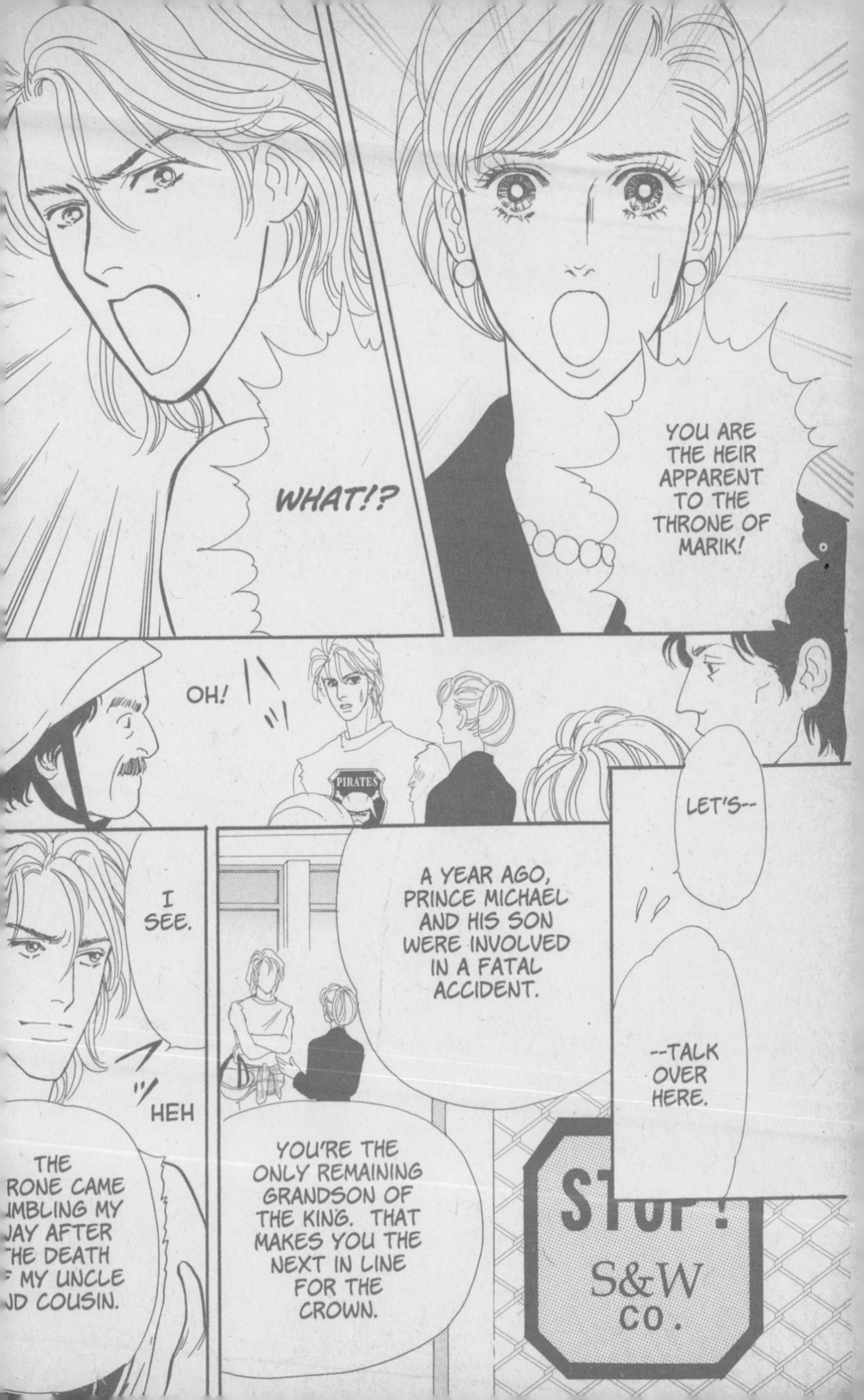
YOU ARE THE HEIR APPARENT TO THE THRONE OF MARIK!
WHAT!?
LET'S--
OH!
--TALK OVER HERE.
A YEAR AGO, PRINCE MICHAEL AND HIS SON WERE INVOLVED IN A FATAL ACCIDENT.
YOU'RE THE ONLY REMAINING GRANDSON OF THE KING. THAT MAKES YOU THE NEXT IN LINE FOR THE CROWN.
S&W CO.
I SEE.
HEH
THE RONE CAME MBLING MY JAY AFTER HE DEATH F MY UNCLE JD COUSIN.

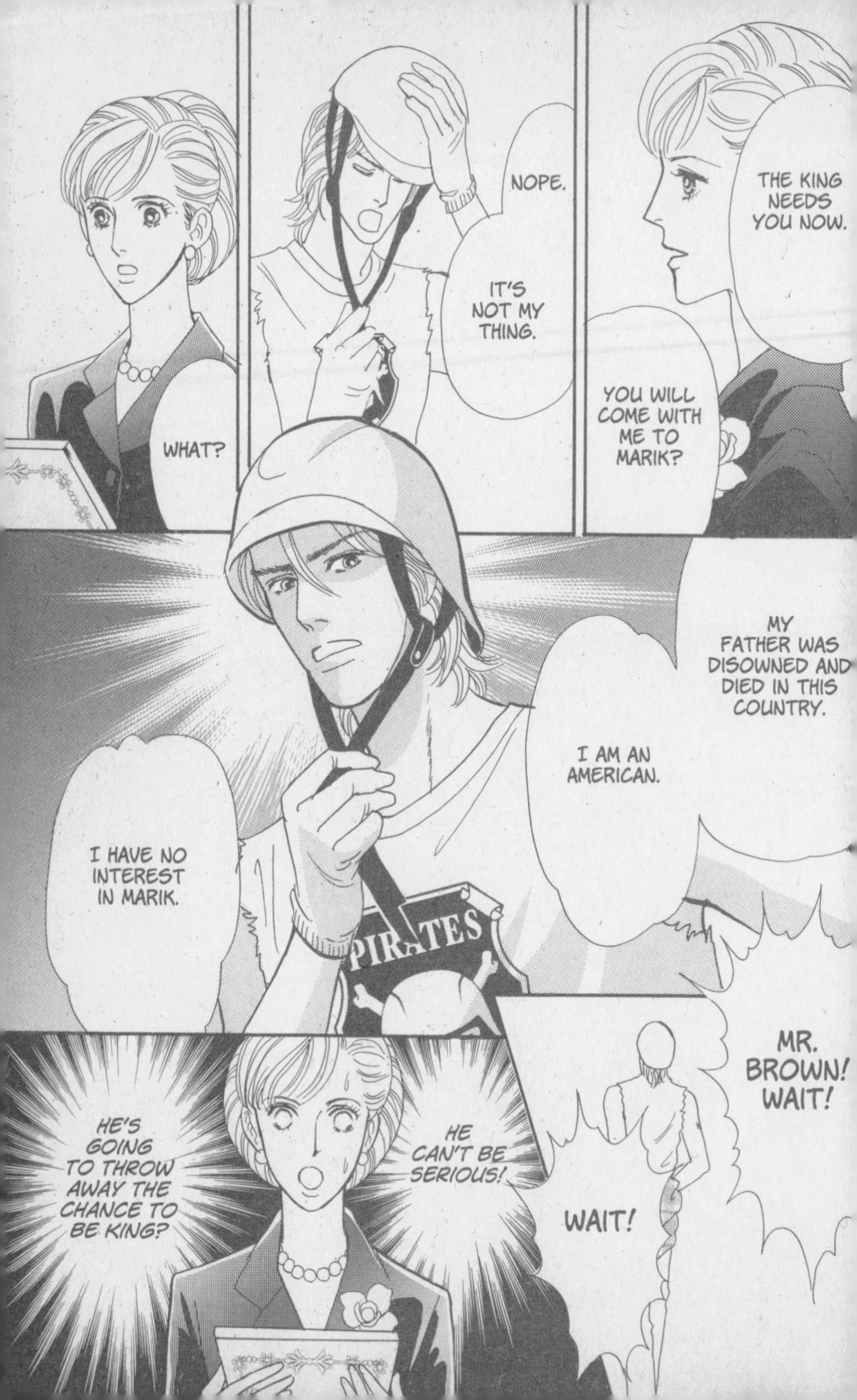
THE KING NEEDS YOU NOW.
YOU WILL COME WITH ME TO MARIK?
NOPE.
IT'S NOT MY THING.
WHAT?
MY FATHER WAS DISOWNED AND DIED IN THIS COUNTRY.
I AM AN AMERICAN.
I HAVE NO INTEREST IN MARIK.
PIRATES
MR. BROWN! WAIT!
WAIT!
HE CAN'T BE SERIOUS!
HE'S GOING TO THROW AWAY THE CHANCE TO BE KING?

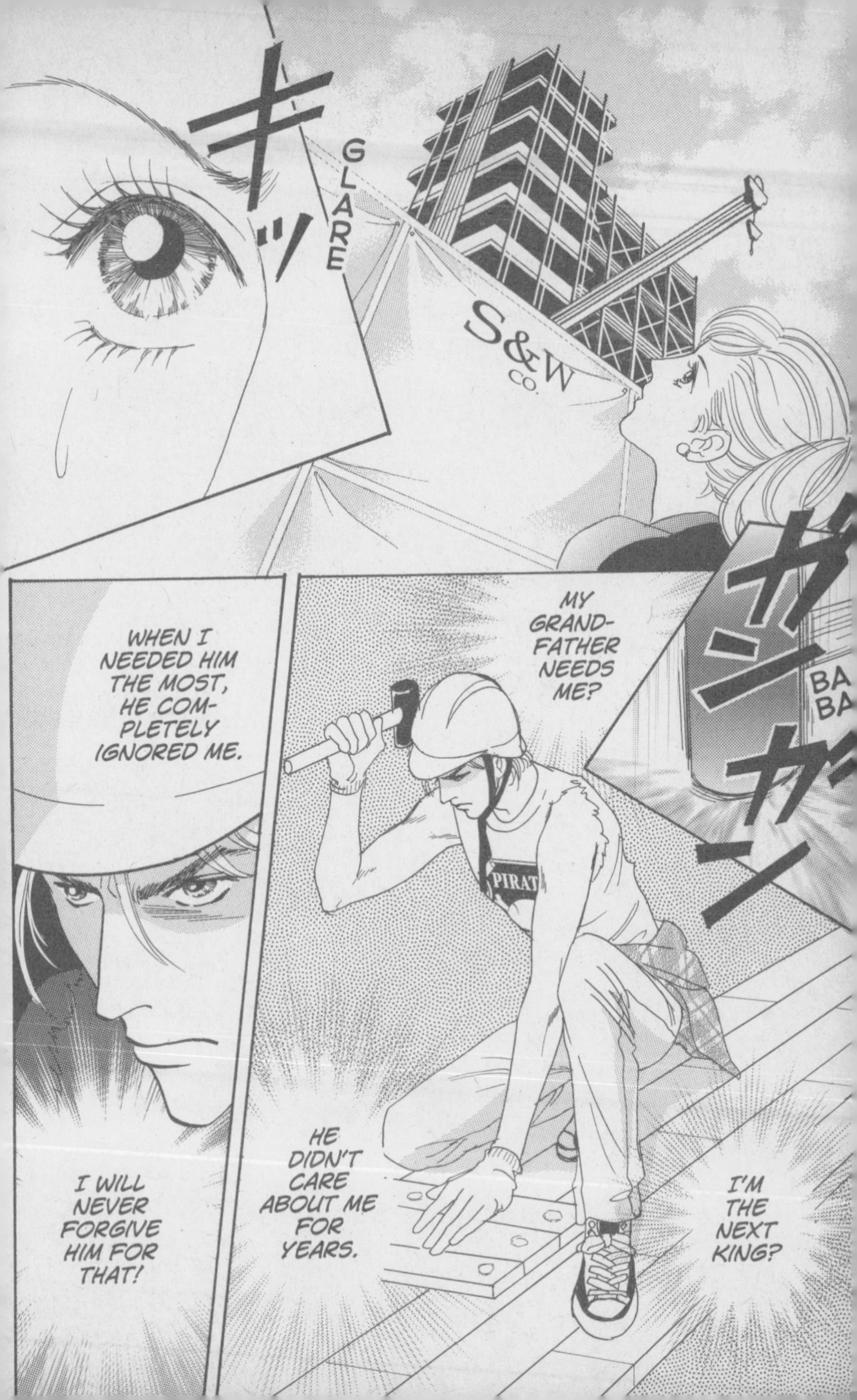
キッ
GLARE
S&W CO.
ガシャーン
BA
BA
MY GRANDFATHER NEEDS ME?
I'M THE NEXT KING?
HE DIDN'T CARE ABOUT ME FOR YEARS.
WHEN I NEEDED HIM THE MOST, HE COMPLETELY IGNORED ME.
I WILL NEVER FORGIVE HIM FOR THAT!

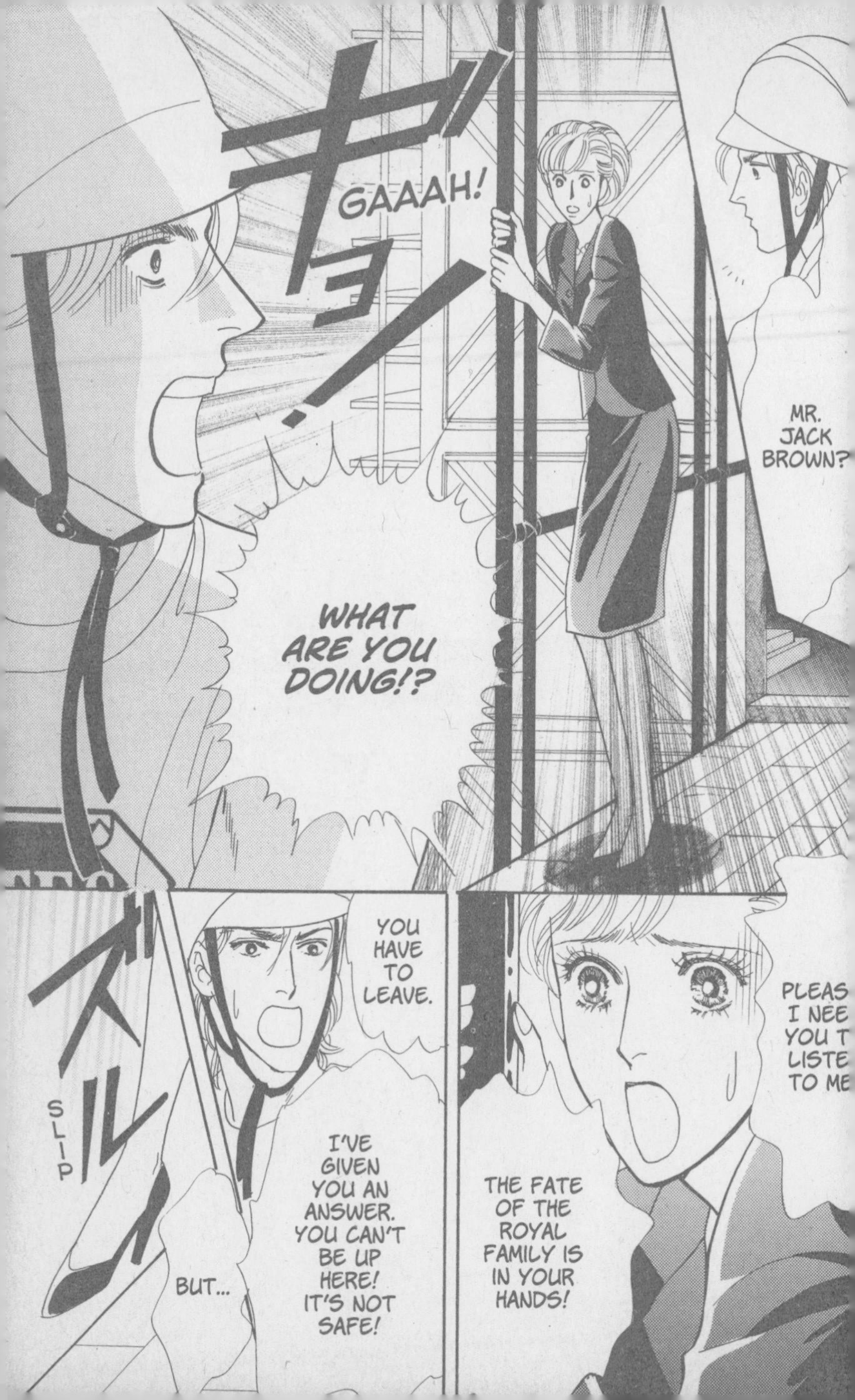
MR. JACK BROWN?
GAAAH!
WHAT ARE YOU DOING!?
PLEAS I NEE YOU T LISTE TO ME
THE FATE OF THE ROYAL FAMILY IS IN YOUR HANDS!
YOU HAVE TO LEAVE.
I'VE GIVEN YOU AN ANSWER. YOU CAN'T BE UP HERE! IT'S NOT SAFE!
BUT...
SLIP

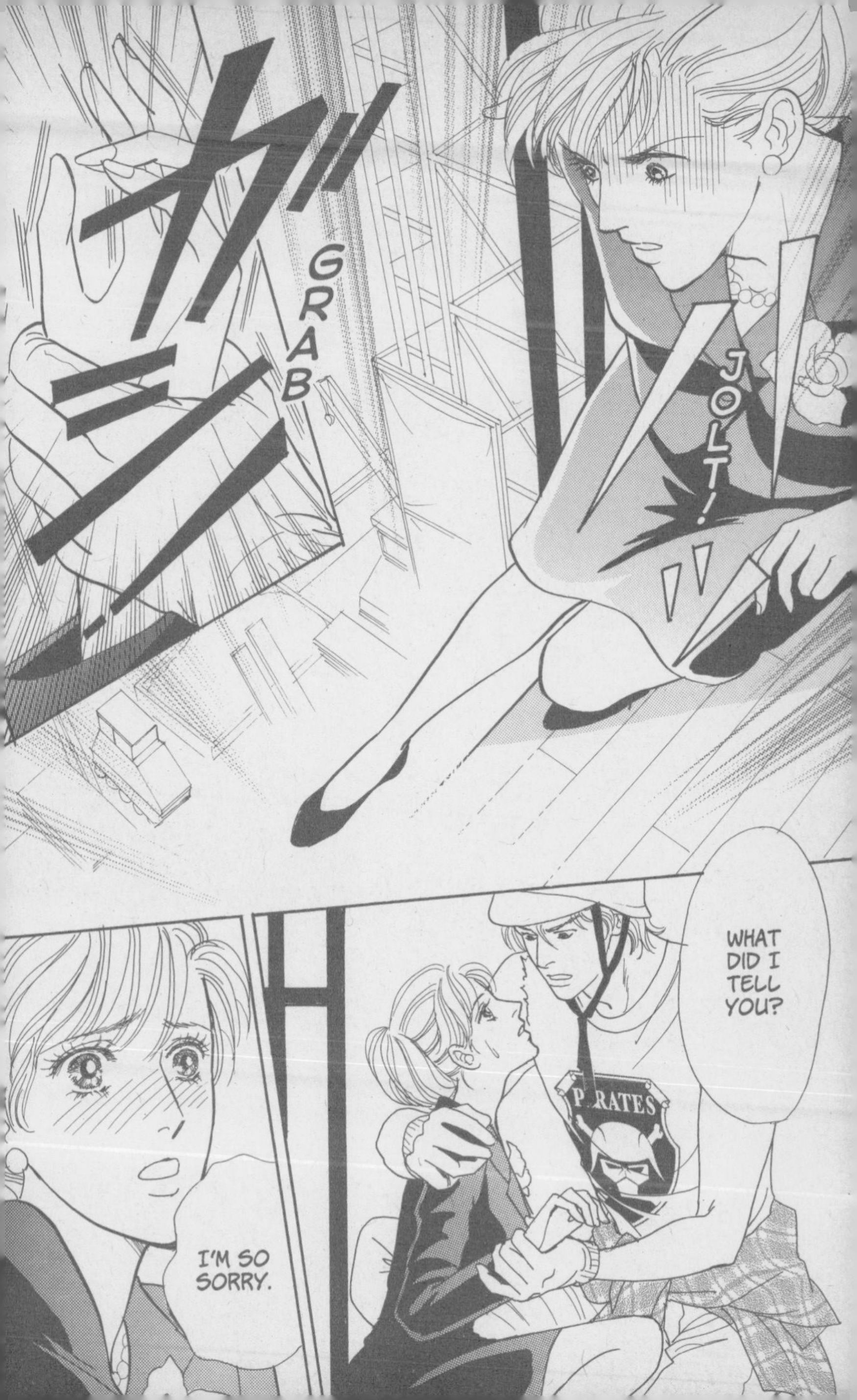
JOLT!
GRAB
WHAT DID I TELL YOU?
I'M SO SORRY.

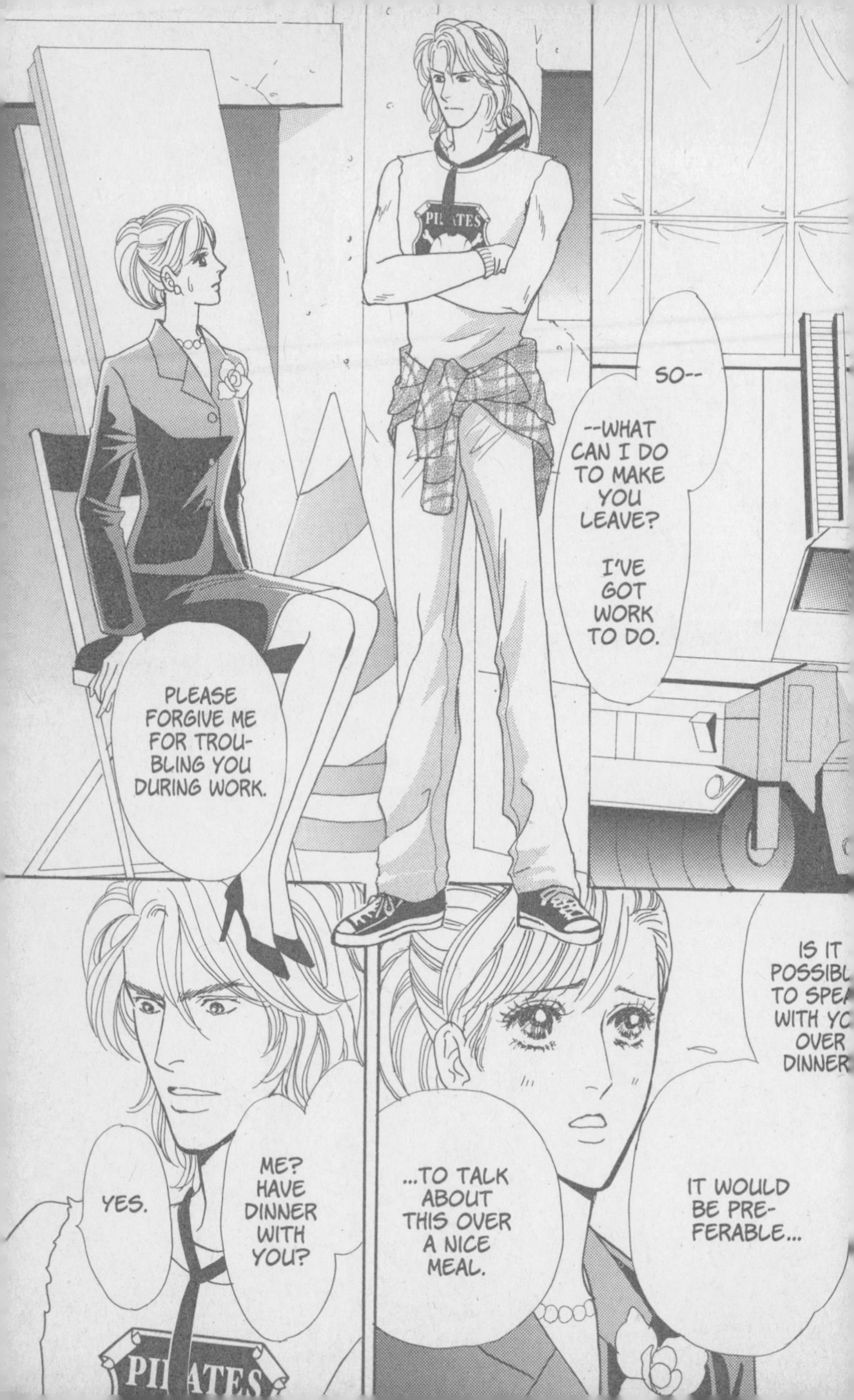
PIRATES
SO--
--WHAT CAN I DO TO MAKE YOU LEAVE?
I'VE GOT WORK TO DO.
PLEASE FORGIVE ME FOR TROU-BLING YOU DURING WORK.
IS IT POSSIBL TO SPEA WITH YO OVER DINNER
IT WOULD BE PRE-FERABLE...
...TO TALK ABOUT THIS OVER A NICE MEAL.
ME? HAVE DINNER WITH YOU?
YES.

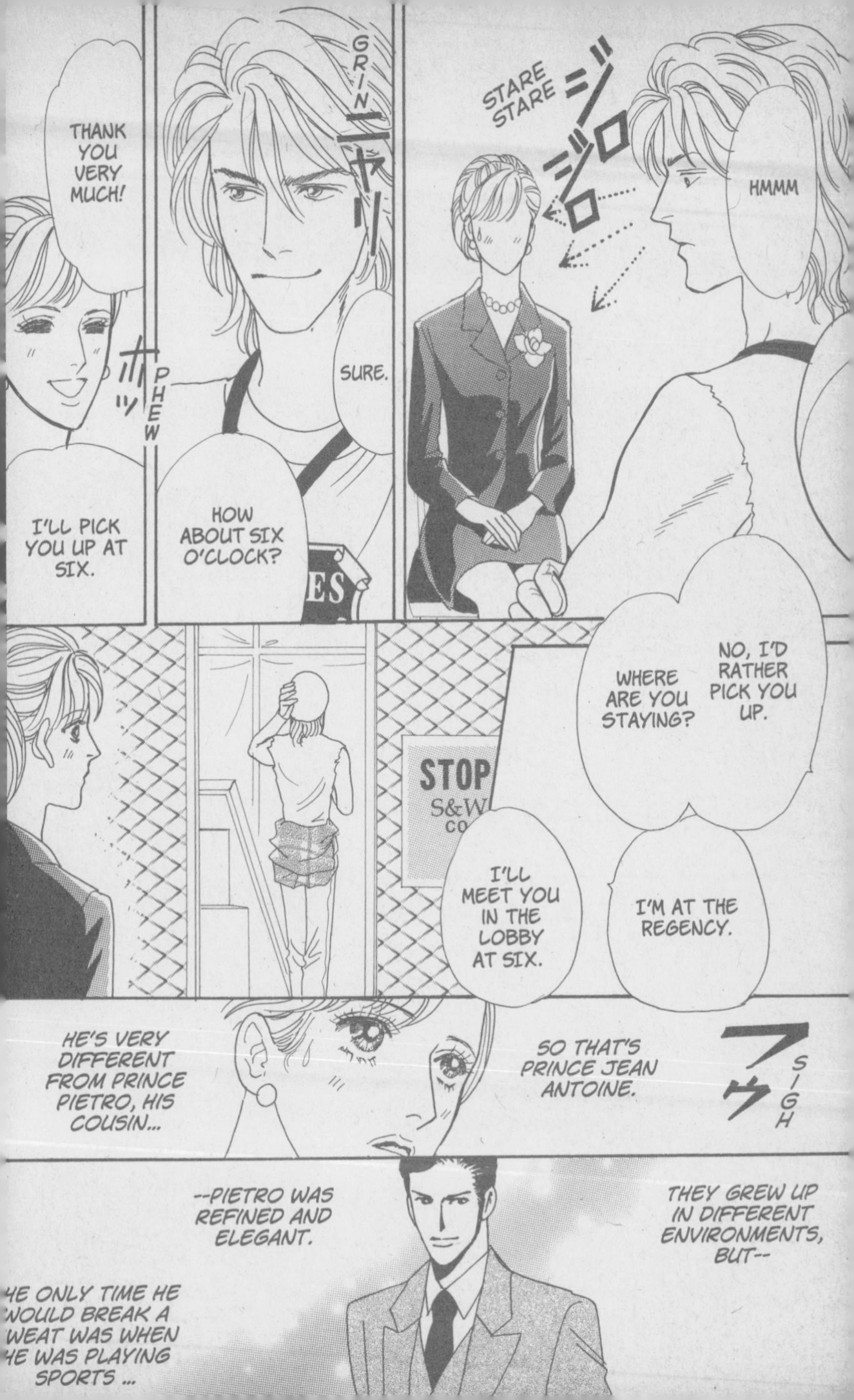

ジロジロ
STARE STARE
HMMM
ニヤリ
GRIN
SURE.
HOW ABOUT SIX O'CLOCK?
THANK YOU VERY MUCH!
ホッ
PHEW
I'LL PICK YOU UP AT SIX.
NO, I'D RATHER PICK YOU UP.
WHERE ARE YOU STAYING?
I'M AT THE REGENCY.
I'LL MEET YOU IN THE LOBBY AT SIX.
STOP
S&W
フゥ
SIGH
SO THAT'S PRINCE JEAN ANTOINE.
HE'S VERY DIFFERENT FROM PRINCE PIETRO, HIS COUSIN...
THEY GREW UP IN DIFFERENT ENVIRONMENTS, BUT--
--PIETRO WAS REFINED AND ELEGANT.
HE ONLY TIME HE WOULD BREAK A WEAT WAS WHEN HE WAS PLAYING SPORTS ...

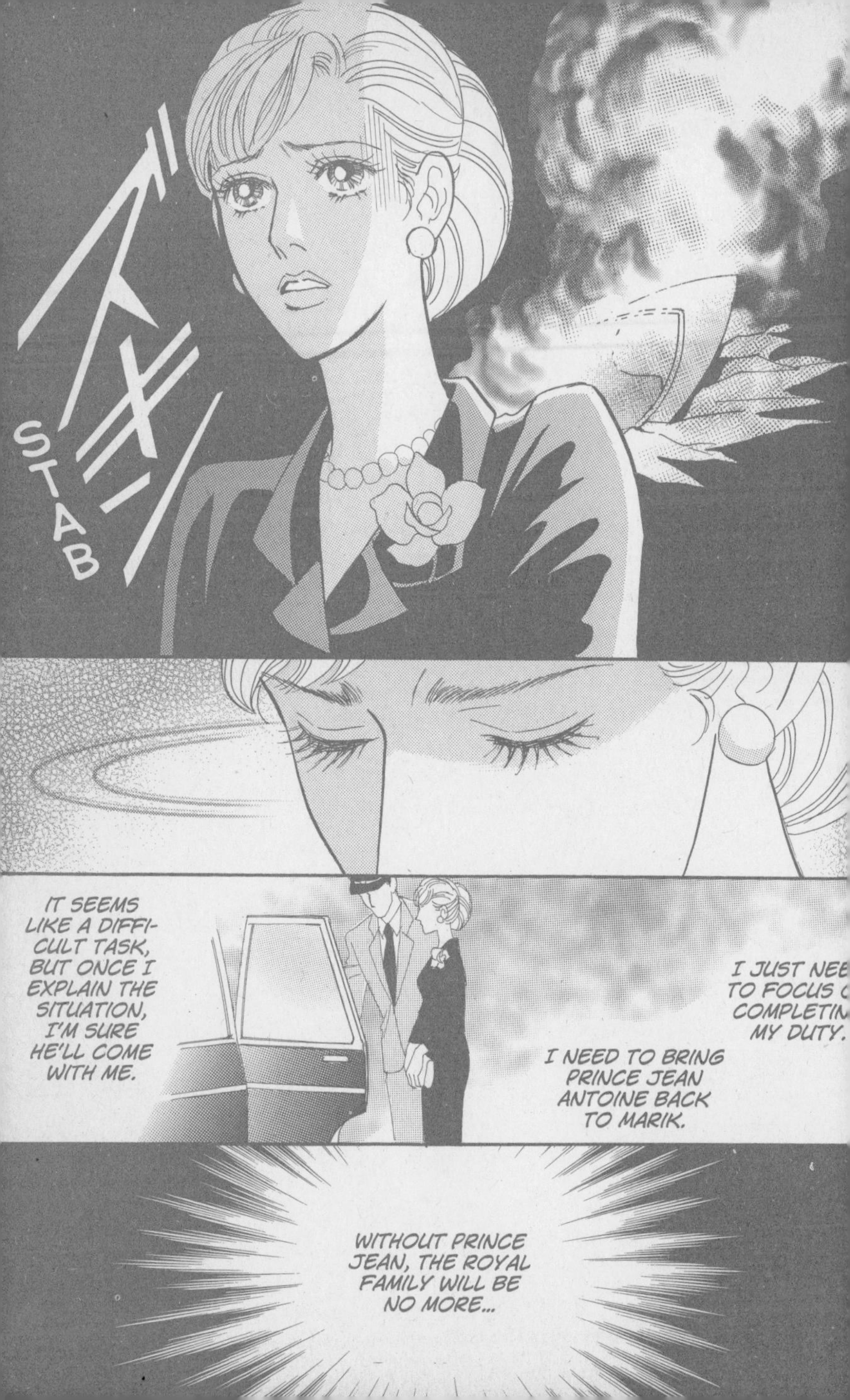
STAB
I JUST NEE TO FOCUS COMPLETIN MY DUTY.
I NEED TO BRING PRINCE JEAN ANTOINE BACK TO MARIK.
IT SEEMS LIKE A DIFFI-CULT TASK, BUT ONCE I EXPLAIN THE SITUATION, I'M SURE HE'LL COME WITH ME.
WITHOUT PRINCE JEAN, THE ROYAL FAMILY WILL BE NO MORE...

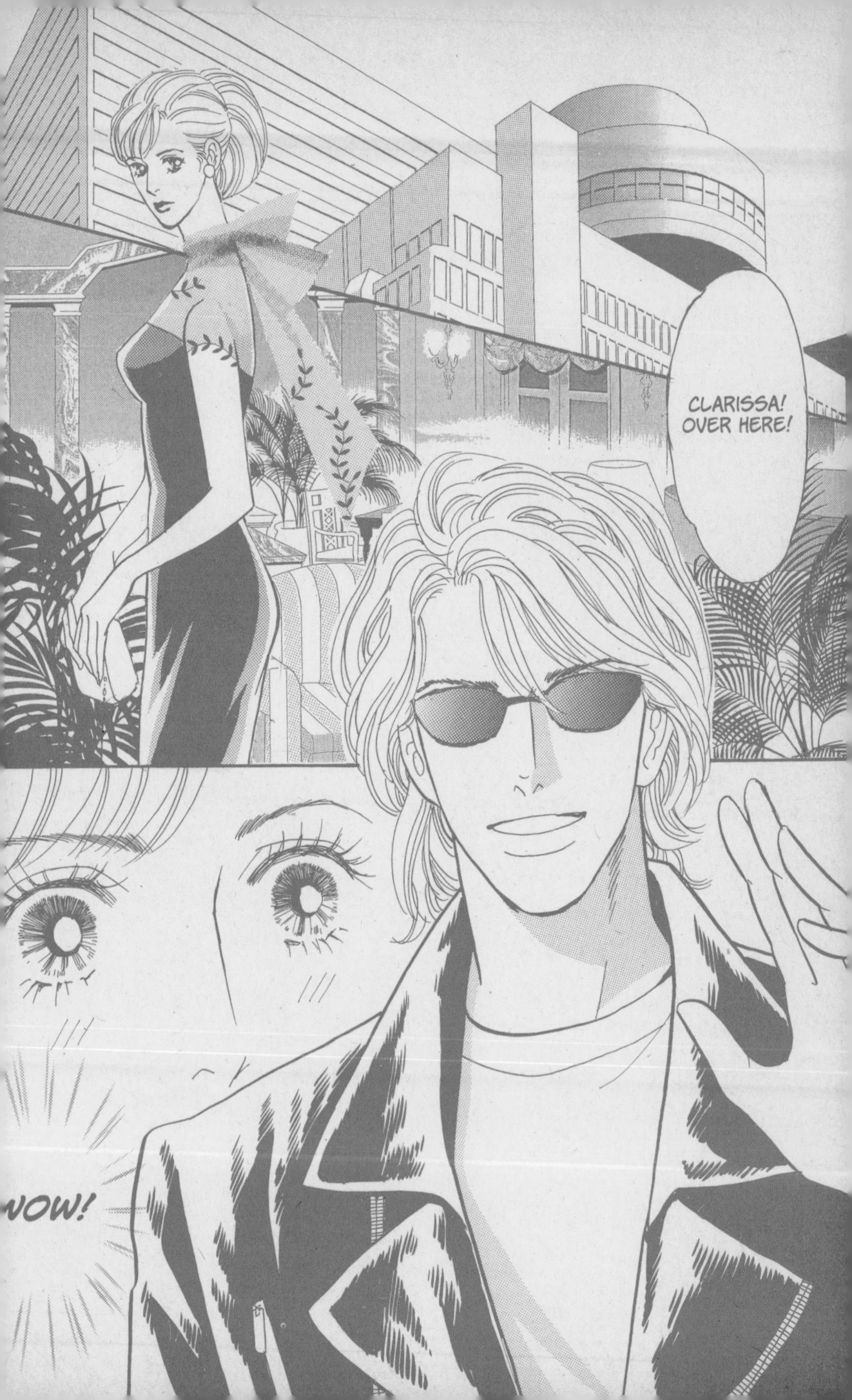
CLARISSA! OVER HERE!
WOW!

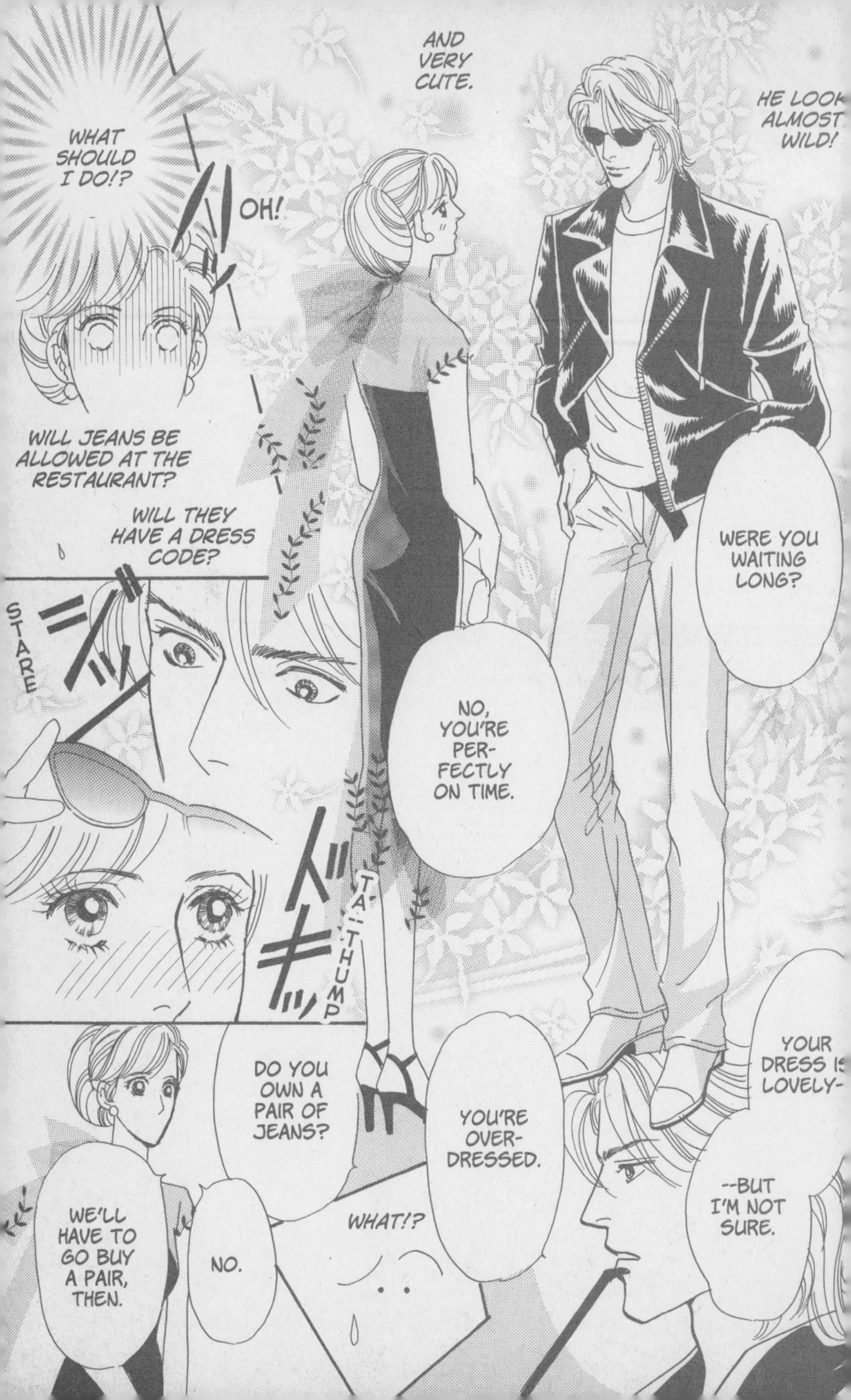
HE LOOK ALMOST WILD!
AND VERY CUTE.
WERE YOU WAITING LONG?
NO, YOU'RE PER-FECTLY ON TIME.
OH!
WHAT SHOULD I DO!?
WILL JEANS BE ALLOWED AT THE RESTAURANT?
WILL THEY HAVE A DRESS CODE?
STARE
TA-THUMP
YOUR DRESS IS LOVELY-
--BUT I'M NOT SURE.
YOU'RE OVER-DRESSED.
WHAT!?
DO YOU OWN A PAIR OF JEANS?
NO.
WE'LL HAVE TO GO BUY A PAIR, THEN.

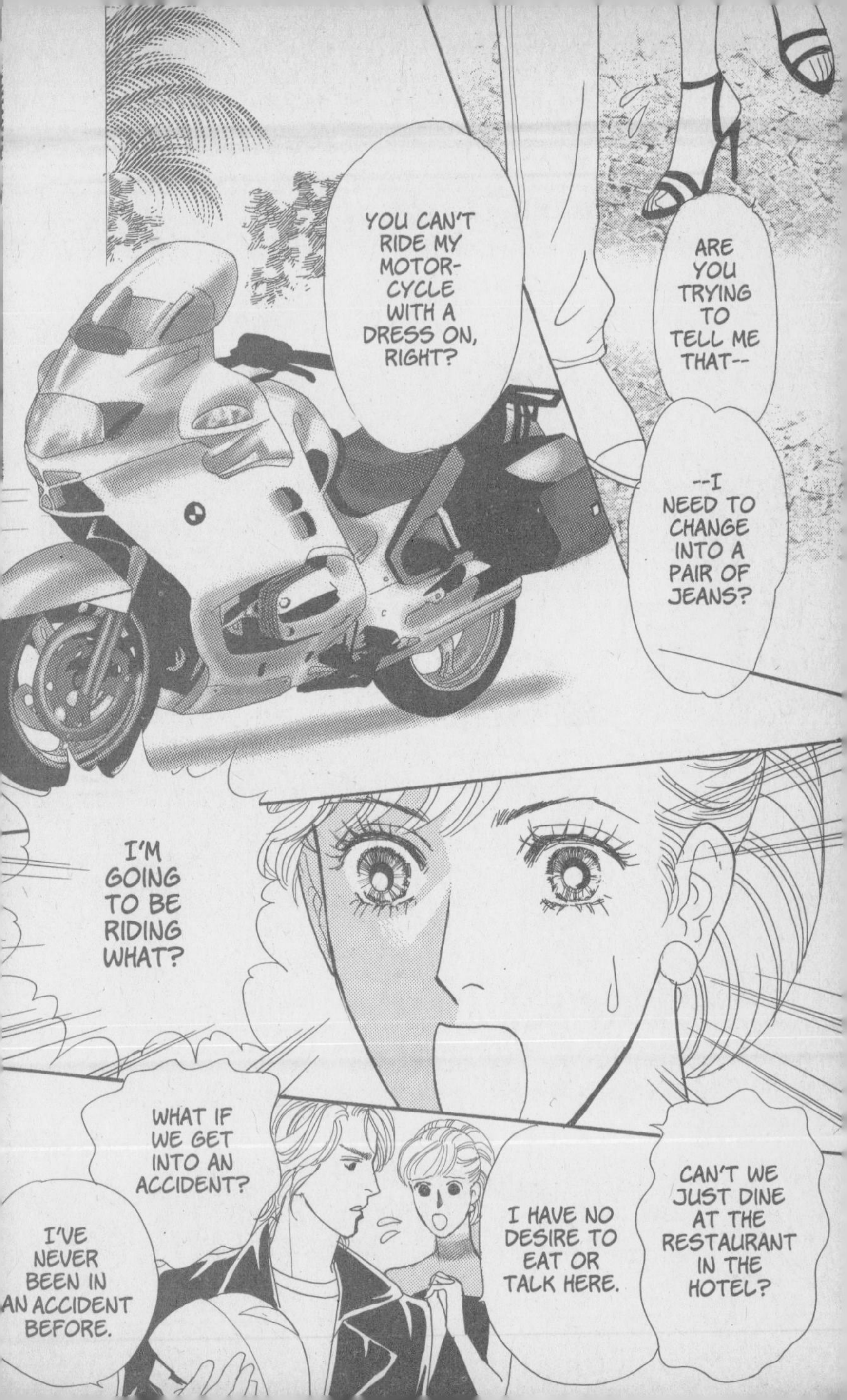
ARE YOU TRYING TO TELL ME THAT--
--I NEED TO CHANGE INTO A PAIR OF JEANS?
YOU CAN'T RIDE MY MOTOR-CYCLE WITH A DRESS ON, RIGHT?
I'M GOING TO BE RIDING WHAT?
CAN'T WE JUST DINE AT THE RESTAURANT IN THE HOTEL?
I HAVE NO DESIRE TO EAT OR TALK HERE.
WHAT IF WE GET INTO AN ACCIDENT?
I'VE NEVER BEEN IN AN ACCIDENT BEFORE.

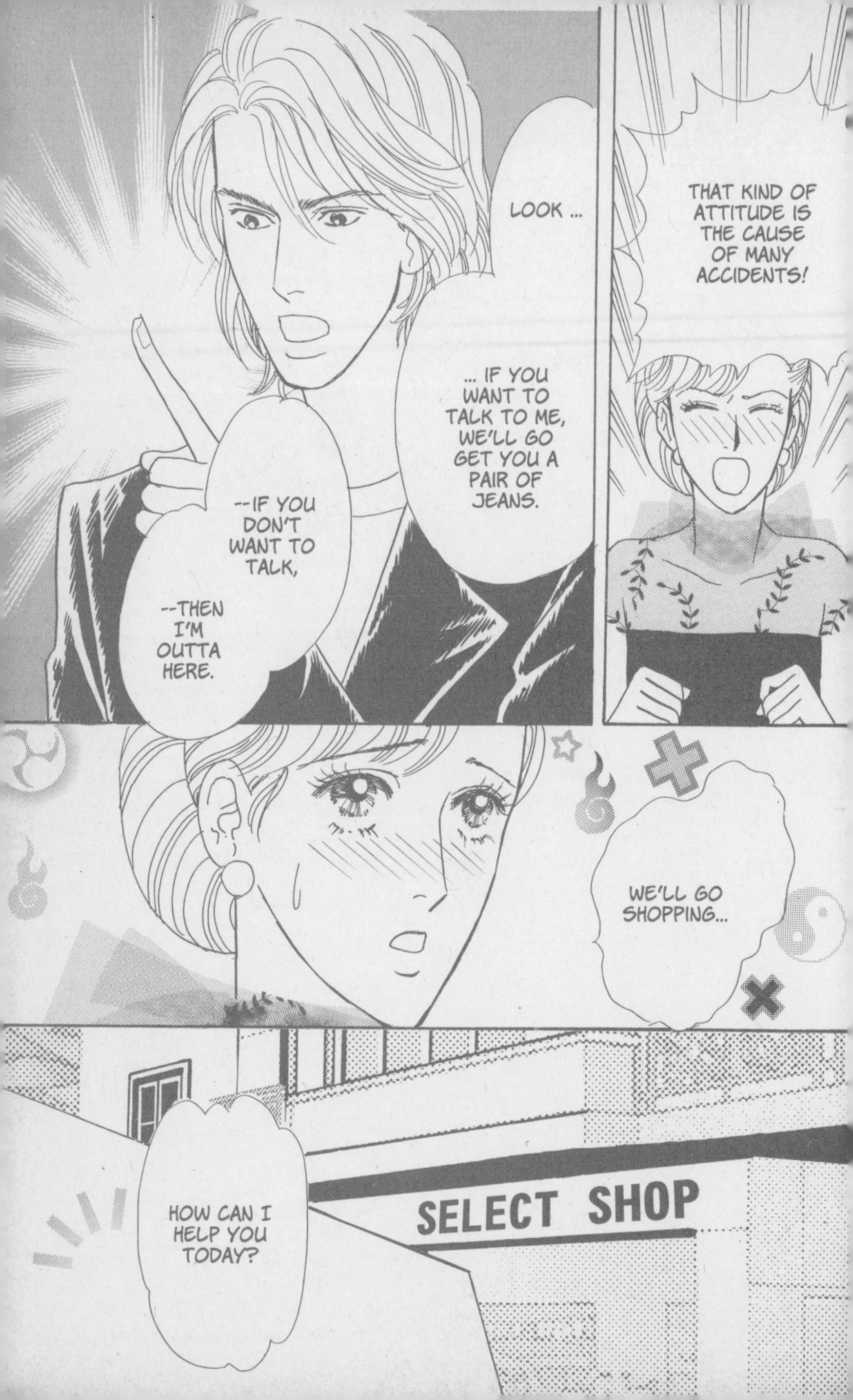
THAT KIND OF ATTITUDE IS THE CAUSE OF MANY ACCIDENTS!
LOOK ...
... IF YOU WANT TO TALK TO ME, WE'LL GO GET YOU A PAIR OF JEANS.
--IF YOU DON'T WANT TO TALK,
--THEN I'M OUTTA HERE.
WE'LL GO SHOPPING...
SELECT SHOP
HOW CAN I HELP YOU TODAY?

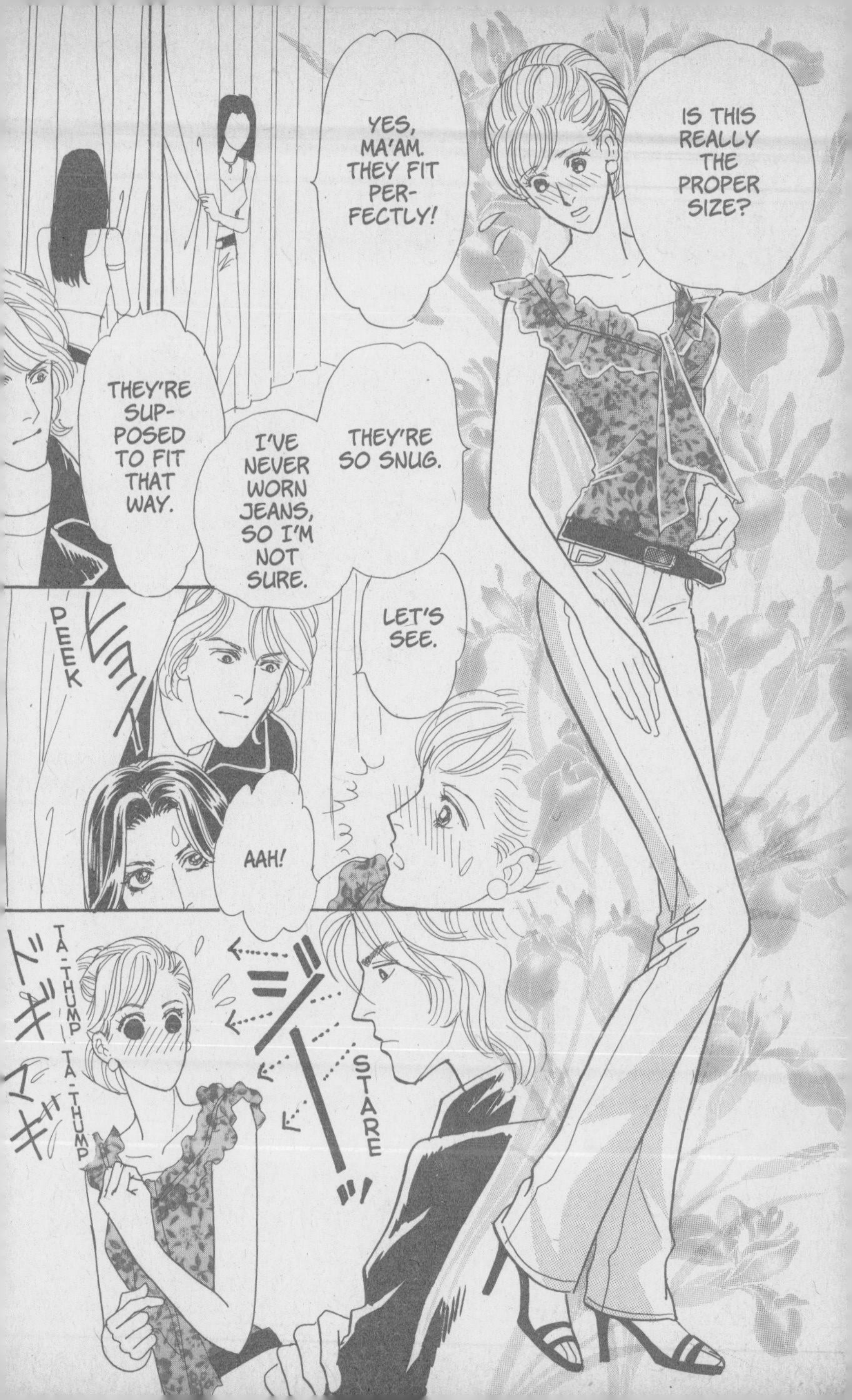
IS THIS REALLY THE PROPER SIZE?
YES, MA'AM. THEY FIT PER-FECTLY!
THEY'RE SO SNUG.
I'VE NEVER WORN JEANS, SO I'M NOT SURE.
THEY'RE SUP-POSED TO FIT THAT WAY.
LET'S SEE.
PEEK
AAH!
STARE
TA-THUMP TA-THUMP

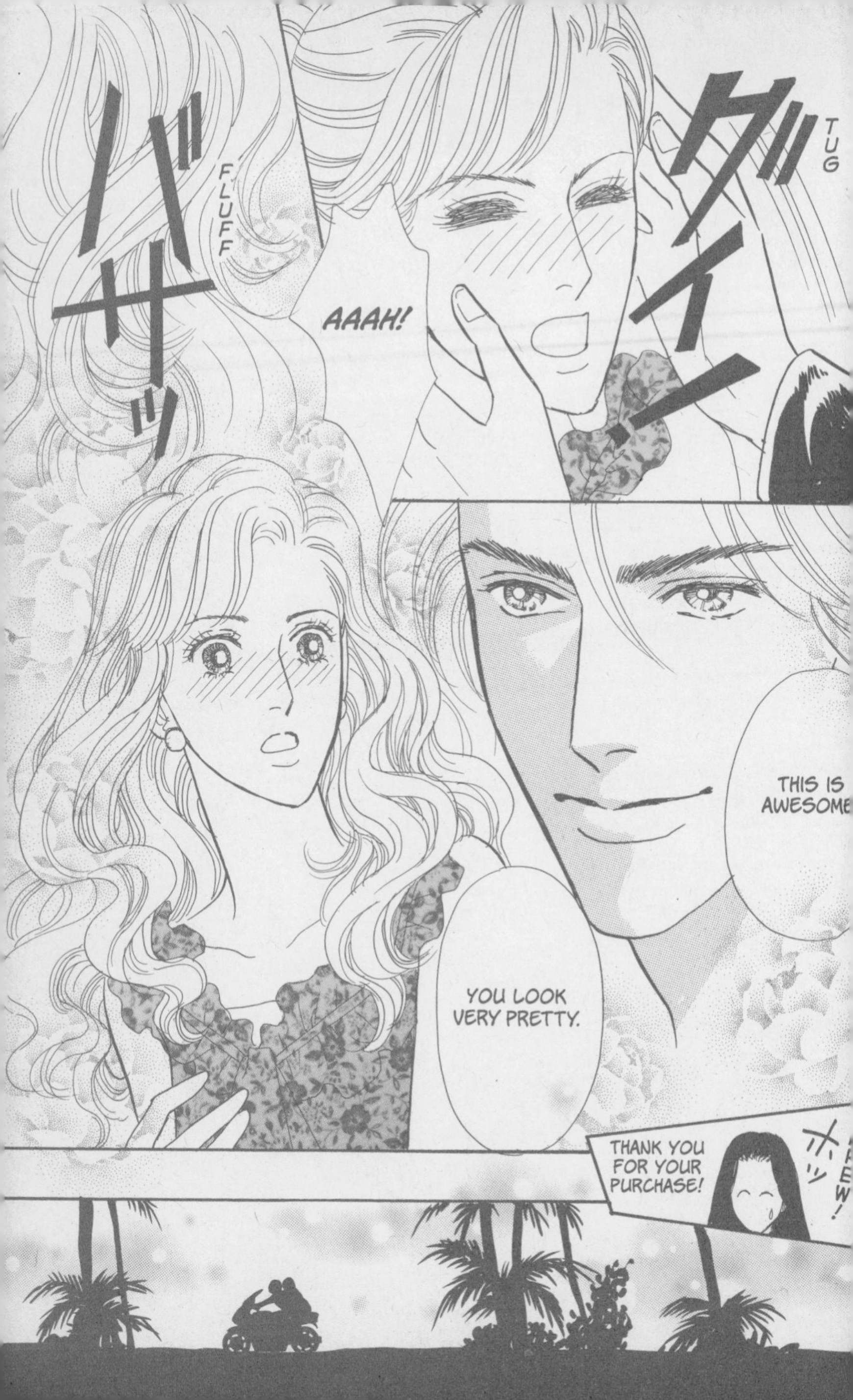
グイッ
TUG
AAAH!
バサッ
FLUFF
THIS IS AWESOME
YOU LOOK VERY PRETTY.
ホッ
PHEW!
THANK YOU FOR YOUR PURCHASE!

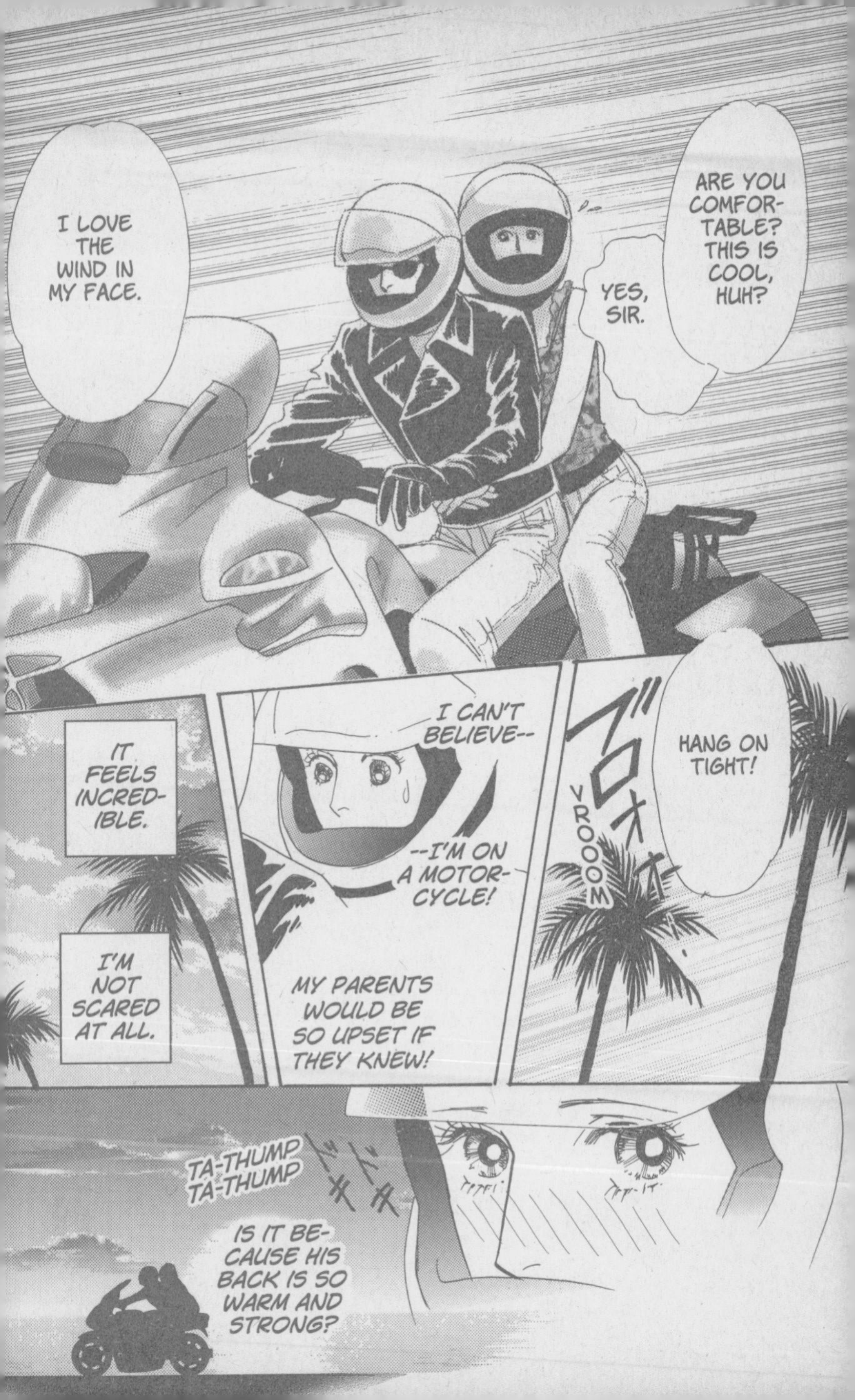
ARE YOU COMFORTABLE? THIS IS COOL, HUH?
YES, SIR.
I LOVE THE WIND IN MY FACE.
HANG ON TIGHT!
VROOOM
I CAN'T BELIEVE--
--I'M ON A MOTORCYCLE!
MY PARENTS WOULD BE SO UPSET IF THEY KNEW!
IT FEELS INCREDIBLE.
I'M NOT SCARED AT ALL.
TA-THUMP TA-THUMP
IS IT BECAUSE HIS BACK IS SO WARM AND STRONG?

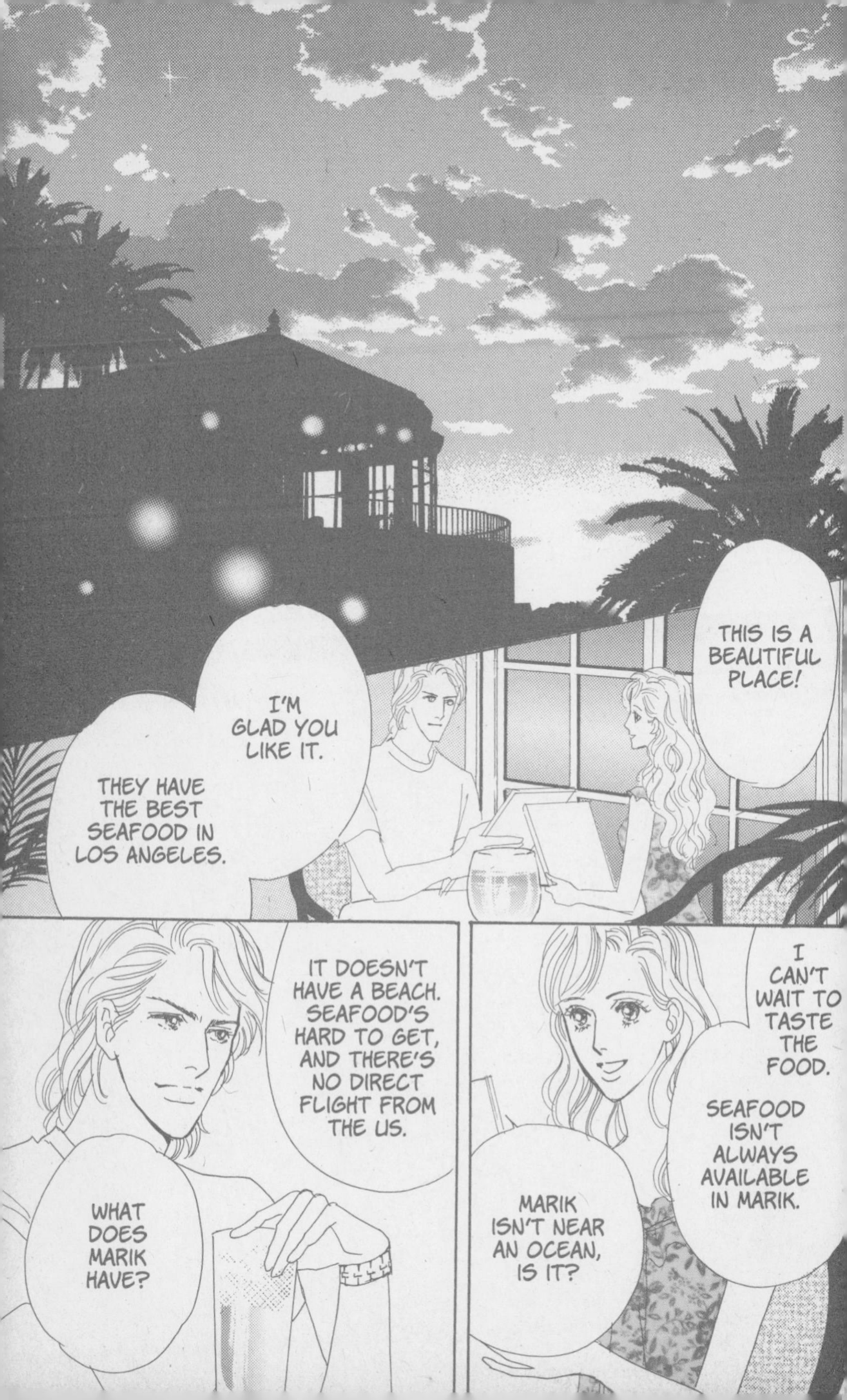
THIS IS A BEAUTIFUL PLACE!
I'M GLAD YOU LIKE IT.
THEY HAVE THE BEST SEAFOOD IN LOS ANGELES.
I CAN'T WAIT TO TASTE THE FOOD.
SEAFOOD ISN'T ALWAYS AVAILABLE IN MARIK.
MARIK ISN'T NEAR AN OCEAN, IS IT?
IT DOESN'T HAVE A BEACH. SEAFOOD'S HARD TO GET, AND THERE'S NO DIRECT FLIGHT FROM THE US.
WHAT DOES MARIK HAVE?

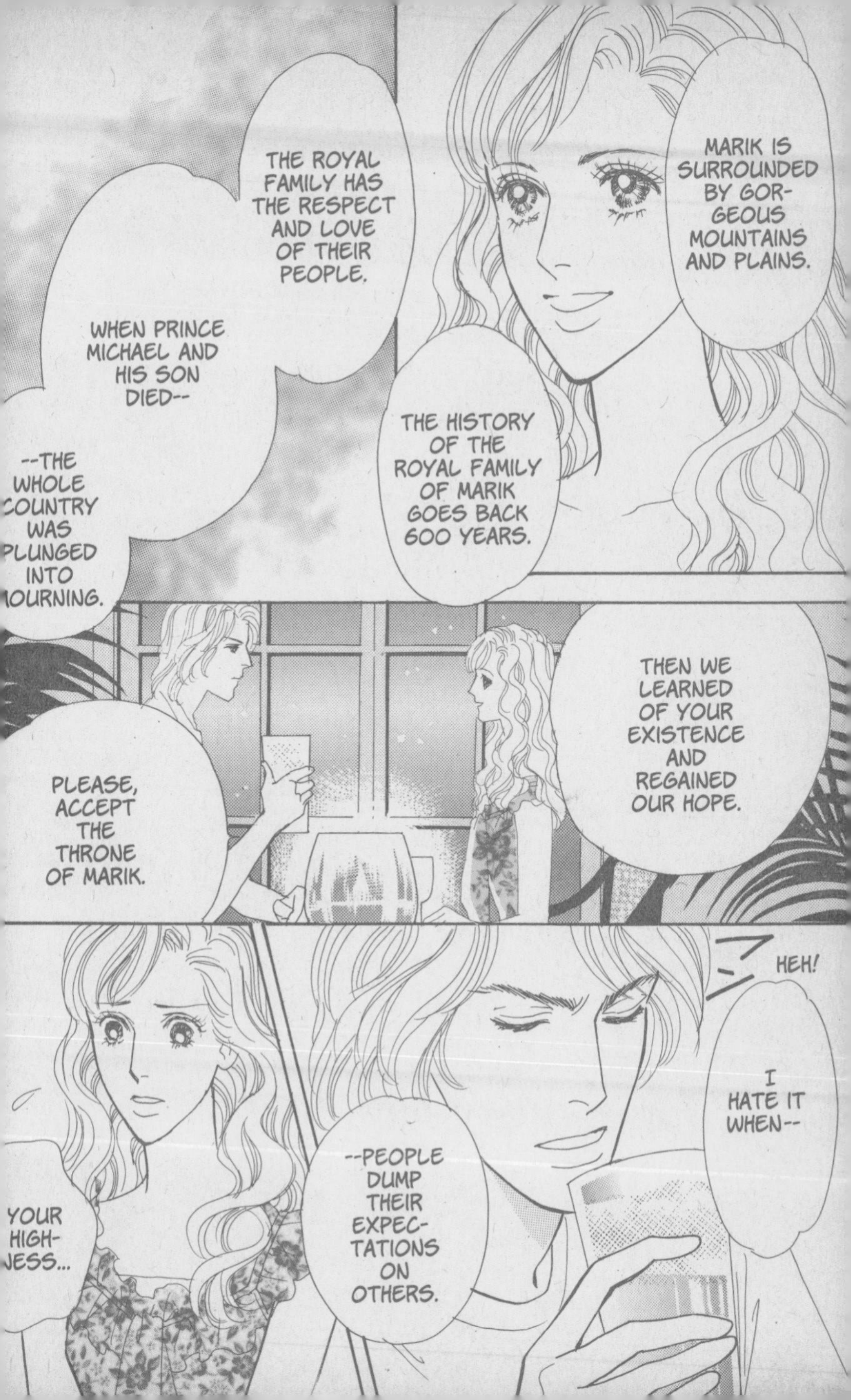
MARIK IS SURROUNDED BY GOR-GEOUS MOUNTAINS AND PLAINS.
THE HISTORY OF THE ROYAL FAMILY OF MARIK GOES BACK 600 YEARS.
THE ROYAL FAMILY HAS THE RESPECT AND LOVE OF THEIR PEOPLE.
WHEN PRINCE MICHAEL AND HIS SON DIED--
--THE WHOLE COUNTRY WAS PLUNGED INTO MOURNING.
THEN WE LEARNED OF YOUR EXISTENCE AND REGAINED OUR HOPE.
PLEASE, ACCEPT THE THRONE OF MARIK.
HEH!
I HATE IT WHEN--
--PEOPLE DUMP THEIR EXPECTATIONS ON OTHERS.
YOUR HIGHNESS...

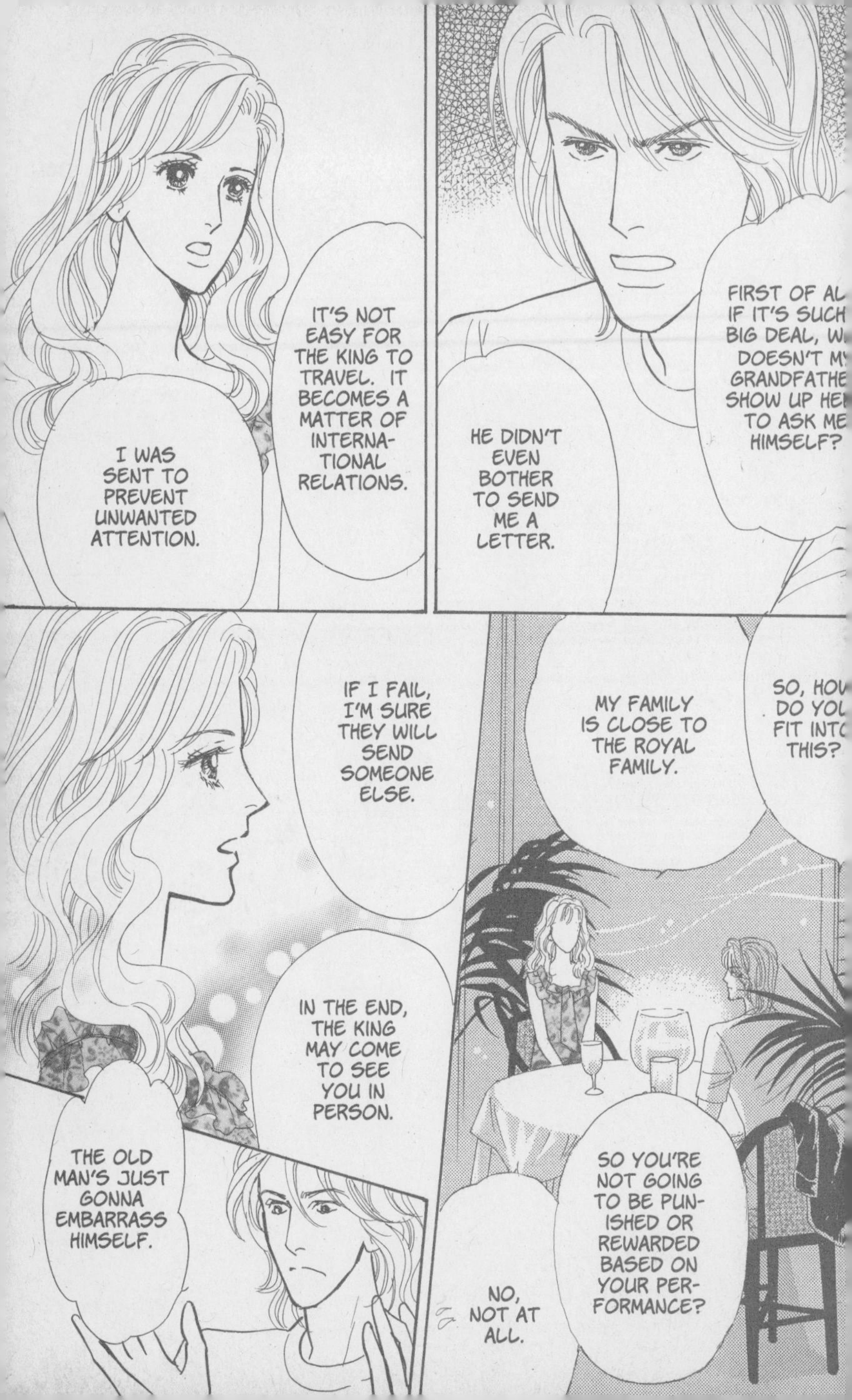

FIRST OF AL IF IT'S SUCH BIG DEAL, W DOESN'T MY GRANDFATHE SHOW UP HE TO ASK ME HIMSELF?
HE DIDN'T EVEN BOTHER TO SEND ME A LETTER.
IT'S NOT EASY FOR THE KING TO TRAVEL. IT BECOMES A MATTER OF INTERNA-TIONAL RELATIONS.
I WAS SENT TO PREVENT UNWANTED ATTENTION.
SO, HOV DO YOL FIT INTC THIS?
MY FAMILY IS CLOSE TO THE ROYAL FAMILY.
SO YOU'RE NOT GOING TO BE PUN-ISHED OR REWARDED BASED ON YOUR PER-FORMANCE?
NO, NOT AT ALL.
IF I FAIL, I'M SURE THEY WILL SEND SOMEONE ELSE.
IN THE END, THE KING MAY COME TO SEE YOU IN PERSON.
THE OLD MAN'S JUST GONNA EMBARRASS HIMSELF.

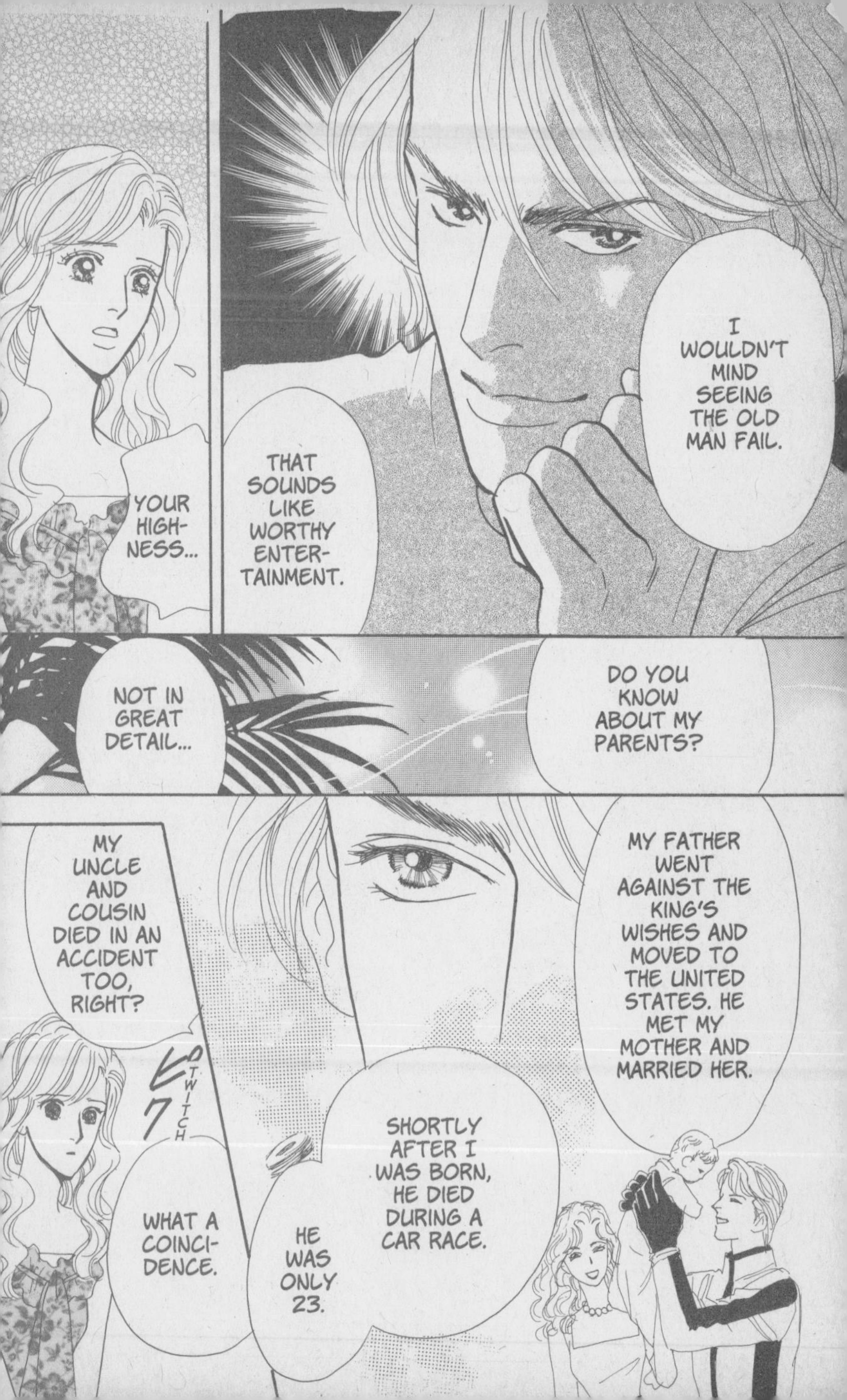
I WOULDN'T MIND SEEING THE OLD MAN FAIL.
THAT SOUNDS LIKE WORTHY ENTERTAINMENT.
YOUR HIGHNESS...
DO YOU KNOW ABOUT MY PARENTS?
NOT IN GREAT DETAIL...
MY FATHER WENT AGAINST THE KING'S WISHES AND MOVED TO THE UNITED STATES. HE MET MY MOTHER AND MARRIED HER.
SHORTLY AFTER I WAS BORN, HE DIED DURING A CAR RACE.
HE WAS ONLY 23.
MY UNCLE AND COUSIN DIED IN AN ACCIDENT TOO, RIGHT?
TWITCH
WHAT A COINCIDENCE.

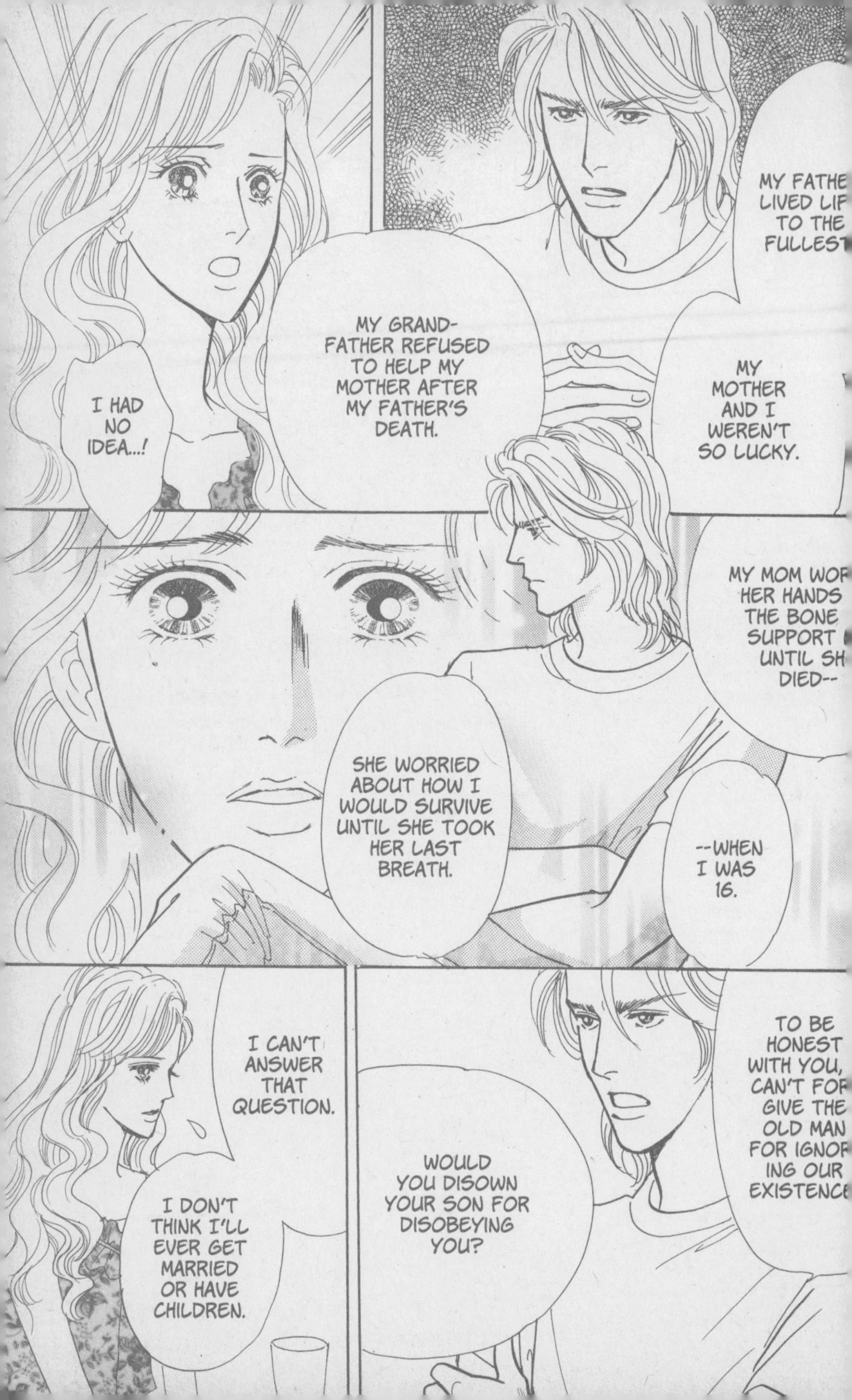

MY FATHE LIVED LIF TO THE FULLEST
MY MOTHER AND I WEREN'T SO LUCKY.
MY GRAND-FATHER REFUSED TO HELP MY MOTHER AFTER MY FATHER'S DEATH.
I HAD NO IDEA...!
MY MOM WOR HER HANDS THE BONE SUPPORT UNTIL SH DIED--
--WHEN I WAS 16.
SHE WORRIED ABOUT HOW I WOULD SURVIVE UNTIL SHE TOOK HER LAST BREATH.
TO BE HONEST WITH YOU, CAN'T FOR GIVE THE OLD MAN FOR IGNOR ING OUR EXISTENC
WOULD YOU DISOWN YOUR SON FOR DISOBEYING YOU?
I CAN'T ANSWER THAT QUESTION.
I DON'T THINK I'LL EVER GET MARRIED OR HAVE CHILDREN.

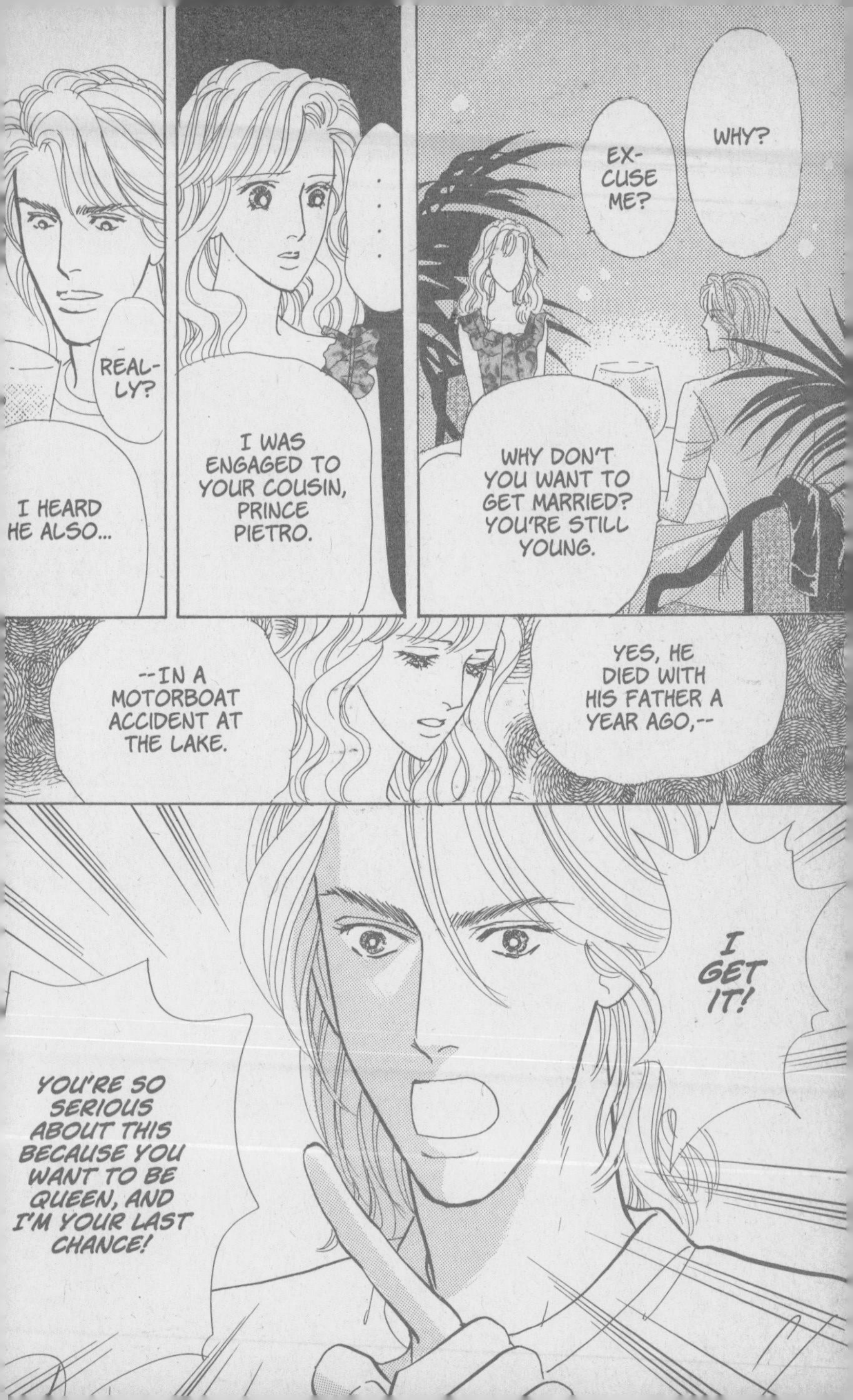
WHY?
EX-CUSE ME?
WHY DON'T YOU WANT TO GET MARRIED? YOU'RE STILL YOUNG.
...
I WAS ENGAGED TO YOUR COUSIN, PRINCE PIETRO.
REAL-LY?
I HEARD HE ALSO...
YES, HE DIED WITH HIS FATHER A YEAR AGO,--
--IN A MOTORBOAT ACCIDENT AT THE LAKE.
I GET IT!
YOU'RE SO SERIOUS ABOUT THIS BECAUSE YOU WANT TO BE QUEEN, AND I'M YOUR LAST CHANCE!

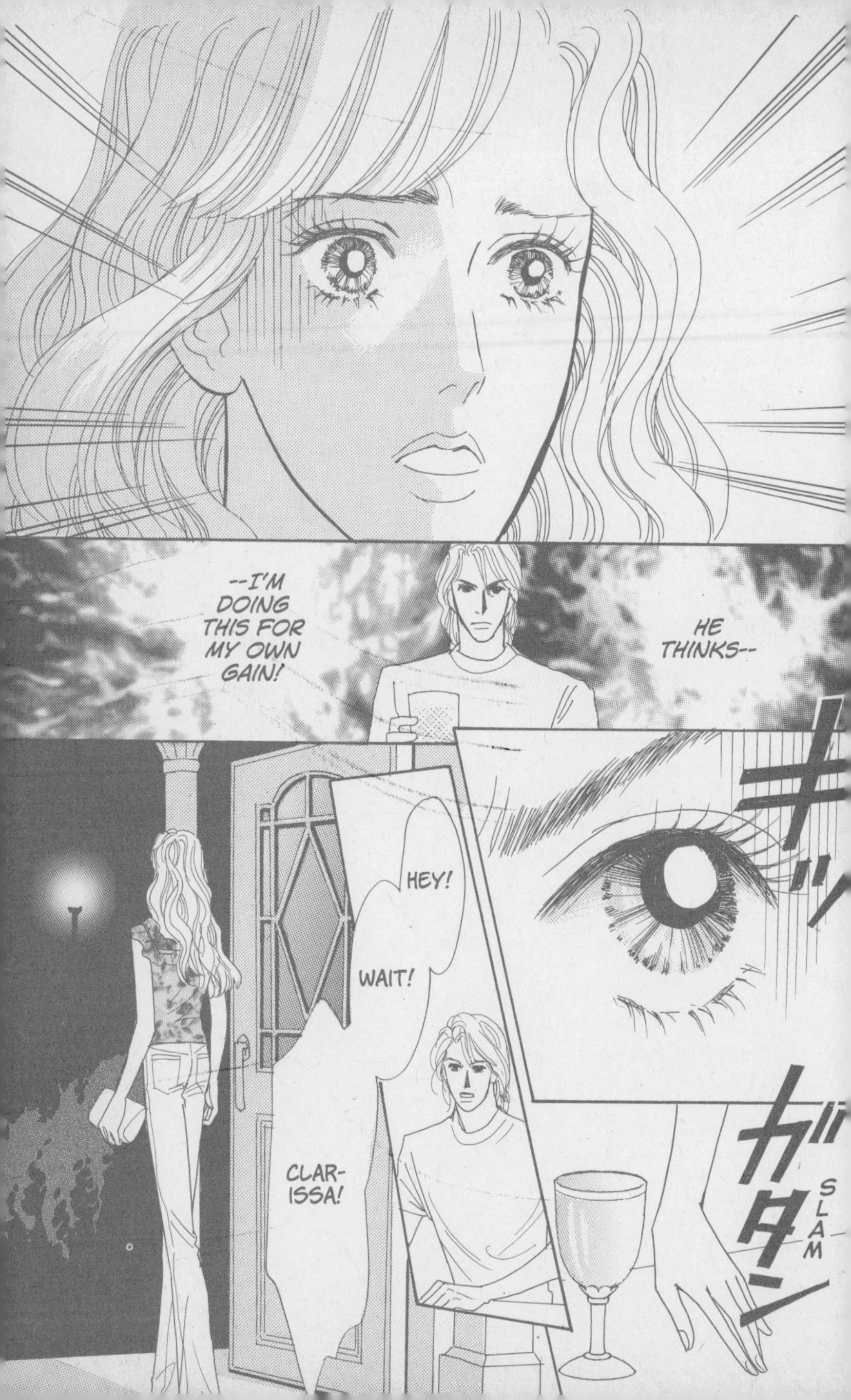
HE THINKS--
--I'M DOING THIS FOR MY OWN GAIN!
キッ
ガタ
SLAM
HEY!
WAIT!
CLARISSA!

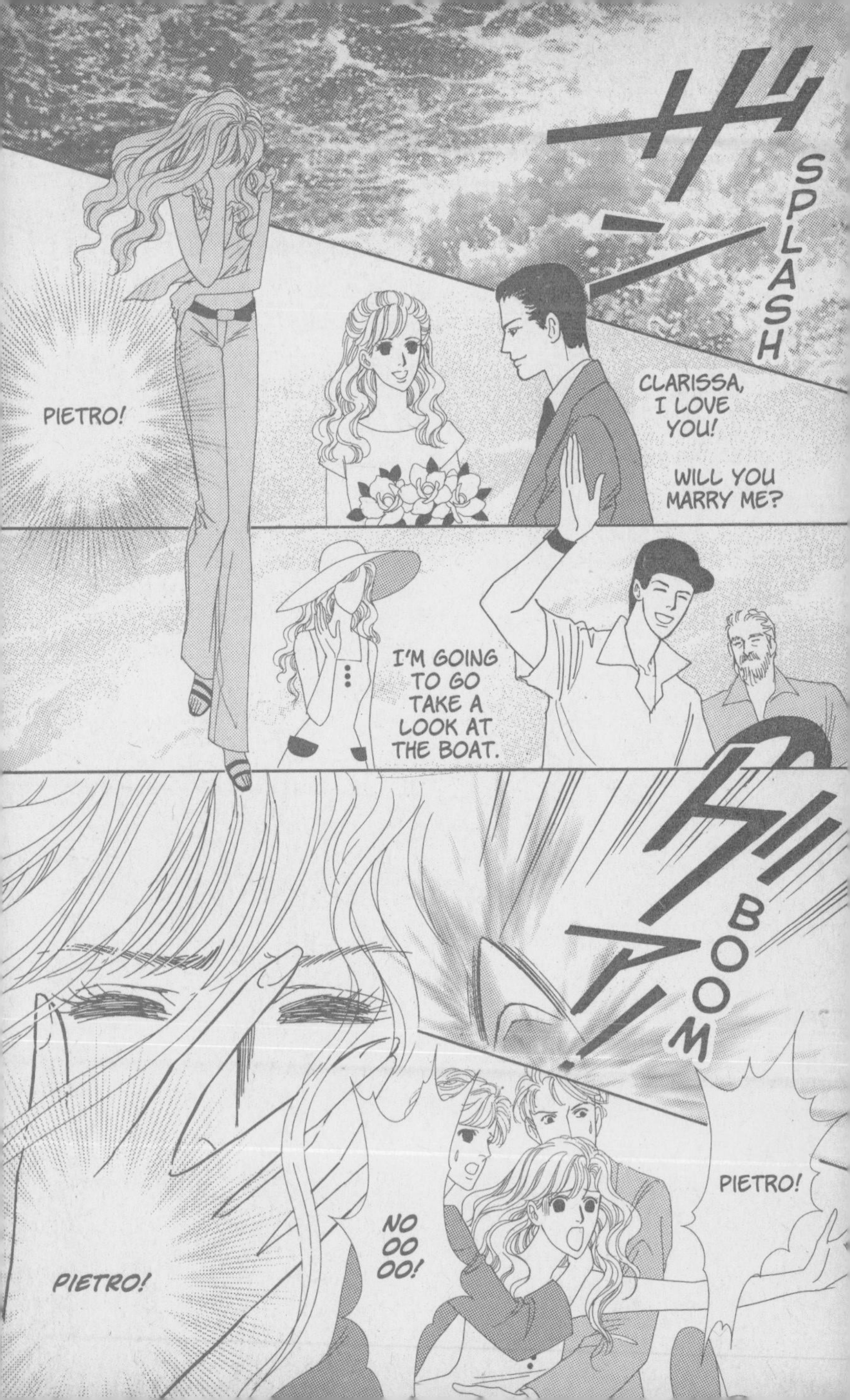
SPLASH
CLARISSA, I LOVE YOU!
WILL YOU MARRY ME?
I'M GOING TO GO TAKE A LOOK AT THE BOAT.
PIETRO!
BOOM
PIETRO!
NO OO OO!
PIETRO!

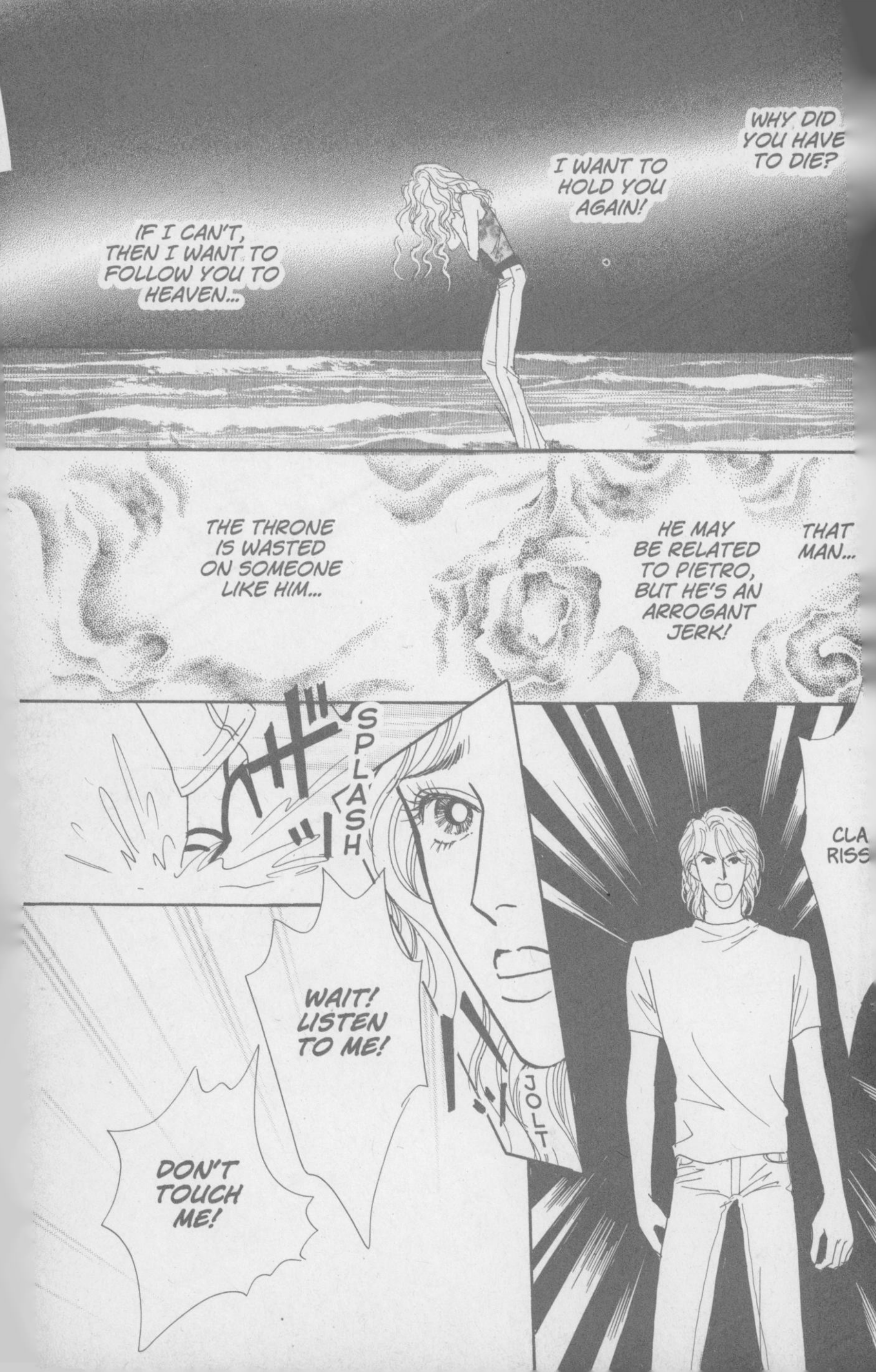
WHY DID YOU HAVE TO DIE?
I WANT TO HOLD YOU AGAIN!
IF I CAN'T, THEN I WANT TO FOLLOW YOU TO HEAVEN...
THAT MAN...
HE MAY BE RELATED TO PIETRO, BUT HE'S AN ARROGANT JERK!
THE THRONE IS WASTED ON SOMEONE LIKE HIM...
CLA RISS
SPLASH
JOLT
WAIT! LISTEN TO ME!
DON'T TOUCH ME!

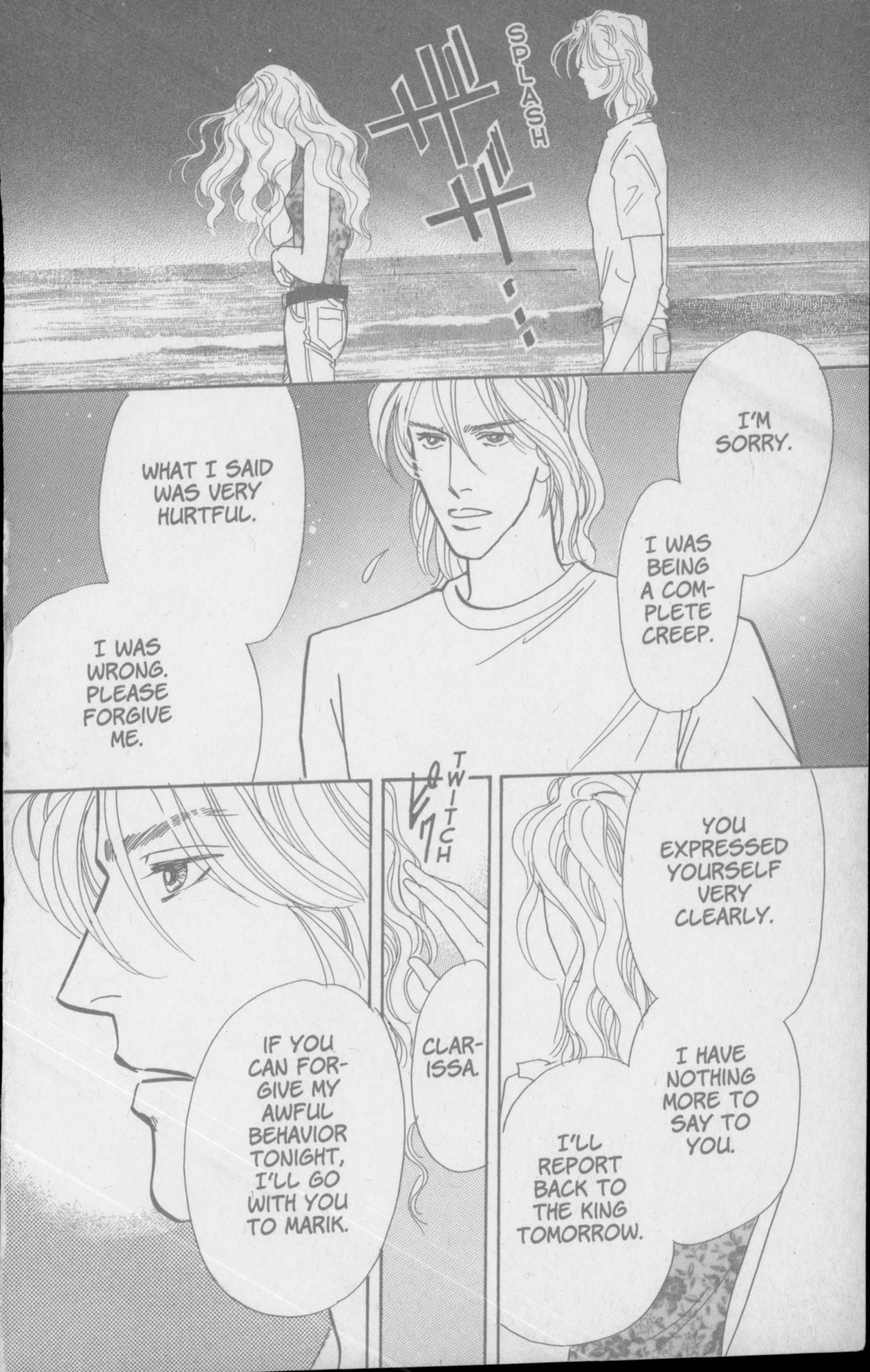
SPLASH
I'M SORRY.
I WAS BEING A COMPLETE CREEP.
WHAT I SAID WAS VERY HURTFUL.
I WAS WRONG. PLEASE FORGIVE ME.
YOU EXPRESSED YOURSELF VERY CLEARLY.
I HAVE NOTHING MORE TO SAY TO YOU.
I'LL REPORT BACK TO THE KING TOMORROW.
TWITCH
CLARISSA.
IF YOU CAN FORGIVE MY AWFUL BEHAVIOR TONIGHT, I'LL GO WITH YOU TO MARIK.

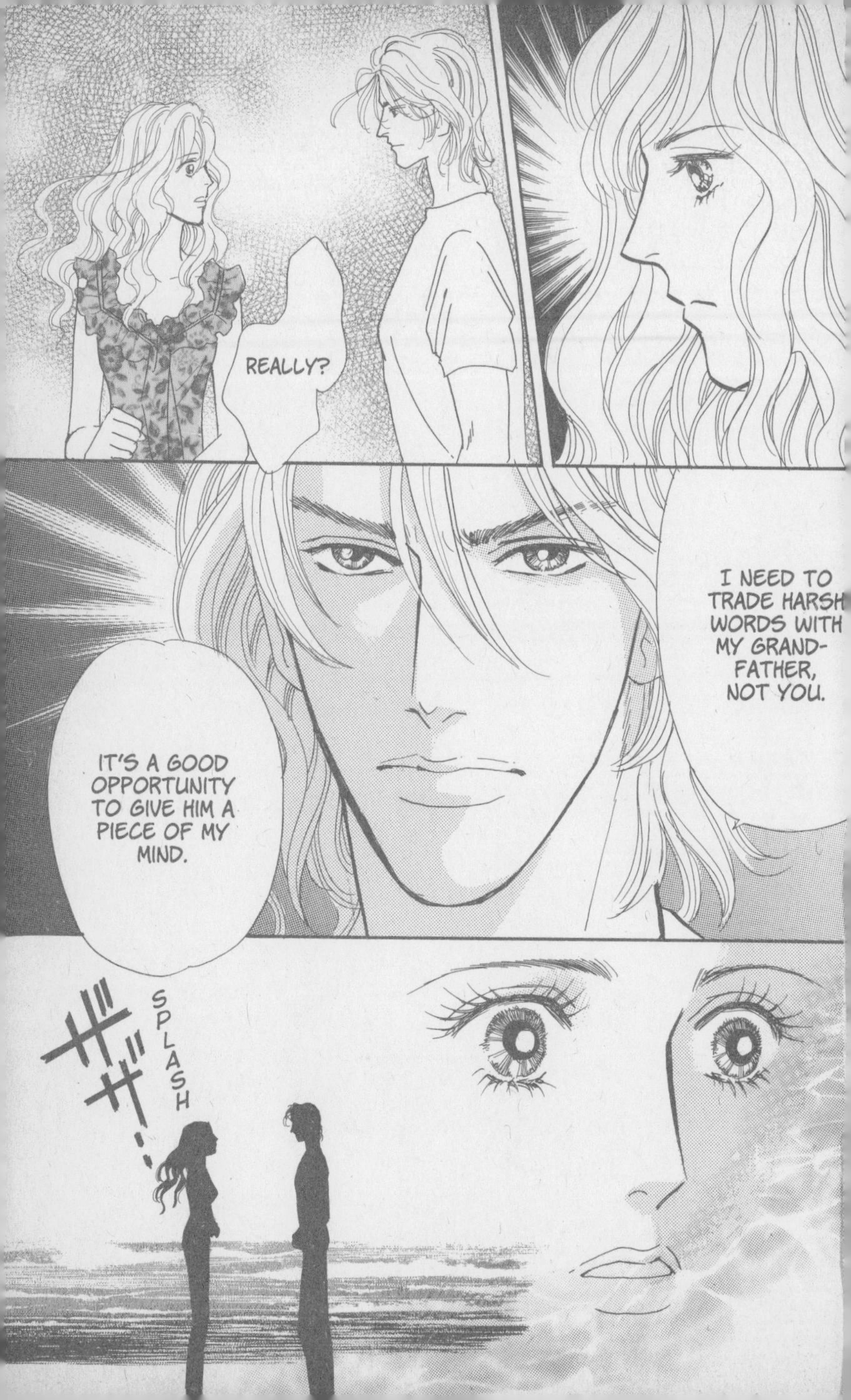
REALLY?
I NEED TO TRADE HARSH WORDS WITH MY GRAND-FATHER, NOT YOU.
IT'S A GOOD OPPORTUNITY TO GIVE HIM A PIECE OF MY MIND.
SPLASH

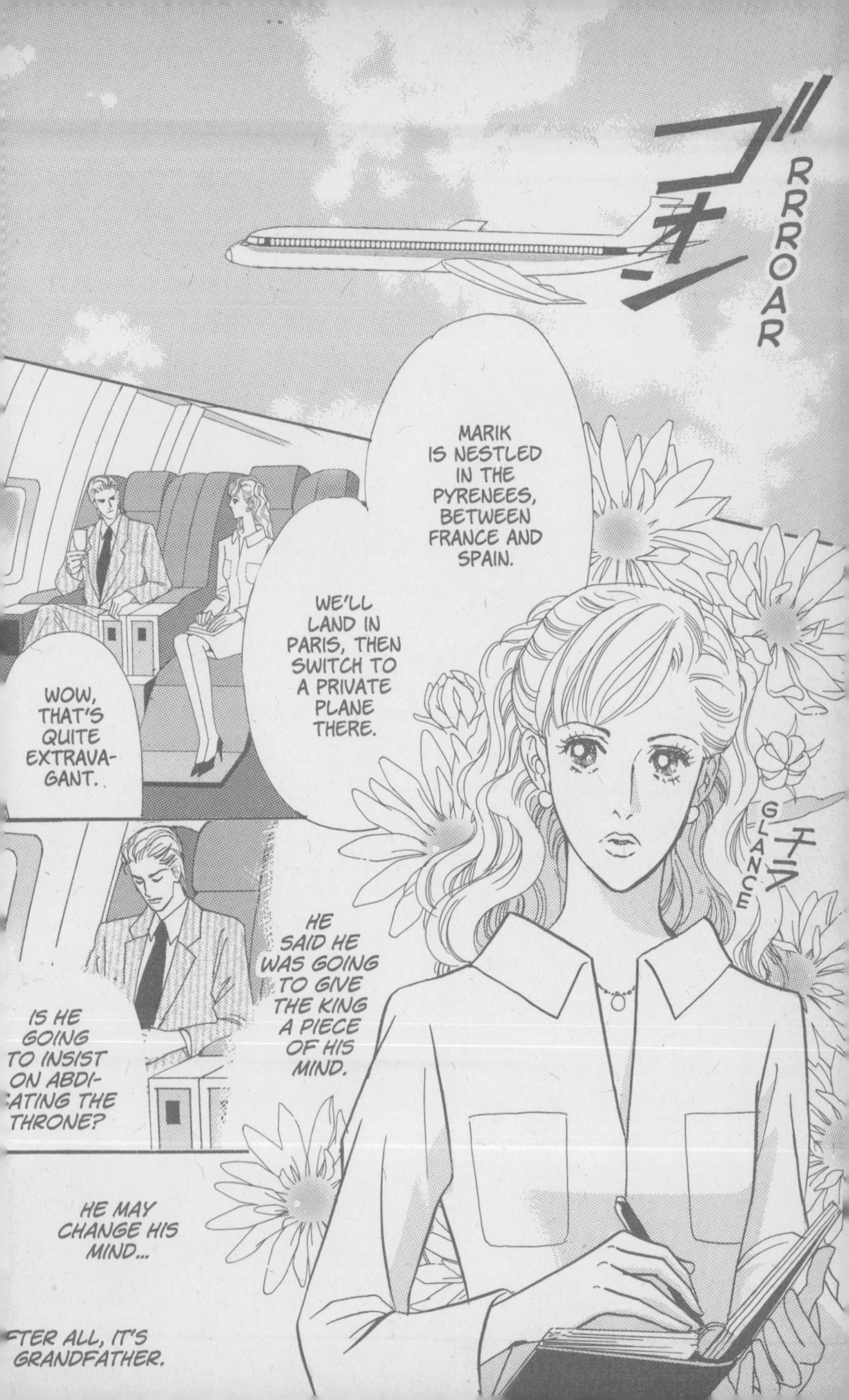

ゴォン
RRROAR
チラ
GLANCE
MARIK IS NESTLED IN THE PYRENEES, BETWEEN FRANCE AND SPAIN.
WE'LL LAND IN PARIS, THEN SWITCH TO A PRIVATE PLANE THERE.
WOW, THAT'S QUITE EXTRAVA-GANT.
HE SAID HE WAS GOING TO GIVE THE KING A PIECE OF HIS MIND.
IS HE GOING TO INSIST ON ABDI-CATING THE THRONE?
HE MAY CHANGE HIS MIND...
FTER ALL, IT'S GRANDFATHER.

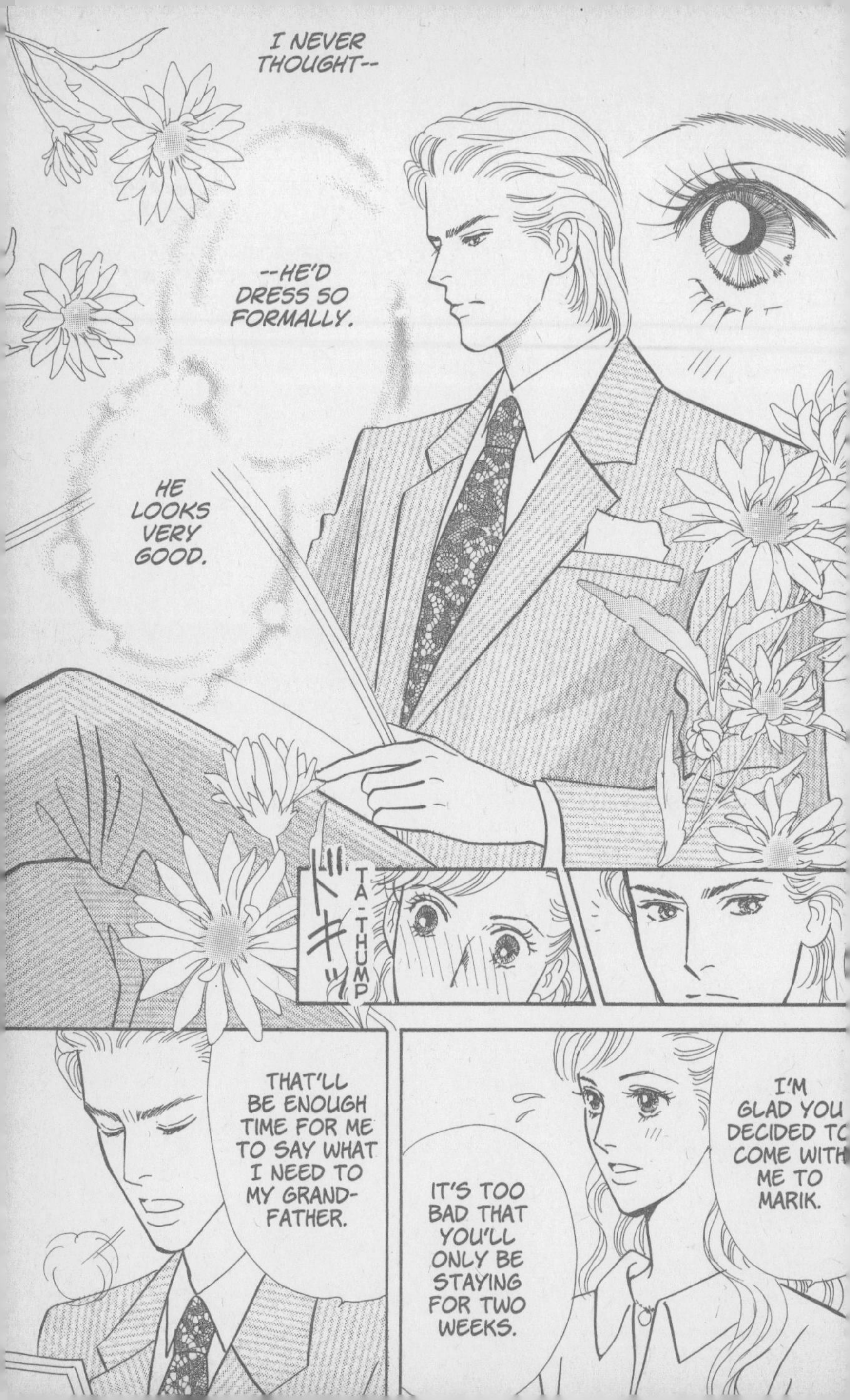
I NEVER THOUGHT--
--HE'D DRESS SO FORMALLY.
HE LOOKS VERY GOOD.
ドキッ
TA-THUMP
I'M GLAD YOU DECIDED TO COME WITH ME TO MARIK.
IT'S TOO BAD THAT YOU'LL ONLY BE STAYING FOR TWO WEEKS.
THAT'LL BE ENOUGH TIME FOR ME TO SAY WHAT I NEED TO MY GRAND-FATHER.

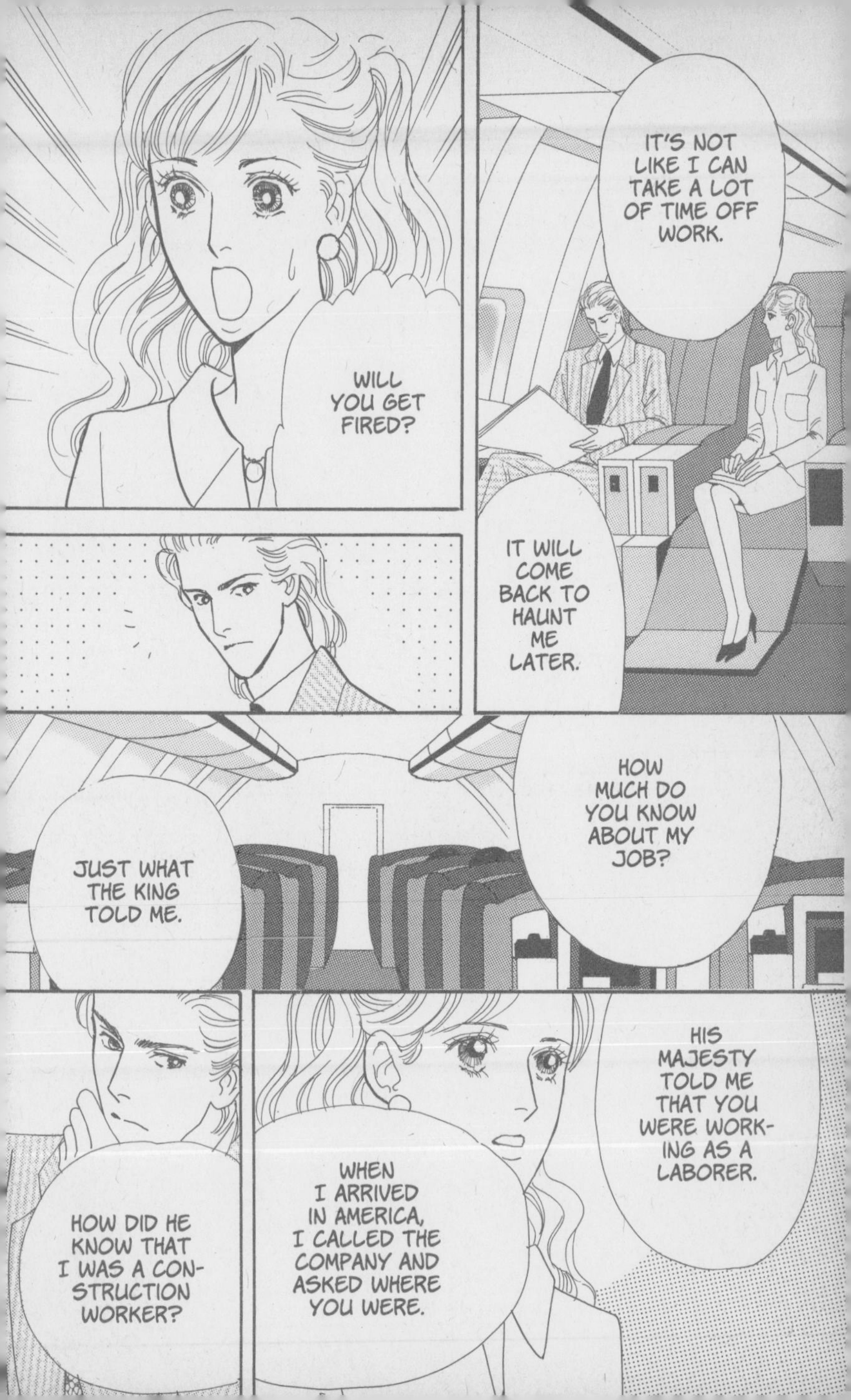
IT'S NOT LIKE I CAN TAKE A LOT OF TIME OFF WORK.
IT WILL COME BACK TO HAUNT ME LATER.
WILL YOU GET FIRED?
HOW MUCH DO YOU KNOW ABOUT MY JOB?
JUST WHAT THE KING TOLD ME.
HIS MAJESTY TOLD ME THAT YOU WERE WORKING AS A LABORER.
WHEN I ARRIVED IN AMERICA, I CALLED THE COMPANY AND ASKED WHERE YOU WERE.
HOW DID HE KNOW THAT I WAS A CONSTRUCTION WORKER?

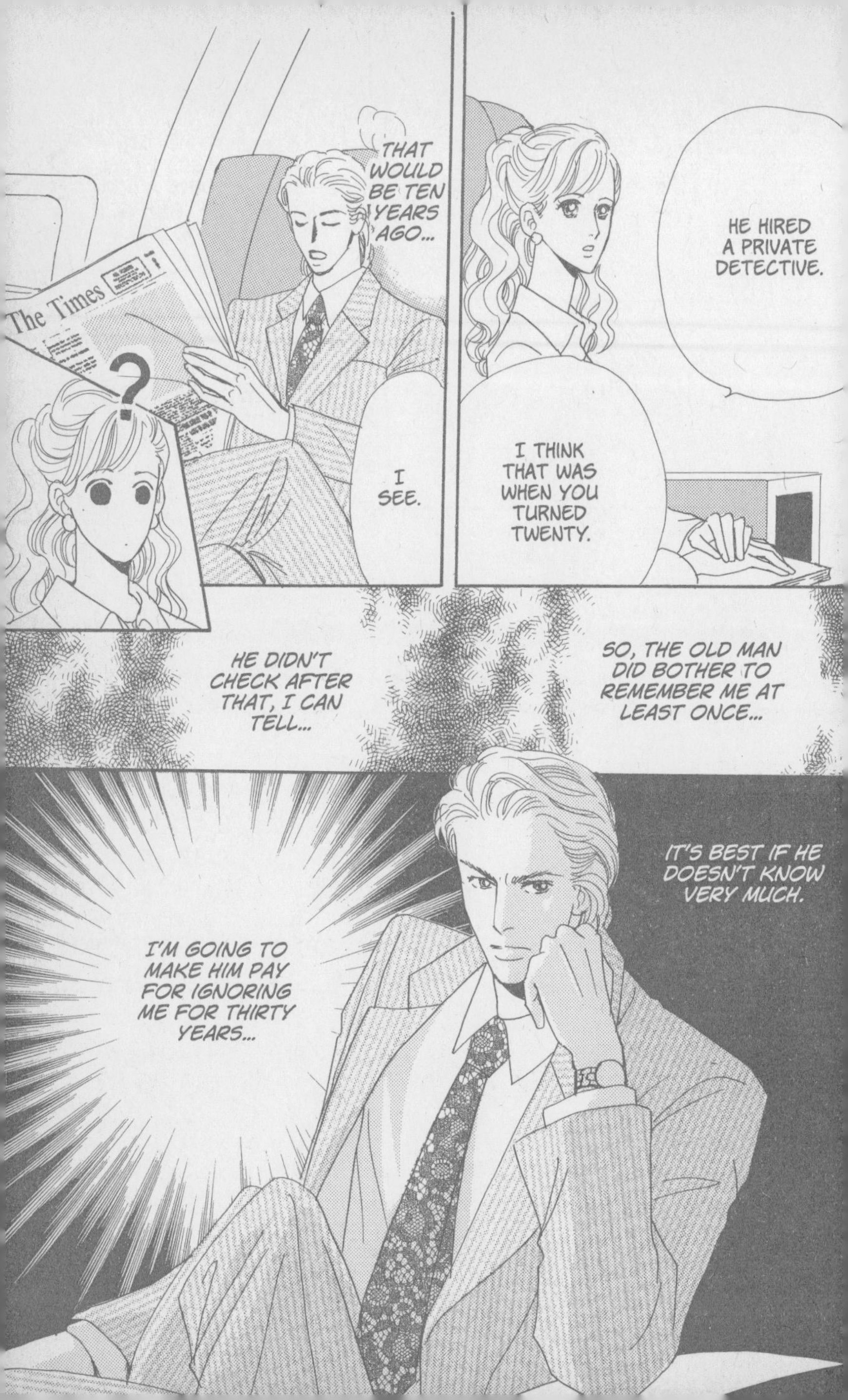
HE HIRED A PRIVATE DETECTIVE.
I THINK THAT WAS WHEN YOU TURNED TWENTY.
THAT WOULD BE TEN YEARS AGO...
The Times
I SEE.
SO, THE OLD MAN DID BOTHER TO REMEMBER ME AT LEAST ONCE...
HE DIDN'T CHECK AFTER THAT, I CAN TELL...
IT'S BEST IF HE DOESN'T KNOW VERY MUCH.
I'M GOING TO MAKE HIM PAY FOR IGNORING ME FOR THIRTY YEARS...

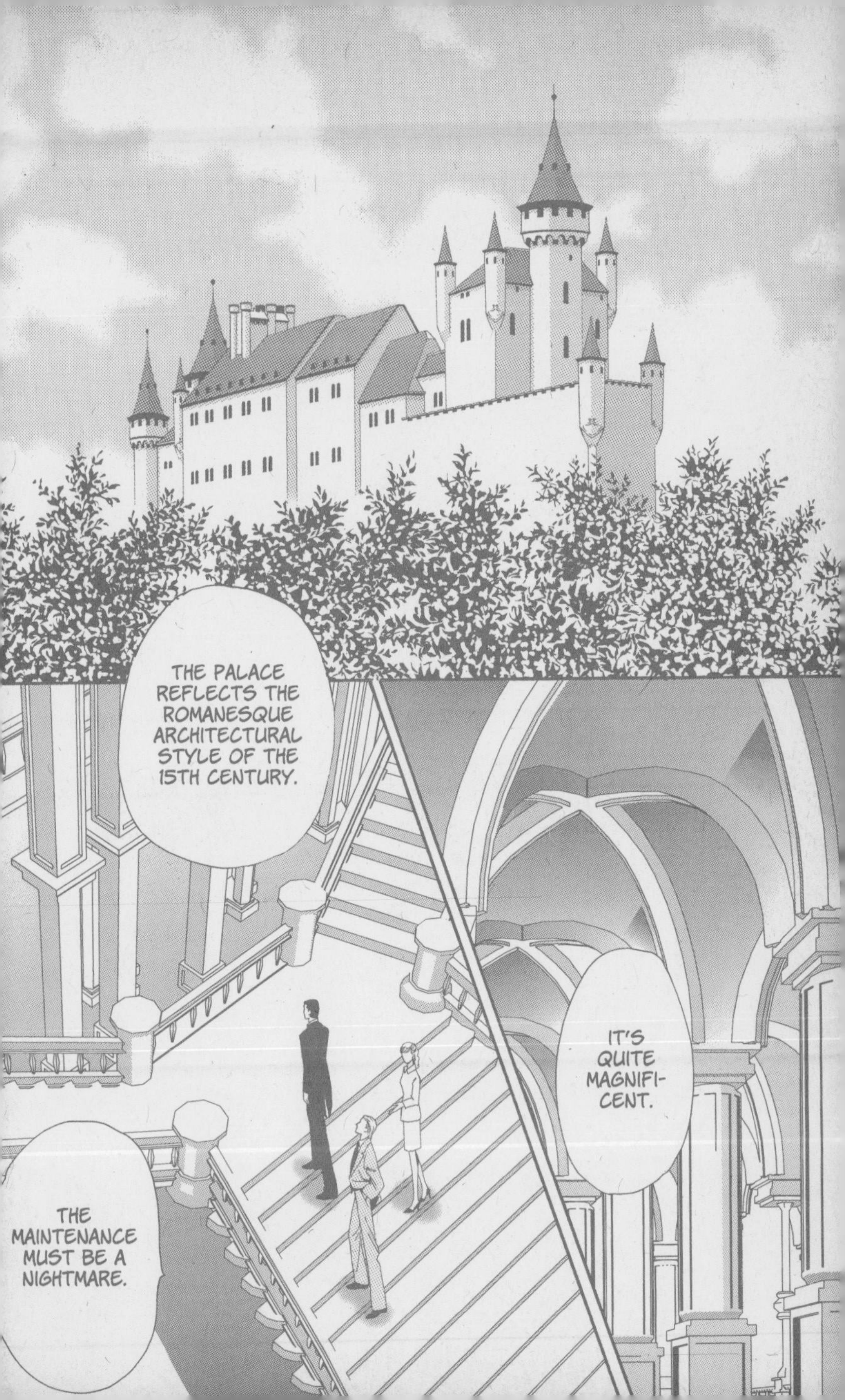
THE PALACE REFLECTS THE ROMANESQUE ARCHITECTURAL STYLE OF THE 15TH CENTURY.
IT'S QUITE MAGNIFI-CENT.
THE MAINTENANCE MUST BE A NIGHTMARE.

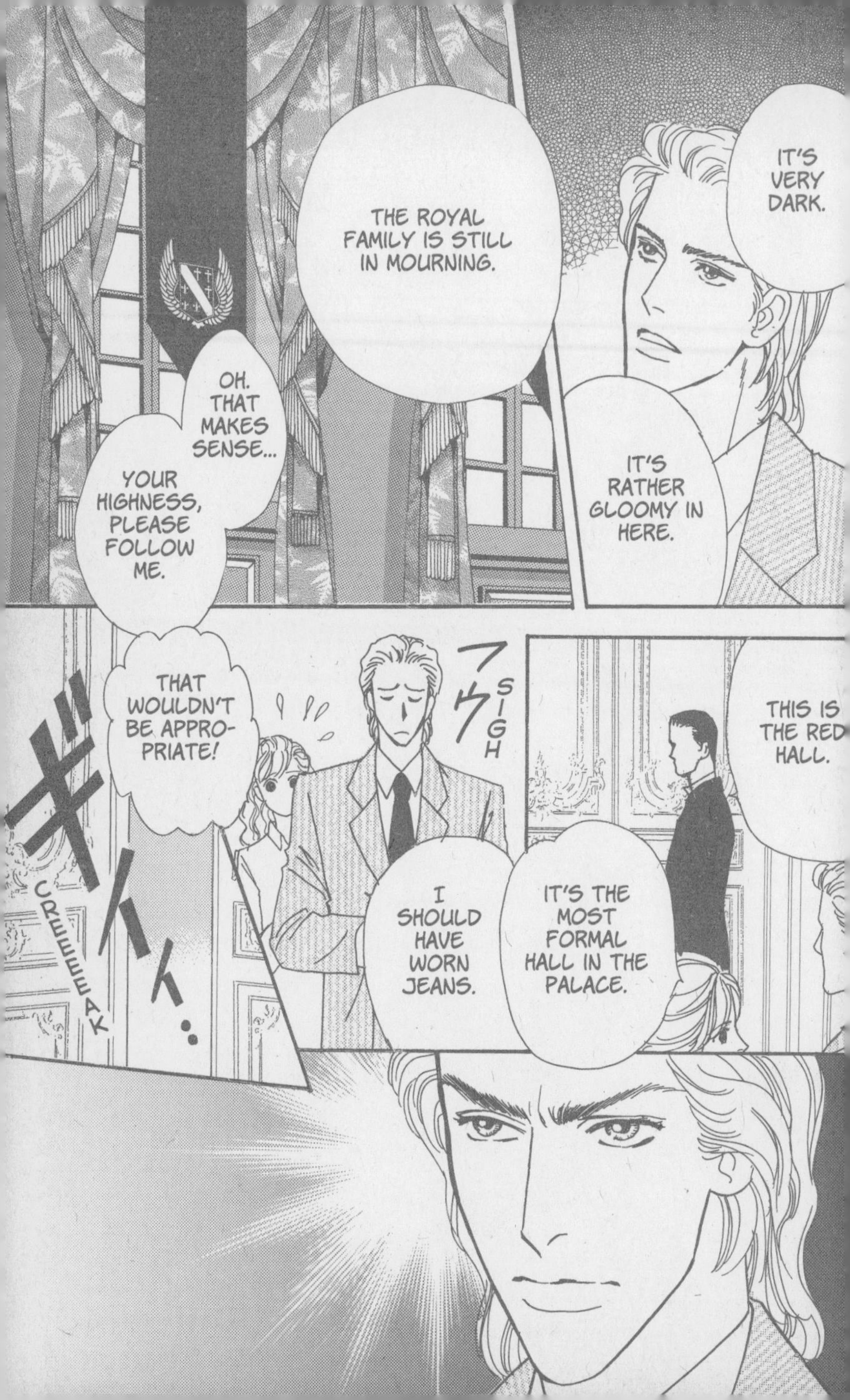
IT'S VERY DARK.
IT'S RATHER GLOOMY IN HERE.
THE ROYAL FAMILY IS STILL IN MOURNING.
OH. THAT MAKES SENSE...
YOUR HIGHNESS, PLEASE FOLLOW ME.
THIS IS THE RED HALL.
IT'S THE MOST FORMAL HALL IN THE PALACE.
SIGH
I SHOULD HAVE WORN JEANS.
THAT WOULDN'T BE APPROPRIATE!
CREEEEAK

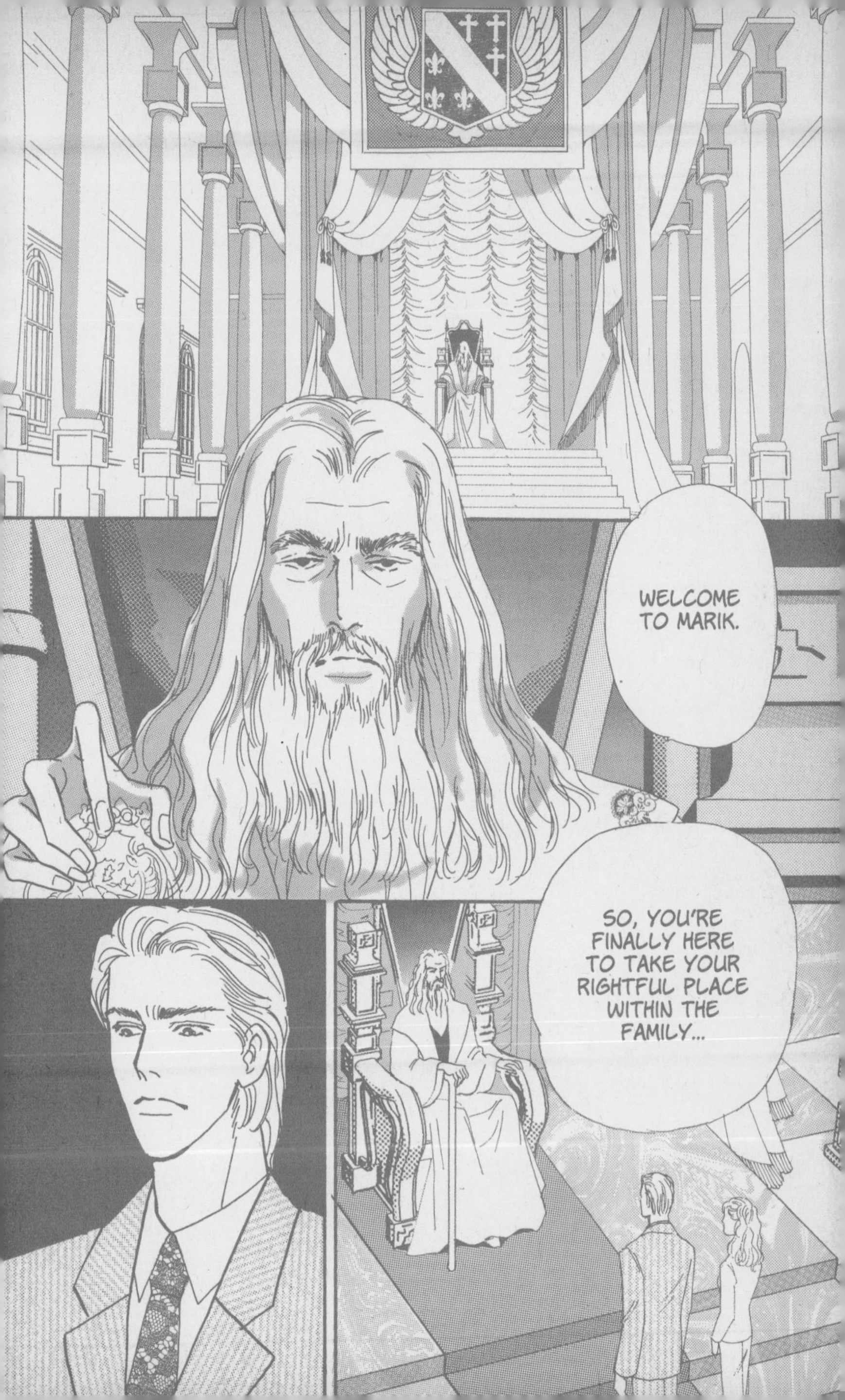
WELCOME TO MARIK.
SO, YOU'RE FINALLY HERE TO TAKE YOUR RIGHTFUL PLACE WITHIN THE FAMILY...

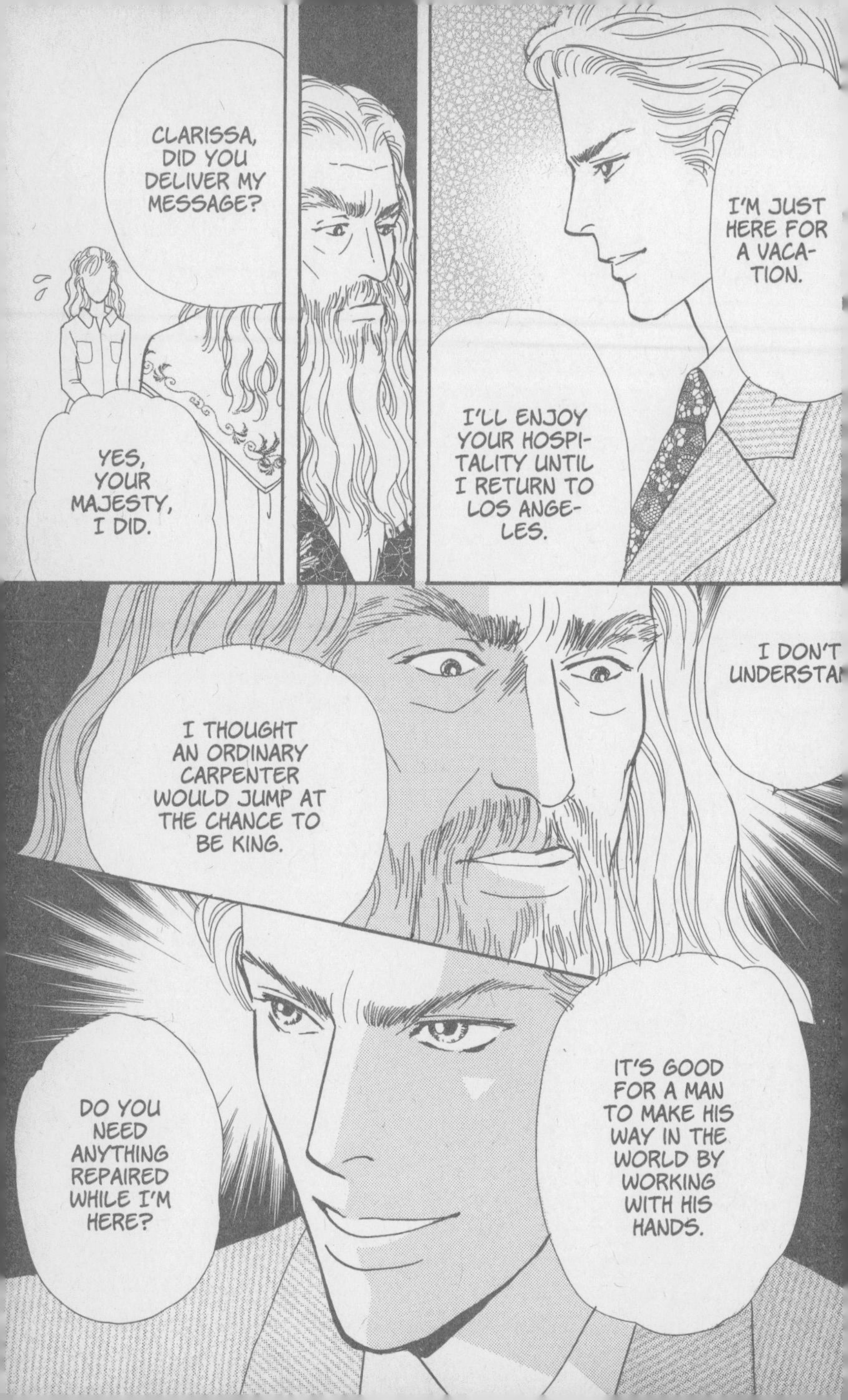
I'M JUST HERE FOR A VACATION.
I'LL ENJOY YOUR HOSPITALITY UNTIL I RETURN TO LOS ANGELES.
CLARISSA, DID YOU DELIVER MY MESSAGE?
YES, YOUR MAJESTY, I DID.
I DON'T UNDERSTAN
I THOUGHT AN ORDINARY CARPENTER WOULD JUMP AT THE CHANCE TO BE KING.
IT'S GOOD FOR A MAN TO MAKE HIS WAY IN THE WORLD BY WORKING WITH HIS HANDS.
DO YOU NEED ANYTHING REPAIRED WHILE I'M HERE?

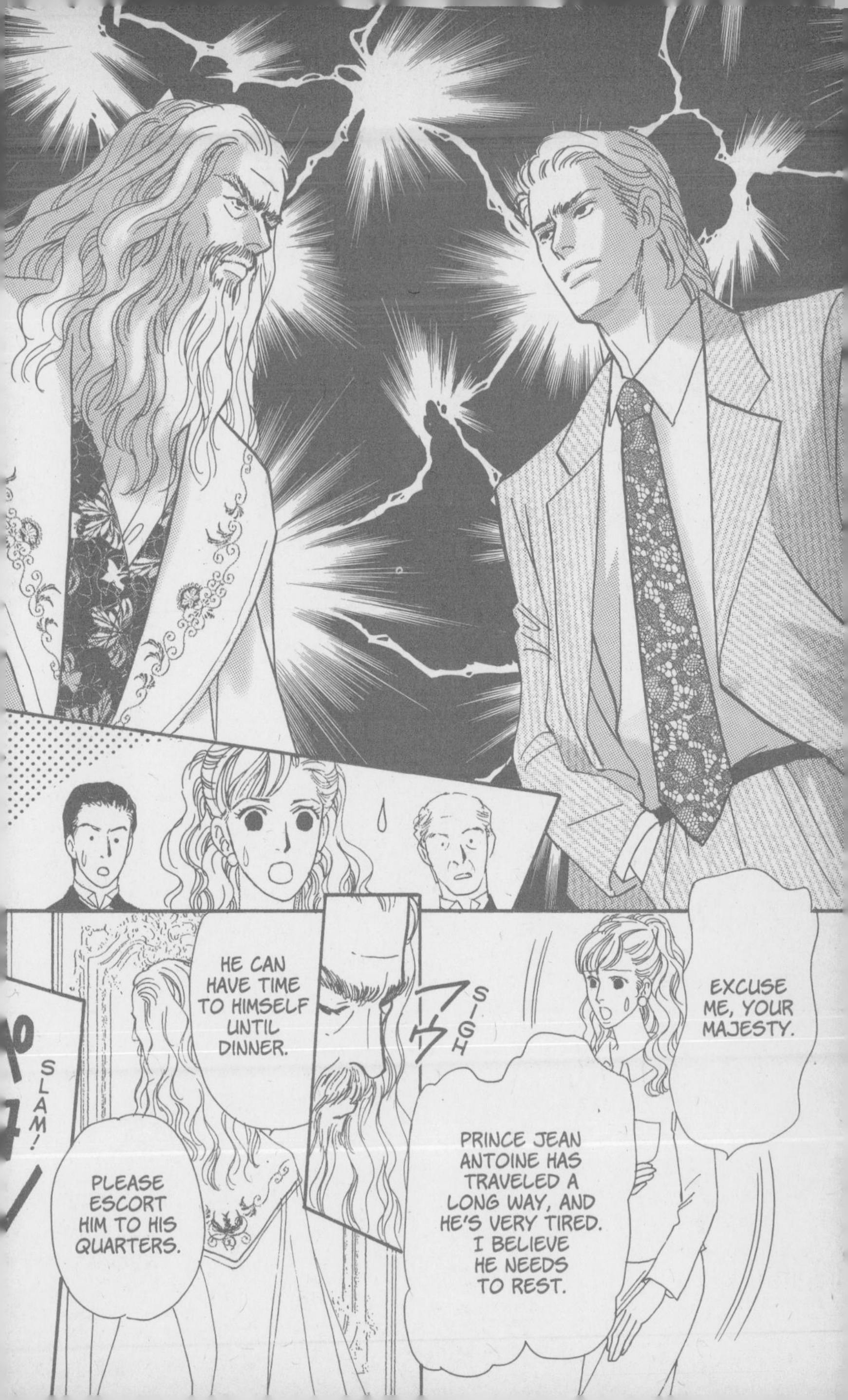
EXCUSE ME, YOUR MAJESTY.
PRINCE JEAN ANTOINE HAS TRAVELED A LONG WAY, AND HE'S VERY TIRED. I BELIEVE HE NEEDS TO REST.
SIGH
HE CAN HAVE TIME TO HIMSELF UNTIL DINNER.
PLEASE ESCORT HIM TO HIS QUARTERS.
SLAM!

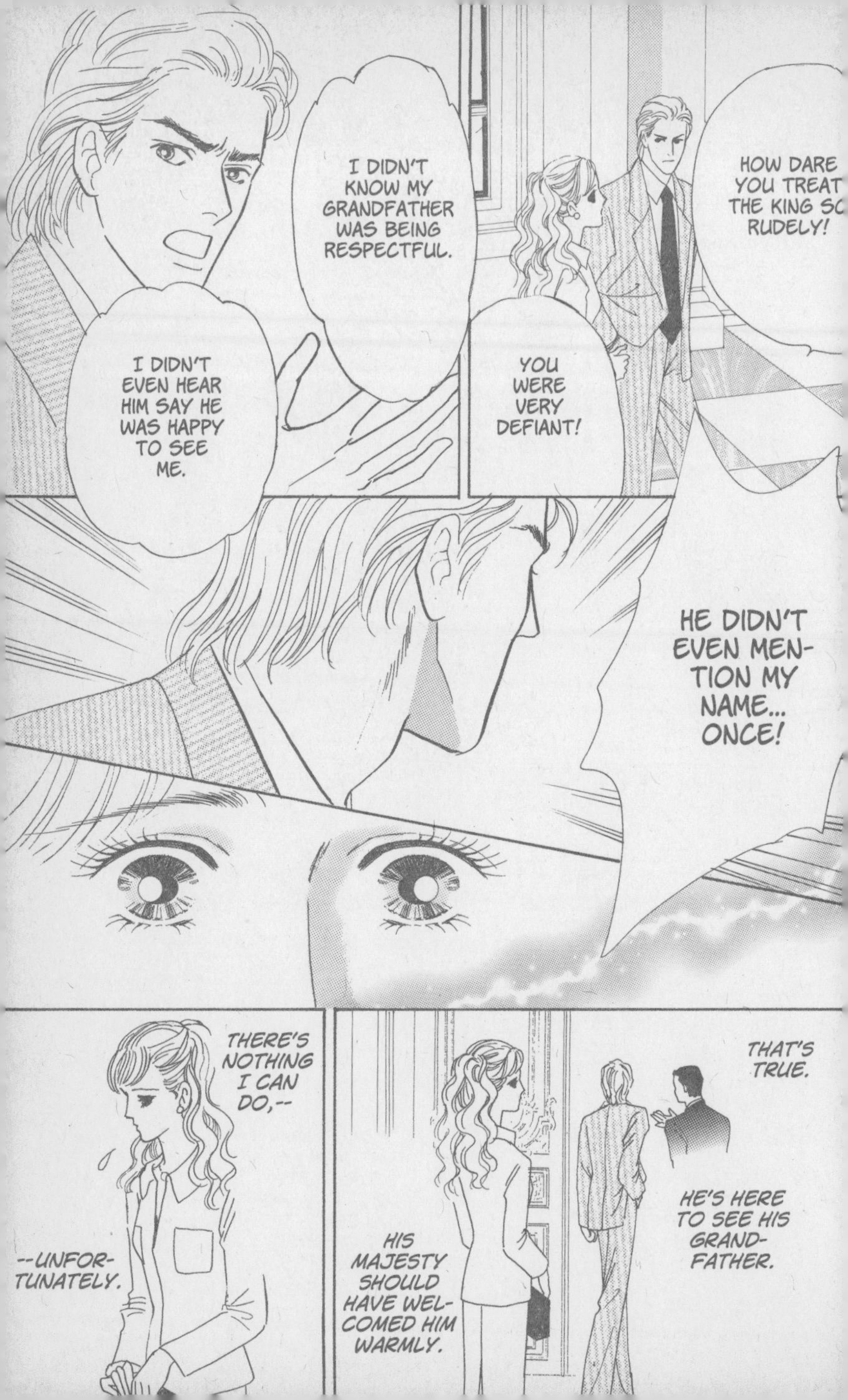
HOW DARE YOU TREAT THE KING SO RUDELY!
YOU WERE VERY DEFIANT!
I DIDN'T KNOW MY GRANDFATHER WAS BEING RESPECTFUL.
I DIDN'T EVEN HEAR HIM SAY HE WAS HAPPY TO SEE ME.
HE DIDN'T EVEN MEN-TION MY NAME... ONCE!
THAT'S TRUE.
HE'S HERE TO SEE HIS GRAND-FATHER.
HIS MAJESTY SHOULD HAVE WEL-COMED HIM WARMLY.
THERE'S NOTHING I CAN DO,--
--UNFOR-TUNATELY.

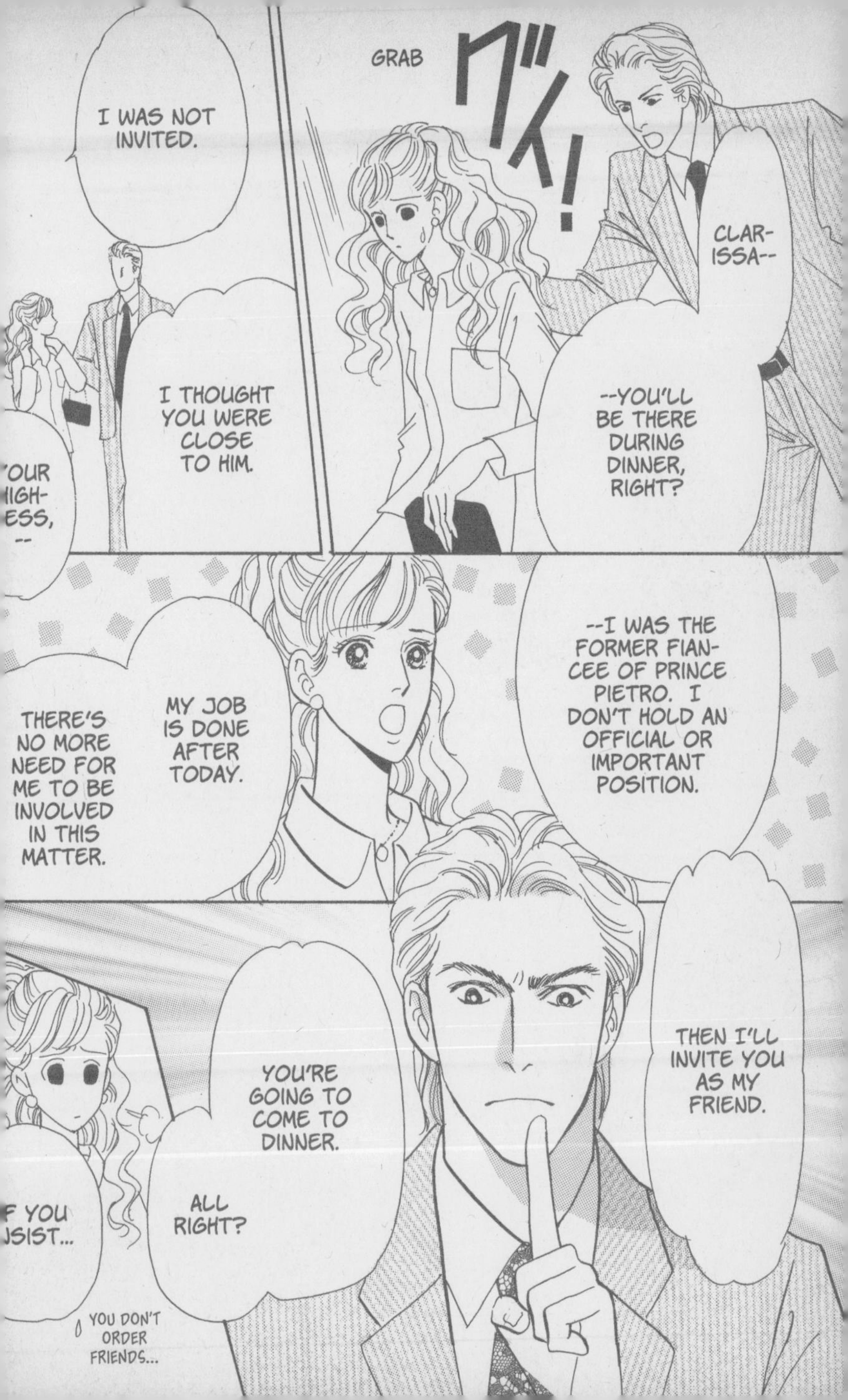
GRAB
グイ!
CLAR-ISSA--
--YOU'LL BE THERE DURING DINNER, RIGHT?
I WAS NOT INVITED.
I THOUGHT YOU WERE CLOSE TO HIM.
OUR IGH-ESS, --
--I WAS THE FORMER FIAN-CEE OF PRINCE PIETRO. I DON'T HOLD AN OFFICIAL OR IMPORTANT POSITION.
MY JOB IS DONE AFTER TODAY.
THERE'S NO MORE NEED FOR ME TO BE INVOLVED IN THIS MATTER.
THEN I'LL INVITE YOU AS MY FRIEND.
YOU'RE GOING TO COME TO DINNER.
ALL RIGHT?
F YOU NSIST...
YOU DON'T ORDER FRIENDS...

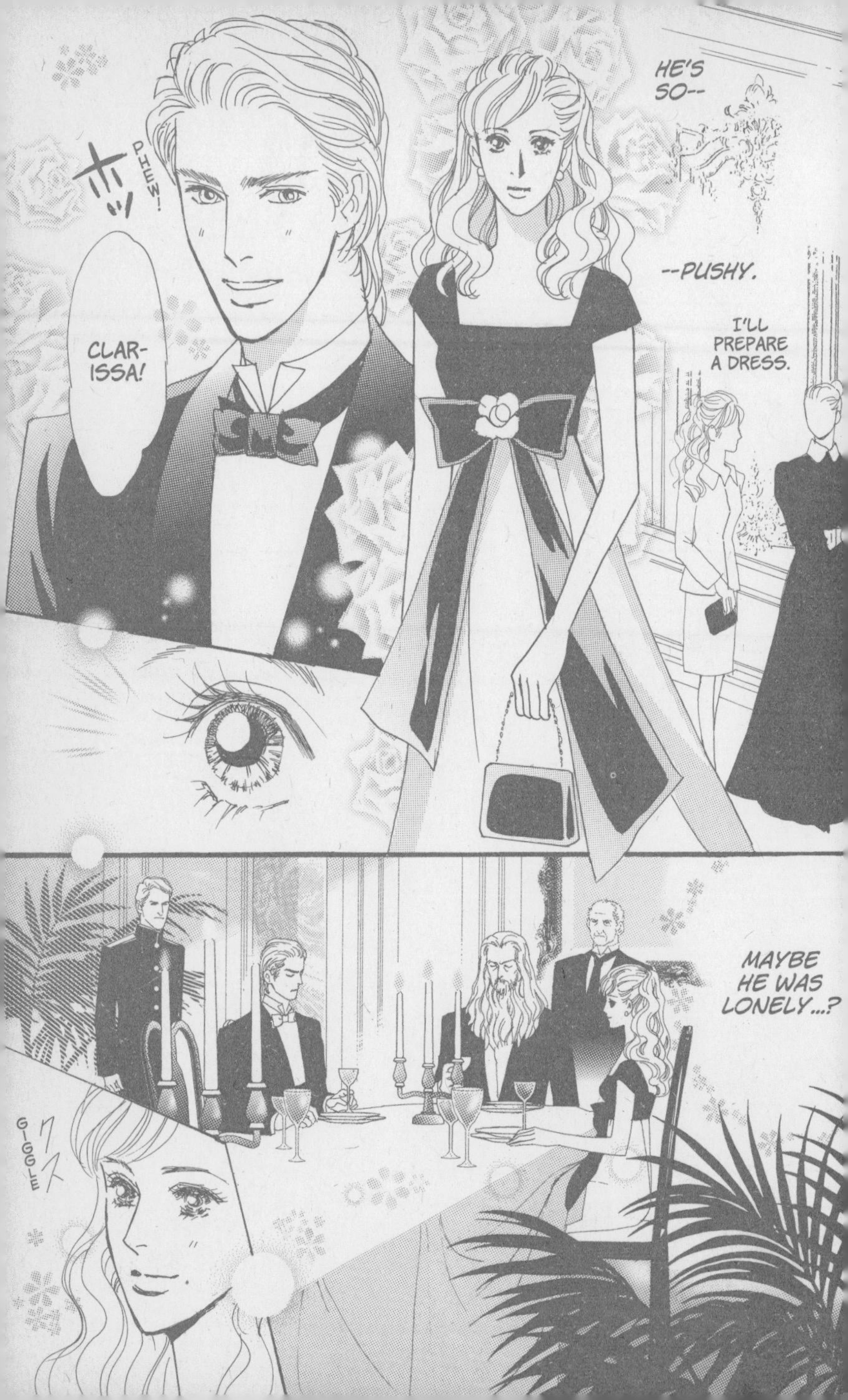
HE'S SO--
--PUSHY.
I'LL PREPARE A DRESS.
PHEW!
ホッ
CLARISSA!
MAYBE HE WAS LONELY...?
クス
GIGGLE

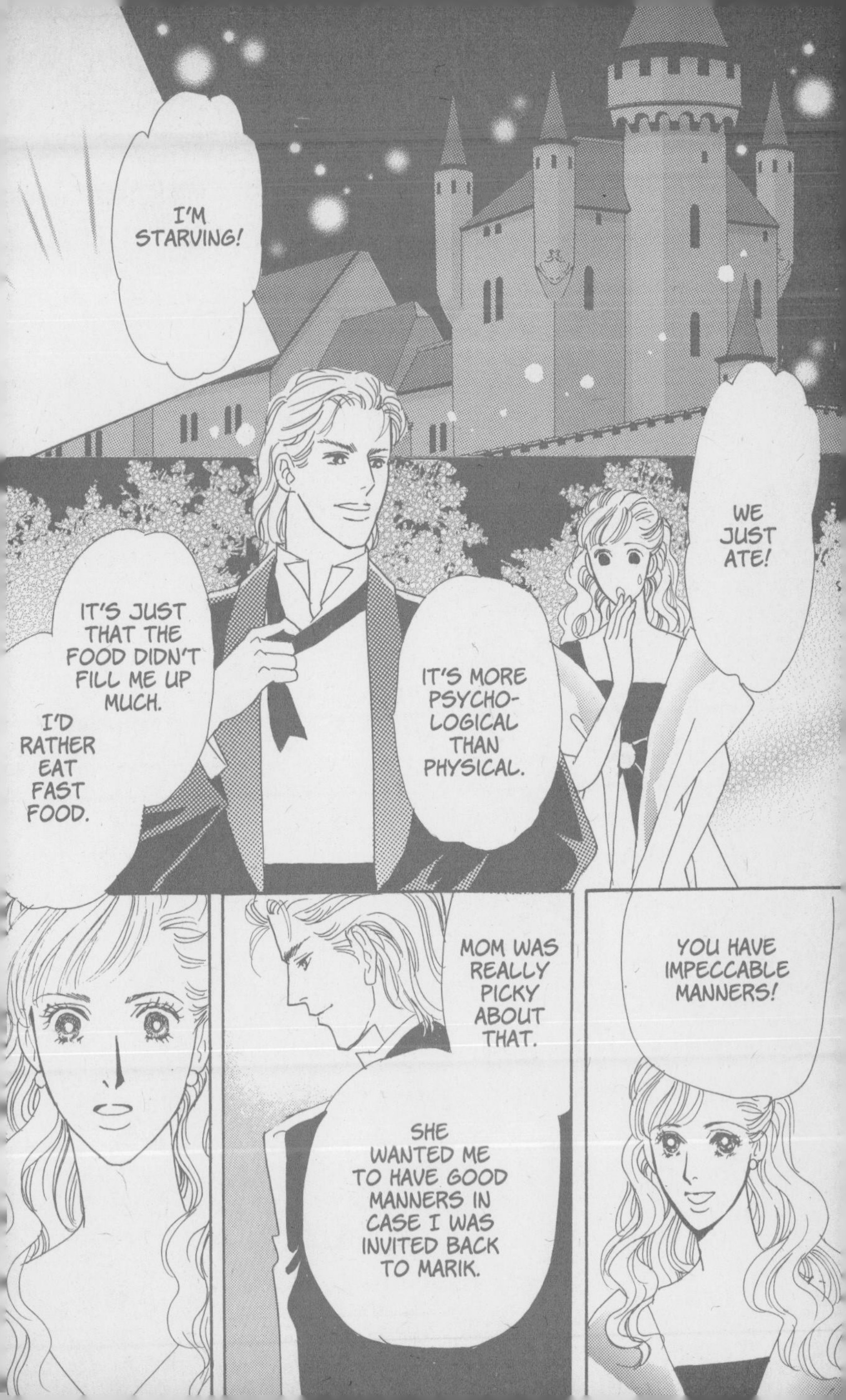
I'M STARVING!
WE JUST ATE!
IT'S MORE PSYCHOLOGICAL THAN PHYSICAL.
IT'S JUST THAT THE FOOD DIDN'T FILL ME UP MUCH.
I'D RATHER EAT FAST FOOD.
YOU HAVE IMPECCABLE MANNERS!
MOM WAS REALLY PICKY ABOUT THAT.
SHE WANTED ME TO HAVE GOOD MANNERS IN CASE I WAS INVITED BACK TO MARIK.

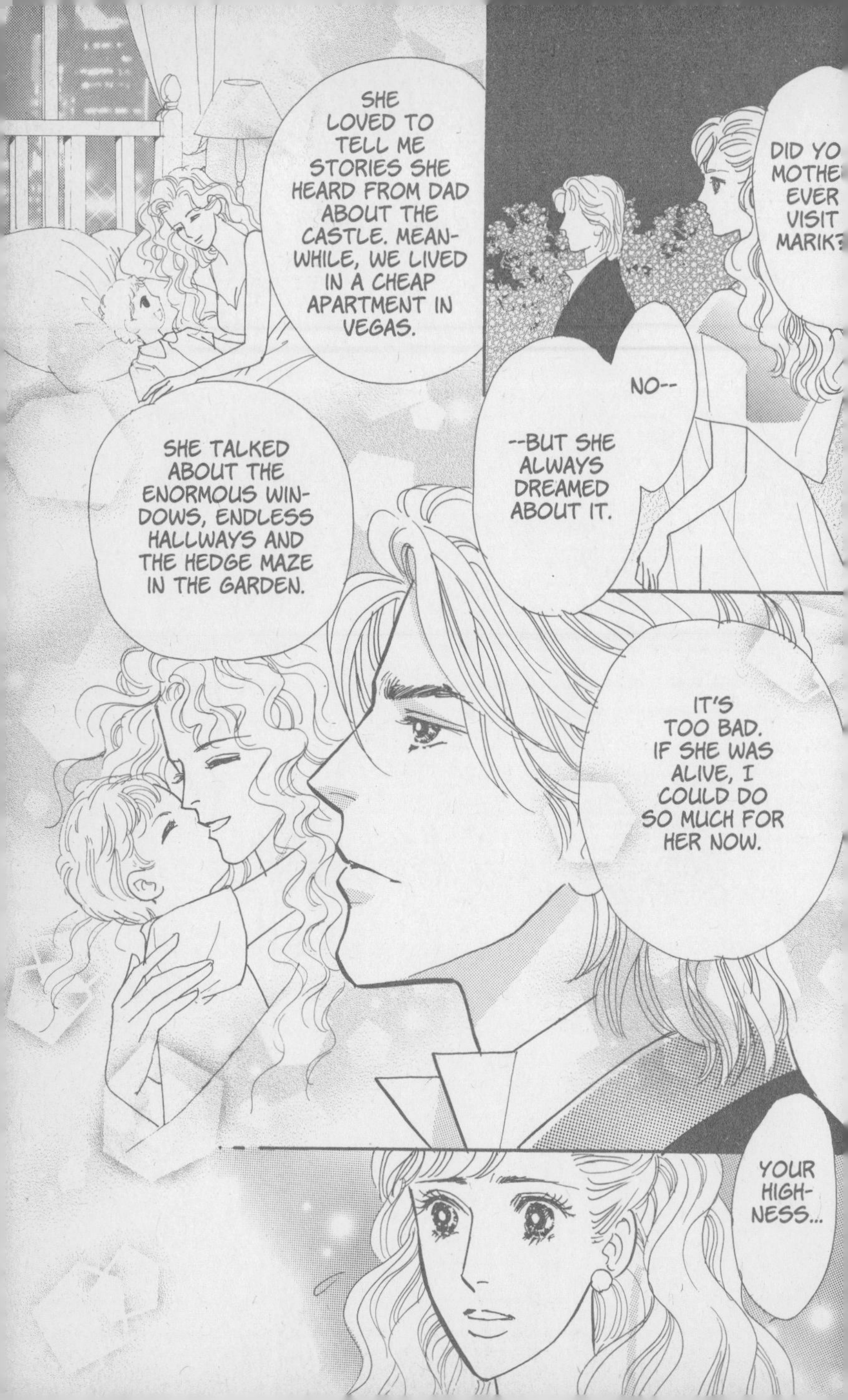
DID YO MOTHE EVER VISIT MARIK?
NO--
--BUT SHE ALWAYS DREAMED ABOUT IT.
SHE LOVED TO TELL ME STORIES SHE HEARD FROM DAD ABOUT THE CASTLE. MEAN-WHILE, WE LIVED IN A CHEAP APARTMENT IN VEGAS.
SHE TALKED ABOUT THE ENORMOUS WIN-DOWS, ENDLESS HALLWAYS AND THE HEDGE MAZE IN THE GARDEN.
IT'S TOO BAD. IF SHE WAS ALIVE, I COULD DO SO MUCH FOR HER NOW.
YOUR HIGH-NESS...

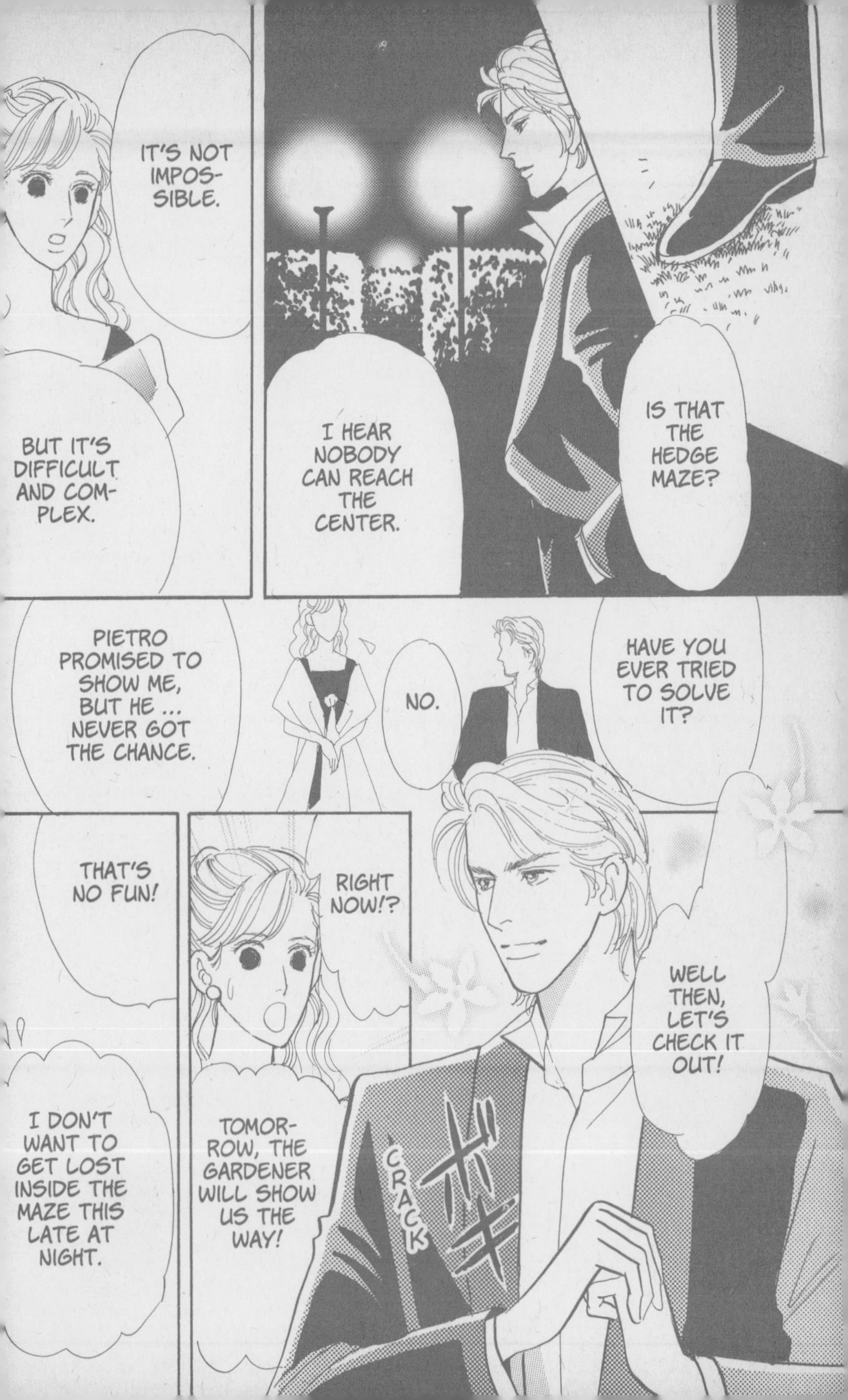
IS THAT THE HEDGE MAZE?
I HEAR NOBODY CAN REACH THE CENTER.
IT'S NOT IMPOSSIBLE.
BUT IT'S DIFFICULT AND COMPLEX.
HAVE YOU EVER TRIED TO SOLVE IT?
NO.
PIETRO PROMISED TO SHOW ME, BUT HE ... NEVER GOT THE CHANCE.
WELL THEN, LET'S CHECK IT OUT!
CRACK
RIGHT NOW!?
TOMORROW, THE GARDENER WILL SHOW US THE WAY!
THAT'S NO FUN!
I DON'T WANT TO GET LOST INSIDE THE MAZE THIS LATE AT NIGHT.

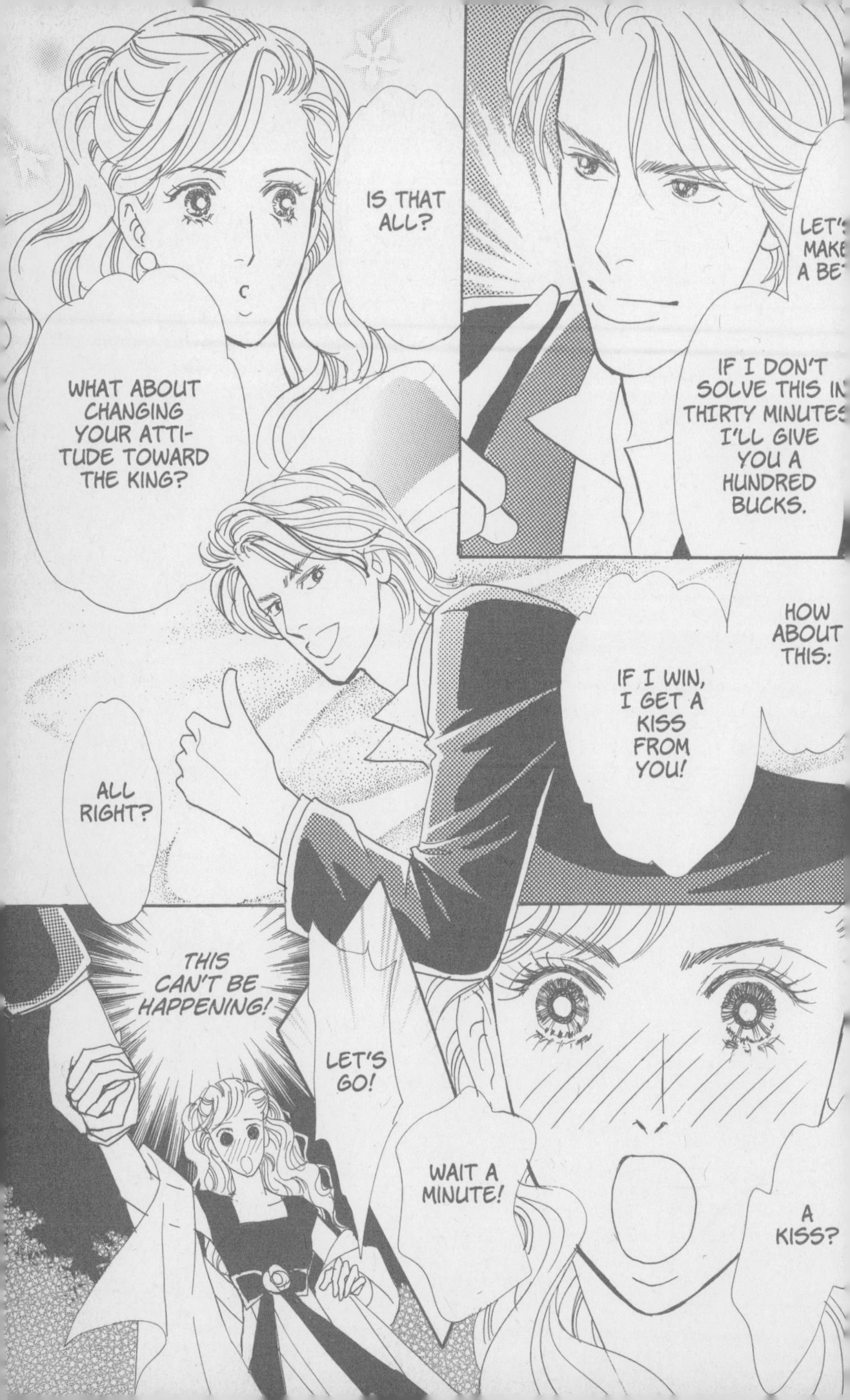
LET'S MAKE A BET
IF I DON'T SOLVE THIS IN THIRTY MINUTES I'LL GIVE YOU A HUNDRED BUCKS.
IS THAT ALL?
WHAT ABOUT CHANGING YOUR ATTI-TUDE TOWARD THE KING?
HOW ABOUT THIS:
IF I WIN, I GET A KISS FROM YOU!
ALL RIGHT?
A KISS?
WAIT A MINUTE!
LET'S GO!
THIS CAN'T BE HAPPENING!

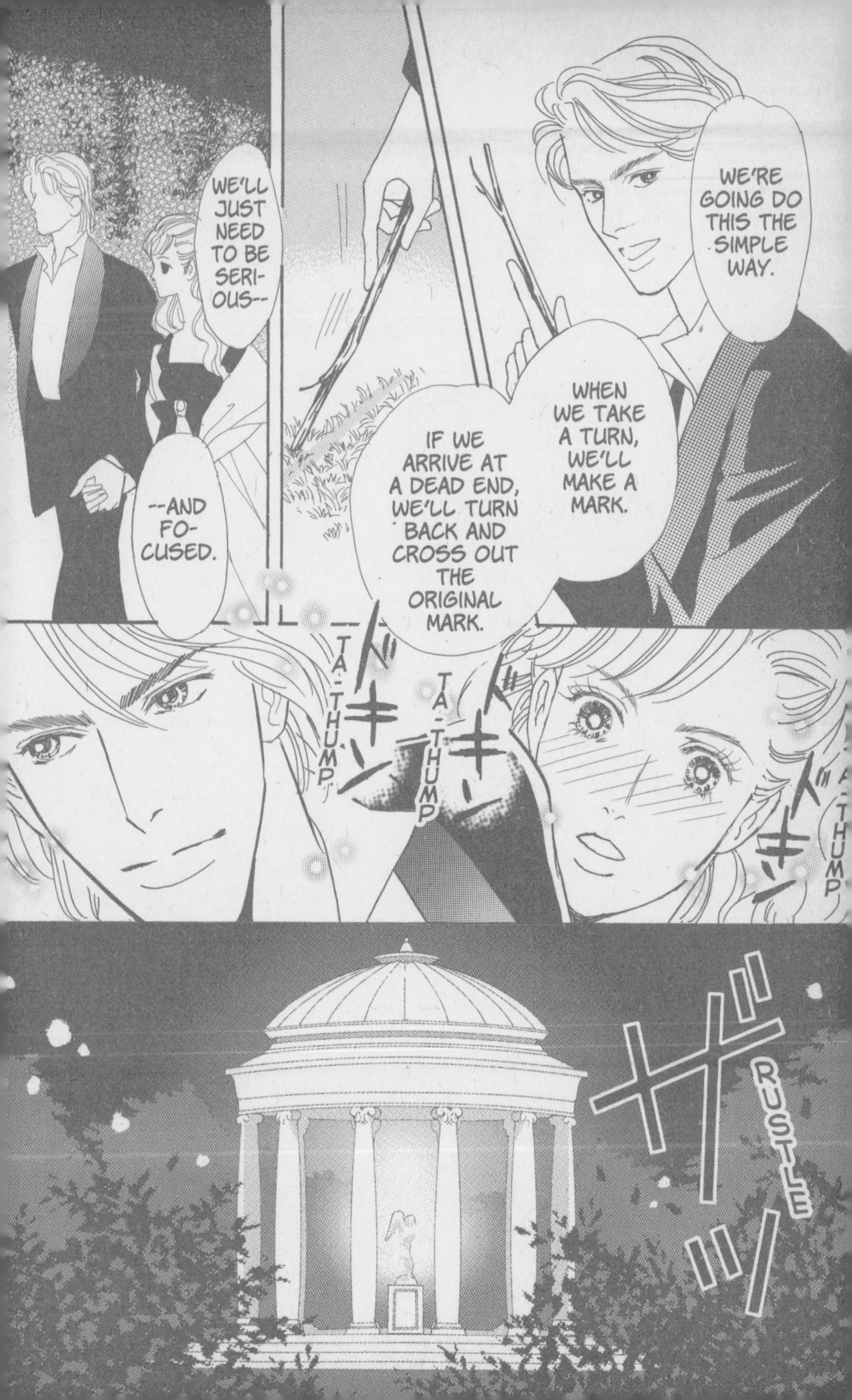
WE'RE GOING DO THIS THE SIMPLE WAY.
WHEN WE TAKE A TURN, WE'LL MAKE A MARK.
IF WE ARRIVE AT A DEAD END, WE'LL TURN BACK AND CROSS OUT THE ORIGINAL MARK.
WE'LL JUST NEED TO BE SERI-OUS--
--AND FO-CUSED.
A-THUMP
TA-THUMP
TA-THUMP
RUSTLE

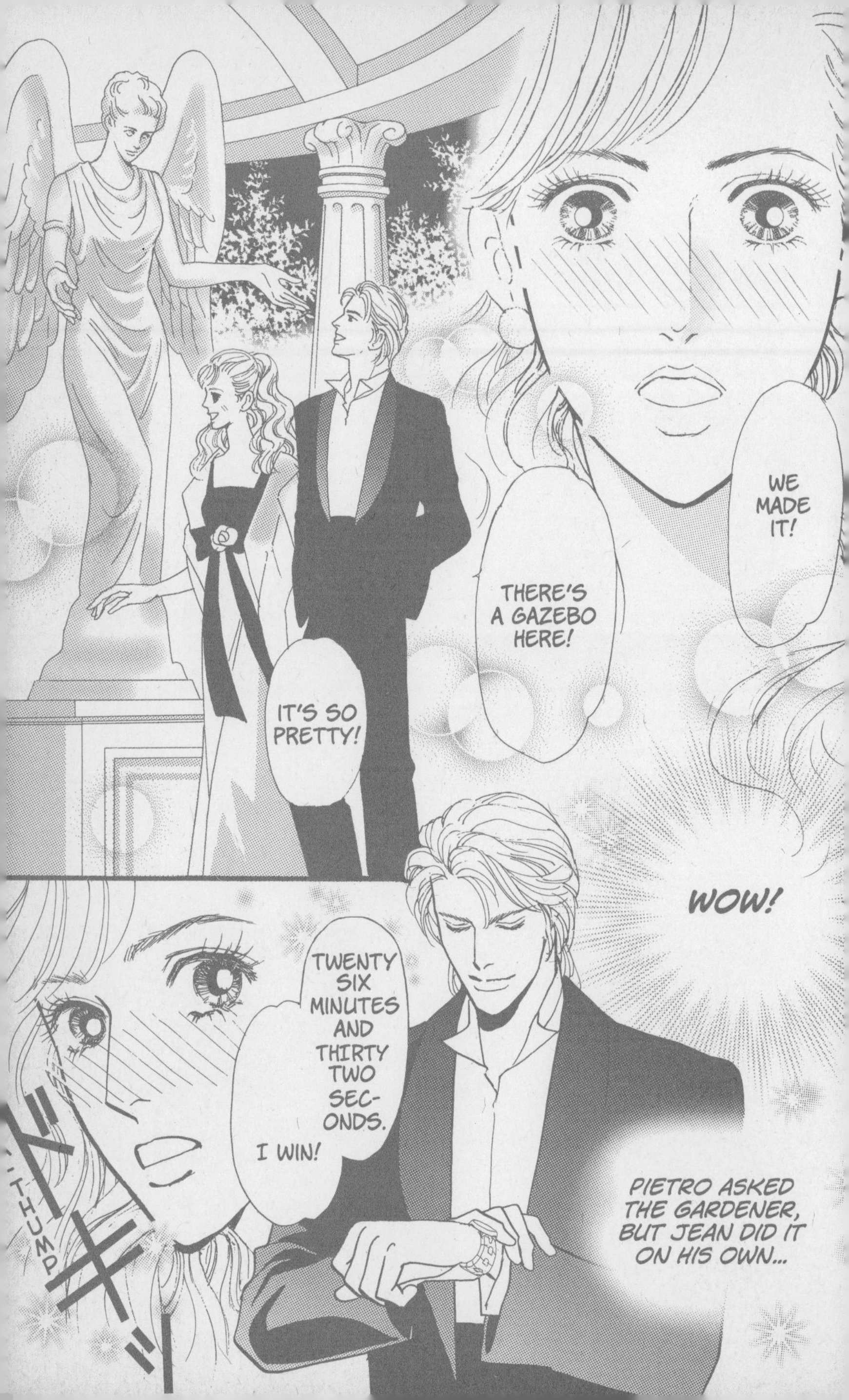
WE MADE IT!
THERE'S A GAZEBO HERE!
WOW!
IT'S SO PRETTY!
PIETRO ASKED THE GARDENER, BUT JEAN DID IT ON HIS OWN...
TWENTY SIX MINUTES AND THIRTY TWO SECONDS.
I WIN!
THUMP

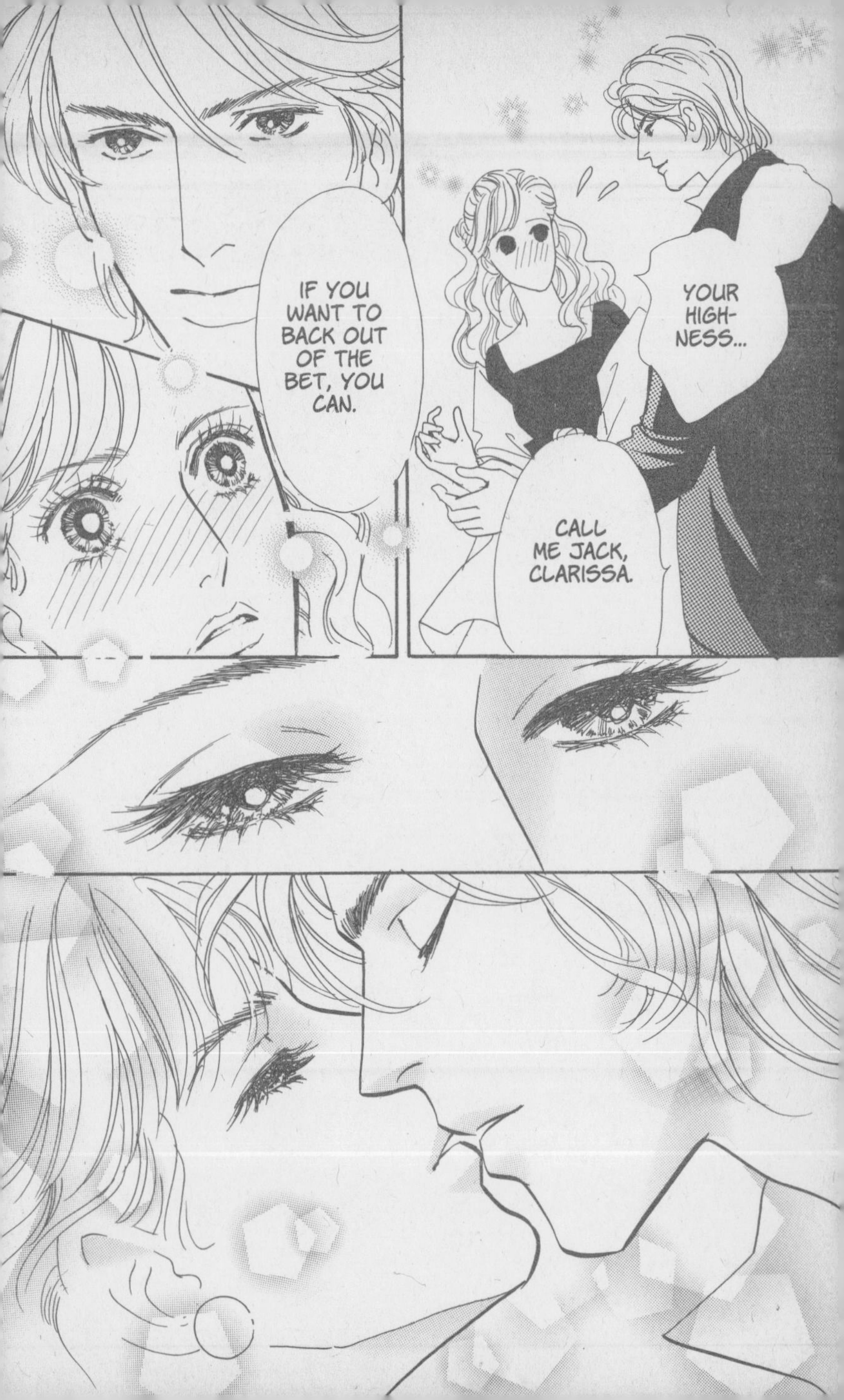
YOUR HIGH-NESS...
CALL ME JACK, CLARISSA.
IF YOU WANT TO BACK OUT OF THE BET, YOU CAN.

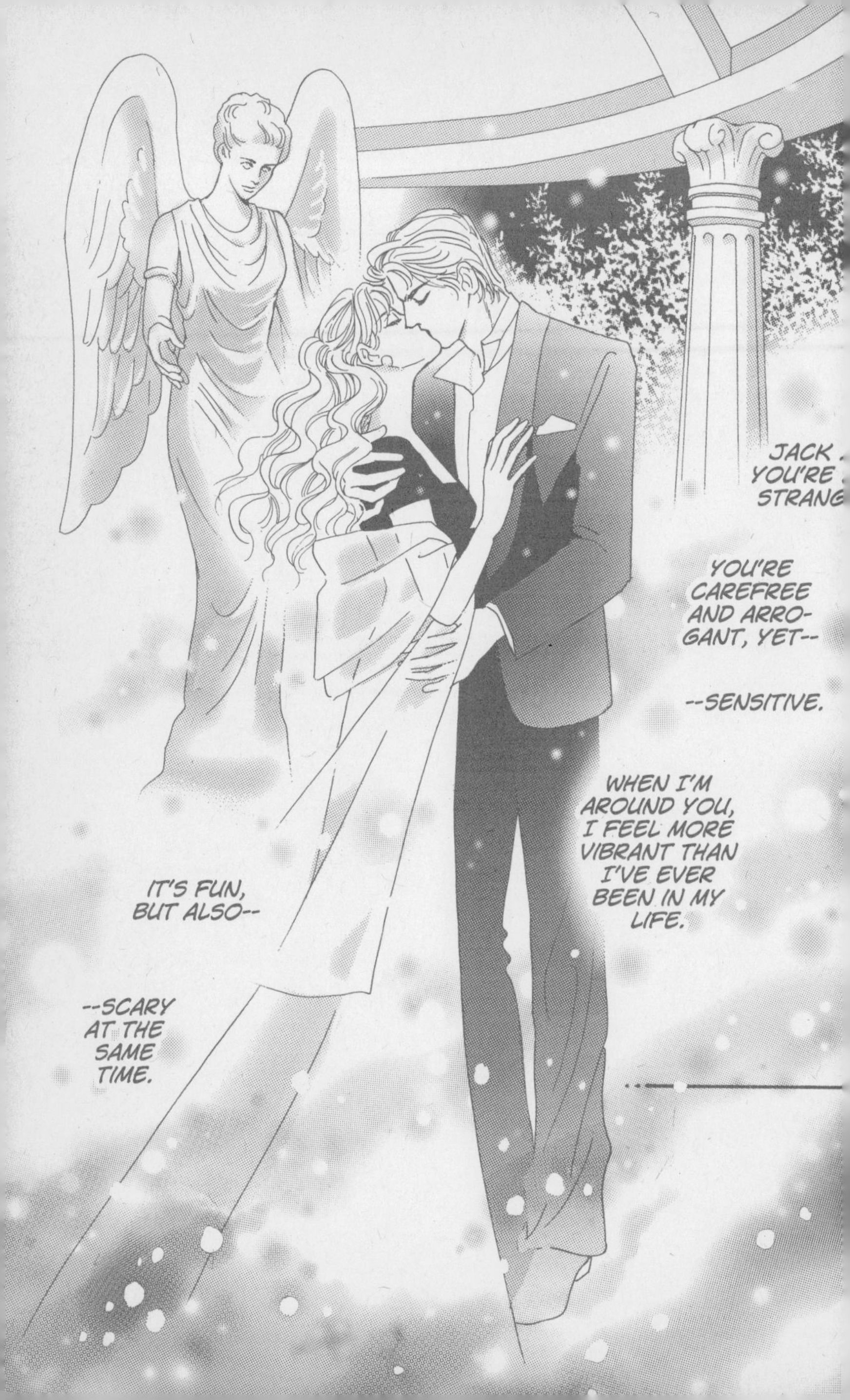
JACK . YOU'RE . STRANG
YOU'RE CAREFREE AND ARRO- GANT, YET--
--SENSITIVE.
WHEN I'M AROUND YOU, I FEEL MORE VIBRANT THAN I'VE EVER BEEN IN MY LIFE.
IT'S FUN, BUT ALSO--
--SCARY AT THE SAME TIME.

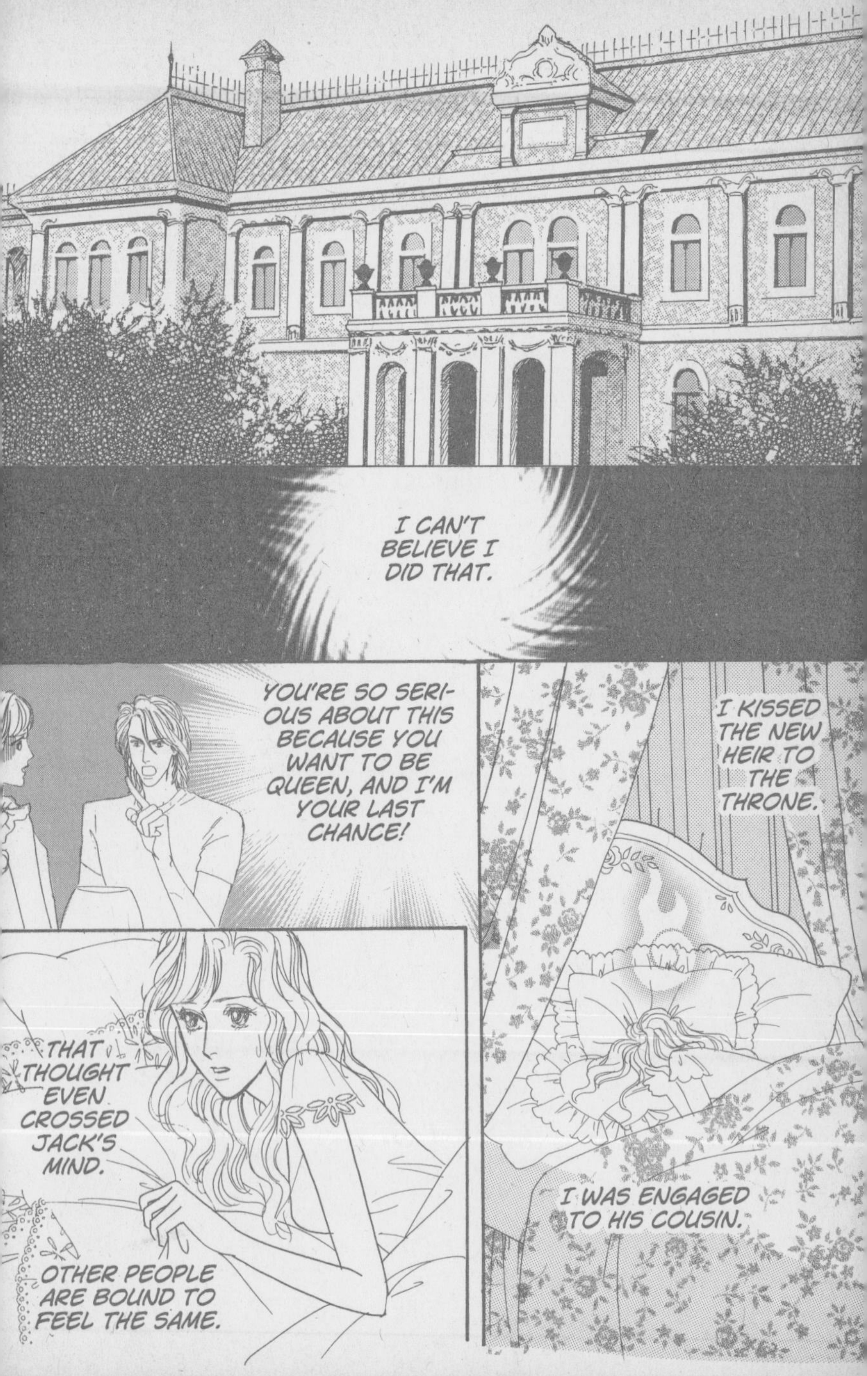
I CAN'T BELIEVE I DID THAT.
I KISSED THE NEW HEIR TO THE THRONE.
I WAS ENGAGED TO HIS COUSIN.
YOU'RE SO SERI-OUS ABOUT THIS BECAUSE YOU WANT TO BE QUEEN, AND I'M YOUR LAST CHANCE!
THAT THOUGHT EVEN CROSSED JACK'S MIND.
OTHER PEOPLE ARE BOUND TO FEEL THE SAME.

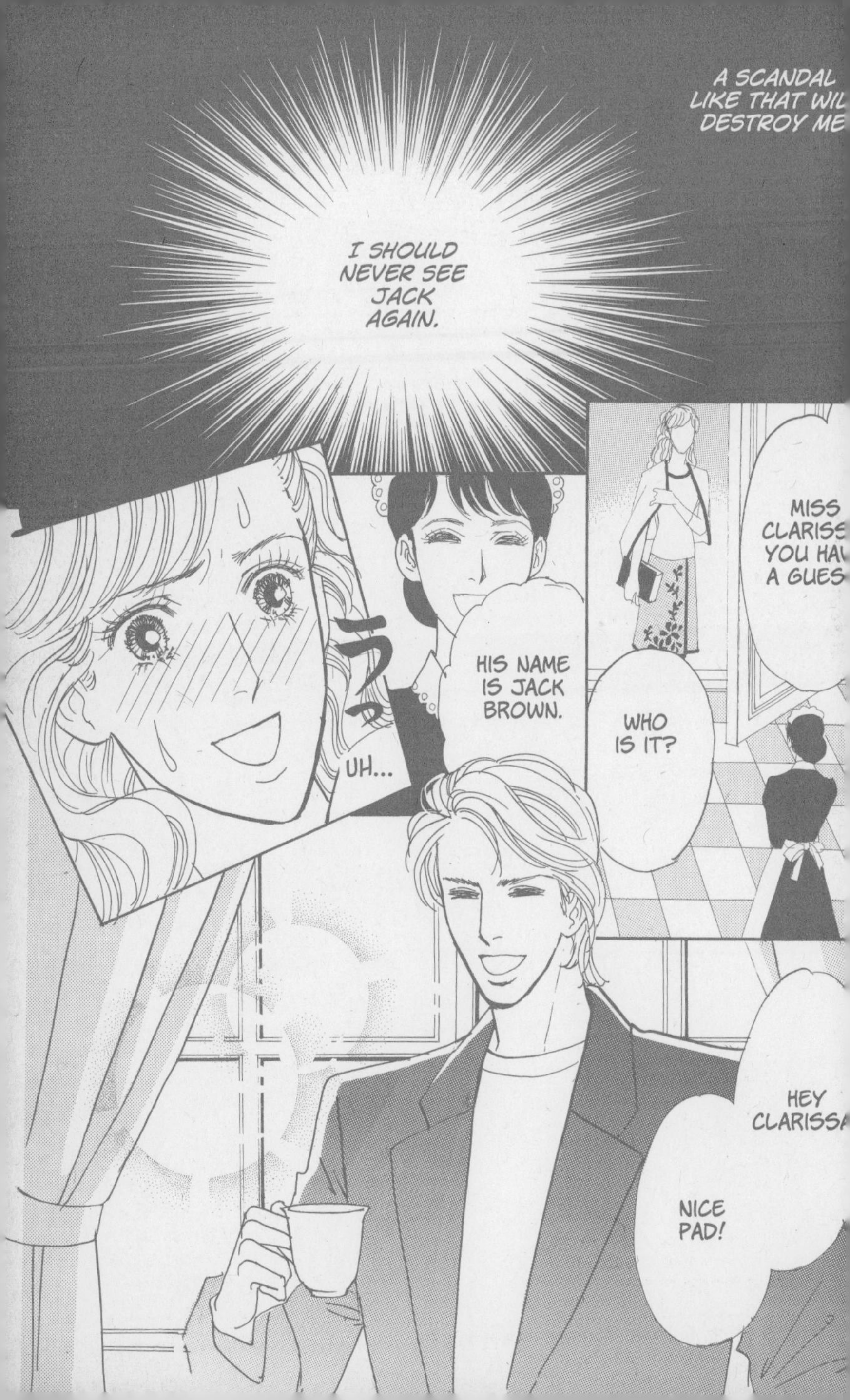
A SCANDAL LIKE THAT WIL DESTROY ME
I SHOULD NEVER SEE JACK AGAIN.
MISS CLARISS YOU HAV A GUES
WHO IS IT?
HIS NAME IS JACK BROWN.
うっ
UH...
HEY CLARISS
NICE PAD!

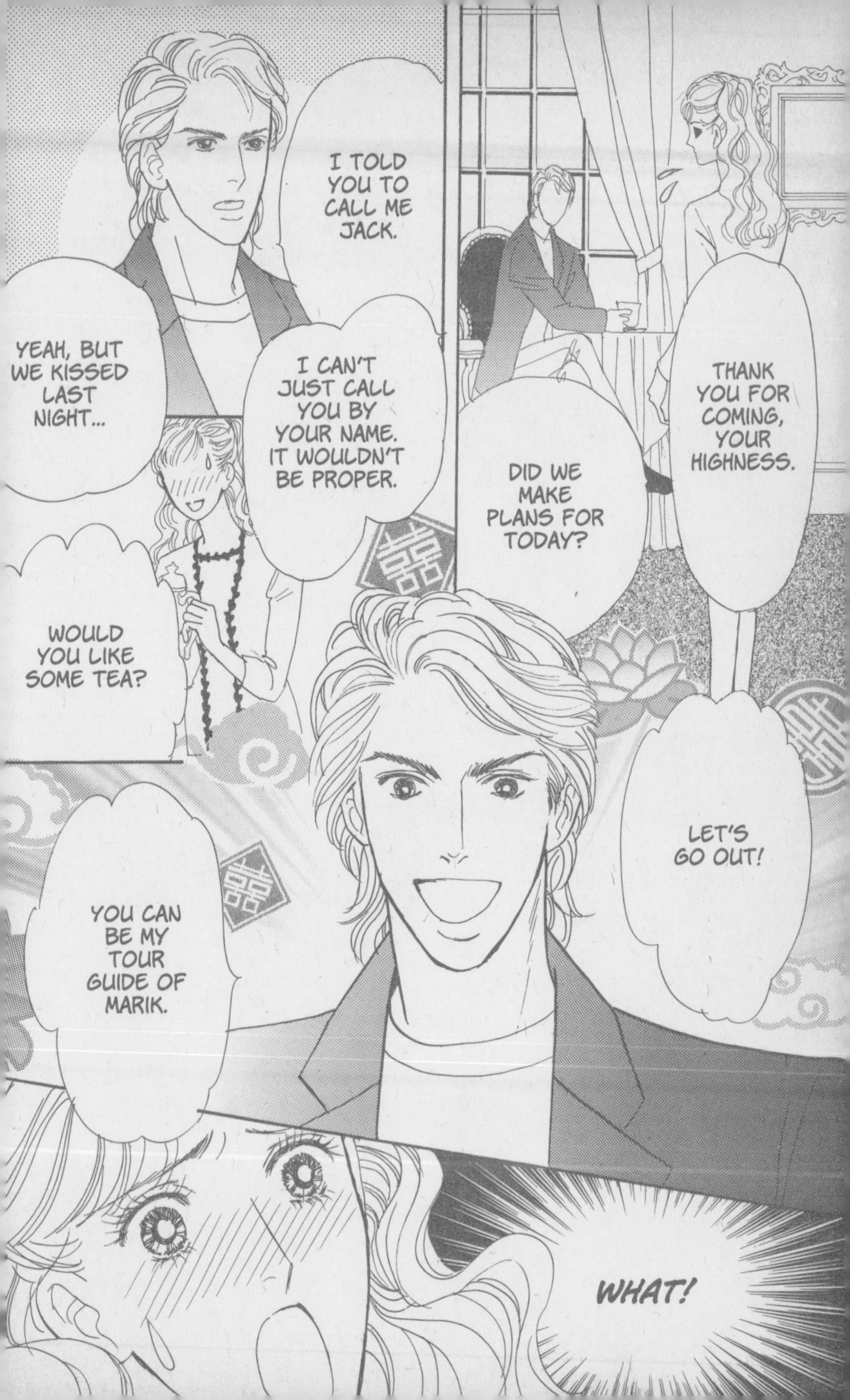
THANK YOU FOR COMING, YOUR HIGHNESS.
DID WE MAKE PLANS FOR TODAY?
I TOLD YOU TO CALL ME JACK.
I CAN'T JUST CALL YOU BY YOUR NAME. IT WOULDN'T BE PROPER.
YEAH, BUT WE KISSED LAST NIGHT...
WOULD YOU LIKE SOME TEA?
LET'S GO OUT!
YOU CAN BE MY TOUR GUIDE OF MARIK.
WHAT!

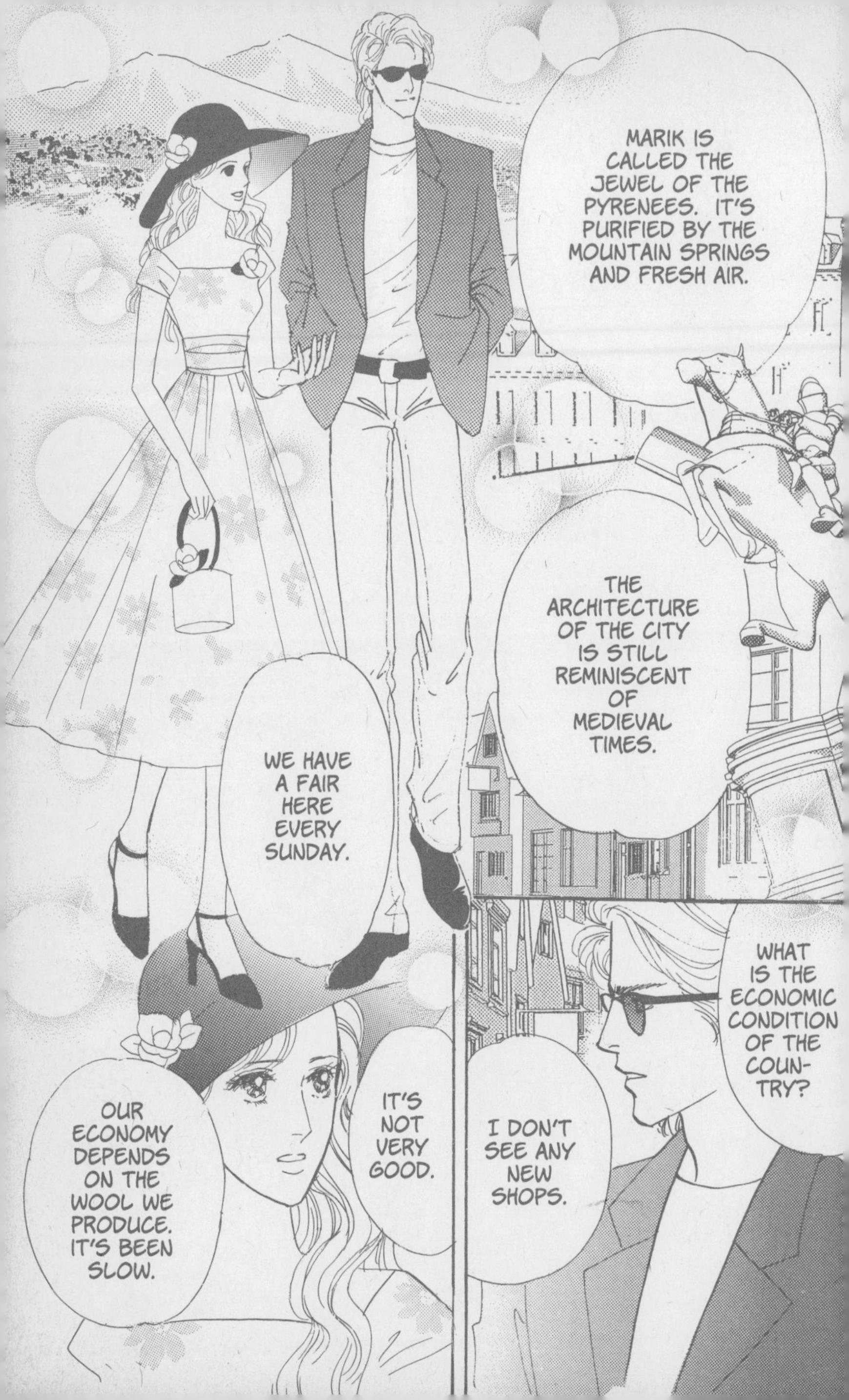
MARIK IS CALLED THE JEWEL OF THE PYRENEES. IT'S PURIFIED BY THE MOUNTAIN SPRINGS AND FRESH AIR.
THE ARCHITECTURE OF THE CITY IS STILL REMINISCENT OF MEDIEVAL TIMES.
WE HAVE A FAIR HERE EVERY SUNDAY.
WHAT IS THE ECONOMIC CONDITION OF THE COUN-TRY?
I DON'T SEE ANY NEW SHOPS.
IT'S NOT VERY GOOD.
OUR ECONOMY DEPENDS ON THE WOOL WE PRODUCE. IT'S BEEN SLOW.

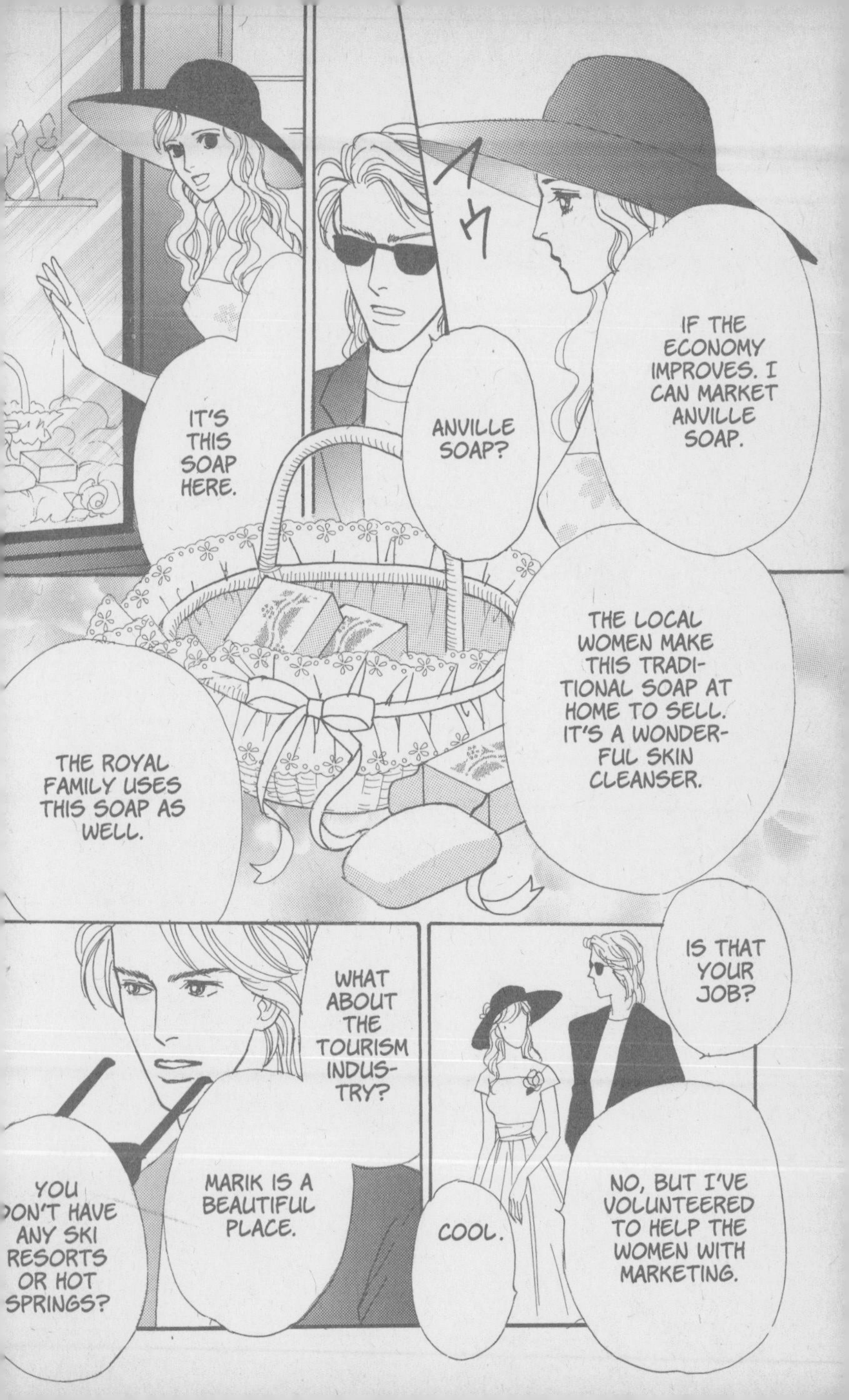
IF THE ECONOMY IMPROVES. I CAN MARKET ANVILLE SOAP.
ANVILLE SOAP?
IT'S THIS SOAP HERE.
THE LOCAL WOMEN MAKE THIS TRADITIONAL SOAP AT HOME TO SELL. IT'S A WONDERFUL SKIN CLEANSER.
THE ROYAL FAMILY USES THIS SOAP AS WELL.
IS THAT YOUR JOB?
NO, BUT I'VE VOLUNTEERED TO HELP THE WOMEN WITH MARKETING.
COOL.
WHAT ABOUT THE TOURISM INDUSTRY?
MARIK IS A BEAUTIFUL PLACE.
YOU DON'T HAVE ANY SKI RESORTS OR HOT SPRINGS?

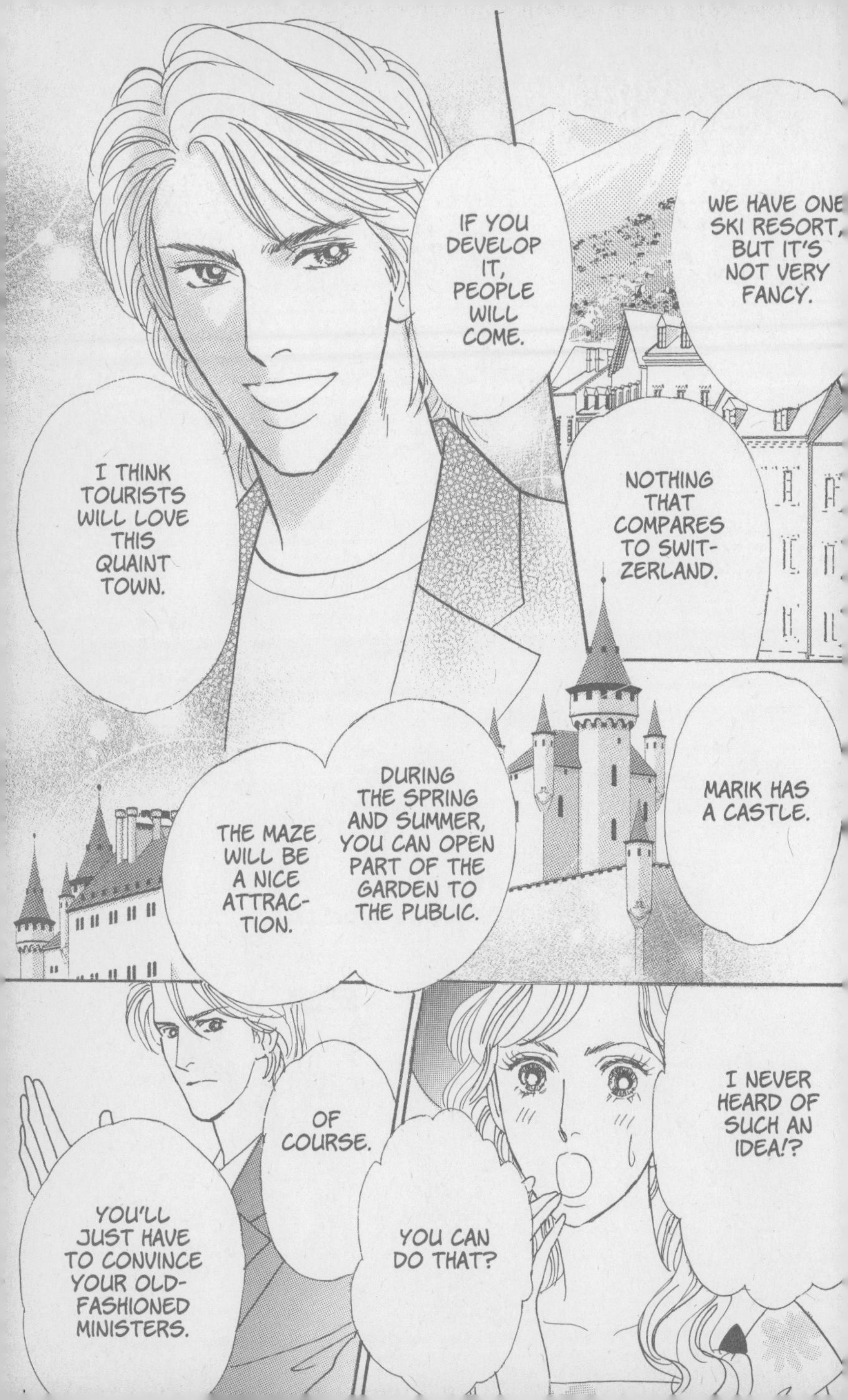
WE HAVE ONE SKI RESORT, BUT IT'S NOT VERY FANCY.
NOTHING THAT COMPARES TO SWIT-ZERLAND.
MARIK HAS A CASTLE.
IF YOU DEVELOP IT, PEOPLE WILL COME.
I THINK TOURISTS WILL LOVE THIS QUAINT TOWN.
DURING THE SPRING AND SUMMER, YOU CAN OPEN PART OF THE GARDEN TO THE PUBLIC.
THE MAZE WILL BE A NICE ATTRAC-TION.
I NEVER HEARD OF SUCH AN IDEA!?
YOU CAN DO THAT?
OF COURSE.
YOU'LL JUST HAVE TO CONVINCE YOUR OLD-FASHIONED MINISTERS.

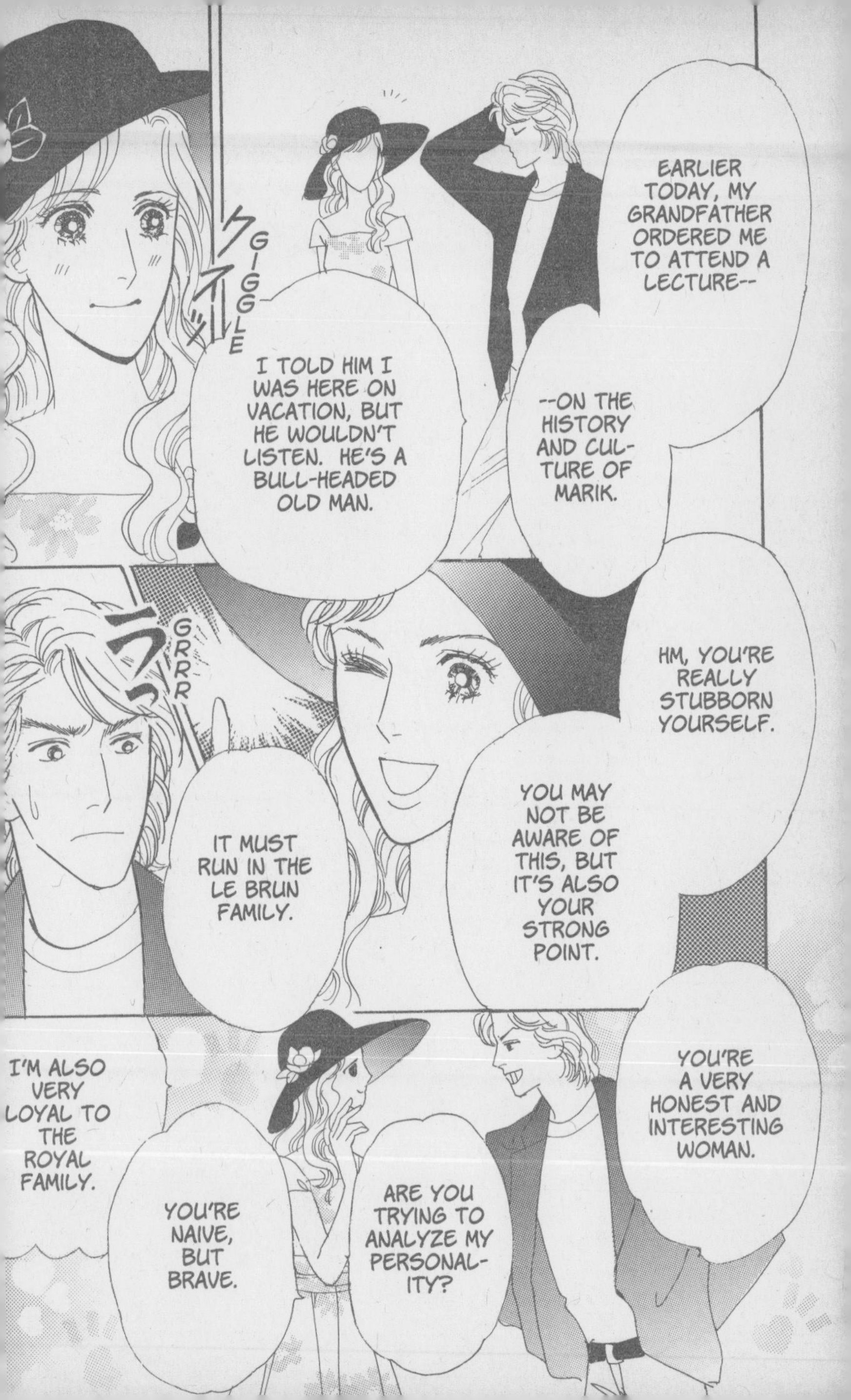
EARLIER TODAY, MY GRANDFATHER ORDERED ME TO ATTEND A LECTURE--
--ON THE HISTORY AND CUL-TURE OF MARIK.
I TOLD HIM I WAS HERE ON VACATION, BUT HE WOULDN'T LISTEN. HE'S A BULL-HEADED OLD MAN.
GIGGLE
HM, YOU'RE REALLY STUBBORN YOURSELF.
YOU MAY NOT BE AWARE OF THIS, BUT IT'S ALSO YOUR STRONG POINT.
IT MUST RUN IN THE LE BRUN FAMILY.
GRRR
YOU'RE A VERY HONEST AND INTERESTING WOMAN.
ARE YOU TRYING TO ANALYZE MY PERSONAL-ITY?
YOU'RE NAIVE, BUT BRAVE.
I'M ALSO VERY LOYAL TO THE ROYAL FAMILY.

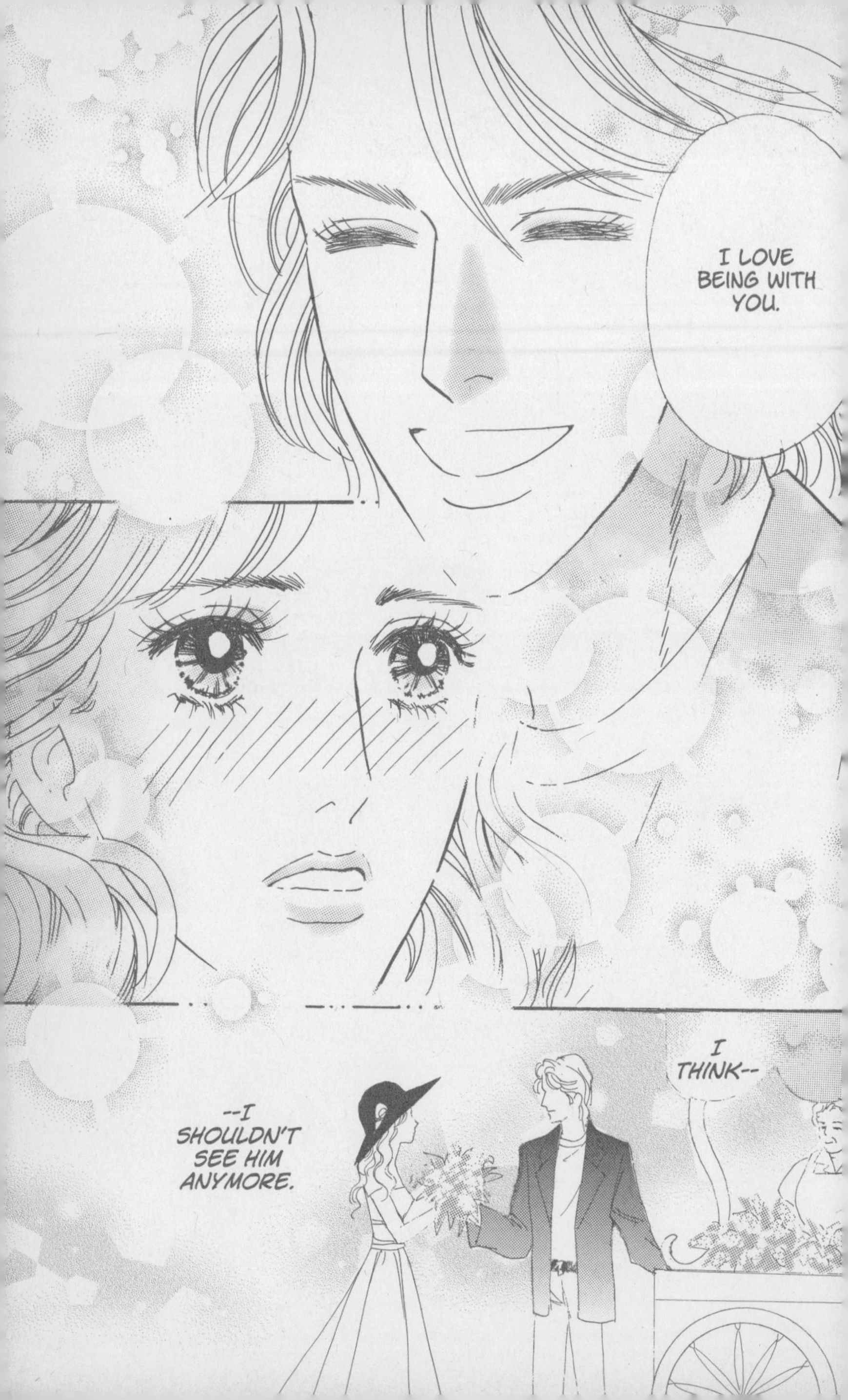
I LOVE BEING WITH YOU.
I THINK--
--I SHOULDN'T SEE HIM ANYMORE.

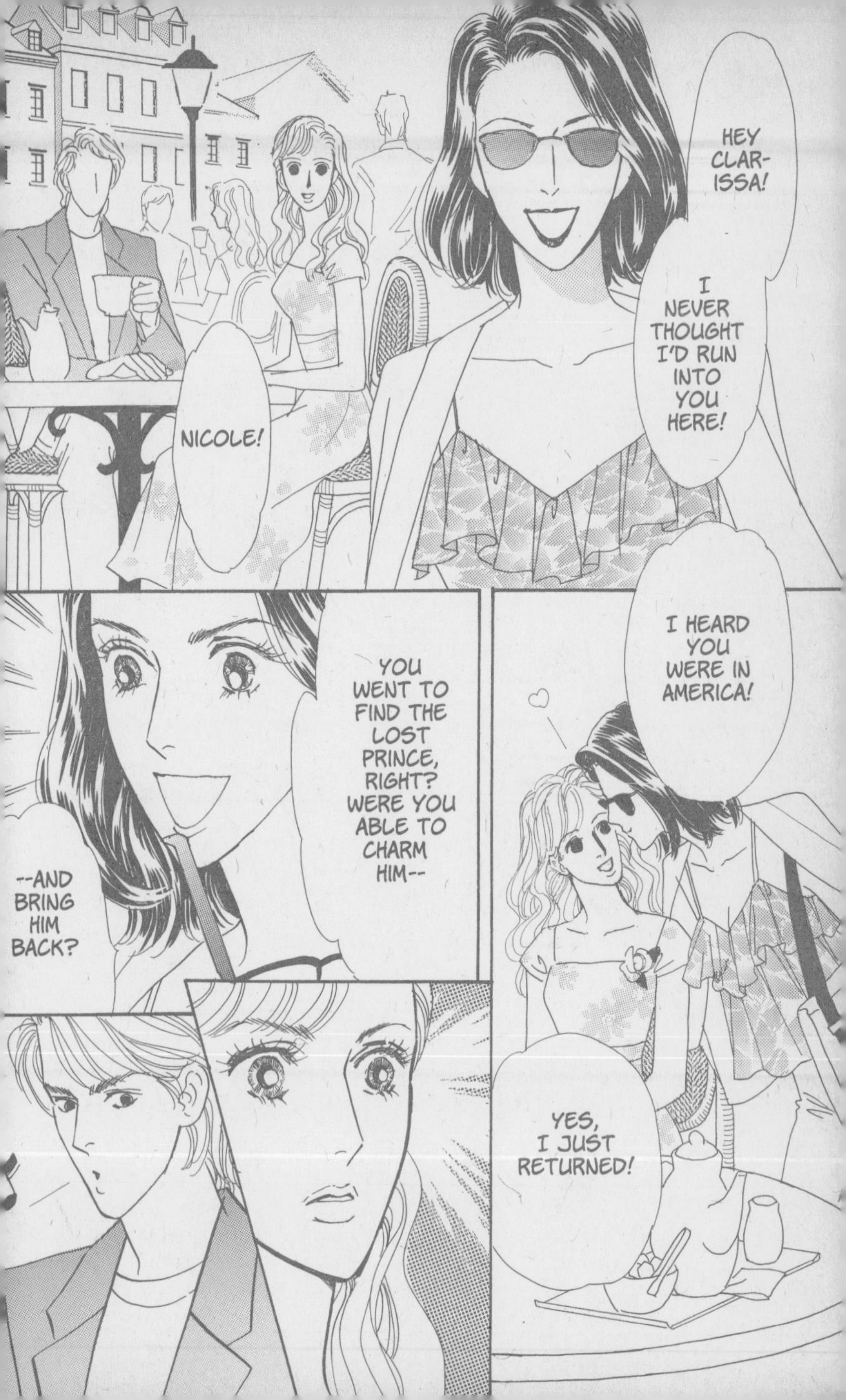
HEY CLARISSA!
I NEVER THOUGHT I'D RUN INTO YOU HERE!
NICOLE!
I HEARD YOU WERE IN AMERICA!
YES, I JUST RETURNED!
YOU WENT TO FIND THE LOST PRINCE, RIGHT? WERE YOU ABLE TO CHARM HIM--
--AND BRING HIM BACK?

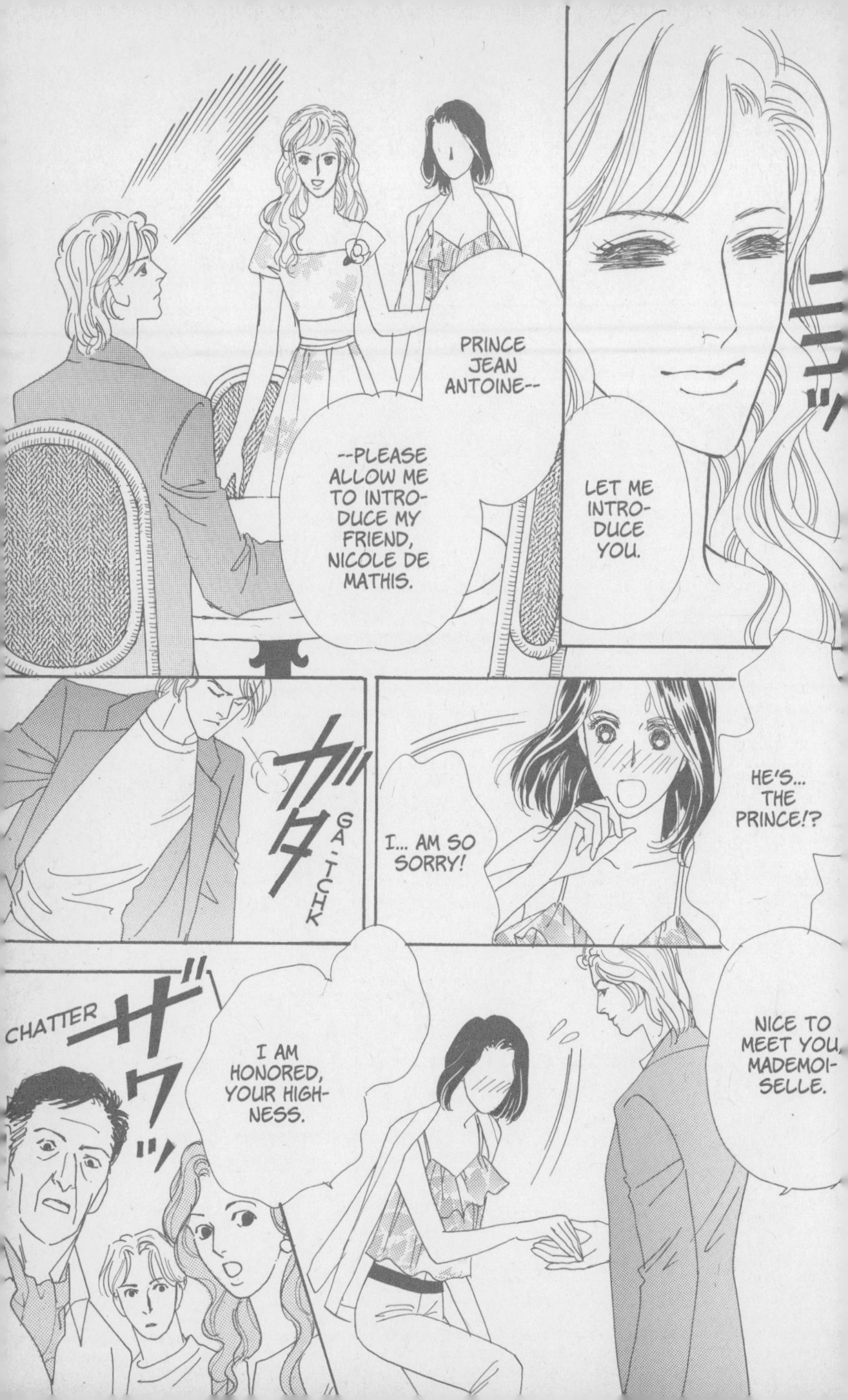
LET ME INTRODUCE YOU.
ニコッ
PRINCE JEAN ANTOINE--
--PLEASE ALLOW ME TO INTRODUCE MY FRIEND, NICOLE DE MATHIS.
HE'S... THE PRINCE!?
I... AM SO SORRY!
ガタ
GA-TCHK
NICE TO MEET YOU, MADEMOISELLE.
I AM HONORED, YOUR HIGHNESS.
ザワッ
CHATTER

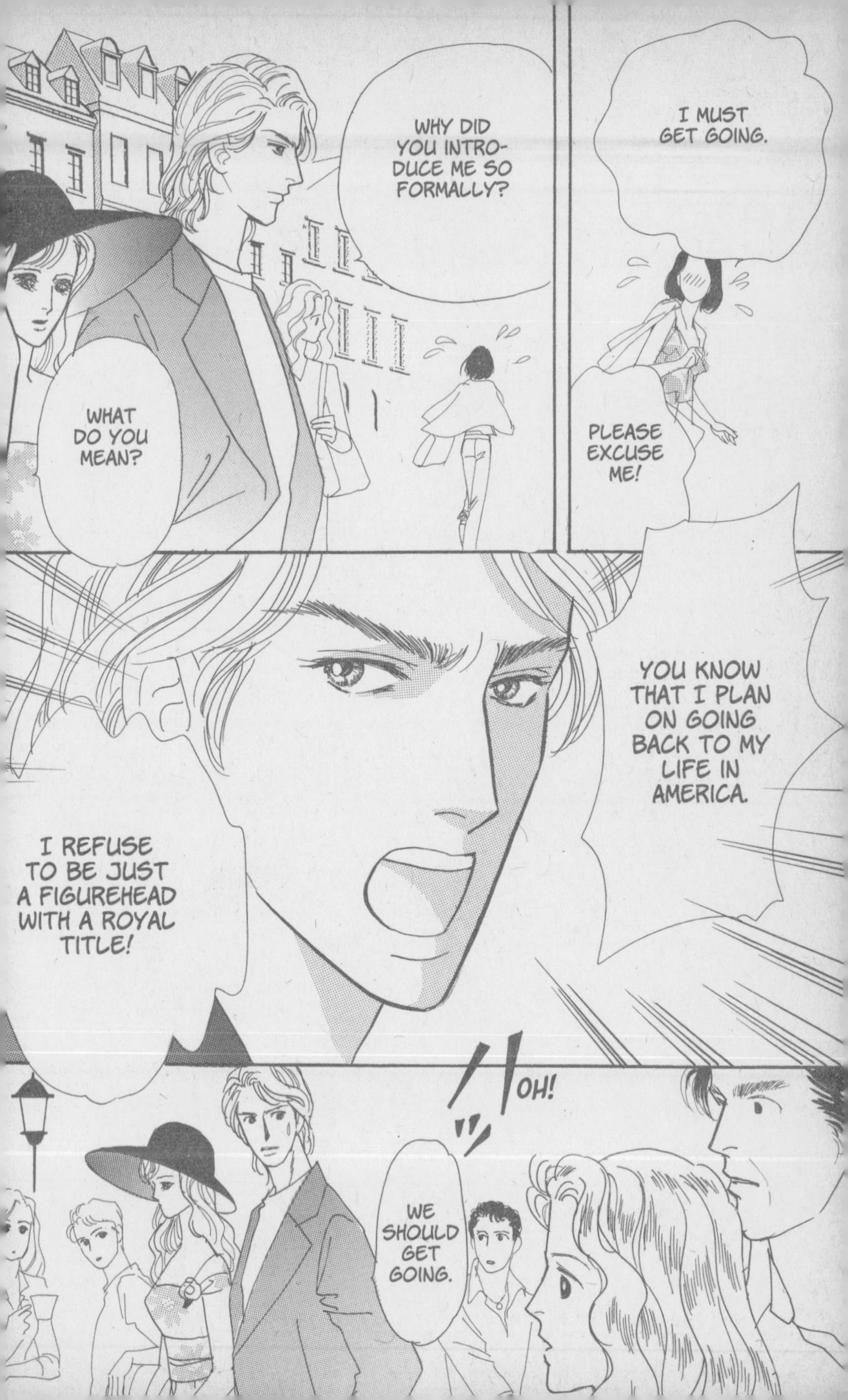
I MUST GET GOING.
PLEASE EXCUSE ME!
WHY DID YOU INTRODUCE ME SO FORMALLY?
WHAT DO YOU MEAN?
YOU KNOW THAT I PLAN ON GOING BACK TO MY LIFE IN AMERICA.
I REFUSE TO BE JUST A FIGUREHEAD WITH A ROYAL TITLE!
OH!
WE SHOULD GET GOING.

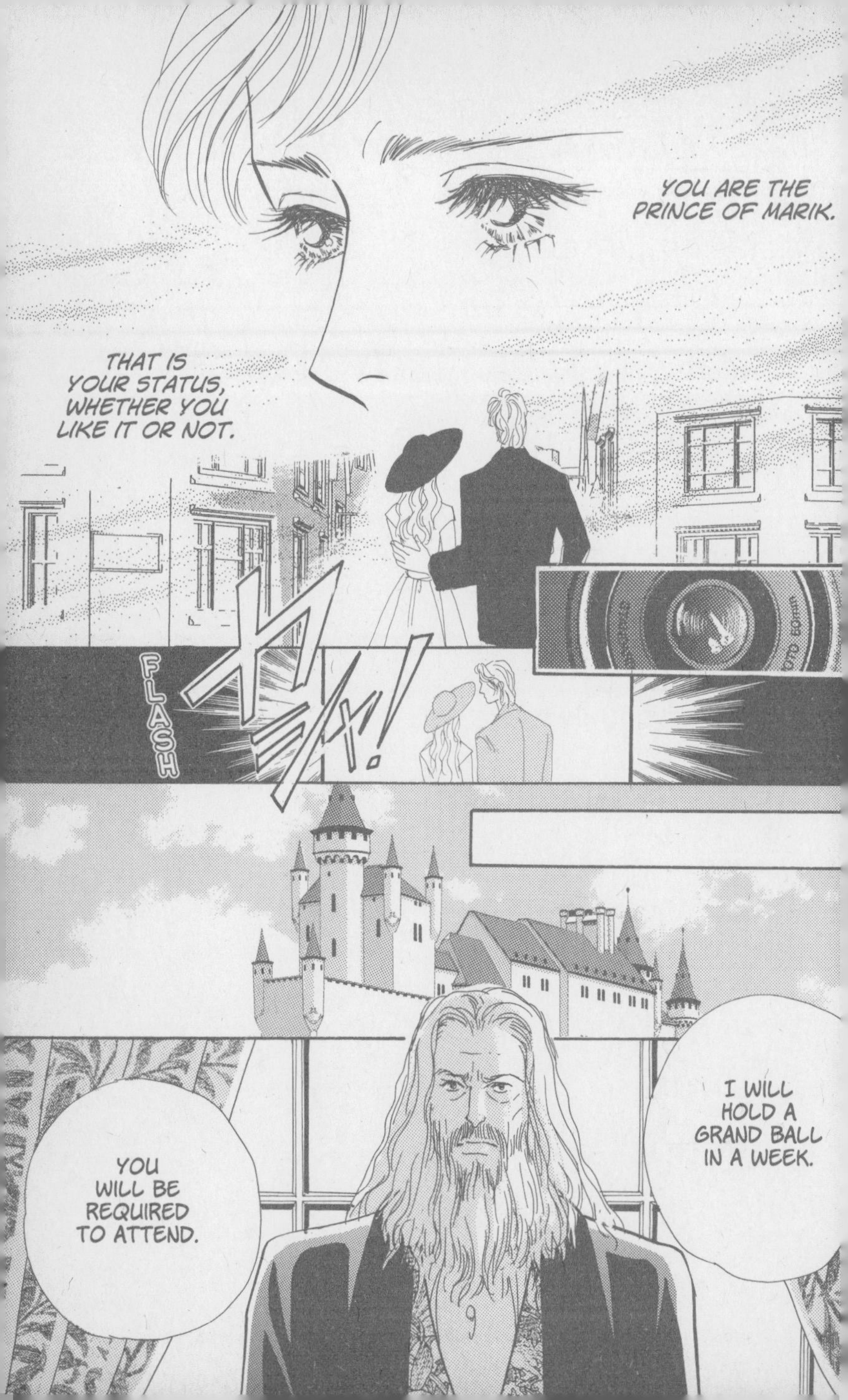
YOU ARE THE PRINCE OF MARIK.
THAT IS YOUR STATUS, WHETHER YOU LIKE IT OR NOT.
FLASH
I WILL HOLD A GRAND BALL IN A WEEK.
YOU WILL BE REQUIRED TO ATTEND.

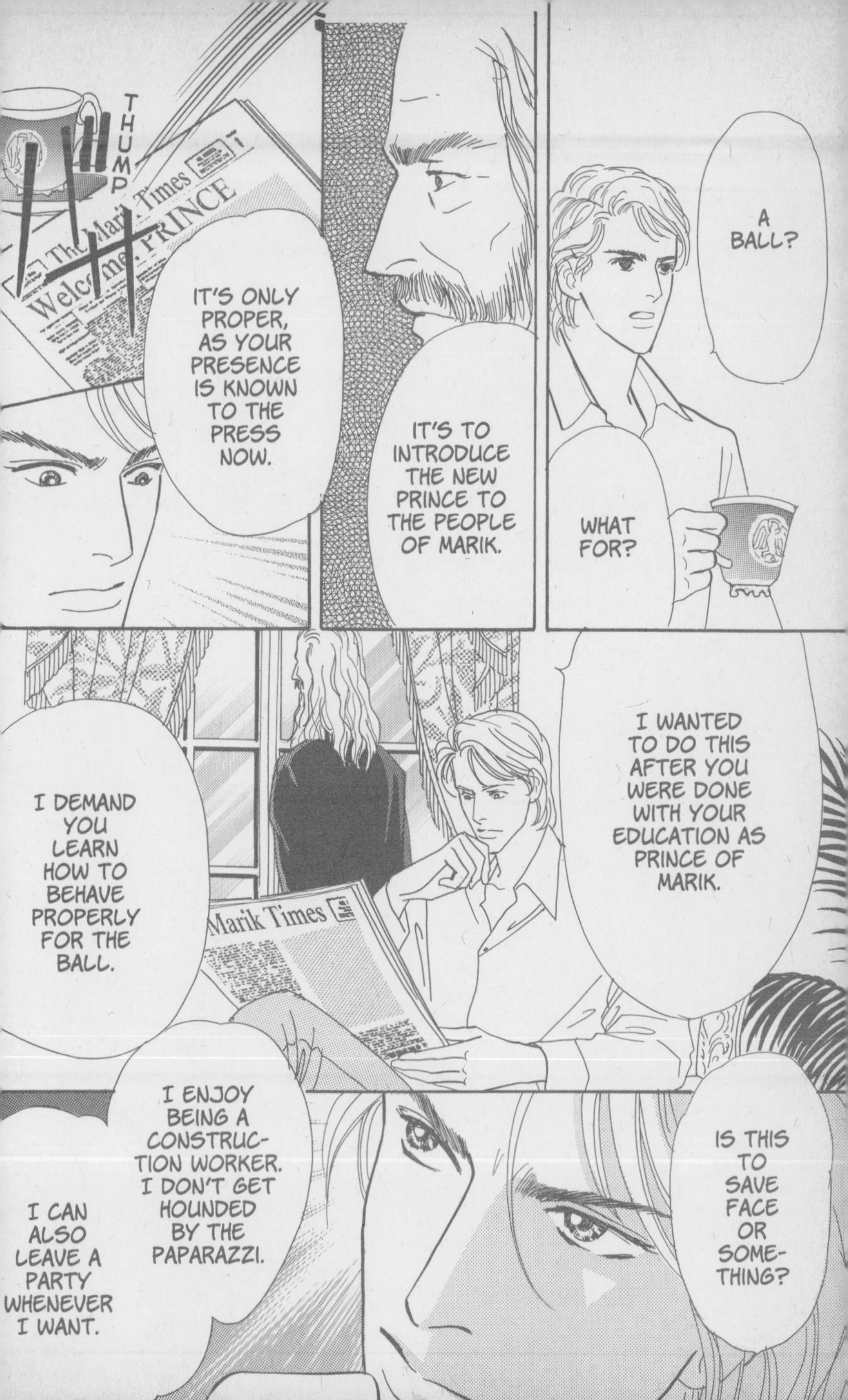
A BALL?
WHAT FOR?
IT'S TO INTRODUCE THE NEW PRINCE TO THE PEOPLE OF MARIK.
THUMP
PRINCE
IT'S ONLY PROPER, AS YOUR PRESENCE IS KNOWN TO THE PRESS NOW.
I WANTED TO DO THIS AFTER YOU WERE DONE WITH YOUR EDUCATION AS PRINCE OF MARIK.
Marik Times
I DEMAND YOU LEARN HOW TO BEHAVE PROPERLY FOR THE BALL.
IS THIS TO SAVE FACE OR SOME-THING?
I ENJOY BEING A CONSTRUC-TION WORKER. I DON'T GET HOUNDED BY THE PAPARAZZI.
I CAN ALSO LEAVE A PARTY WHENEVER I WANT.

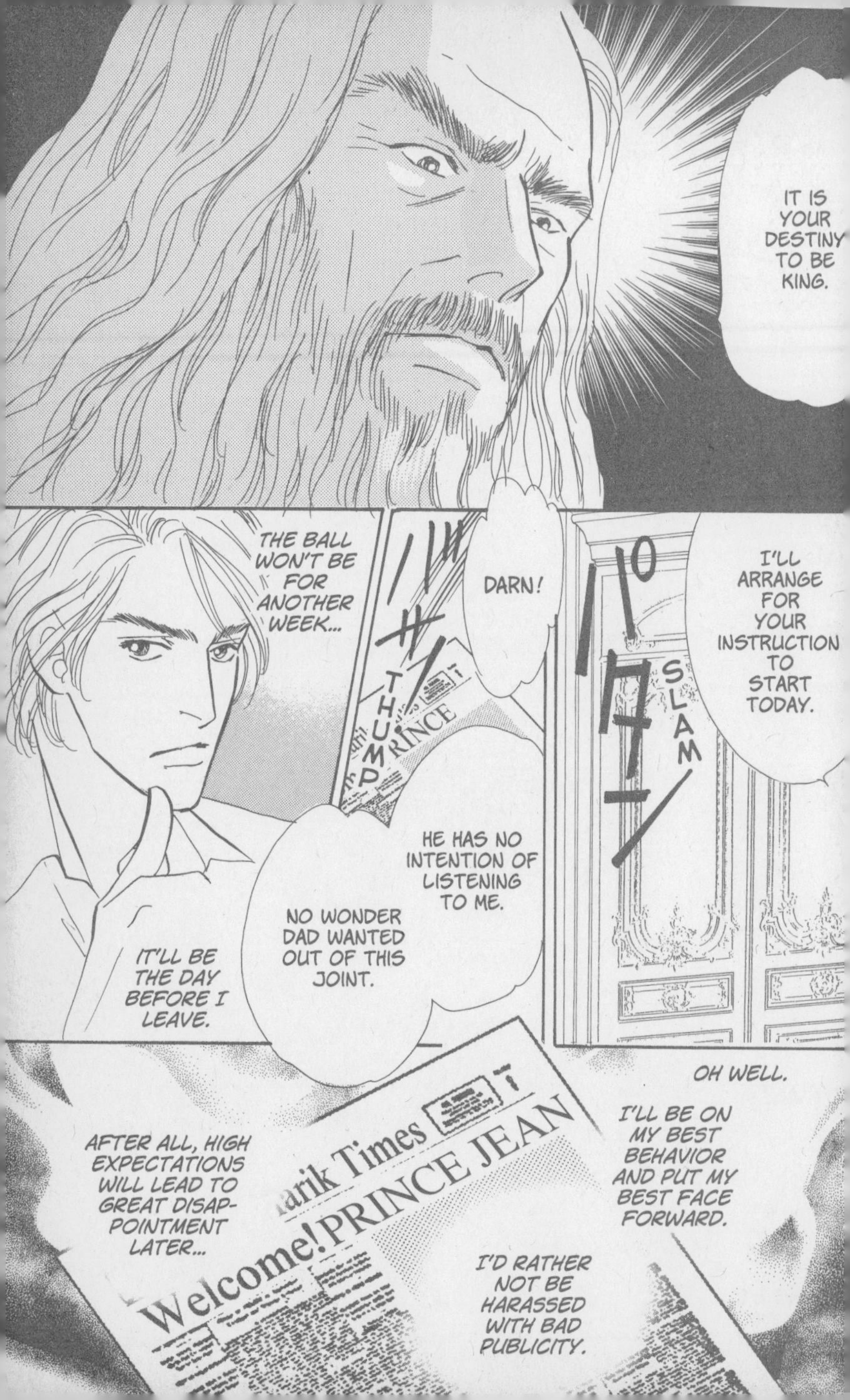
IT IS YOUR DESTINY TO BE KING.
I'LL ARRANGE FOR YOUR INSTRUCTION TO START TODAY.
SLAM
DARN!
THUMP
PRINCE
THE BALL WON'T BE FOR ANOTHER WEEK...
IT'LL BE THE DAY BEFORE I LEAVE.
HE HAS NO INTENTION OF LISTENING TO ME.
NO WONDER DAD WANTED OUT OF THIS JOINT.
OH WELL.
I'LL BE ON MY BEST BEHAVIOR AND PUT MY BEST FACE FORWARD.
I'D RATHER NOT BE HARASSED WITH BAD PUBLICITY.
arik Times
Welcome! PRINCE JEAN
AFTER ALL, HIGH EXPECTATIONS WILL LEAD TO GREAT DISAP-POINTMENT LATER...

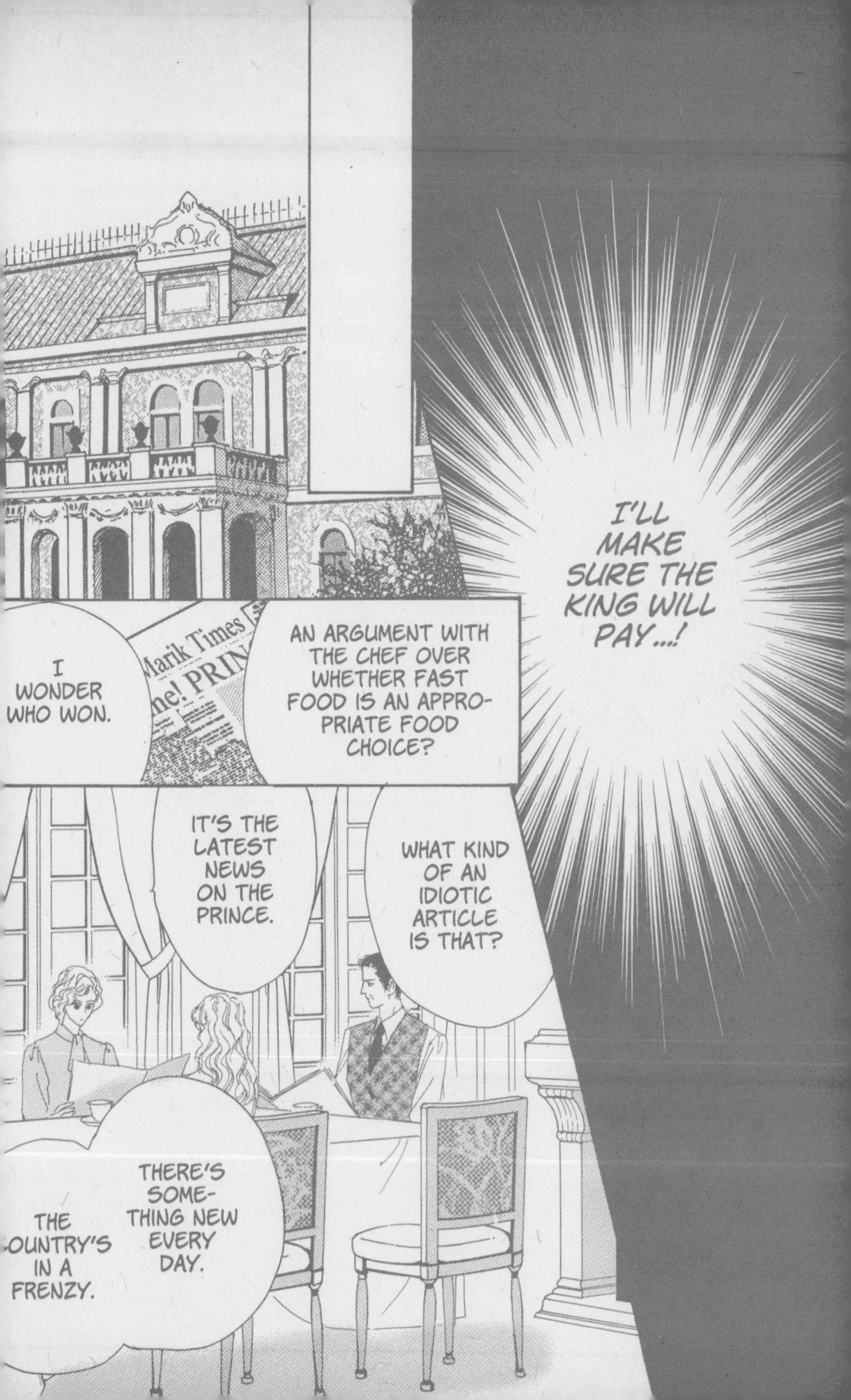
I'LL MAKE SURE THE KING WILL PAY...!
AN ARGUMENT WITH THE CHEF OVER WHETHER FAST FOOD IS AN APPRO-PRIATE FOOD CHOICE?
Marik Times
I WONDER WHO WON.
WHAT KIND OF AN IDIOTIC ARTICLE IS THAT?
IT'S THE LATEST NEWS ON THE PRINCE.
THERE'S SOME-THING NEW EVERY DAY.
THE OUNTRY'S IN A FRENZY.

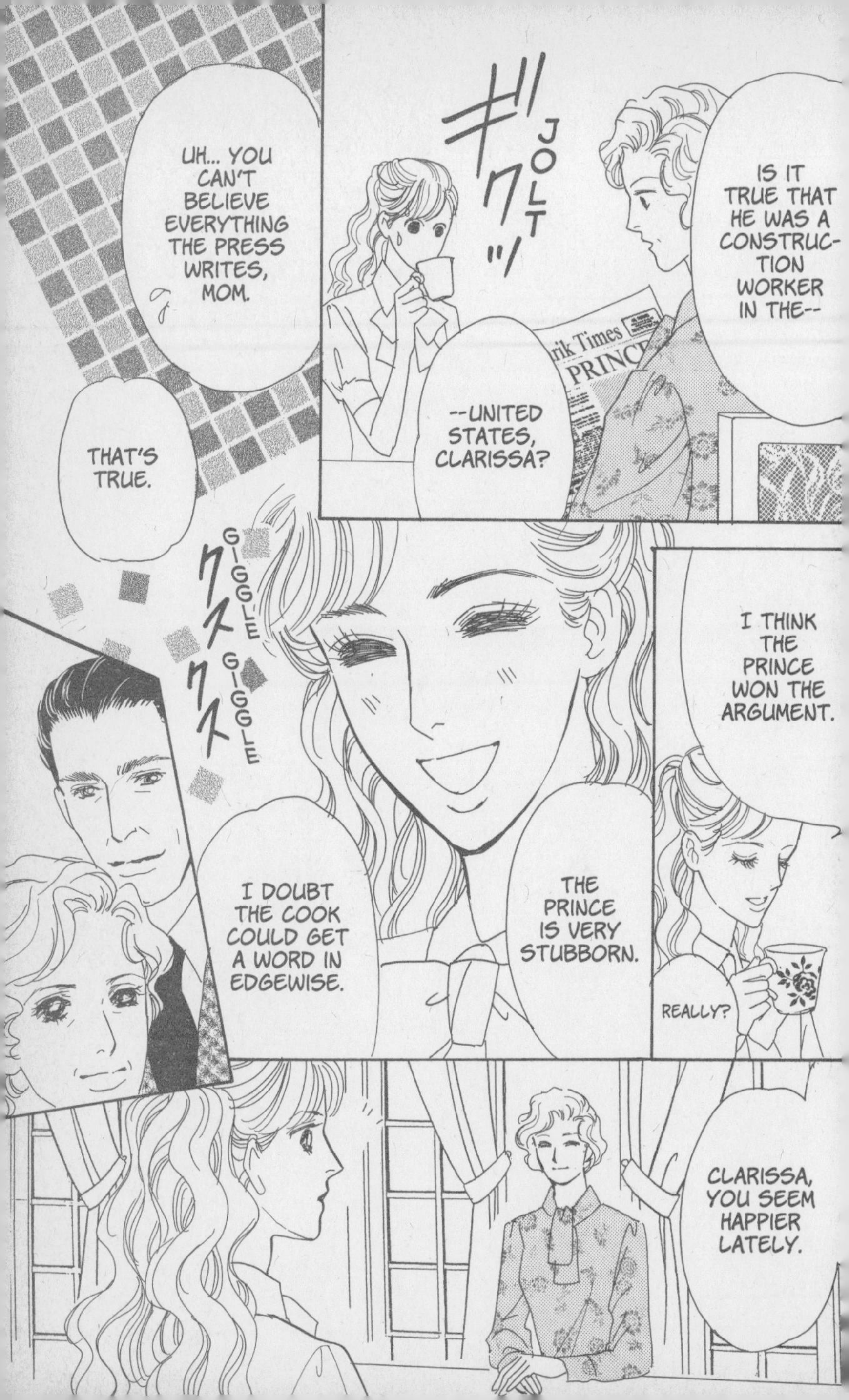
IS IT TRUE THAT HE WAS A CONSTRUCTION WORKER IN THE--
--UNITED STATES, CLARISSA?
ギクッ
JOLT
UH... YOU CAN'T BELIEVE EVERYTHING THE PRESS WRITES, MOM.
THAT'S TRUE.
I THINK THE PRINCE WON THE ARGUMENT.
REALLY?
THE PRINCE IS VERY STUBBORN.
クスクス
GIGGLE GIGGLE
I DOUBT THE COOK COULD GET A WORD IN EDGEWISE.
CLARISSA, YOU SEEM HAPPIER LATELY.

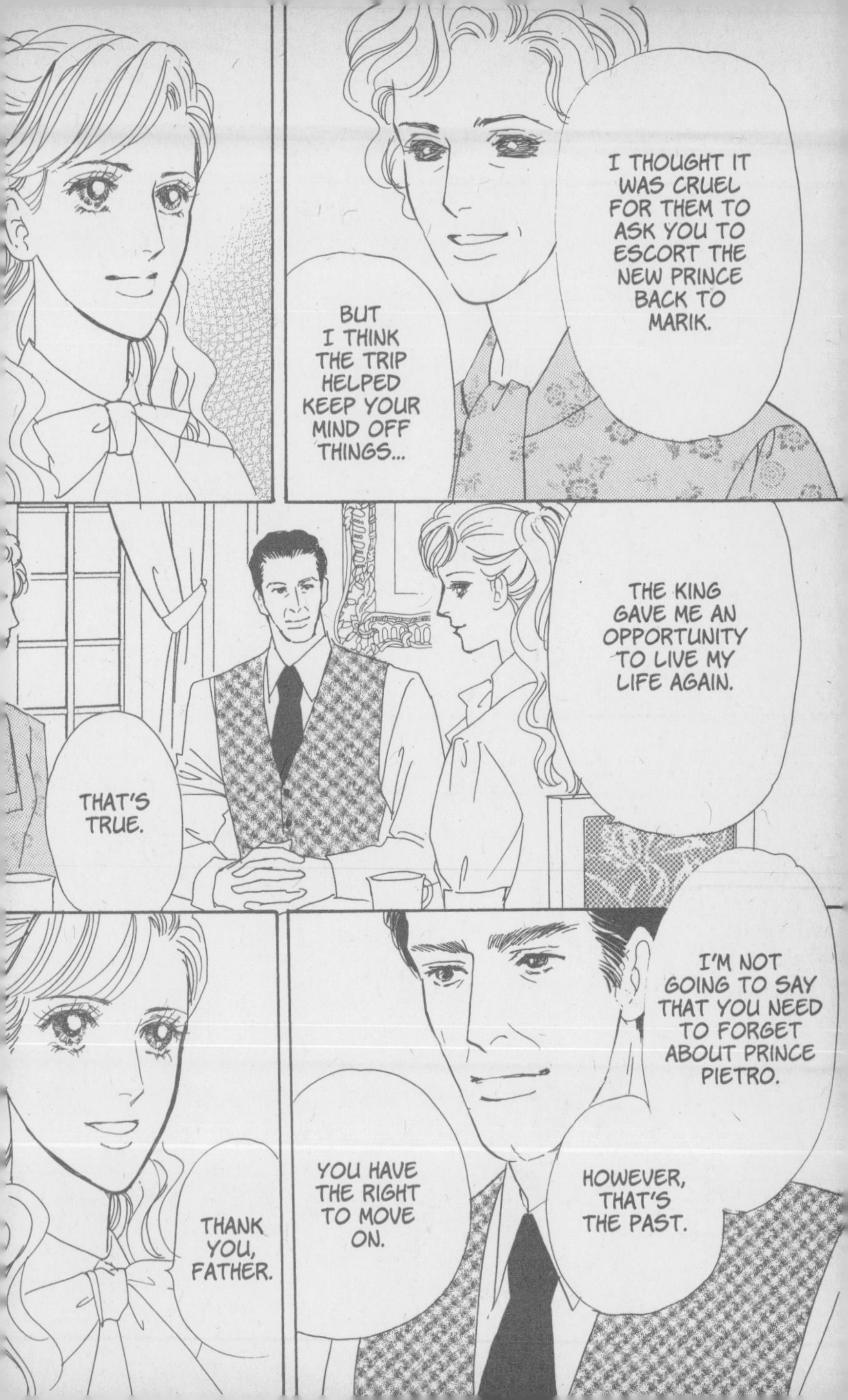
I THOUGHT IT WAS CRUEL FOR THEM TO ASK YOU TO ESCORT THE NEW PRINCE BACK TO MARIK.
BUT I THINK THE TRIP HELPED KEEP YOUR MIND OFF THINGS...
THE KING GAVE ME AN OPPORTUNITY TO LIVE MY LIFE AGAIN.
THAT'S TRUE.
I'M NOT GOING TO SAY THAT YOU NEED TO FORGET ABOUT PRINCE PIETRO.
HOWEVER, THAT'S THE PAST.
YOU HAVE THE RIGHT TO MOVE ON.
THANK YOU, FATHER.

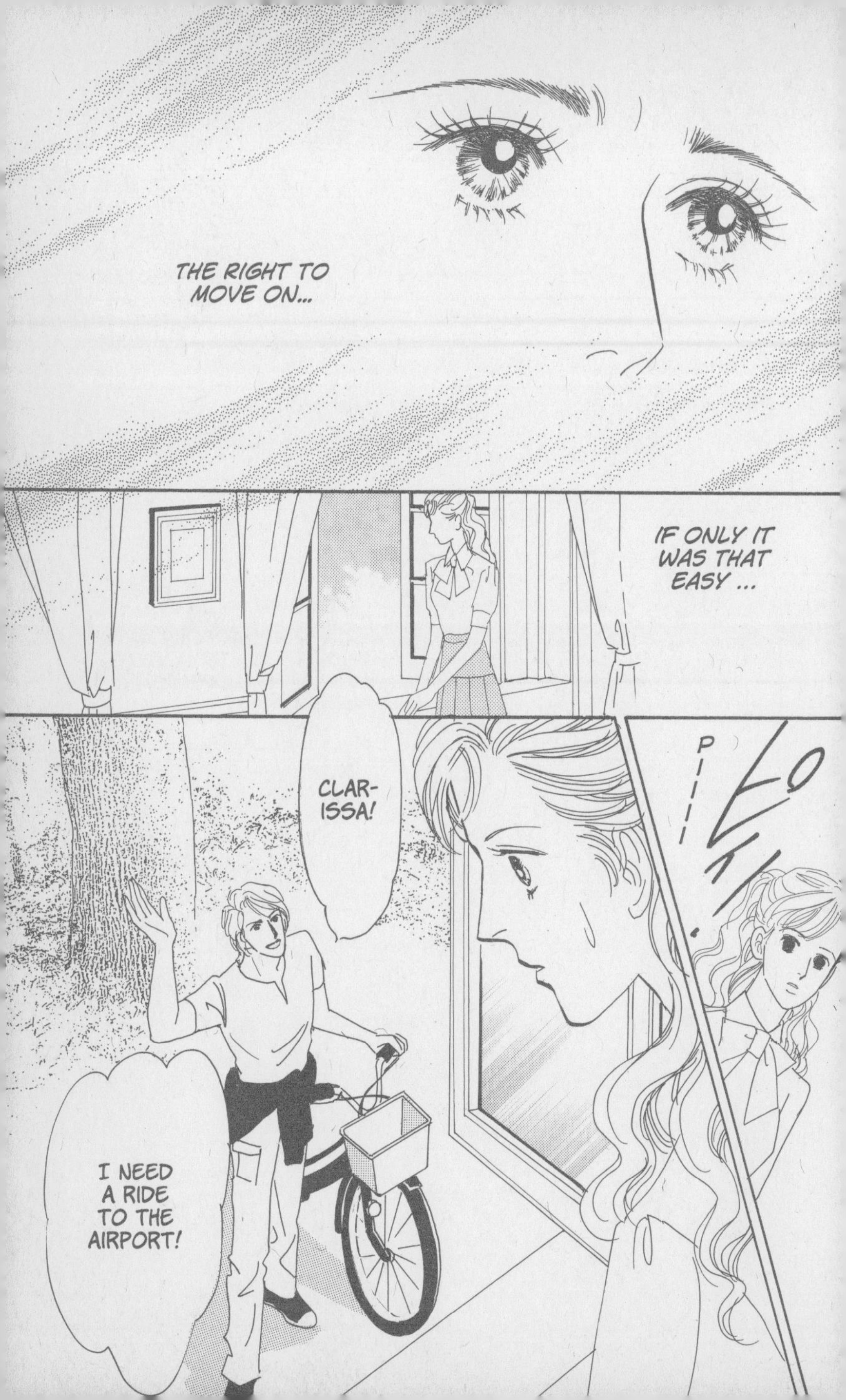
THE RIGHT TO MOVE ON...
IF ONLY IT WAS THAT EASY ...
CLAR-ISSA!
I NEED A RIDE TO THE AIRPORT!

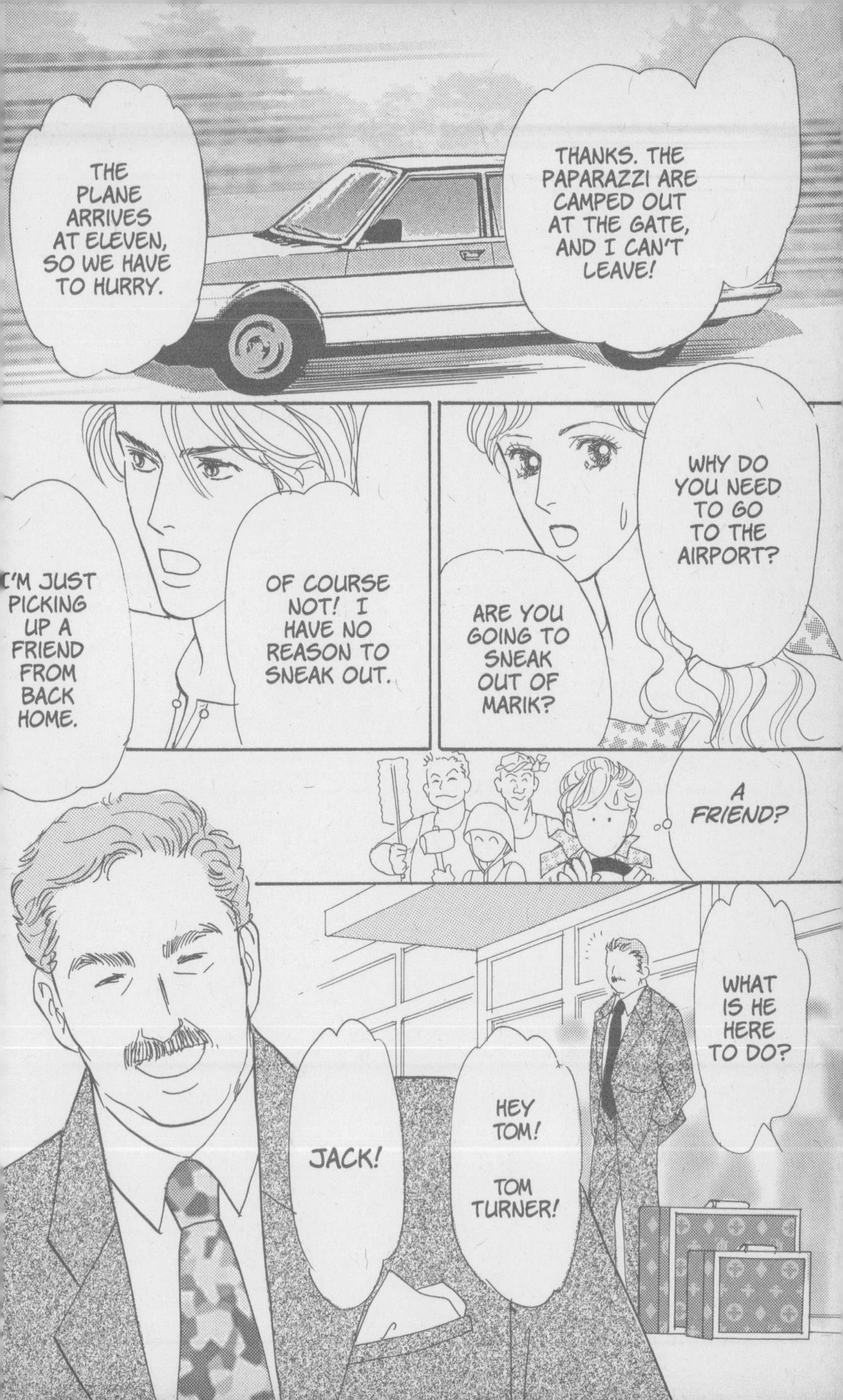
THANKS. THE PAPARAZZI ARE CAMPED OUT AT THE GATE, AND I CAN'T LEAVE!
THE PLANE ARRIVES AT ELEVEN, SO WE HAVE TO HURRY.
WHY DO YOU NEED TO GO TO THE AIRPORT?
ARE YOU GOING TO SNEAK OUT OF MARIK?
OF COURSE NOT! I HAVE NO REASON TO SNEAK OUT.
I'M JUST PICKING UP A FRIEND FROM BACK HOME.
A *FRIEND?*
WHAT IS HE HERE TO DO?
HEY TOM!
TOM TURNER!
JACK!

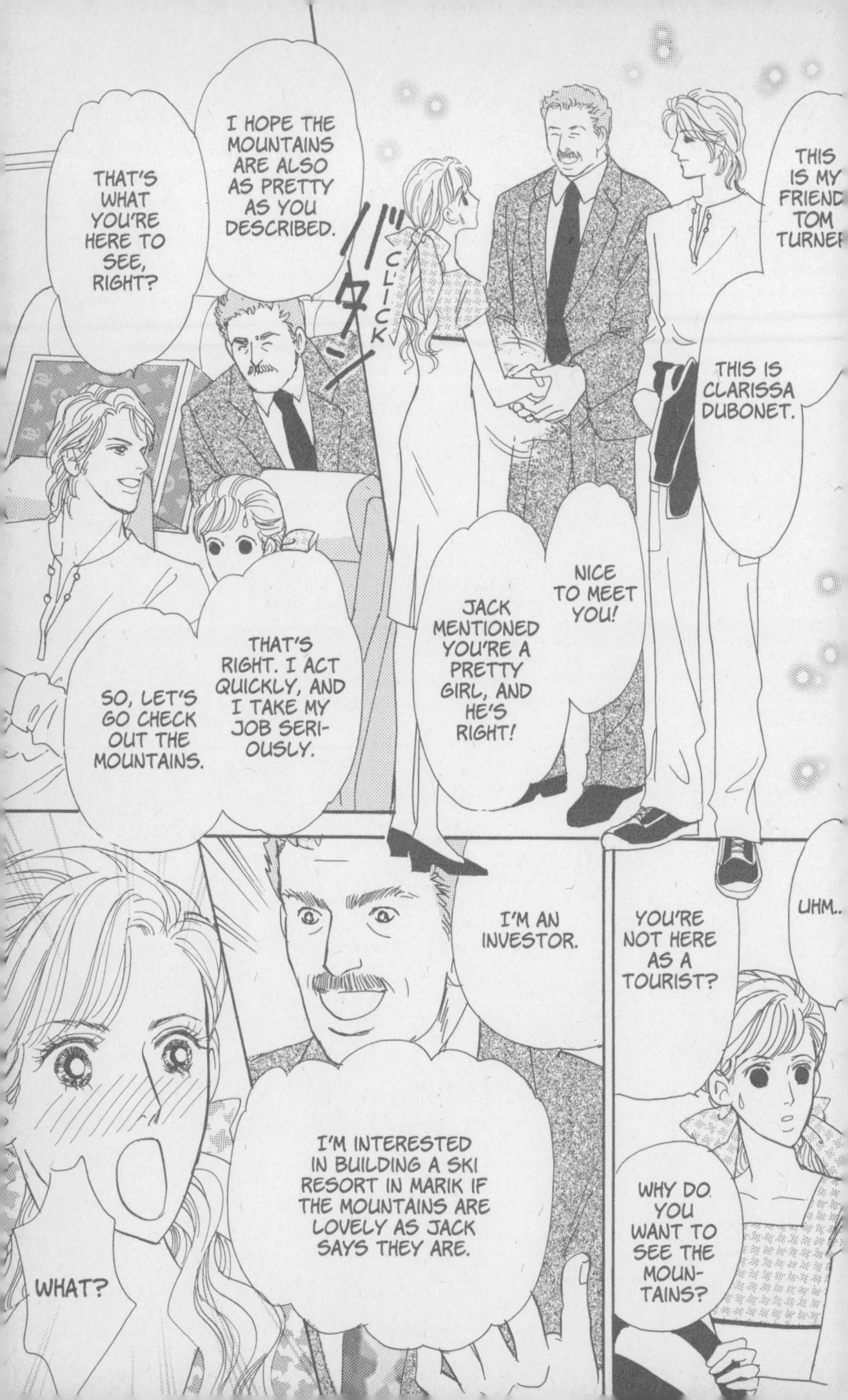
THIS IS MY FRIEND TOM TURNER
THIS IS CLARISSA DUBONET.
NICE TO MEET YOU!
JACK MENTIONED YOU'RE A PRETTY GIRL, AND HE'S RIGHT!
CLICK
I HOPE THE MOUNTAINS ARE ALSO AS PRETTY AS YOU DESCRIBED.
THAT'S WHAT YOU'RE HERE TO SEE, RIGHT?
THAT'S RIGHT. I ACT QUICKLY, AND I TAKE MY JOB SERIOUSLY.
SO, LET'S GO CHECK OUT THE MOUNTAINS.
UHM..
YOU'RE NOT HERE AS A TOURIST?
WHY DO YOU WANT TO SEE THE MOUNTAINS?
I'M AN INVESTOR.
I'M INTERESTED IN BUILDING A SKI RESORT IN MARIK IF THE MOUNTAINS ARE LOVELY AS JACK SAYS THEY ARE.
WHAT?

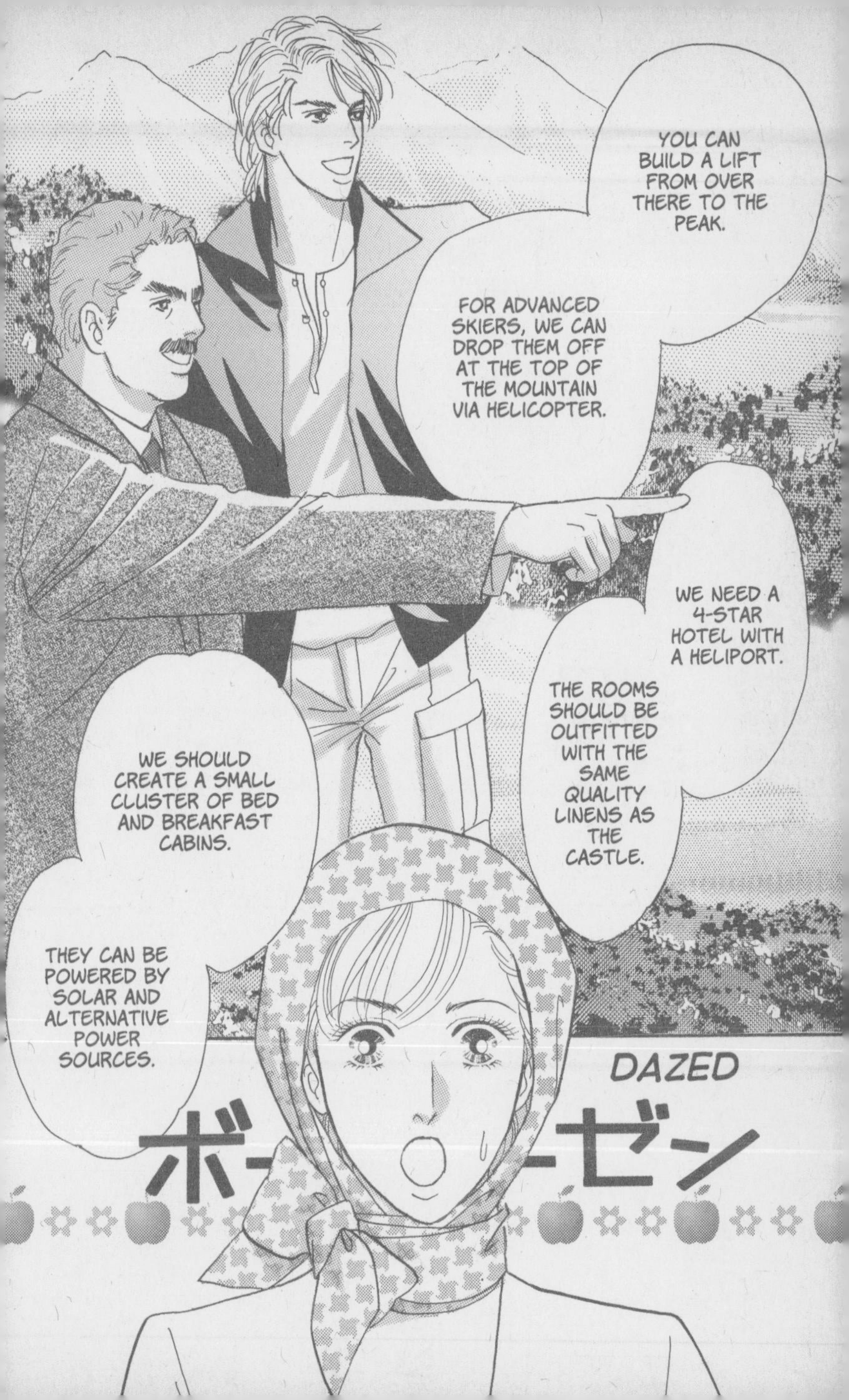
YOU CAN BUILD A LIFT FROM OVER THERE TO THE PEAK.
FOR ADVANCED SKIERS, WE CAN DROP THEM OFF AT THE TOP OF THE MOUNTAIN VIA HELICOPTER.
WE NEED A 4-STAR HOTEL WITH A HELIPORT.
THE ROOMS SHOULD BE OUTFITTED WITH THE SAME QUALITY LINENS AS THE CASTLE.
WE SHOULD CREATE A SMALL CLUSTER OF BED AND BREAKFAST CABINS.
THEY CAN BE POWERED BY SOLAR AND ALTERNATIVE POWER SOURCES.
DAZED
ボー ーゼン

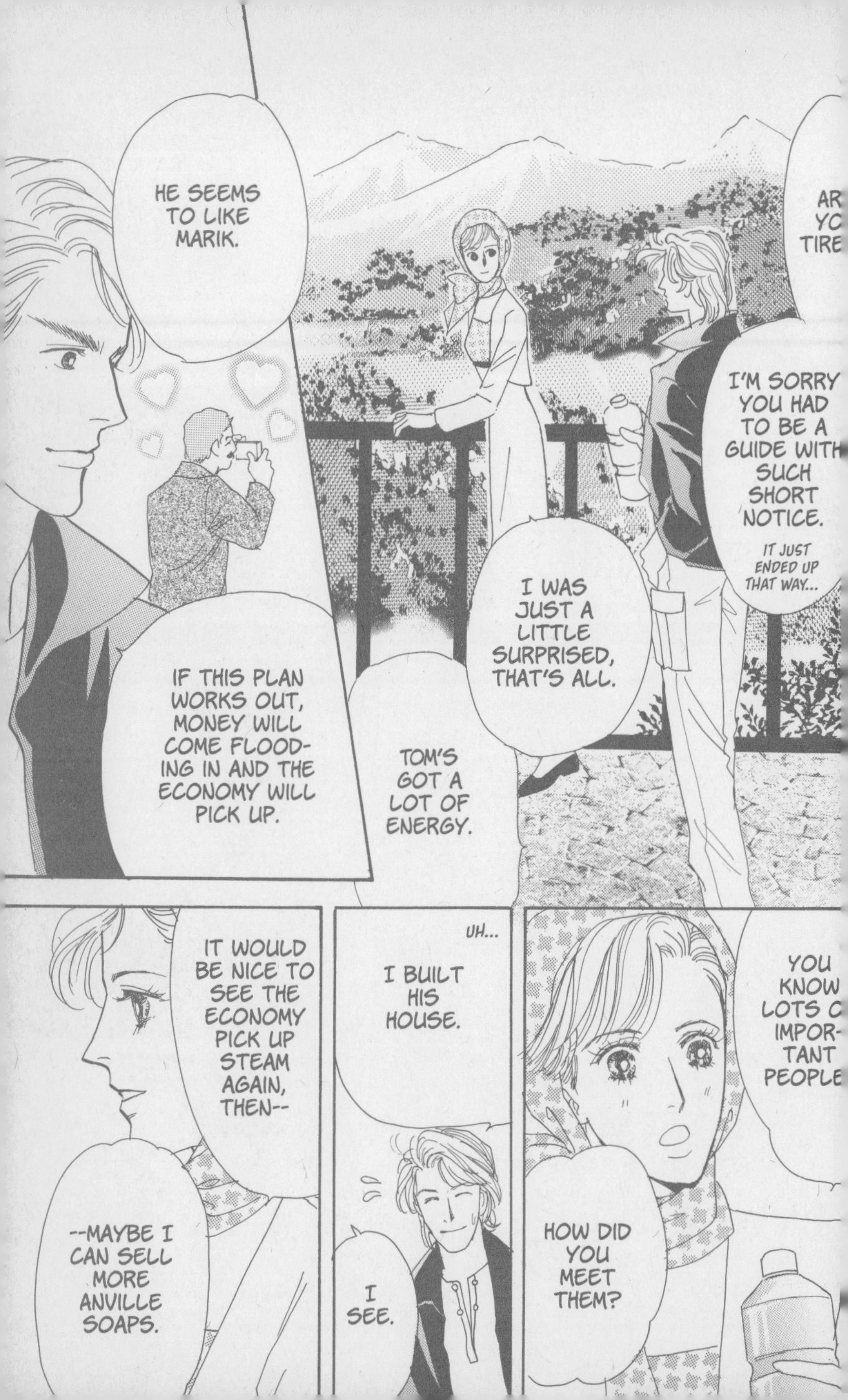
AR YO TIRE
I'M SORRY YOU HAD TO BE A GUIDE WITH SUCH SHORT NOTICE.
IT JUST ENDED UP THAT WAY...
I WAS JUST A LITTLE SURPRISED, THAT'S ALL.
TOM'S GOT A LOT OF ENERGY.
HE SEEMS TO LIKE MARIK.
IF THIS PLAN WORKS OUT, MONEY WILL COME FLOODING IN AND THE ECONOMY WILL PICK UP.
YOU KNOW LOTS O IMPORTANT PEOPLE
HOW DID YOU MEET THEM?
UH...
I BUILT HIS HOUSE.
I SEE.
IT WOULD BE NICE TO SEE THE ECONOMY PICK UP STEAM AGAIN, THEN--
--MAYBE I CAN SELL MORE ANVILLE SOAPS.

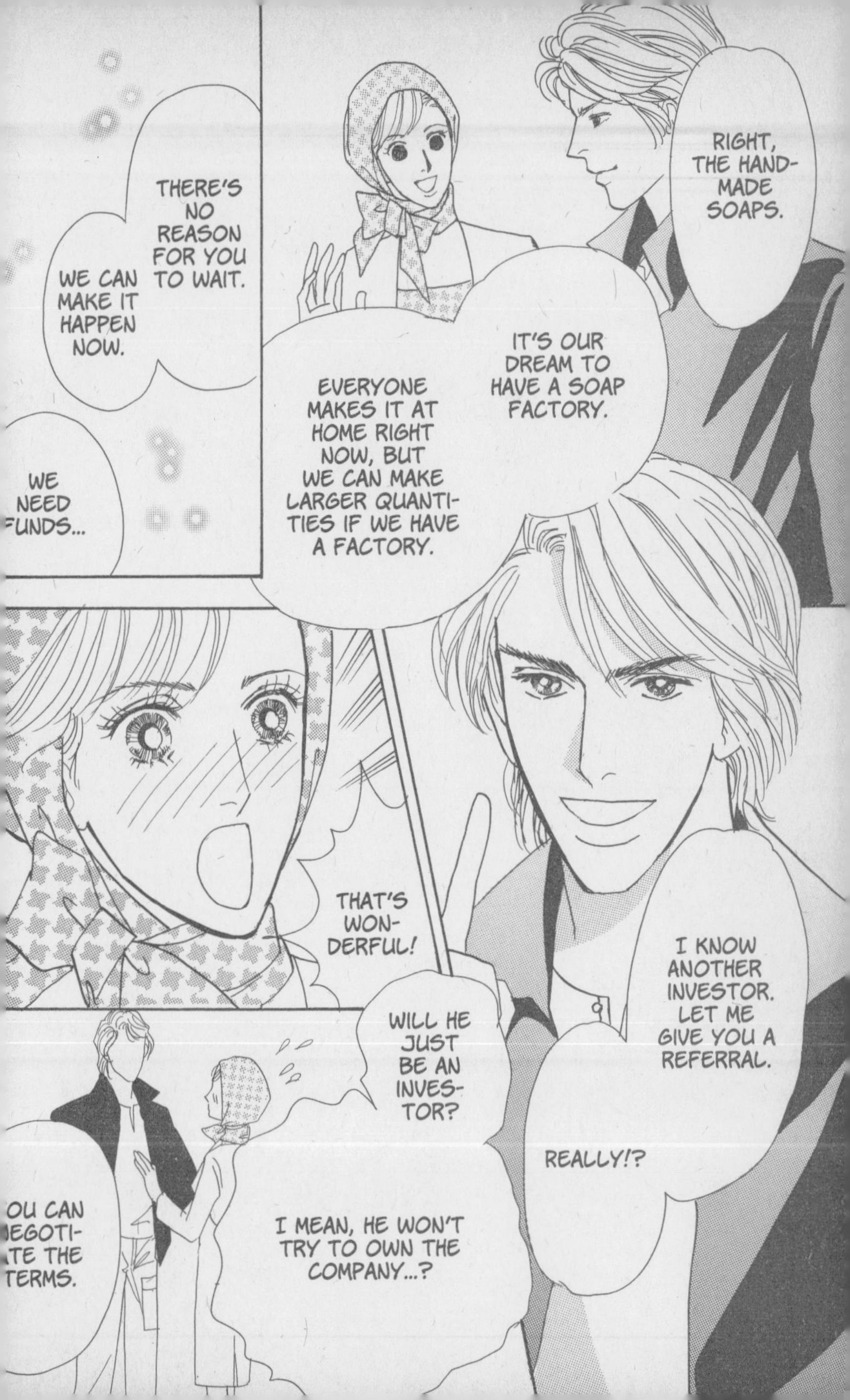
RIGHT, THE HAND-MADE SOAPS.
IT'S OUR DREAM TO HAVE A SOAP FACTORY.
EVERYONE MAKES IT AT HOME RIGHT NOW, BUT WE CAN MAKE LARGER QUANTI-TIES IF WE HAVE A FACTORY.
THERE'S NO REASON FOR YOU TO WAIT.
WE CAN MAKE IT HAPPEN NOW.
WE NEED FUNDS...
I KNOW ANOTHER INVESTOR. LET ME GIVE YOU A REFERRAL.
THAT'S WON-DERFUL!
REALLY!?
WILL HE JUST BE AN INVES-TOR?
I MEAN, HE WON'T TRY TO OWN THE COMPANY...?
OU CAN EGOTI-TE THE TERMS.

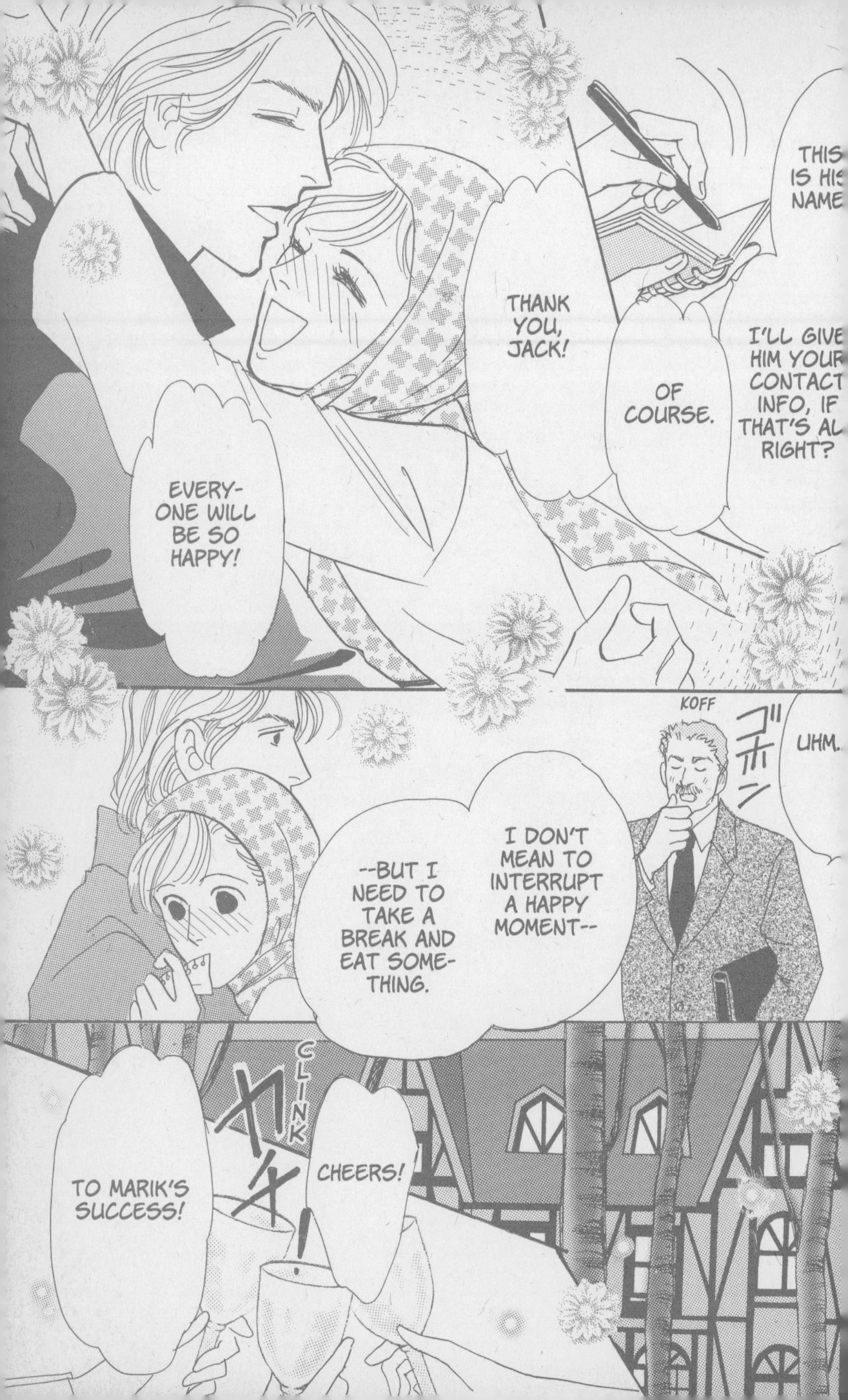
THIS IS HIS NAME
I'LL GIVE HIM YOUR CONTACT INFO, IF THAT'S ALL RIGHT?
OF COURSE.
THANK YOU, JACK!
EVERY-ONE WILL BE SO HAPPY!
KOFF
UHM.
I DON'T MEAN TO INTERRUPT A HAPPY MOMENT--
--BUT I NEED TO TAKE A BREAK AND EAT SOME-THING.
CLINK
CHEERS!
TO MARIK'S SUCCESS!

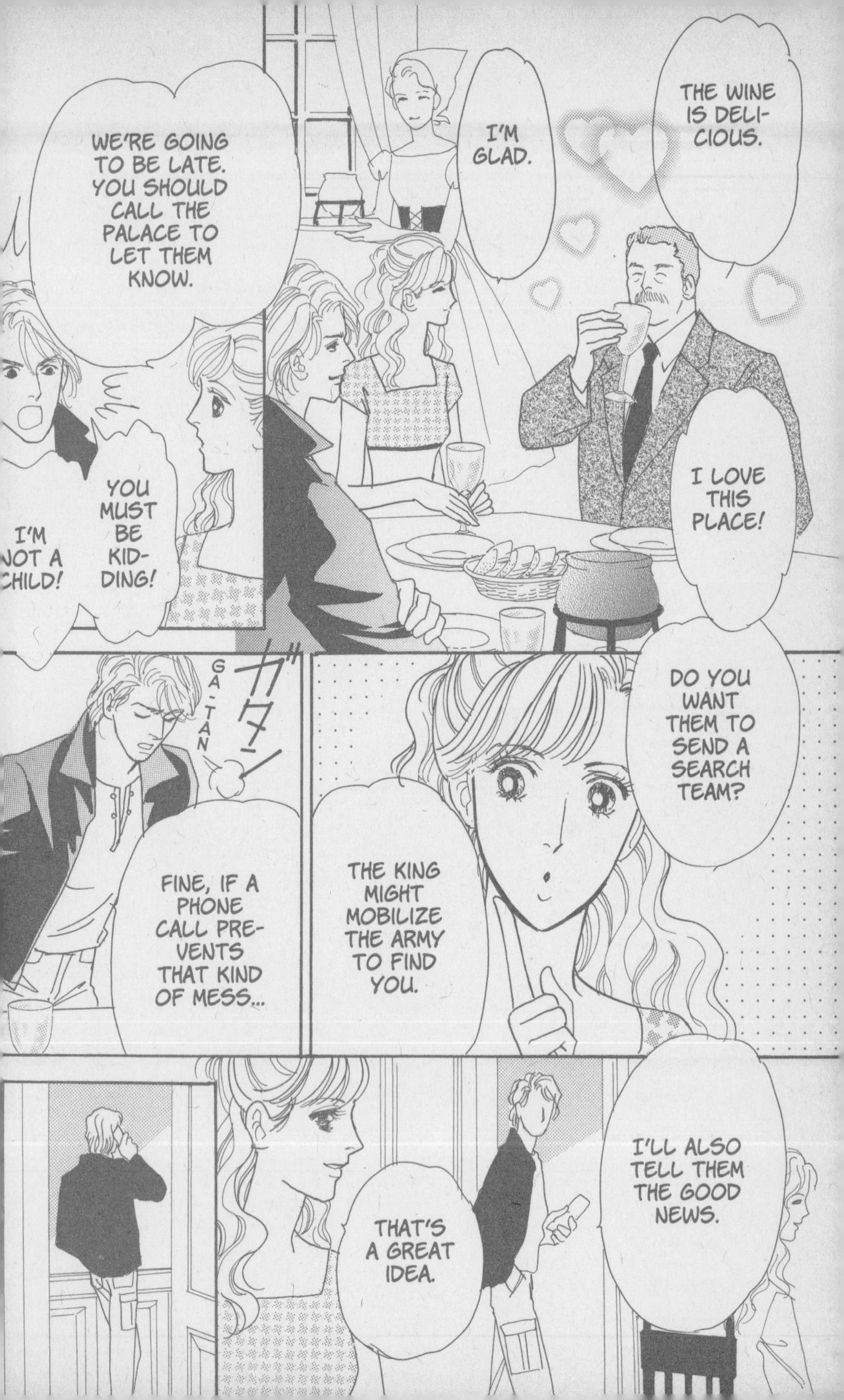
THE WINE IS DELICIOUS.
I'M GLAD.
I LOVE THIS PLACE!
WE'RE GOING TO BE LATE. YOU SHOULD CALL THE PALACE TO LET THEM KNOW.
YOU MUST BE KIDDING!
I'M NOT A CHILD!
DO YOU WANT THEM TO SEND A SEARCH TEAM?
THE KING MIGHT MOBILIZE THE ARMY TO FIND YOU.
ガタン
GA-TAN
FINE, IF A PHONE CALL PREVENTS THAT KIND OF MESS...
I'LL ALSO TELL THEM THE GOOD NEWS.
THAT'S A GREAT IDEA.

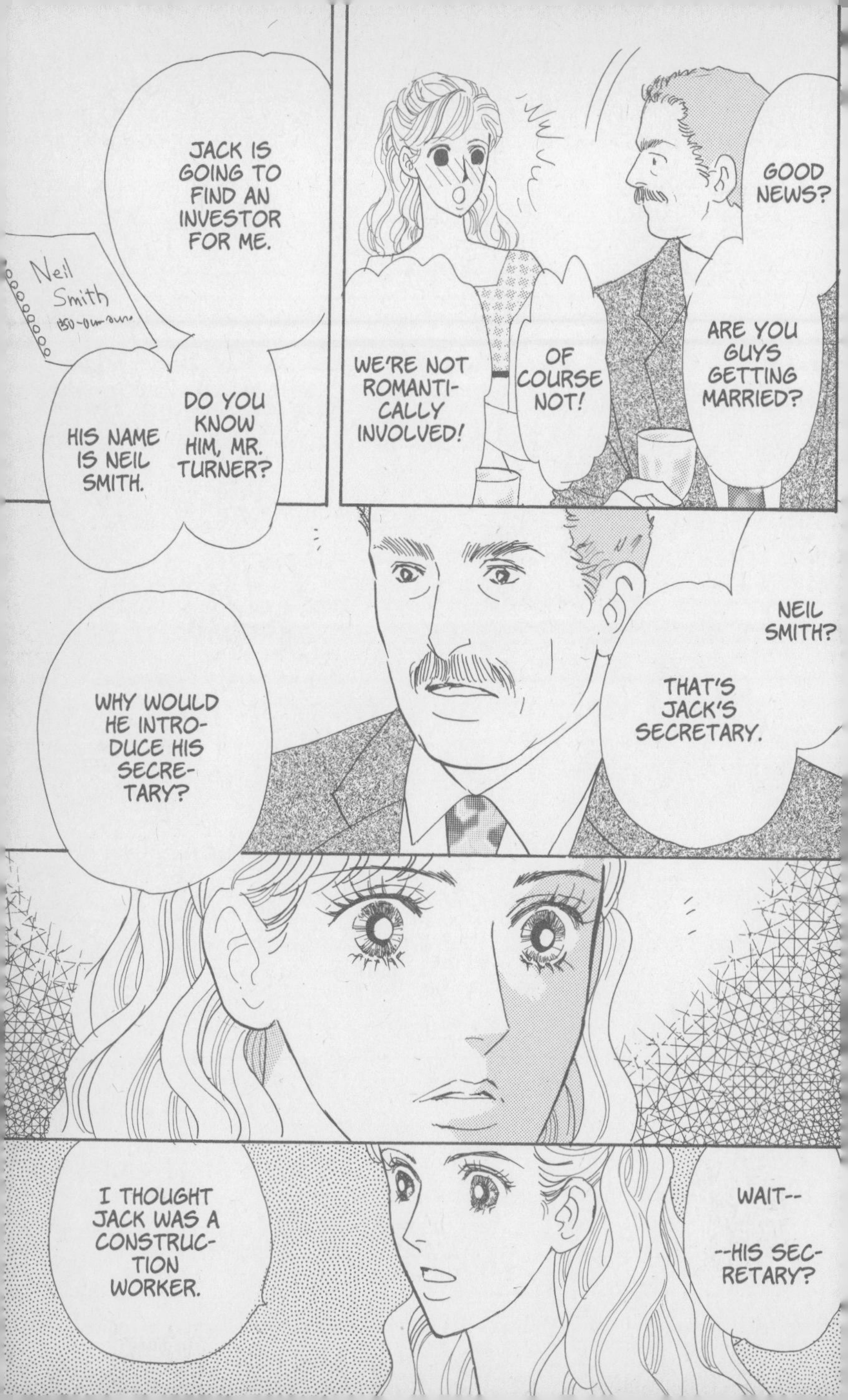
GOOD NEWS?
ARE YOU GUYS GETTING MARRIED?
OF COURSE NOT!
WE'RE NOT ROMANTICALLY INVOLVED!
JACK IS GOING TO FIND AN INVESTOR FOR ME.
Neil Smith
DO YOU KNOW HIM, MR. TURNER?
HIS NAME IS NEIL SMITH.
NEIL SMITH?
THAT'S JACK'S SECRETARY.
WHY WOULD HE INTRODUCE HIS SECRETARY?
WAIT--
--HIS SECRETARY?
I THOUGHT JACK WAS A CONSTRUCTION WORKER.

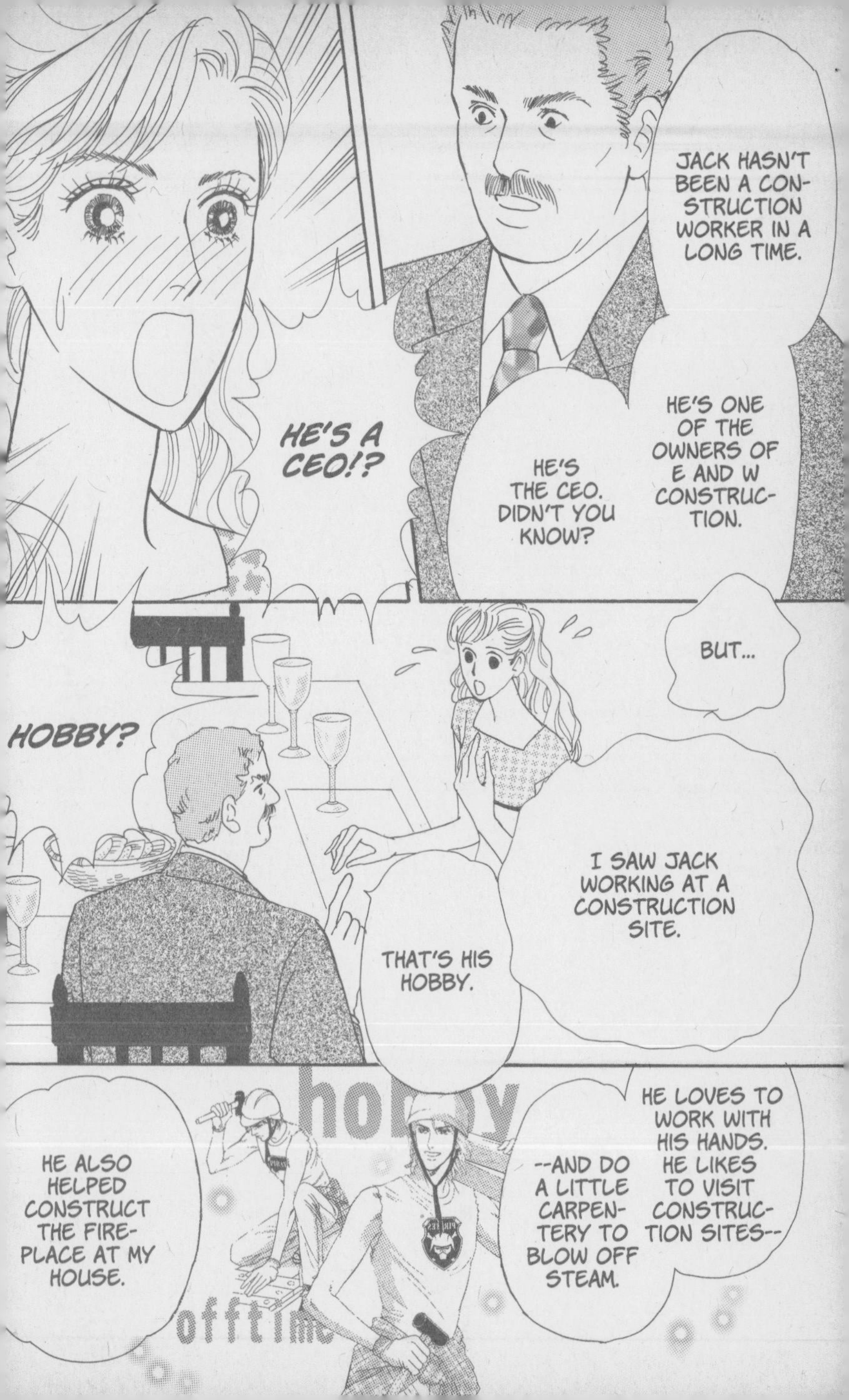
JACK HASN'T BEEN A CONSTRUCTION WORKER IN A LONG TIME.
HE'S ONE OF THE OWNERS OF E AND W CONSTRUCTION.
HE'S THE CEO. DIDN'T YOU KNOW?
HE'S A CEO!?
BUT...
I SAW JACK WORKING AT A CONSTRUCTION SITE.
THAT'S HIS HOBBY.
HOBBY?
HE LOVES TO WORK WITH HIS HANDS. HE LIKES TO VISIT CONSTRUCTION SITES--
--AND DO A LITTLE CARPENTERY TO BLOW OFF STEAM.
HE ALSO HELPED CONSTRUCT THE FIREPLACE AT MY HOUSE.
off time

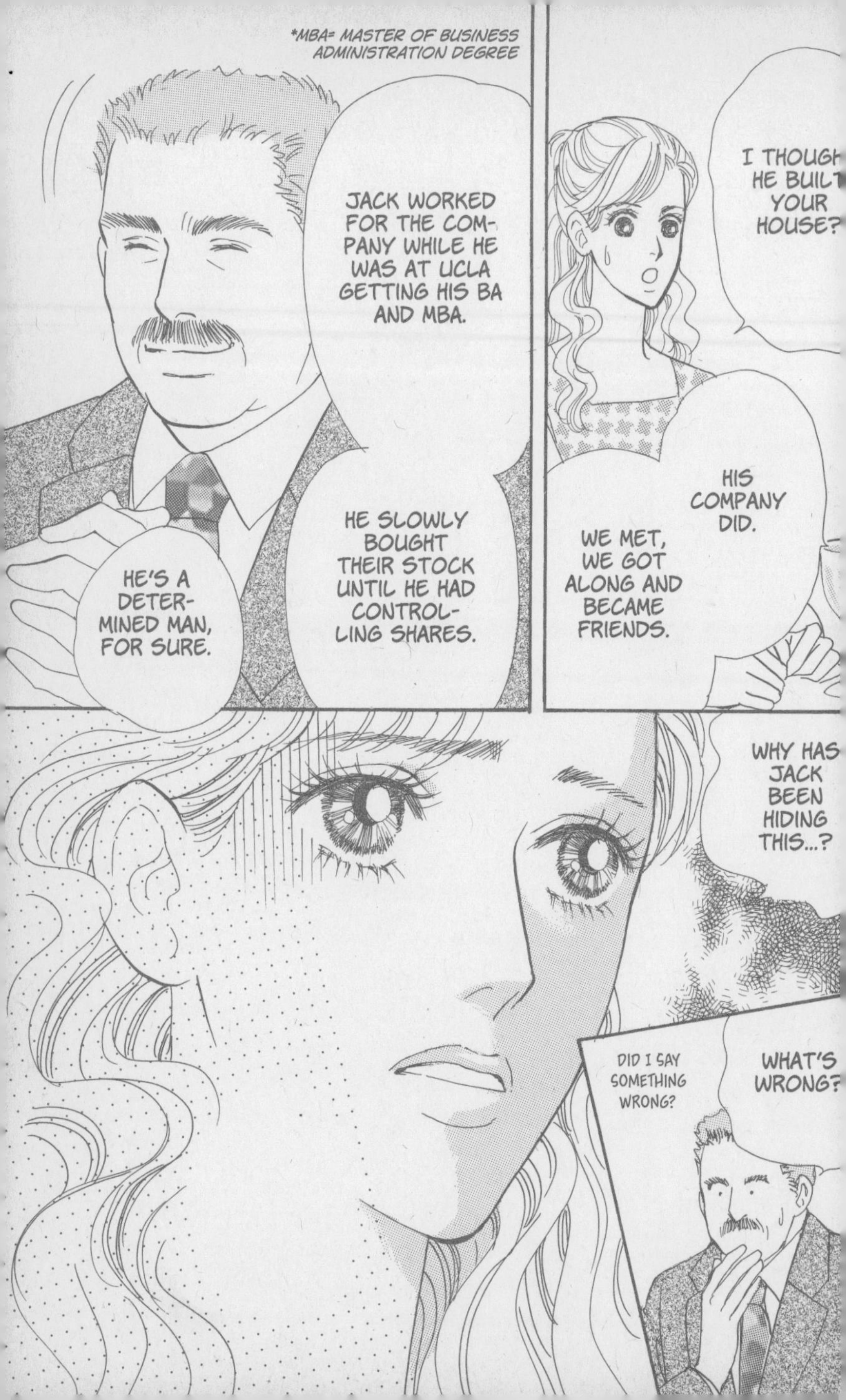
I THOUGH HE BUILT YOUR HOUSE?
HIS COMPANY DID.
WE MET, WE GOT ALONG AND BECAME FRIENDS.
*MBA= MASTER OF BUSINESS ADMINISTRATION DEGREE
JACK WORKED FOR THE COM-PANY WHILE HE WAS AT UCLA GETTING HIS BA AND MBA.
HE SLOWLY BOUGHT THEIR STOCK UNTIL HE HAD CONTROL-LING SHARES.
HE'S A DETER-MINED MAN, FOR SURE.
WHY HAS JACK BEEN HIDING THIS...?
WHAT'S WRONG?
DID I SAY SOMETHING WRONG?

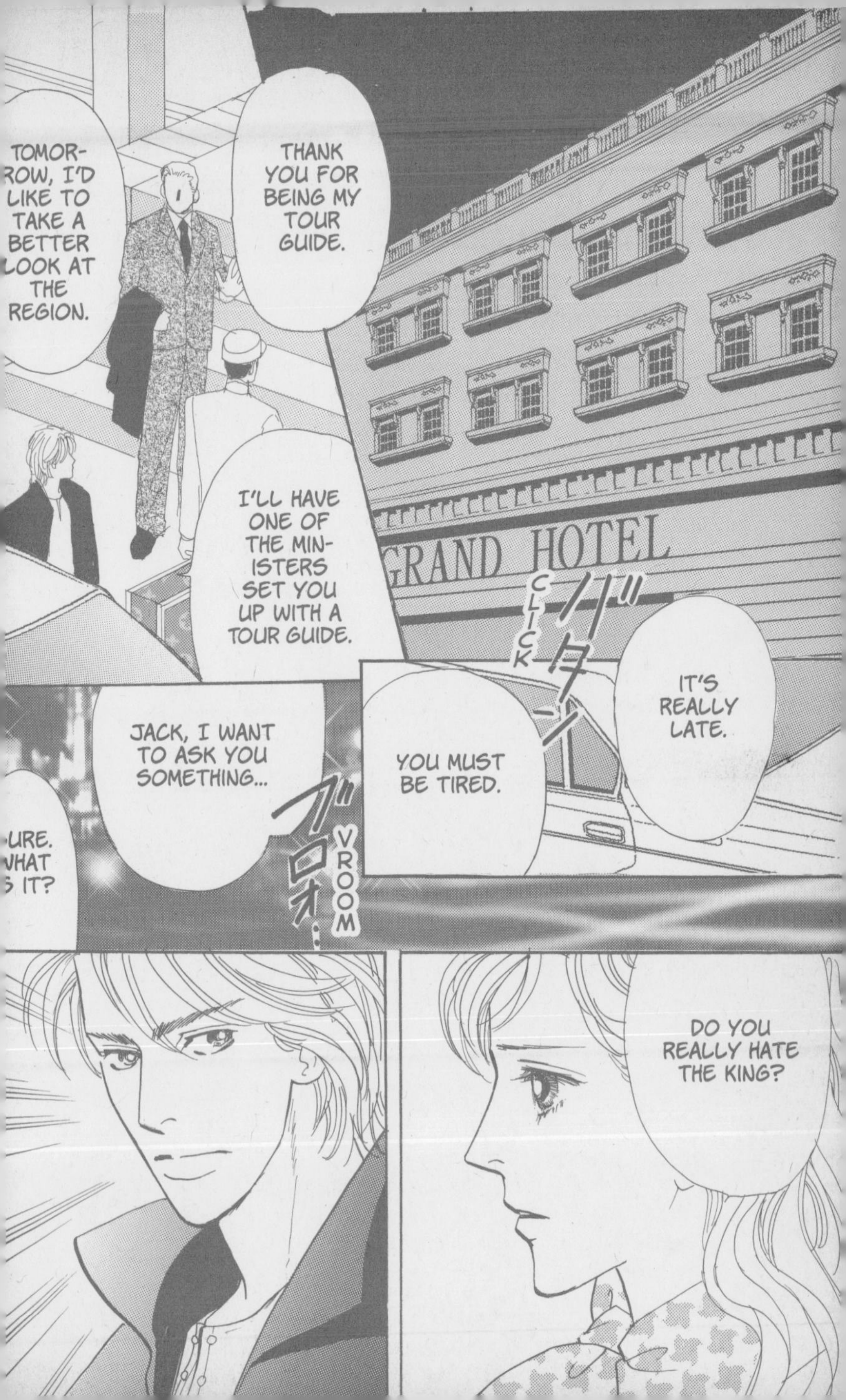
GRAND HOTEL
CLICK
THANK YOU FOR BEING MY TOUR GUIDE.
TOMORROW, I'D LIKE TO TAKE A BETTER LOOK AT THE REGION.
I'LL HAVE ONE OF THE MINISTERS SET YOU UP WITH A TOUR GUIDE.
IT'S REALLY LATE.
YOU MUST BE TIRED.
JACK, I WANT TO ASK YOU SOMETHING...
URE. HAT IT?
VROOM
DO YOU REALLY HATE THE KING?

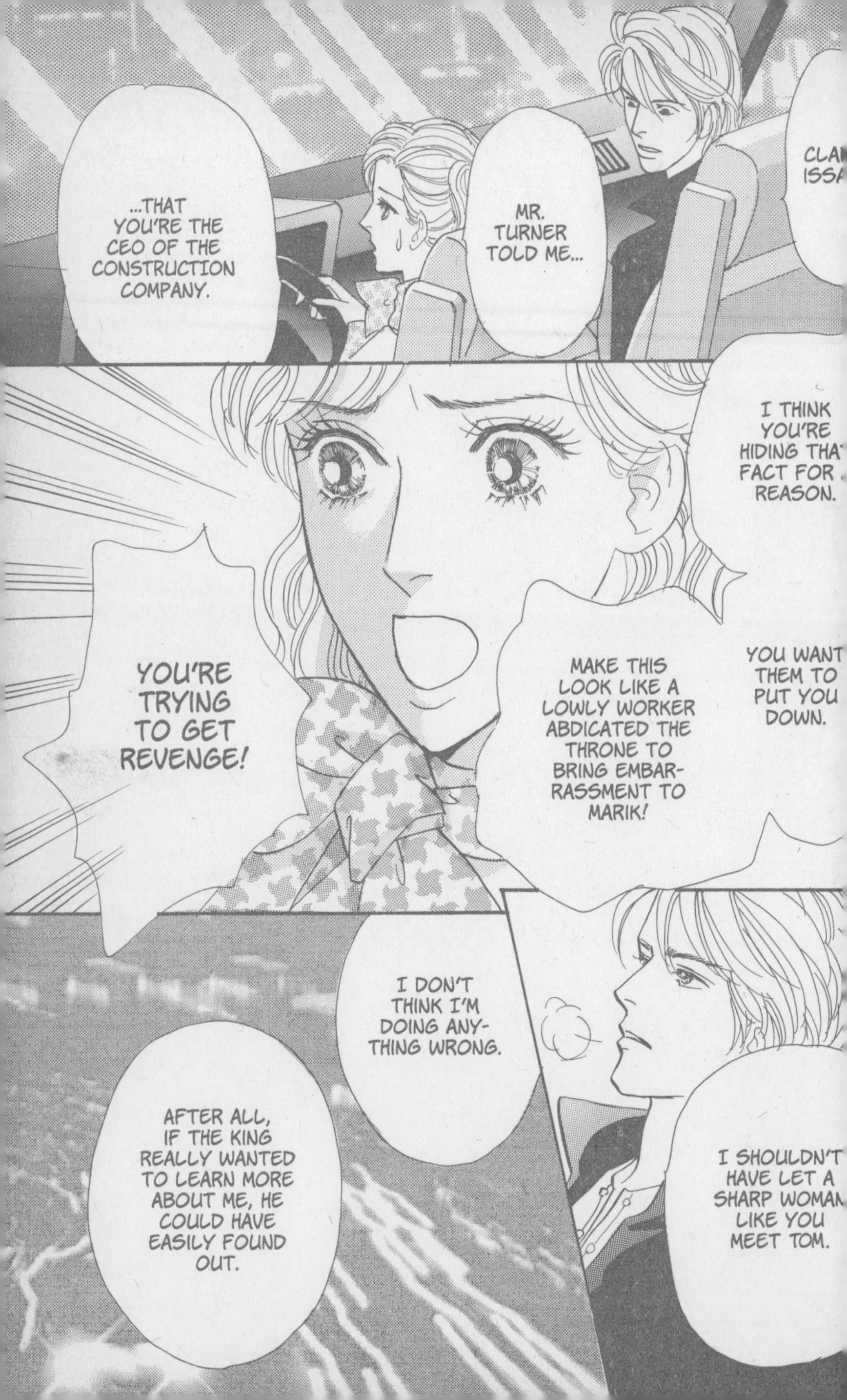
CLA ISSA
MR. TURNER TOLD ME...
...THAT YOU'RE THE CEO OF THE CONSTRUCTION COMPANY.
I THINK YOU'RE HIDING THA FACT FOR REASON.
YOU WANT THEM TO PUT YOU DOWN.
MAKE THIS LOOK LIKE A LOWLY WORKER ABDICATED THE THRONE TO BRING EMBAR-RASSMENT TO MARIK!
YOU'RE TRYING TO GET REVENGE!
I SHOULDN'T HAVE LET A SHARP WOMAN LIKE YOU MEET TOM.
I DON'T THINK I'M DOING ANY-THING WRONG.
AFTER ALL, IF THE KING REALLY WANTED TO LEARN MORE ABOUT ME, HE COULD HAVE EASILY FOUND OUT.

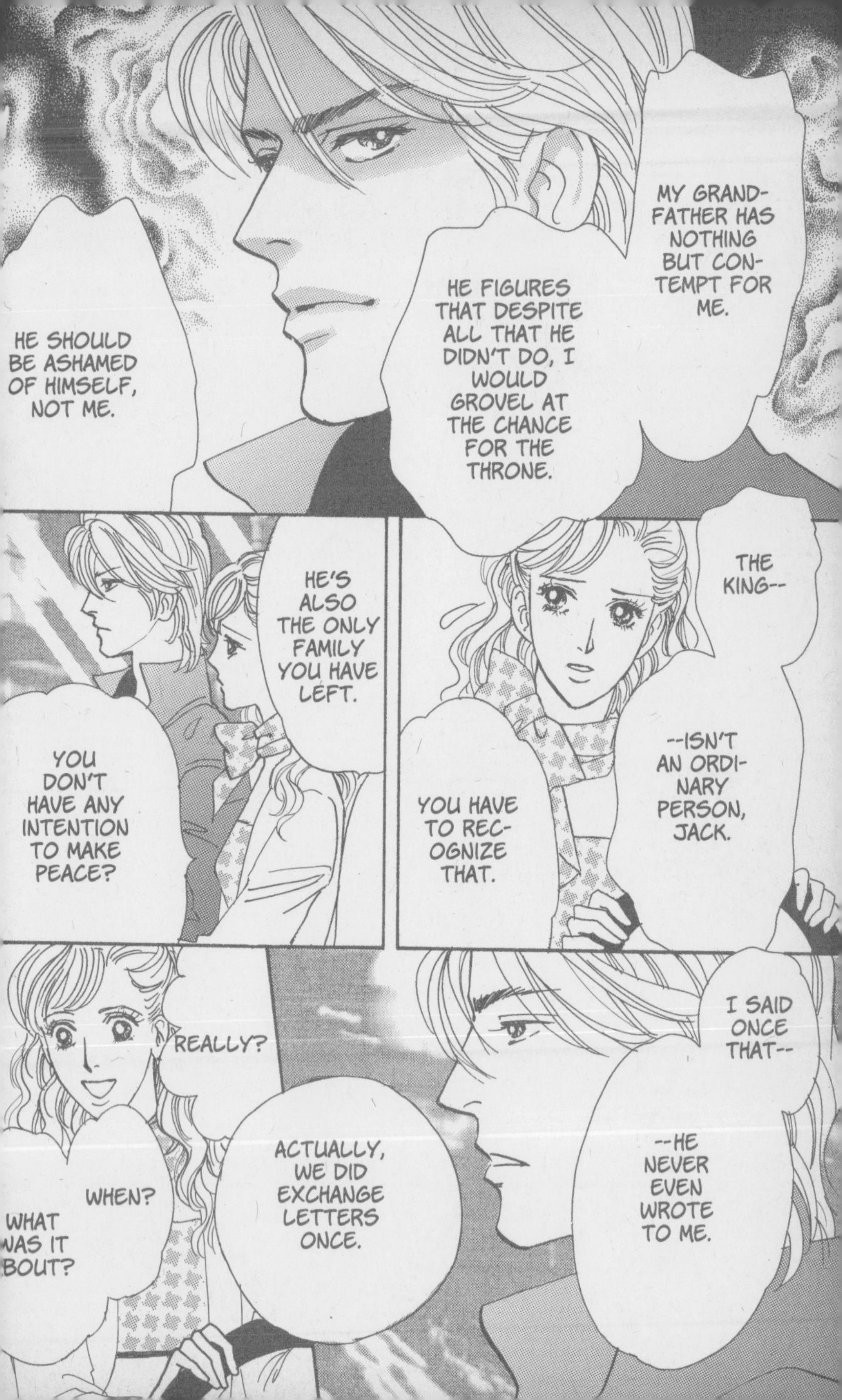
MY GRANDFATHER HAS NOTHING BUT CONTEMPT FOR ME.
HE FIGURES THAT DESPITE ALL THAT HE DIDN'T DO, I WOULD GROVEL AT THE CHANCE FOR THE THRONE.
HE SHOULD BE ASHAMED OF HIMSELF, NOT ME.
THE KING--
--ISN'T AN ORDINARY PERSON, JACK.
YOU HAVE TO RECOGNIZE THAT.
HE'S ALSO THE ONLY FAMILY YOU HAVE LEFT.
YOU DON'T HAVE ANY INTENTION TO MAKE PEACE?
I SAID ONCE THAT--
--HE NEVER EVEN WROTE TO ME.
ACTUALLY, WE DID EXCHANGE LETTERS ONCE.
REALLY?
WHEN?
WHAT WAS IT BOUT?

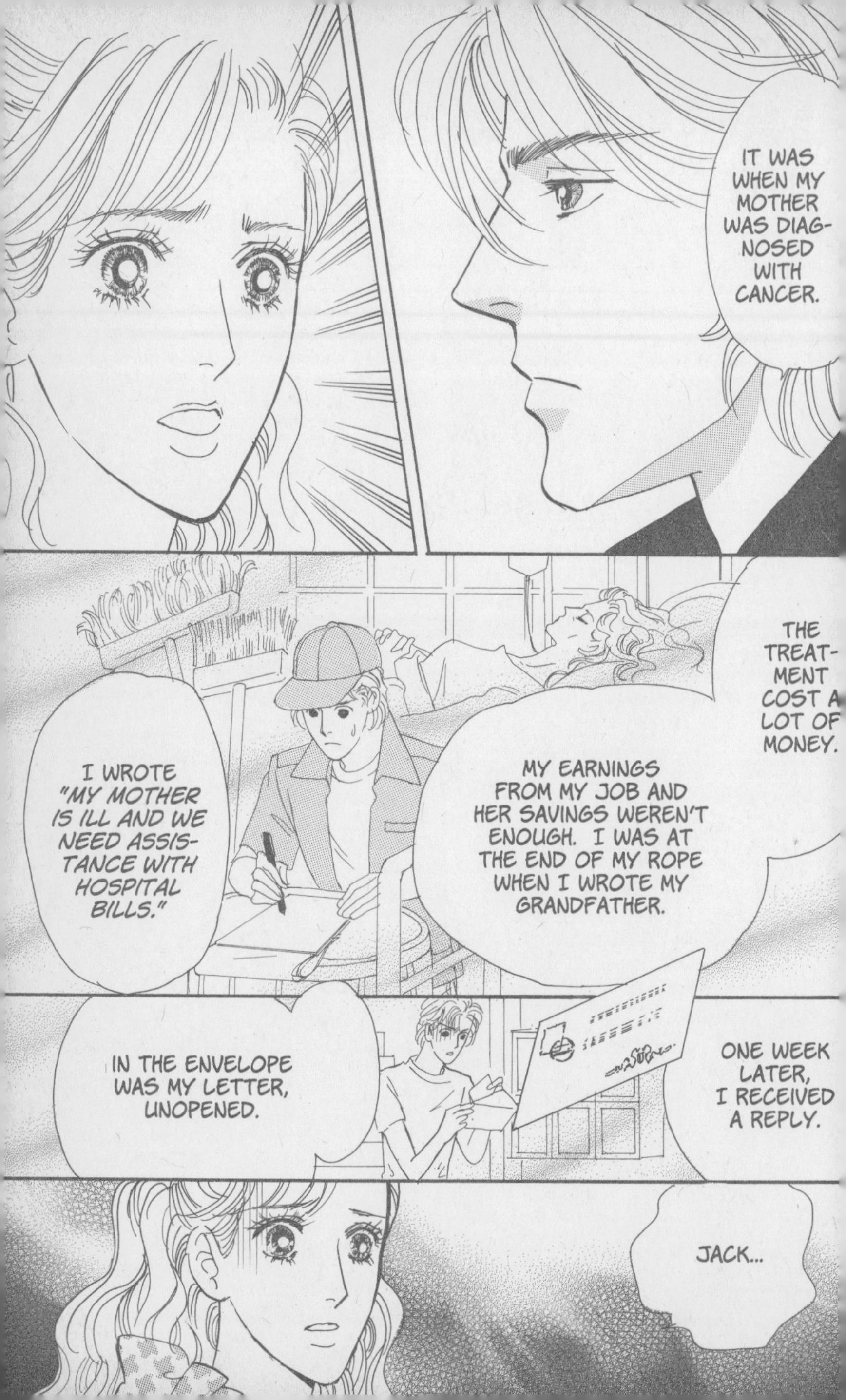
IT WAS WHEN MY MOTHER WAS DIAG-NOSED WITH CANCER.
THE TREAT-MENT COST A LOT OF MONEY.
MY EARNINGS FROM MY JOB AND HER SAVINGS WEREN'T ENOUGH. I WAS AT THE END OF MY ROPE WHEN I WROTE MY GRANDFATHER.
I WROTE "MY MOTHER IS ILL AND WE NEED ASSIS-TANCE WITH HOSPITAL BILLS."
ONE WEEK LATER, I RECEIVED A REPLY.
IN THE ENVELOPE WAS MY LETTER, UNOPENED.
JACK...

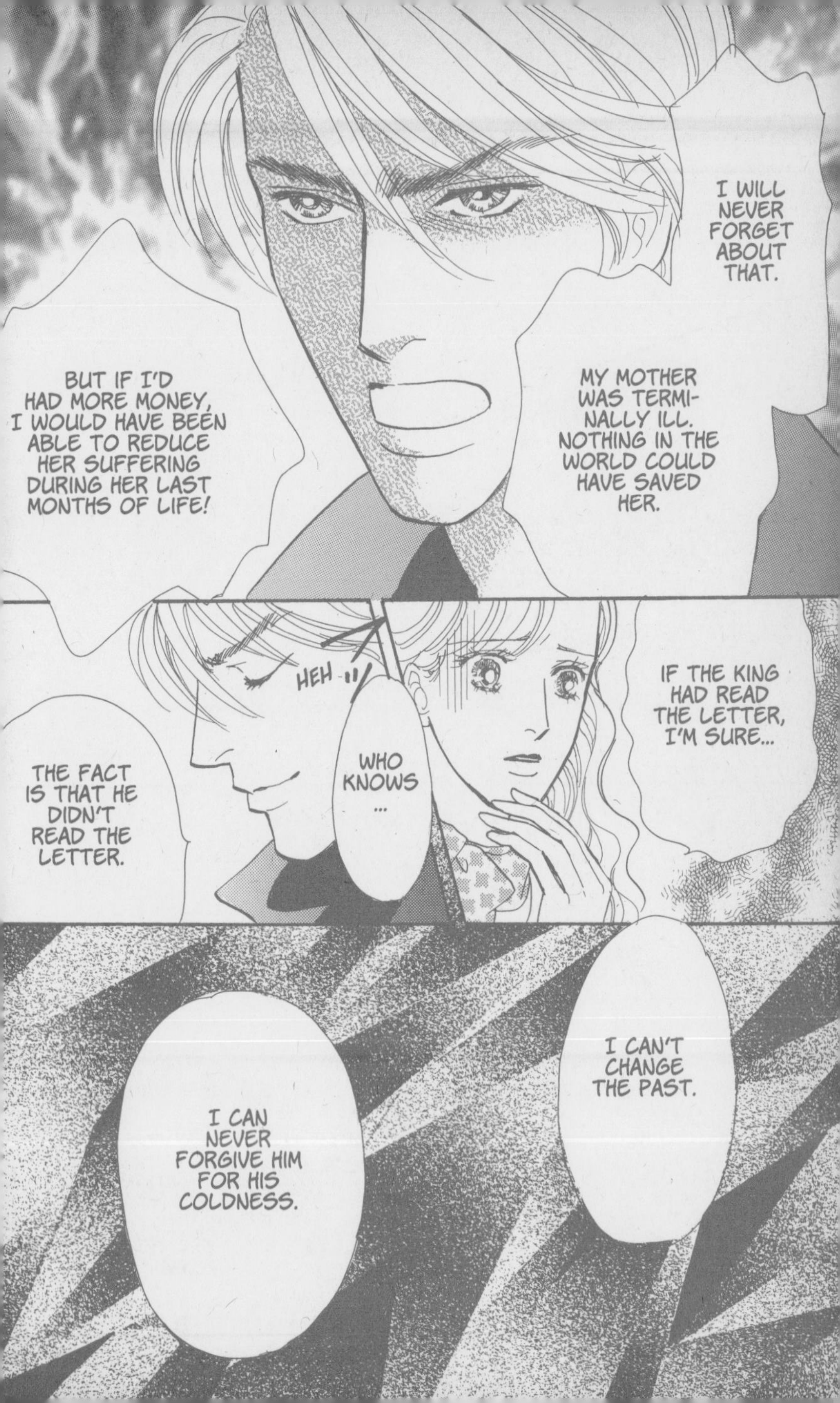
I WILL NEVER FORGET ABOUT THAT.
MY MOTHER WAS TERMI-NALLY ILL. NOTHING IN THE WORLD COULD HAVE SAVED HER.
BUT IF I'D HAD MORE MONEY, I WOULD HAVE BEEN ABLE TO REDUCE HER SUFFERING DURING HER LAST MONTHS OF LIFE!
IF THE KING HAD READ THE LETTER, I'M SURE...
WHO KNOWS ...
HEH
THE FACT IS THAT HE DIDN'T READ THE LETTER.
I CAN'T CHANGE THE PAST.
I CAN NEVER FORGIVE HIM FOR HIS COLDNESS.

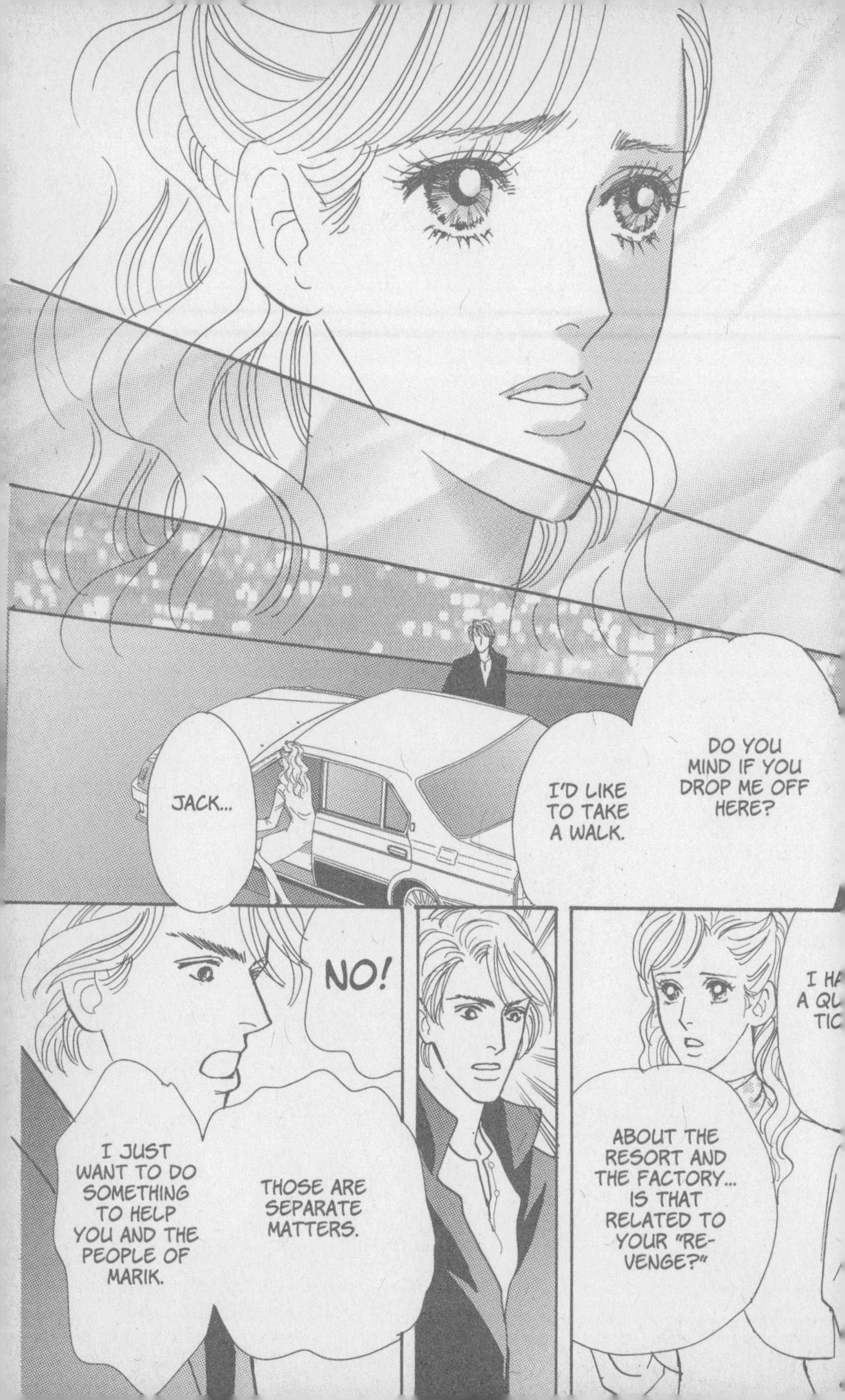
DO YOU MIND IF YOU DROP ME OFF HERE?
I'D LIKE TO TAKE A WALK.
JACK...
ABOUT THE RESORT AND THE FACTORY... IS THAT RELATED TO YOUR "RE-VENGE?"
NO!
THOSE ARE SEPARATE MATTERS.
I JUST WANT TO DO SOMETHING TO HELP YOU AND THE PEOPLE OF MARIK.

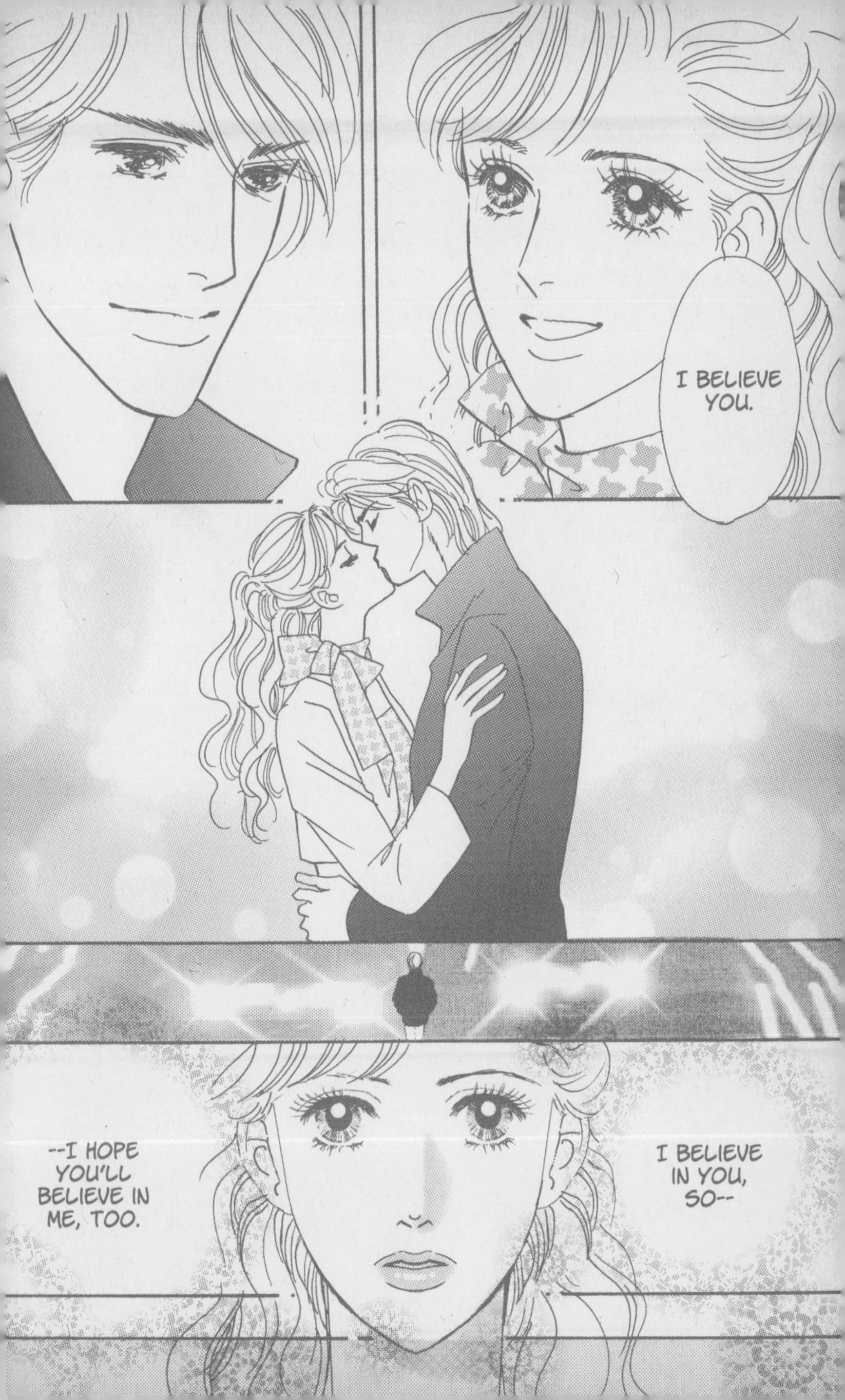
I BELIEVE YOU.
I BELIEVE IN YOU, SO--
--I HOPE YOU'LL BELIEVE IN ME, TOO.

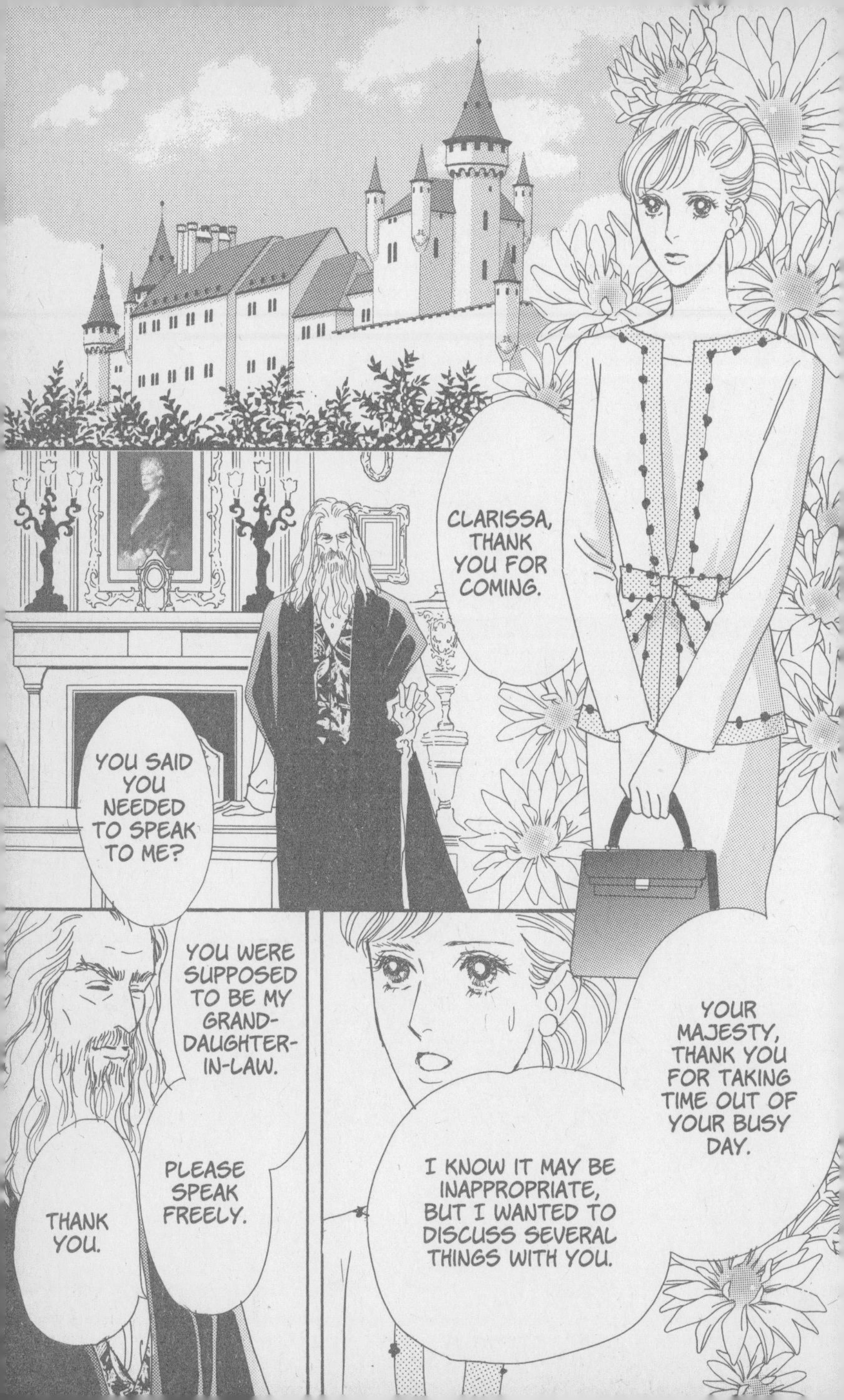
CLARISSA, THANK YOU FOR COMING.
YOUR MAJESTY, THANK YOU FOR TAKING TIME OUT OF YOUR BUSY DAY.
YOU SAID YOU NEEDED TO SPEAK TO ME?
I KNOW IT MAY BE INAPPROPRIATE, BUT I WANTED TO DISCUSS SEVERAL THINGS WITH YOU.
YOU WERE SUPPOSED TO BE MY GRAND-DAUGHTER-IN-LAW.
PLEASE SPEAK FREELY.
THANK YOU.

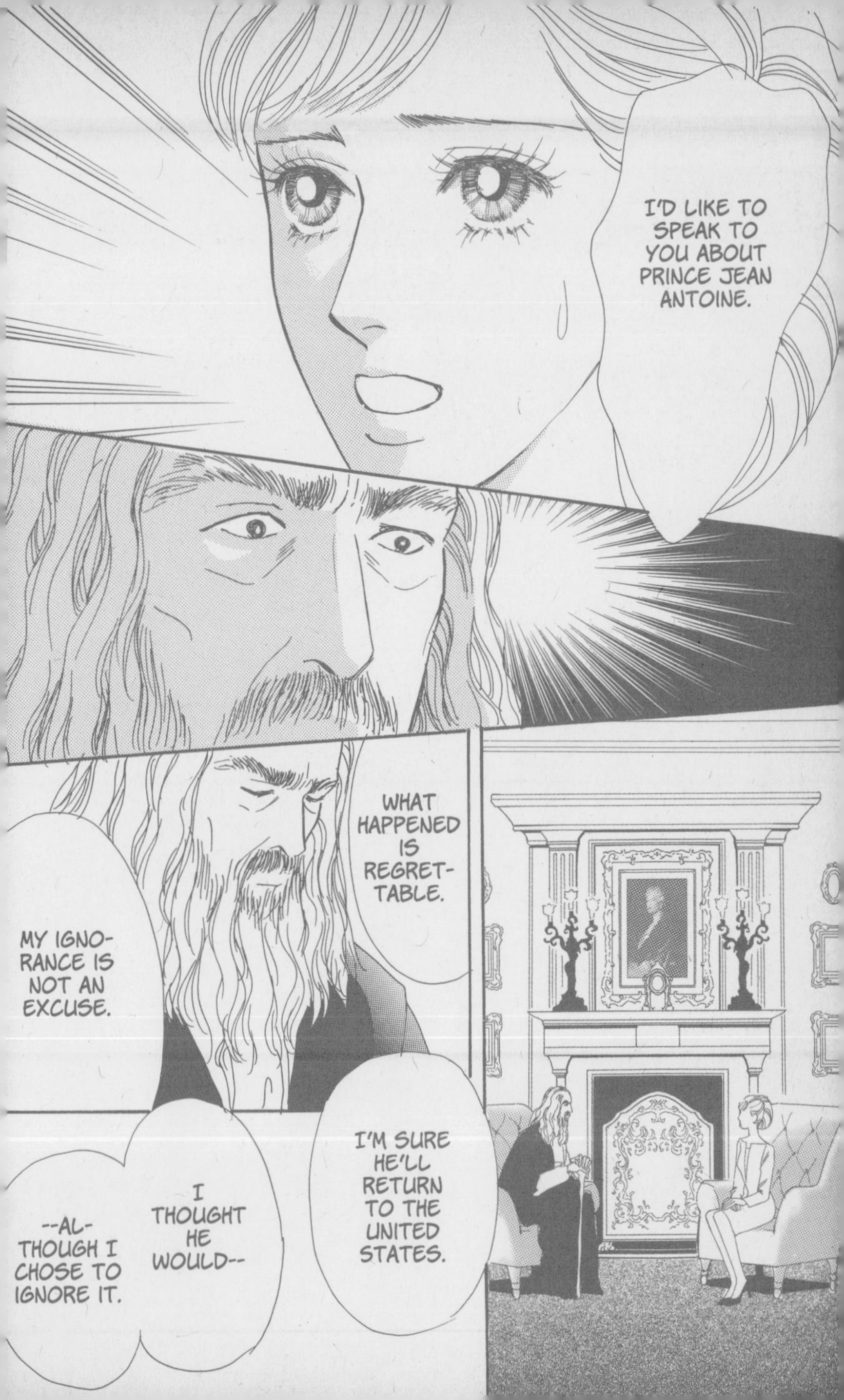
I'D LIKE TO SPEAK TO YOU ABOUT PRINCE JEAN ANTOINE.
WHAT HAPPENED IS REGRET-TABLE.
MY IGNO-RANCE IS NOT AN EXCUSE.
I'M SURE HE'LL RETURN TO THE UNITED STATES.
I THOUGHT HE WOULD--
--AL-THOUGH I CHOSE TO IGNORE IT.

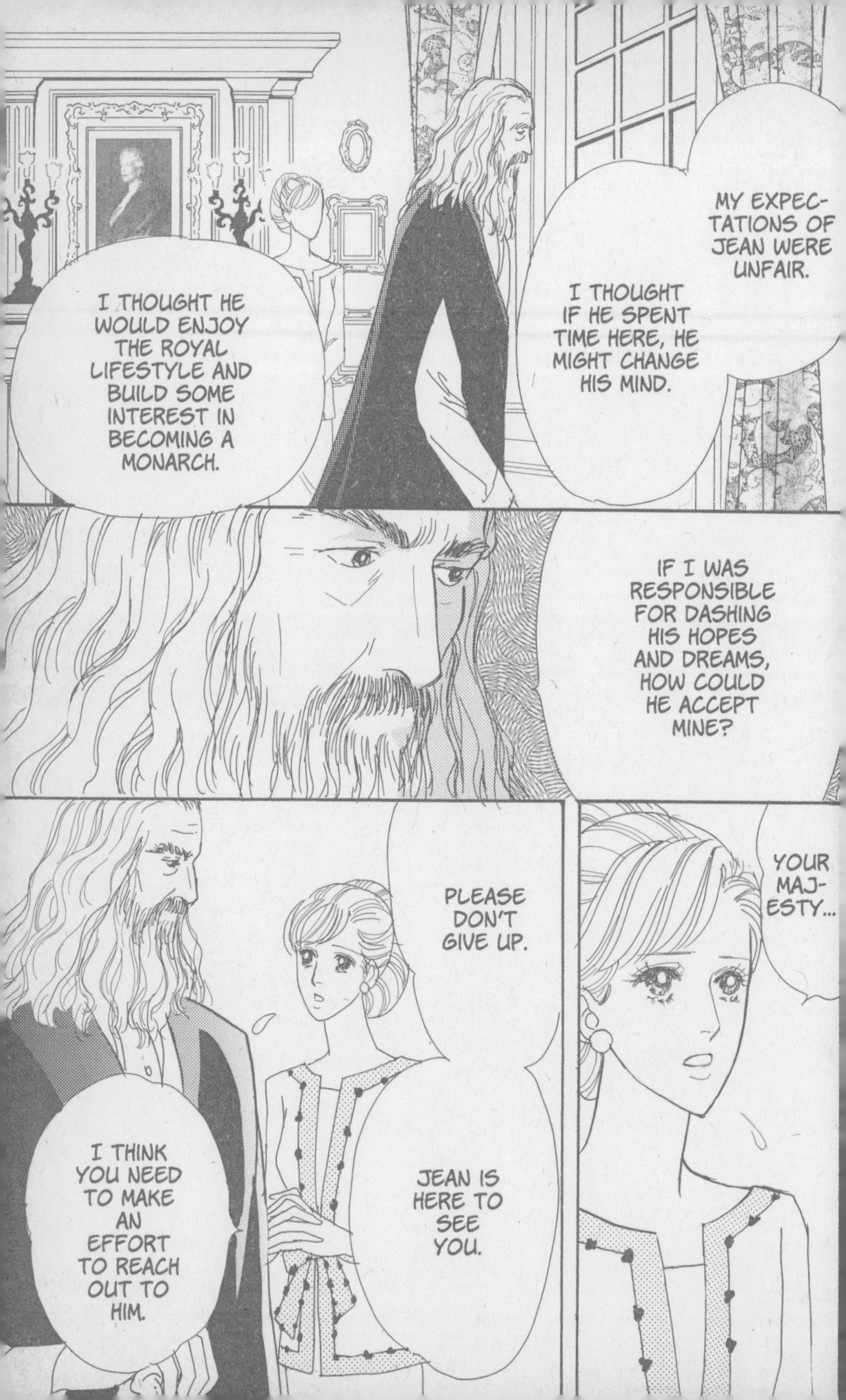
MY EXPECTATIONS OF JEAN WERE UNFAIR.
I THOUGHT IF HE SPENT TIME HERE, HE MIGHT CHANGE HIS MIND.
I THOUGHT HE WOULD ENJOY THE ROYAL LIFESTYLE AND BUILD SOME INTEREST IN BECOMING A MONARCH.
IF I WAS RESPONSIBLE FOR DASHING HIS HOPES AND DREAMS, HOW COULD HE ACCEPT MINE?
YOUR MAJESTY...
PLEASE DON'T GIVE UP.
JEAN IS HERE TO SEE YOU.
I THINK YOU NEED TO MAKE AN EFFORT TO REACH OUT TO HIM.

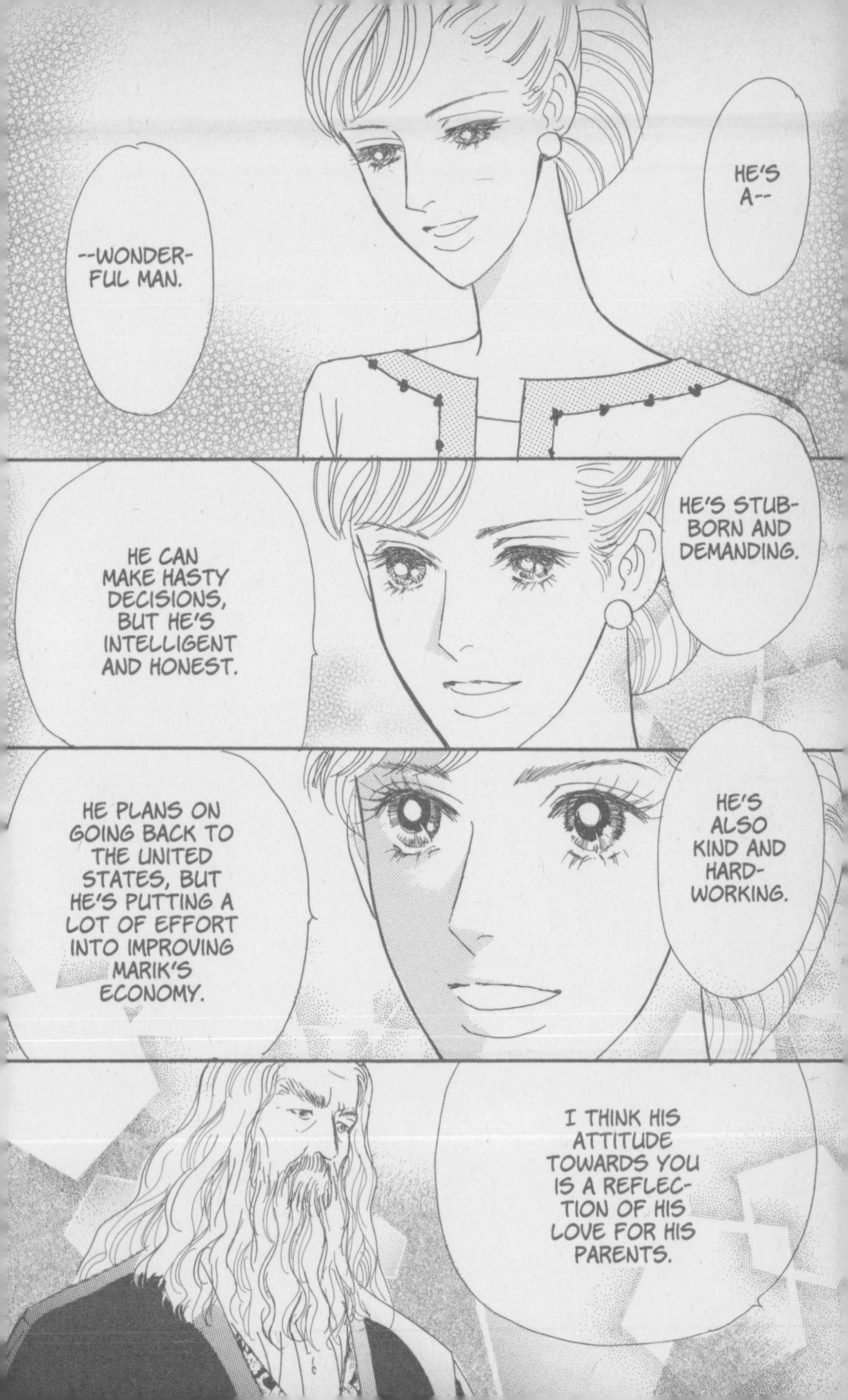
HE'S A--
--WONDERFUL MAN.
HE'S STUBBORN AND DEMANDING.
HE CAN MAKE HASTY DECISIONS, BUT HE'S INTELLIGENT AND HONEST.
HE'S ALSO KIND AND HARD-WORKING.
HE PLANS ON GOING BACK TO THE UNITED STATES, BUT HE'S PUTTING A LOT OF EFFORT INTO IMPROVING MARIK'S ECONOMY.
I THINK HIS ATTITUDE TOWARDS YOU IS A REFLECTION OF HIS LOVE FOR HIS PARENTS.

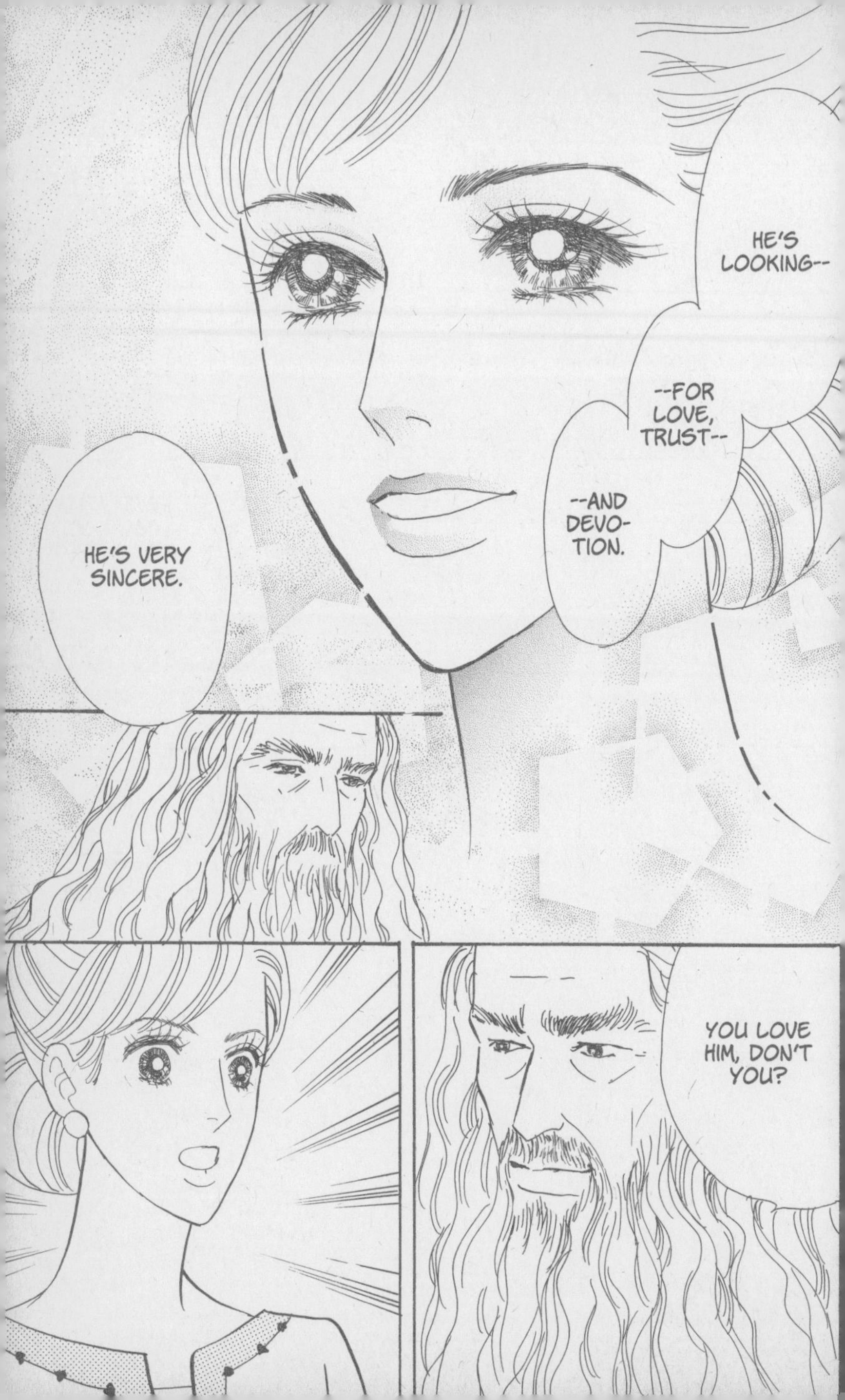
HE'S LOOKING--
--FOR LOVE, TRUST--
--AND DEVOTION.
HE'S VERY SINCERE.
YOU LOVE HIM, DON'T YOU?

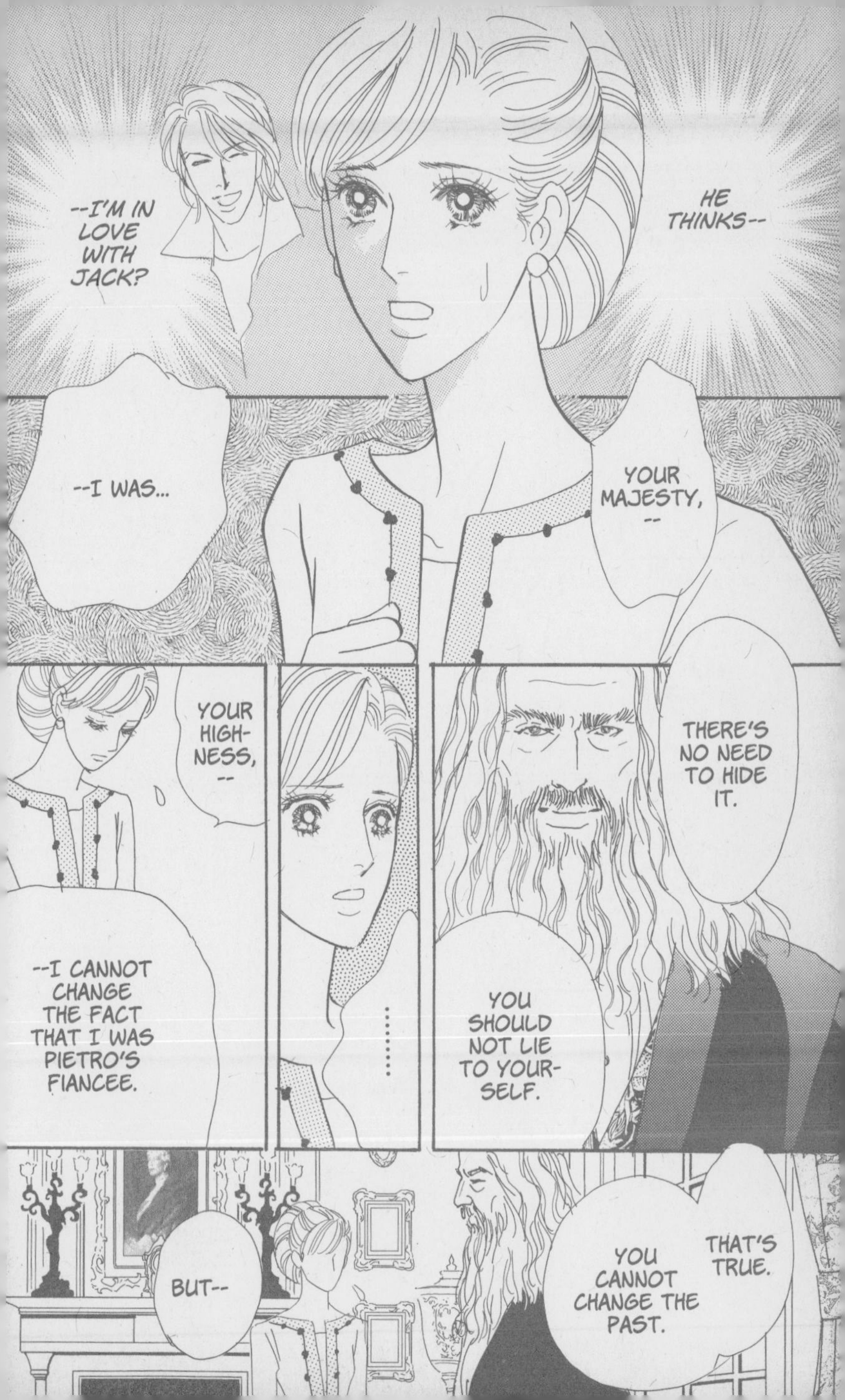
HE THINKS--
--I'M IN LOVE WITH JACK?
YOUR MAJESTY, --
--I WAS...
THERE'S NO NEED TO HIDE IT.
YOU SHOULD NOT LIE TO YOURSELF.
......
YOUR HIGHNESS, --
--I CANNOT CHANGE THE FACT THAT I WAS PIETRO'S FIANCEE.
THAT'S TRUE.
YOU CANNOT CHANGE THE PAST.
BUT--

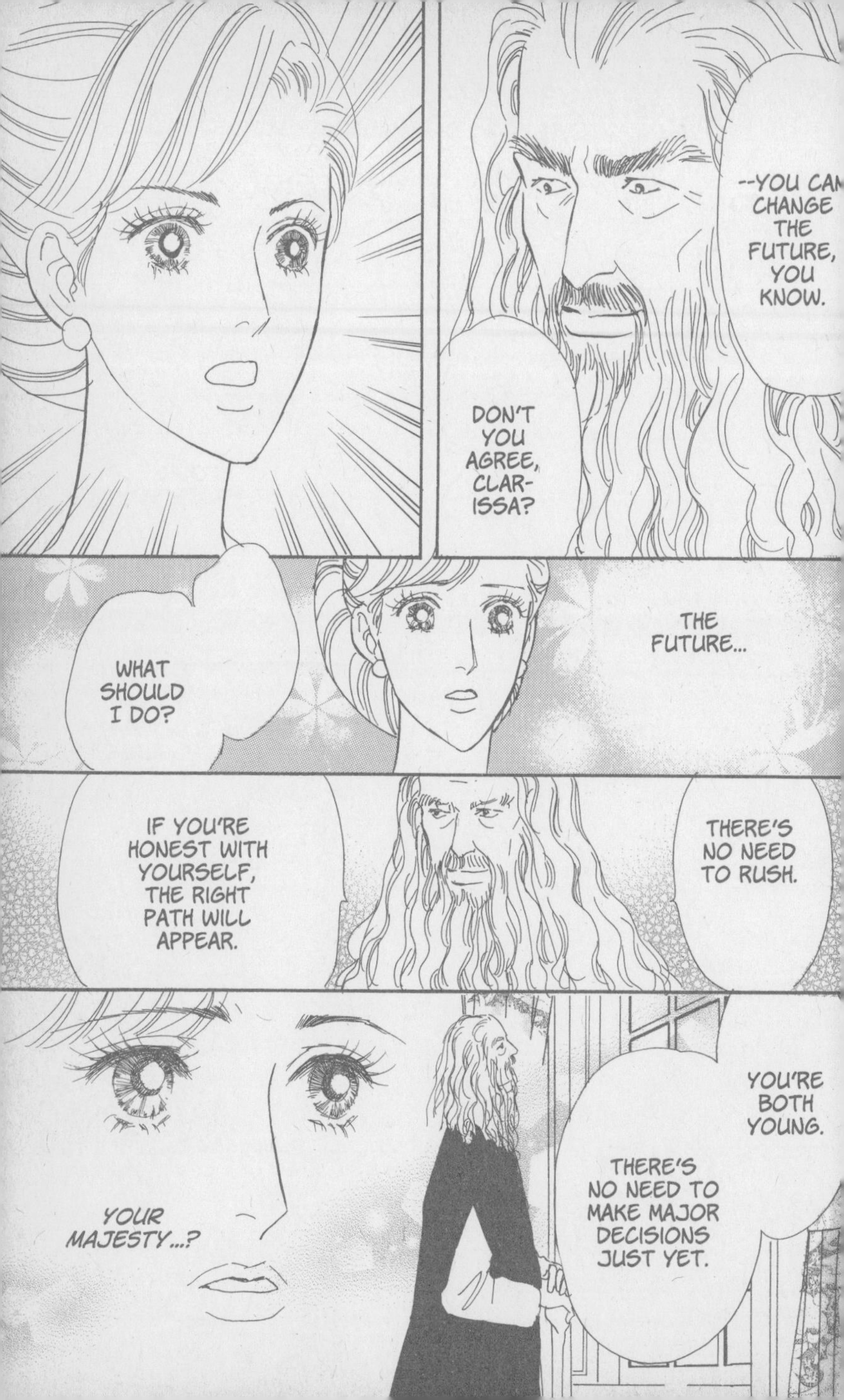
--YOU CAN CHANGE THE FUTURE, YOU KNOW.
DON'T YOU AGREE, CLAR-ISSA?
THE FUTURE...
WHAT SHOULD I DO?
THERE'S NO NEED TO RUSH.
IF YOU'RE HONEST WITH YOURSELF, THE RIGHT PATH WILL APPEAR.
YOU'RE BOTH YOUNG.
THERE'S NO NEED TO MAKE MAJOR DECISIONS JUST YET.
YOUR MAJESTY...?

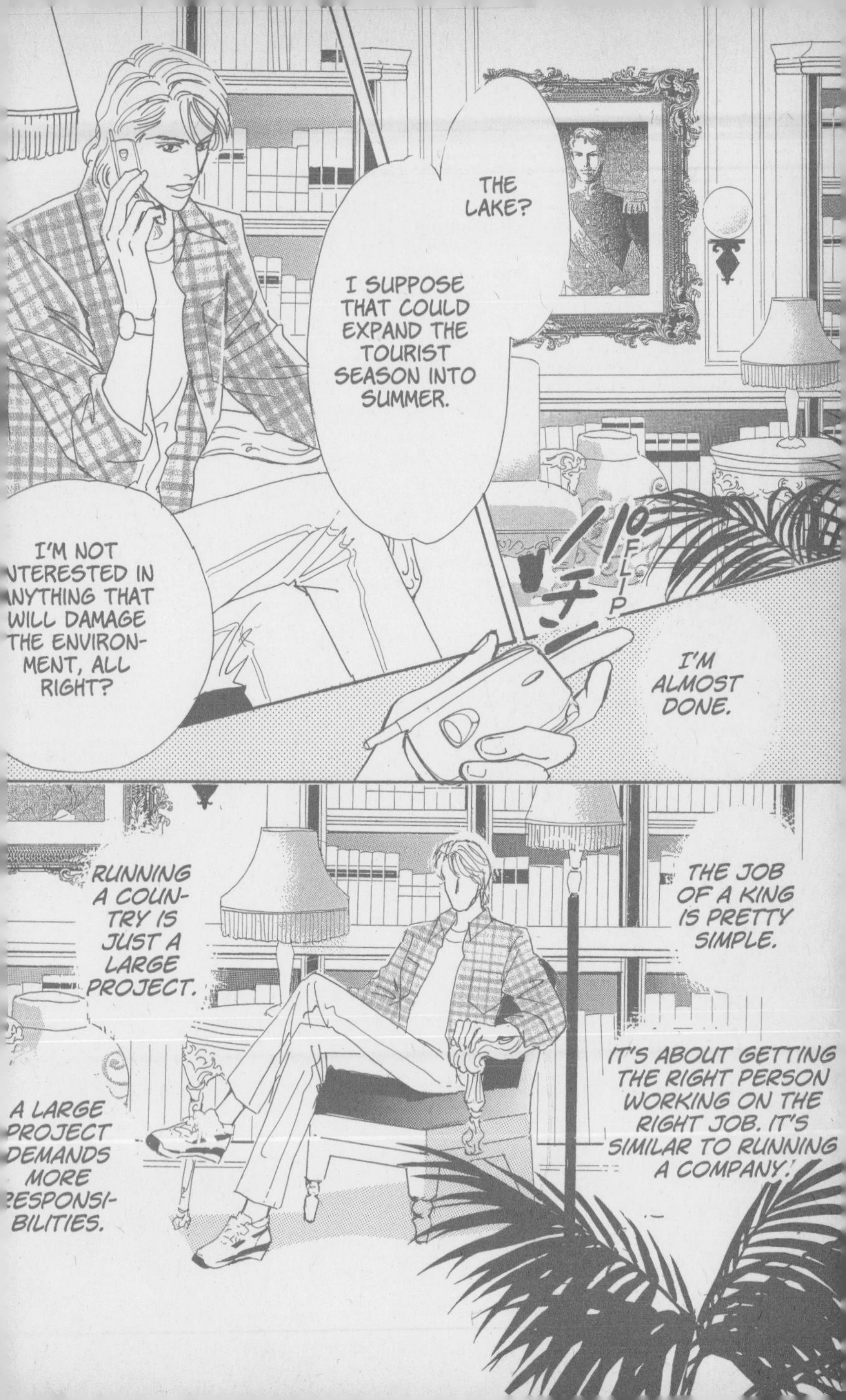
THE LAKE?
I SUPPOSE THAT COULD EXPAND THE TOURIST SEASON INTO SUMMER.
I'M NOT NTERESTED IN NYTHING THAT WILL DAMAGE THE ENVIRON-MENT, ALL RIGHT?
パチン
FLIP
I'M ALMOST DONE.
THE JOB OF A KING IS PRETTY SIMPLE.
IT'S ABOUT GETTING THE RIGHT PERSON WORKING ON THE RIGHT JOB. IT'S SIMILAR TO RUNNING A COMPANY.
RUNNING A COUN-TRY IS JUST A LARGE PROJECT.
A LARGE ROJECT DEMANDS MORE ESPONSI-BILITIES.

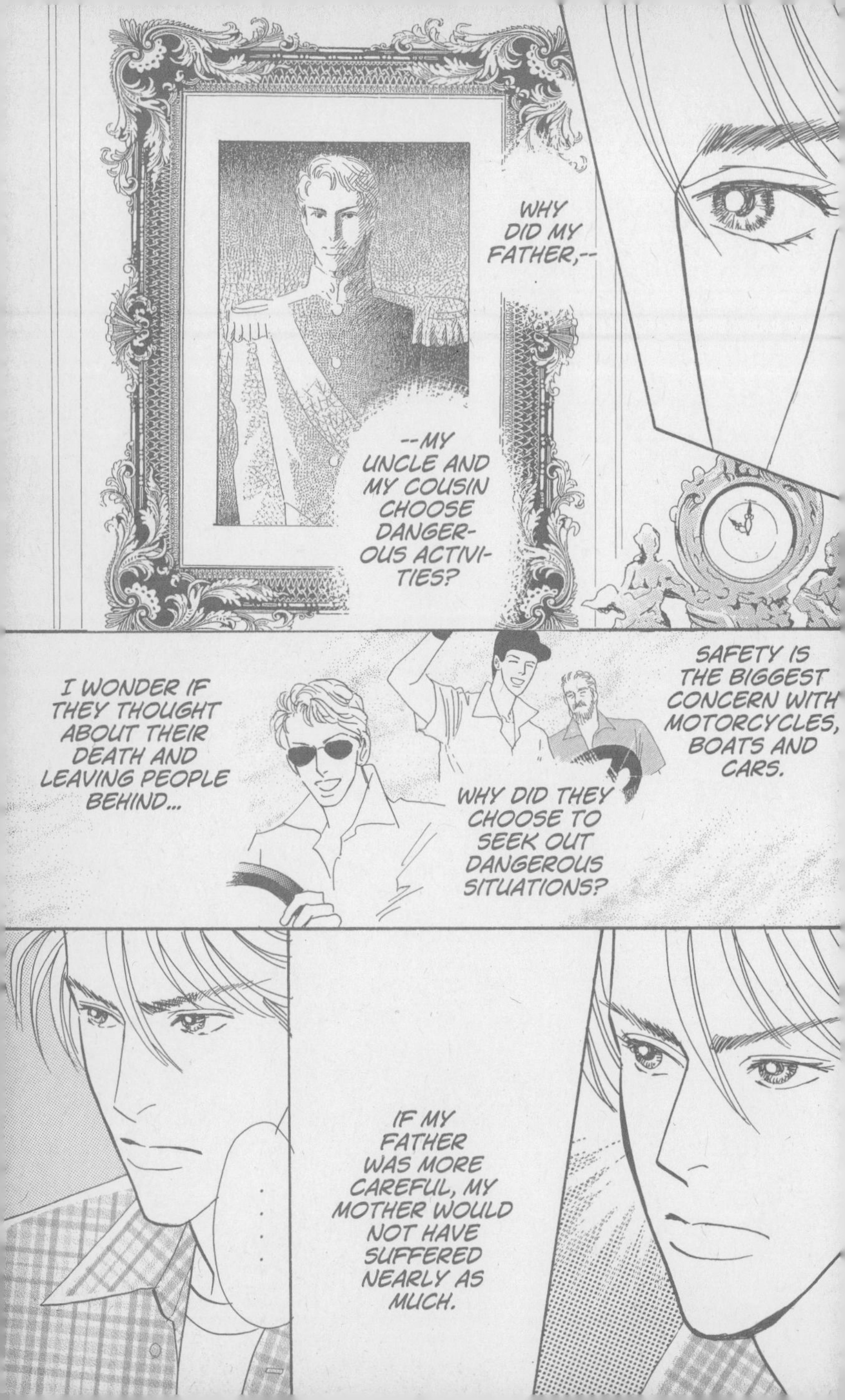
WHY DID MY FATHER,--
--MY UNCLE AND MY COUSIN CHOOSE DANGEROUS ACTIVITIES?
SAFETY IS THE BIGGEST CONCERN WITH MOTORCYCLES, BOATS AND CARS.
WHY DID THEY CHOOSE TO SEEK OUT DANGEROUS SITUATIONS?
I WONDER IF THEY THOUGHT ABOUT THEIR DEATH AND LEAVING PEOPLE BEHIND...
IF MY FATHER WAS MORE CAREFUL, MY MOTHER WOULD NOT HAVE SUFFERED NEARLY AS MUCH.
...

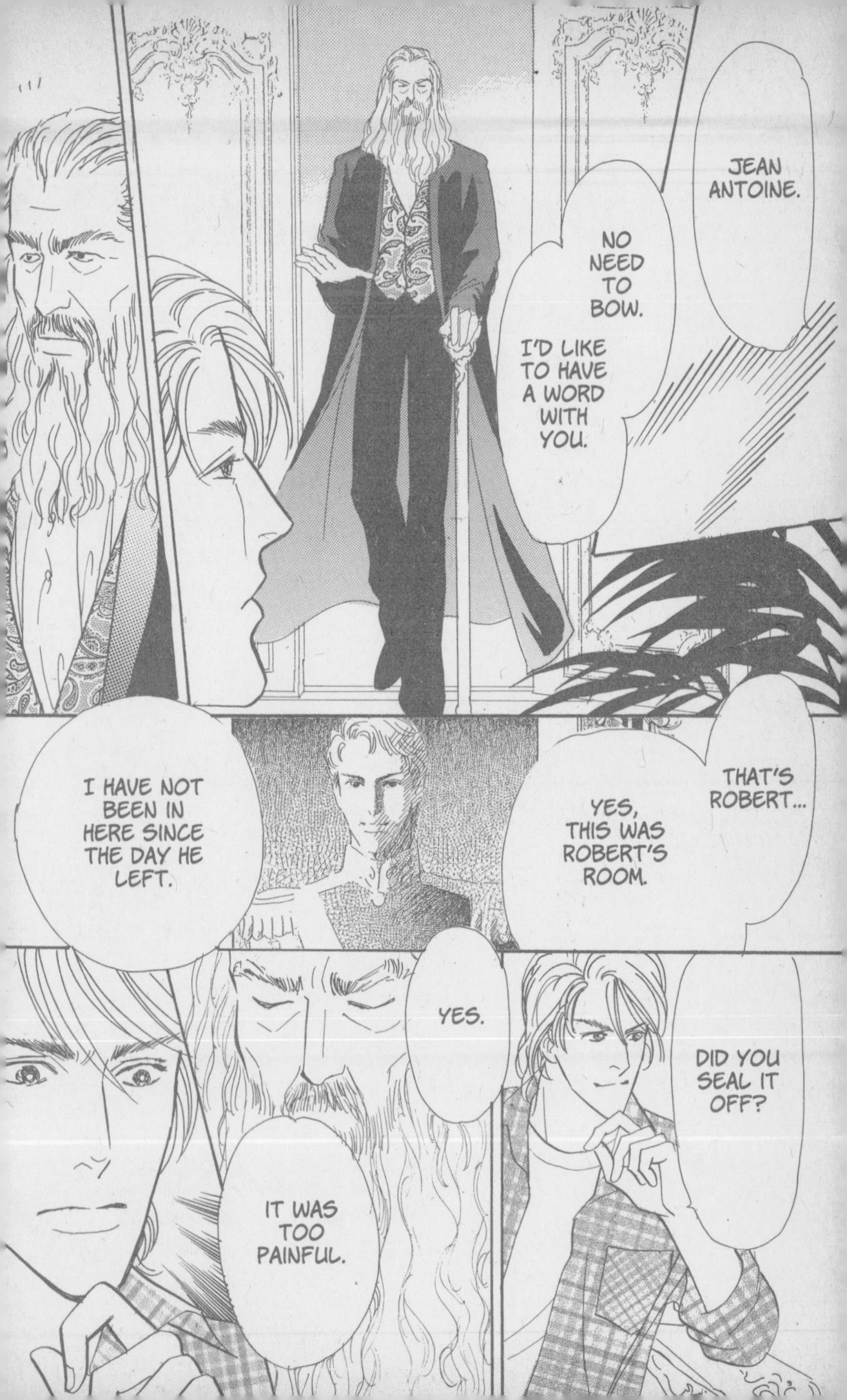
JEAN ANTOINE.
NO NEED TO BOW. I'D LIKE TO HAVE A WORD WITH YOU.
THAT'S ROBERT...
YES, THIS WAS ROBERT'S ROOM.
I HAVE NOT BEEN IN HERE SINCE THE DAY HE LEFT.
DID YOU SEAL IT OFF?
YES.
IT WAS TOO PAINFUL.

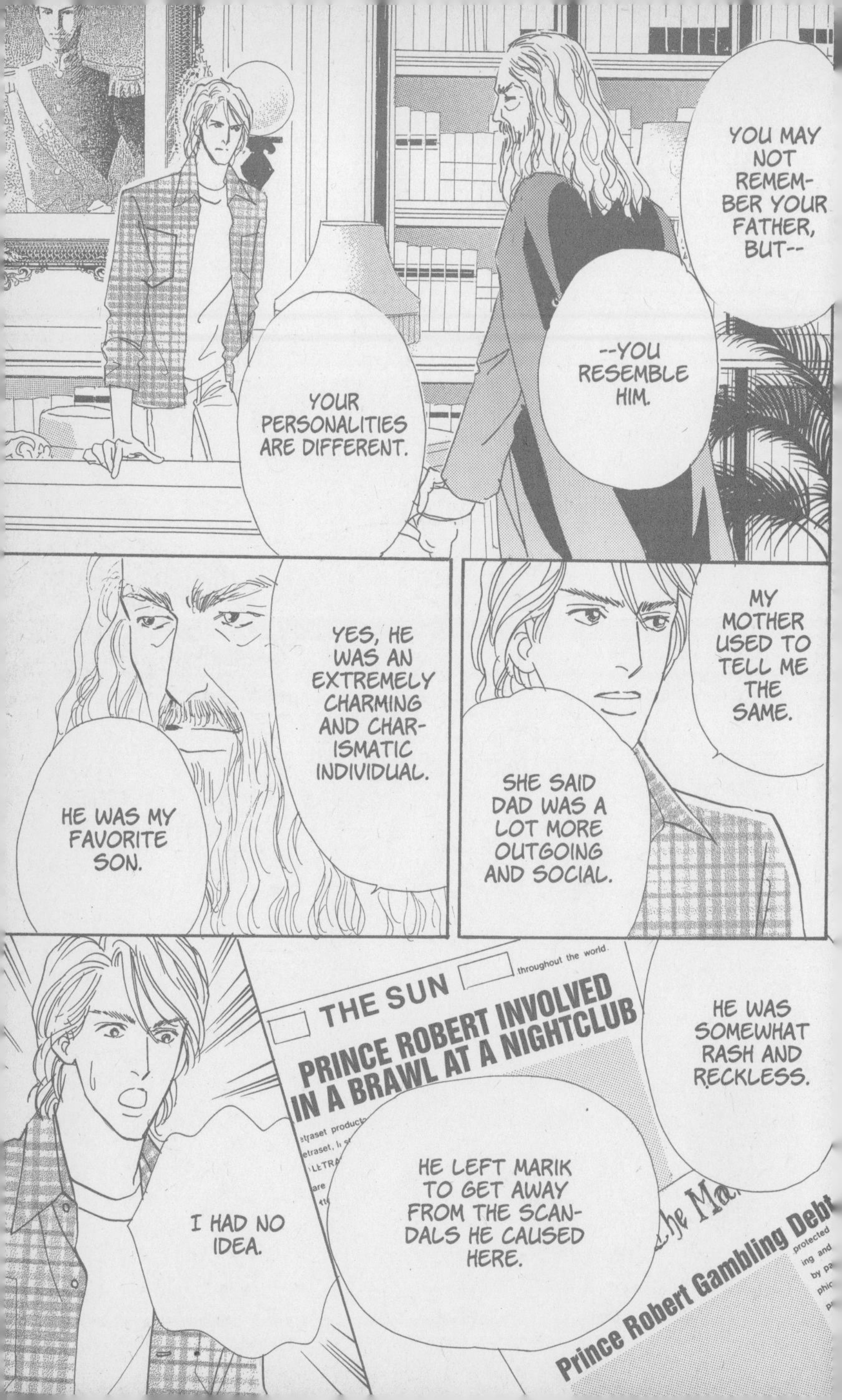
YOU MAY NOT REMEMBER YOUR FATHER, BUT--
--YOU RESEMBLE HIM.
YOUR PERSONALITIES ARE DIFFERENT.
MY MOTHER USED TO TELL ME THE SAME.
SHE SAID DAD WAS A LOT MORE OUTGOING AND SOCIAL.
YES, HE WAS AN EXTREMELY CHARMING AND CHARISMATIC INDIVIDUAL.
HE WAS MY FAVORITE SON.
HE WAS SOMEWHAT RASH AND RECKLESS.
THE SUN
throughout the world.
PRINCE ROBERT INVOLVED IN A BRAWL AT A NIGHTCLUB
Prince Robert Gambling Debt
HE LEFT MARIK TO GET AWAY FROM THE SCANDALS HE CAUSED HERE.
I HAD NO IDEA.

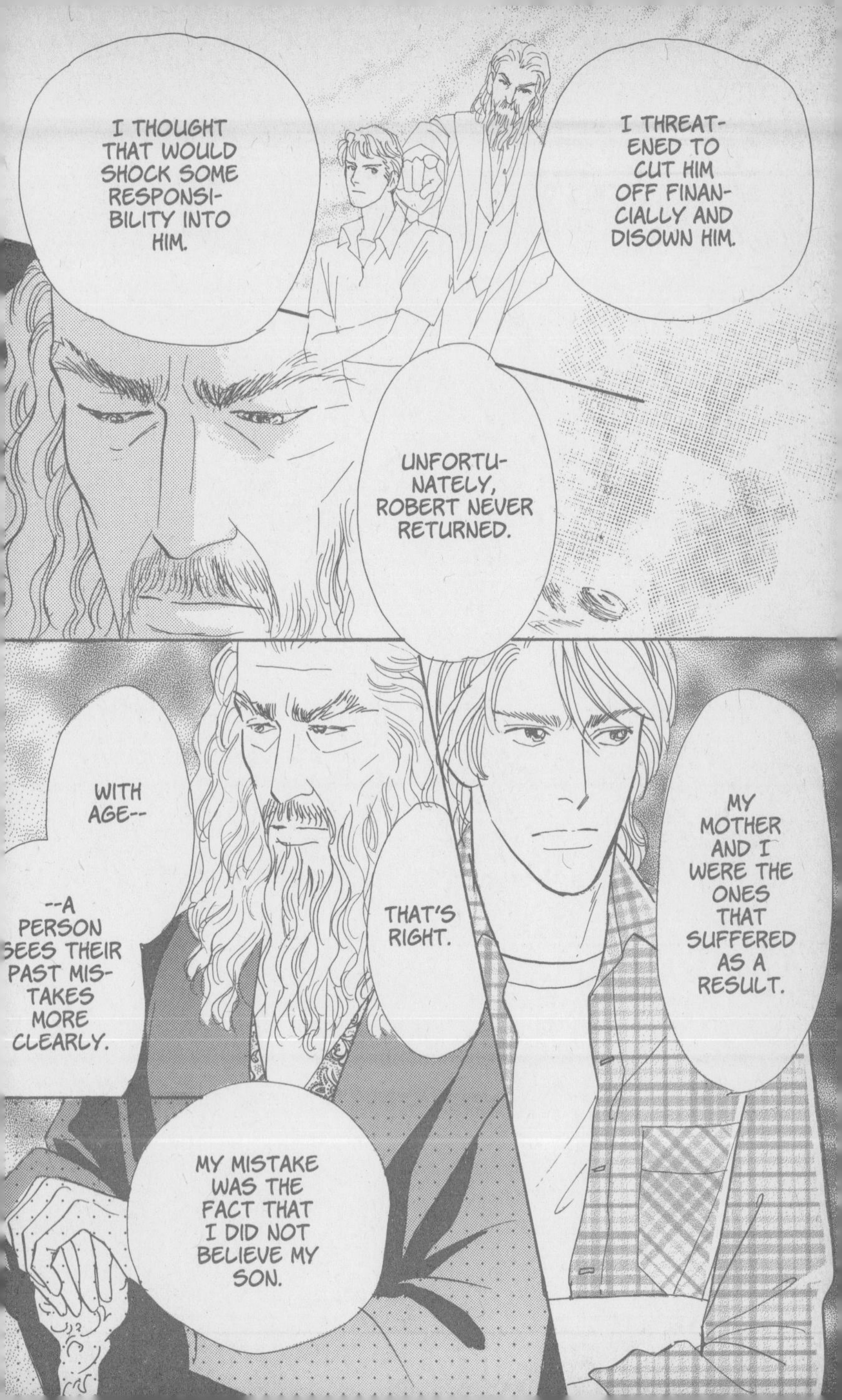
I THREAT-ENED TO CUT HIM OFF FINAN-CIALLY AND DISOWN HIM.
I THOUGHT THAT WOULD SHOCK SOME RESPONSI-BILITY INTO HIM.
UNFORTU-NATELY, ROBERT NEVER RETURNED.
MY MOTHER AND I WERE THE ONES THAT SUFFERED AS A RESULT.
THAT'S RIGHT.
WITH AGE--
--A PERSON SEES THEIR PAST MIS-TAKES MORE CLEARLY.
MY MISTAKE WAS THE FACT THAT I DID NOT BELIEVE MY SON.

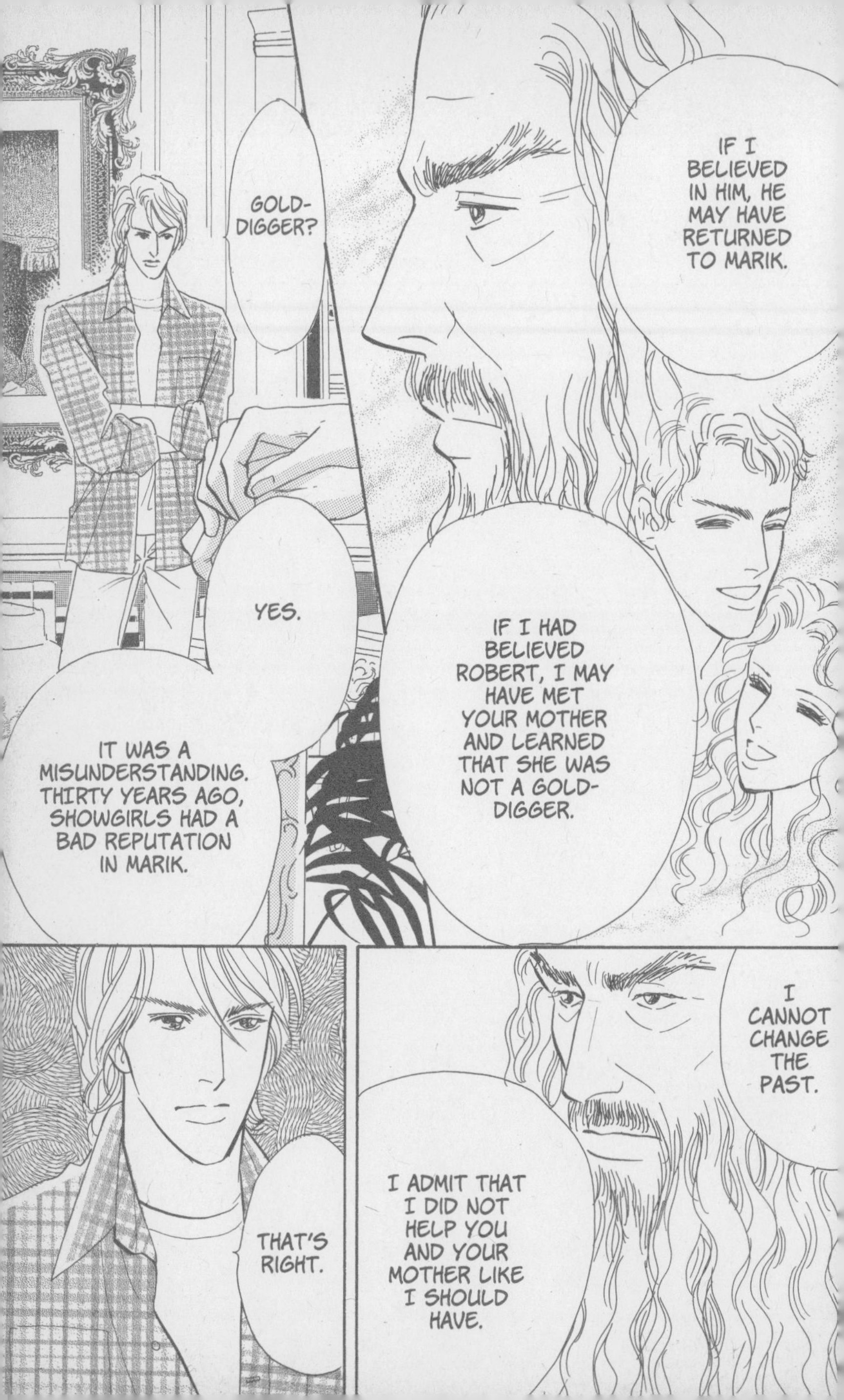
IF I BELIEVED IN HIM, HE MAY HAVE RETURNED TO MARIK.
IF I HAD BELIEVED ROBERT, I MAY HAVE MET YOUR MOTHER AND LEARNED THAT SHE WAS NOT A GOLD-DIGGER.
GOLD-DIGGER?
YES.
IT WAS A MISUNDERSTANDING. THIRTY YEARS AGO, SHOWGIRLS HAD A BAD REPUTATION IN MARIK.
I CANNOT CHANGE THE PAST.
I ADMIT THAT I DID NOT HELP YOU AND YOUR MOTHER LIKE I SHOULD HAVE.
THAT'S RIGHT.

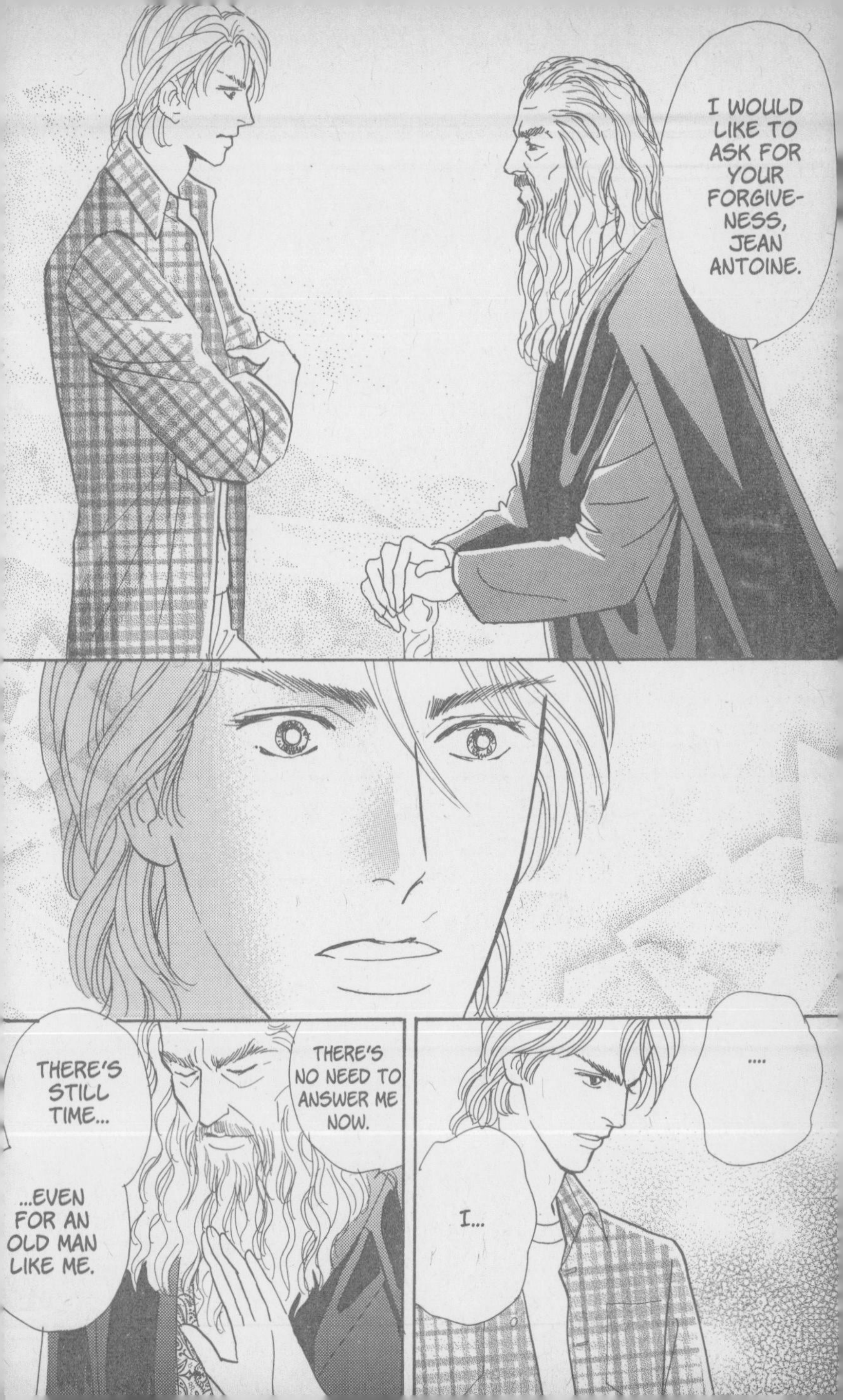
I WOULD LIKE TO ASK FOR YOUR FORGIVENESS, JEAN ANTOINE.
....
I...
THERE'S NO NEED TO ANSWER ME NOW.
THERE'S STILL TIME...
...EVEN FOR AN OLD MAN LIKE ME.

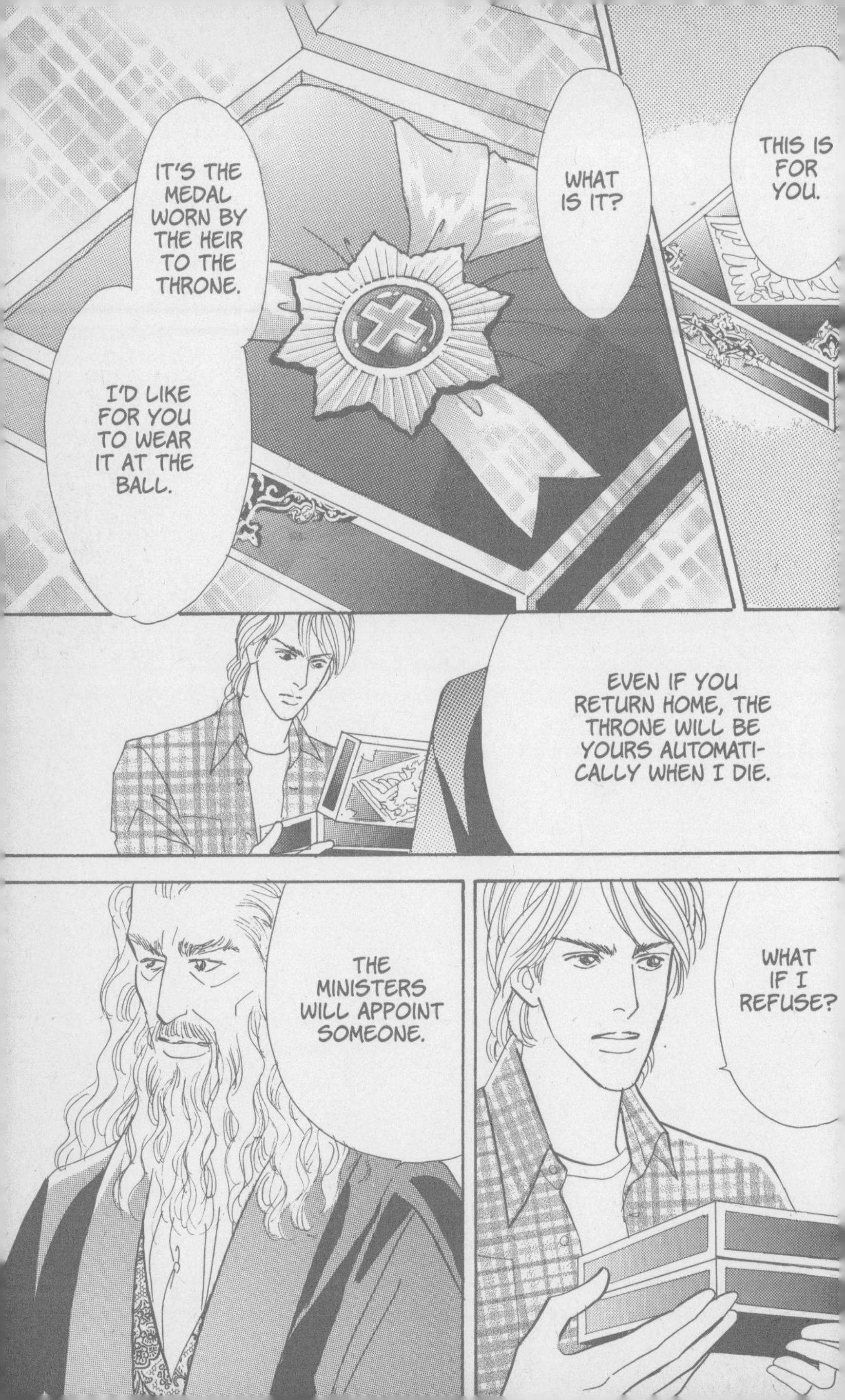
THIS IS FOR YOU.
WHAT IS IT?
IT'S THE MEDAL WORN BY THE HEIR TO THE THRONE.
I'D LIKE FOR YOU TO WEAR IT AT THE BALL.
EVEN IF YOU RETURN HOME, THE THRONE WILL BE YOURS AUTOMATI-CALLY WHEN I DIE.
WHAT IF I REFUSE?
THE MINISTERS WILL APPOINT SOMEONE.

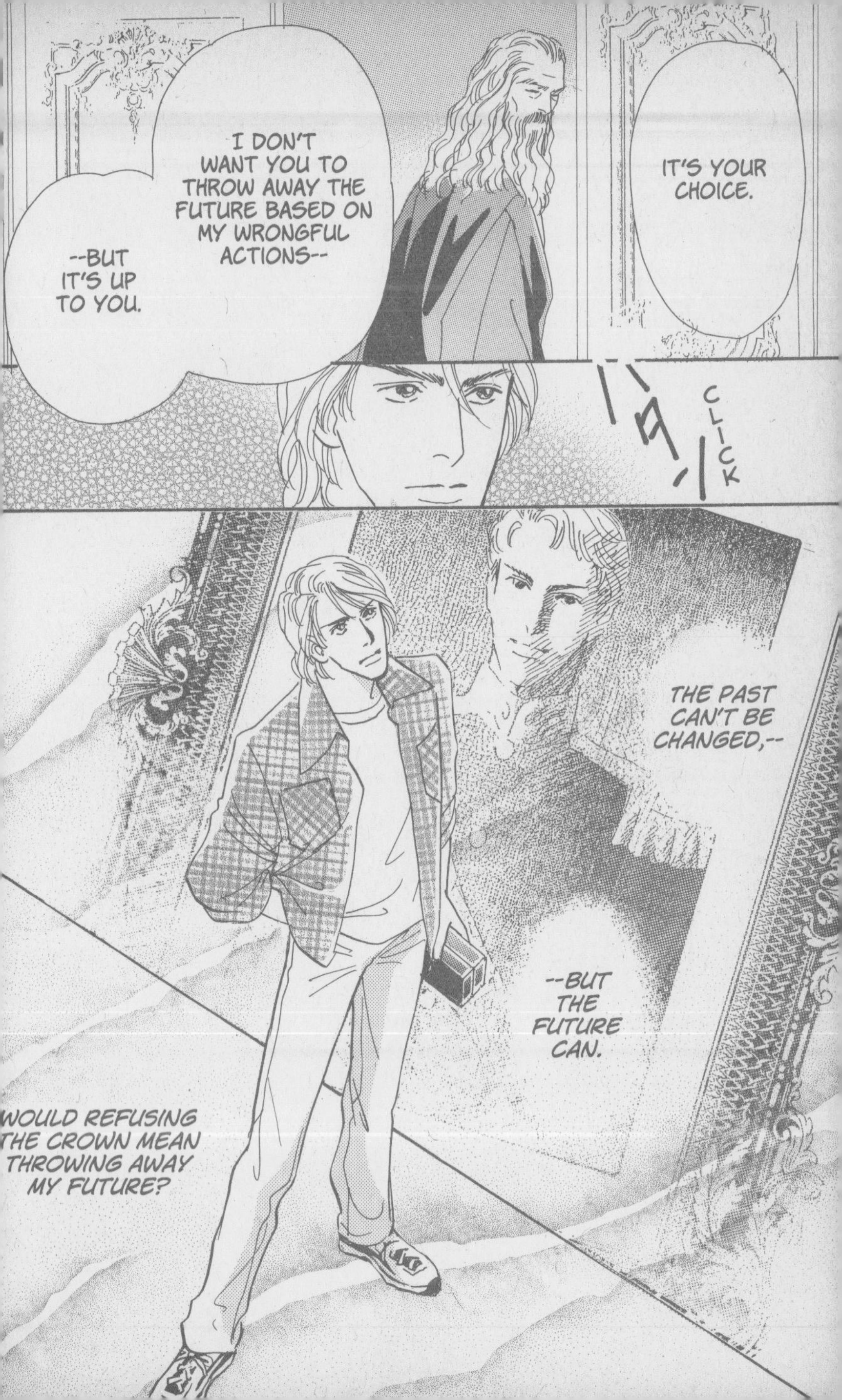
IT'S YOUR CHOICE.
I DON'T WANT YOU TO THROW AWAY THE FUTURE BASED ON MY WRONGFUL ACTIONS--
--BUT IT'S UP TO YOU.
CLICK
THE PAST CAN'T BE CHANGED,--
--BUT THE FUTURE CAN.
WOULD REFUSING THE CROWN MEAN THROWING AWAY MY FUTURE?

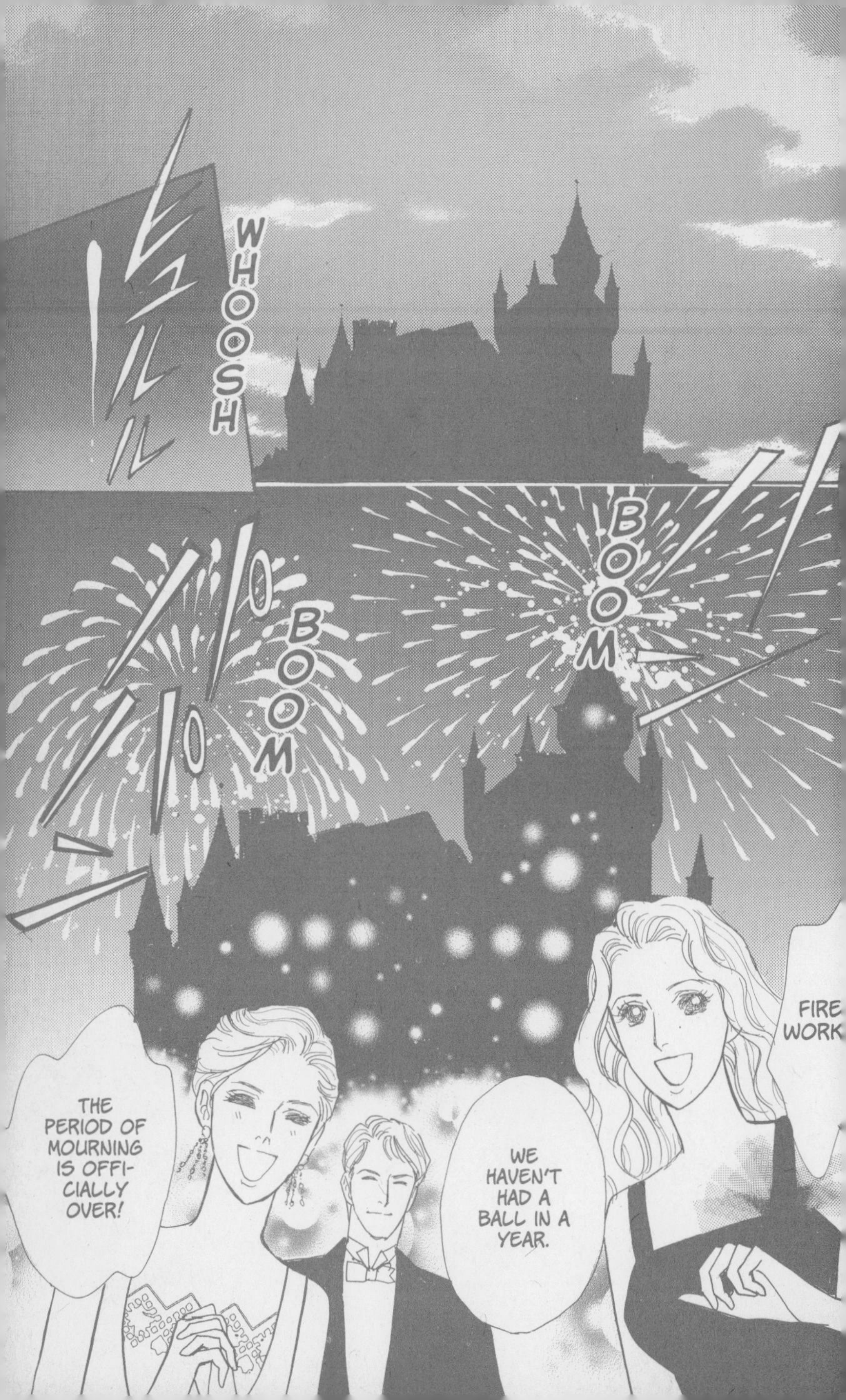
WHOOSH
BOOM
BOOM
FIRE WORK
WE HAVEN'T HAD A BALL IN A YEAR.
THE PERIOD OF MOURNING IS OFFI-CIALLY OVER!

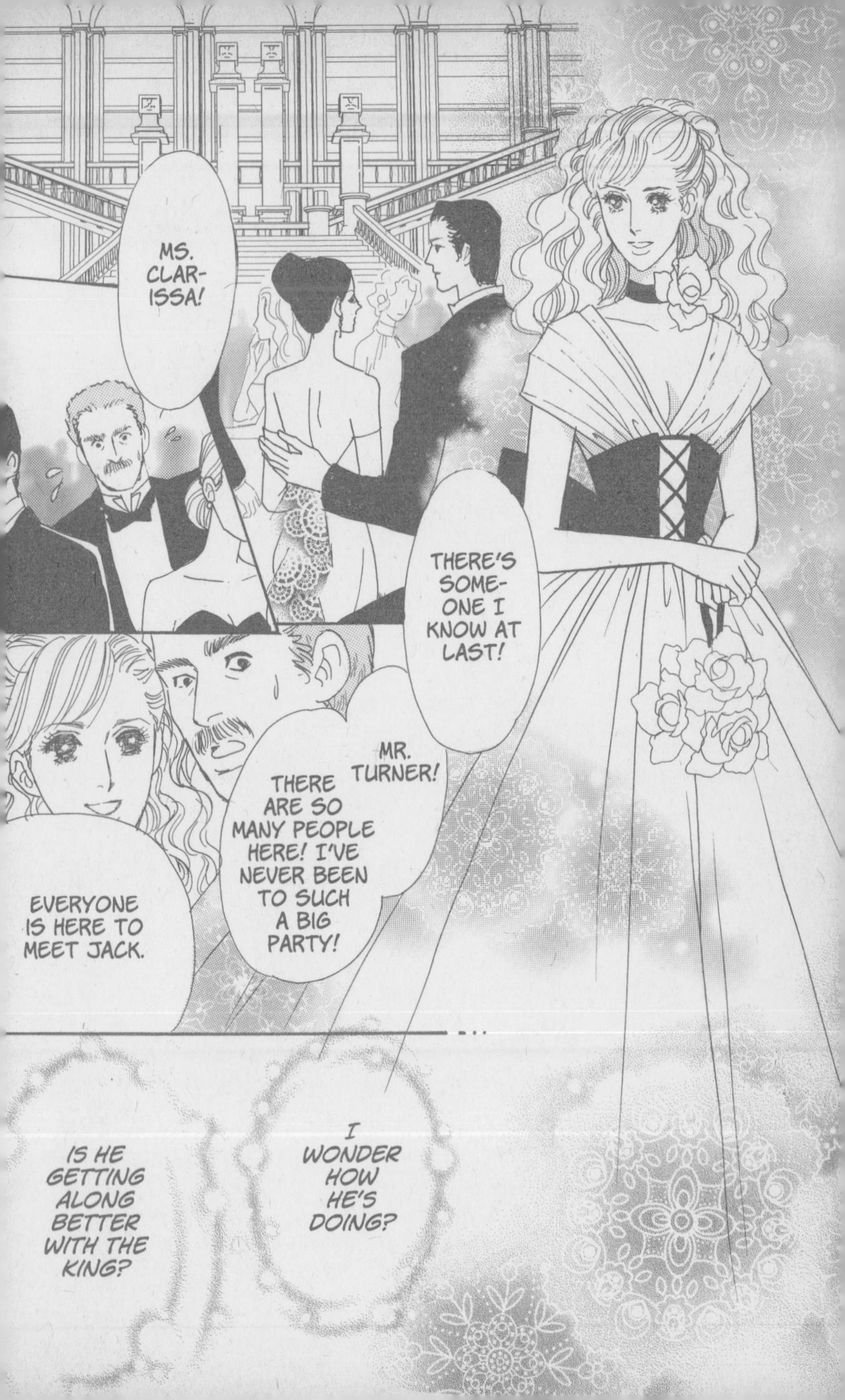
MS. CLARISSA!
THERE'S SOME-ONE I KNOW AT LAST!
MR. TURNER!
THERE ARE SO MANY PEOPLE HERE! I'VE NEVER BEEN TO SUCH A BIG PARTY!
EVERYONE IS HERE TO MEET JACK.
I WONDER HOW HE'S DOING?
IS HE GETTING ALONG BETTER WITH THE KING?

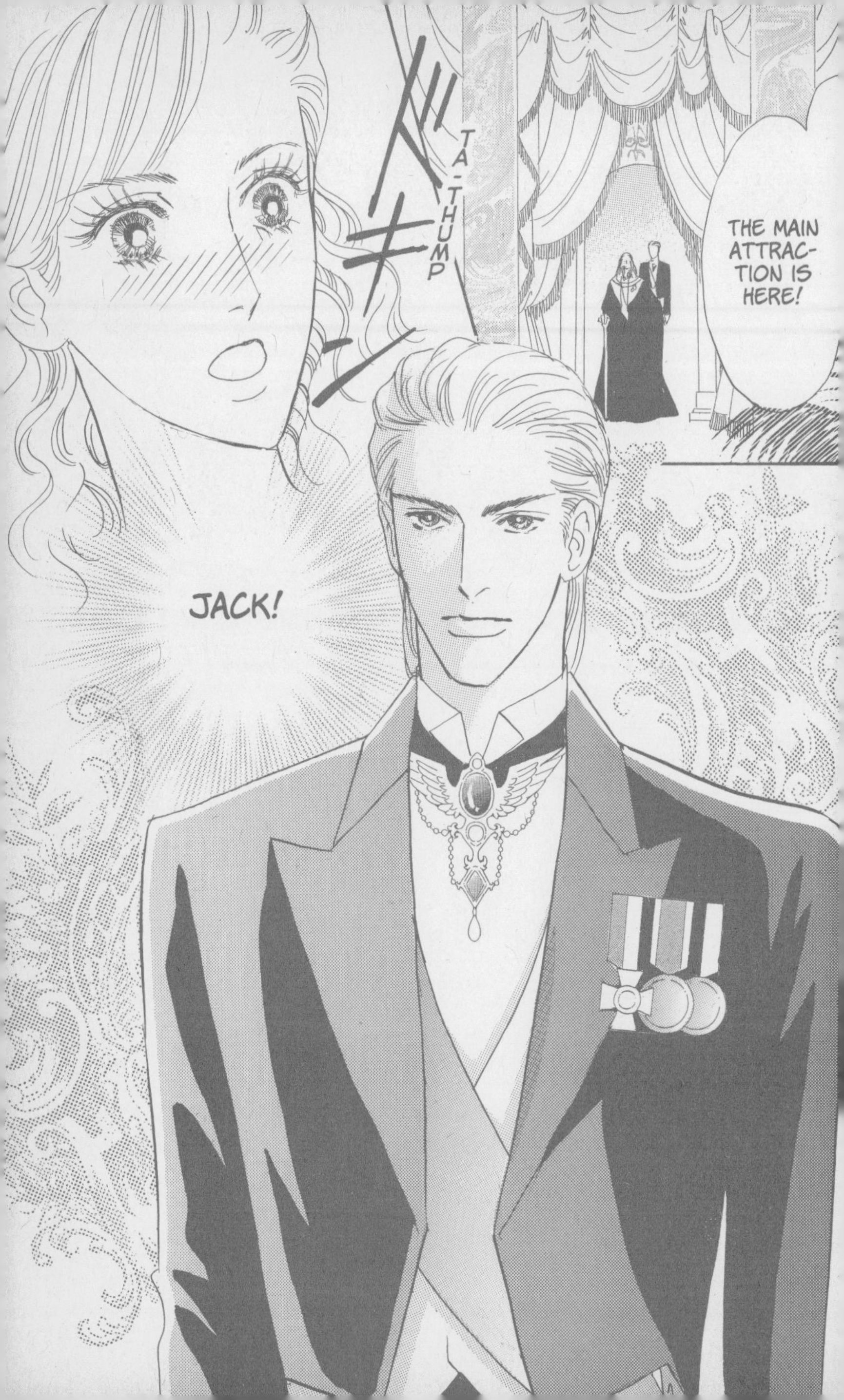
THE MAIN ATTRACTION IS HERE!
TA-THUMP
JACK!

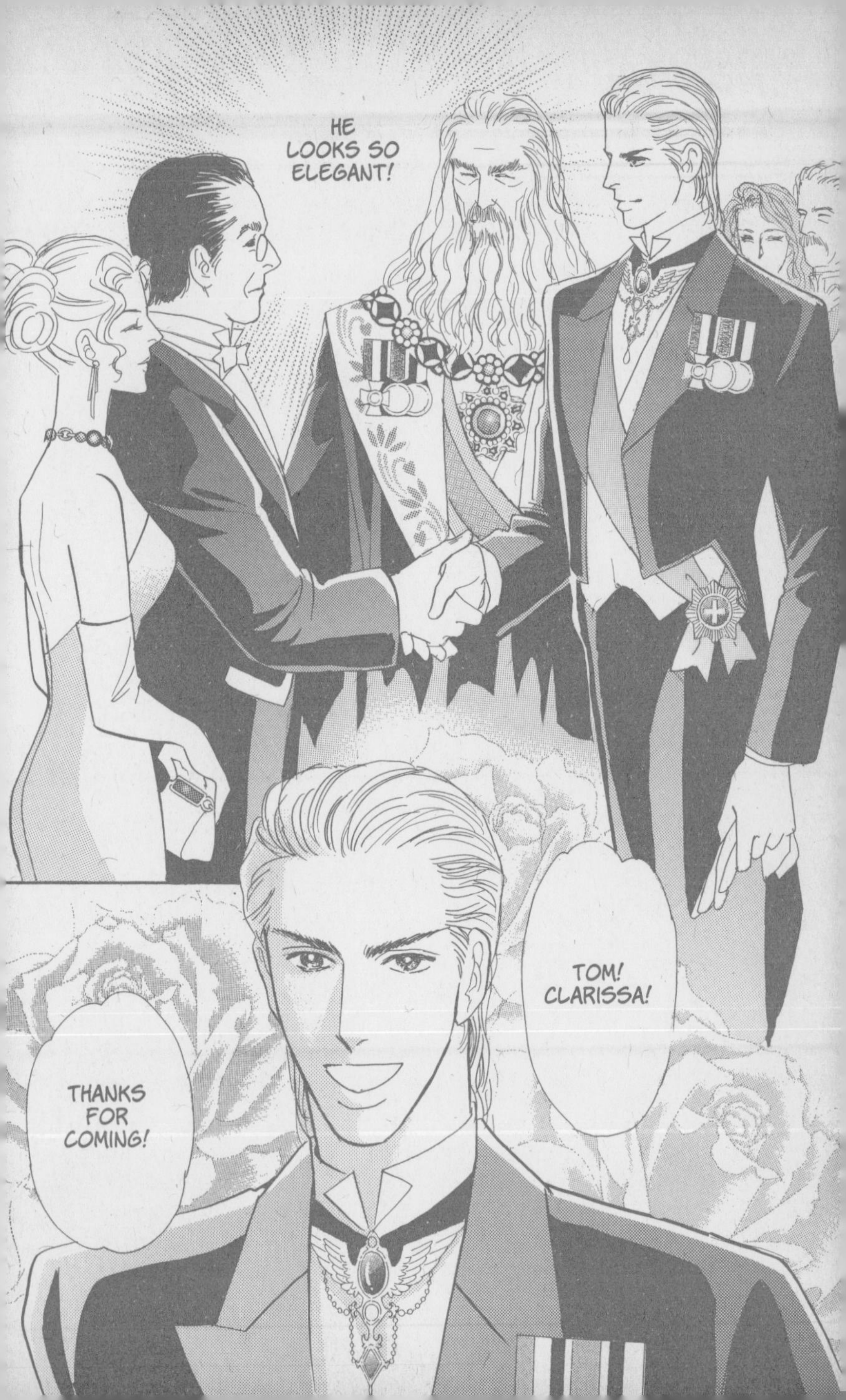
HE LOOKS SO ELEGANT!
TOM! CLARISSA!
THANKS FOR COMING!

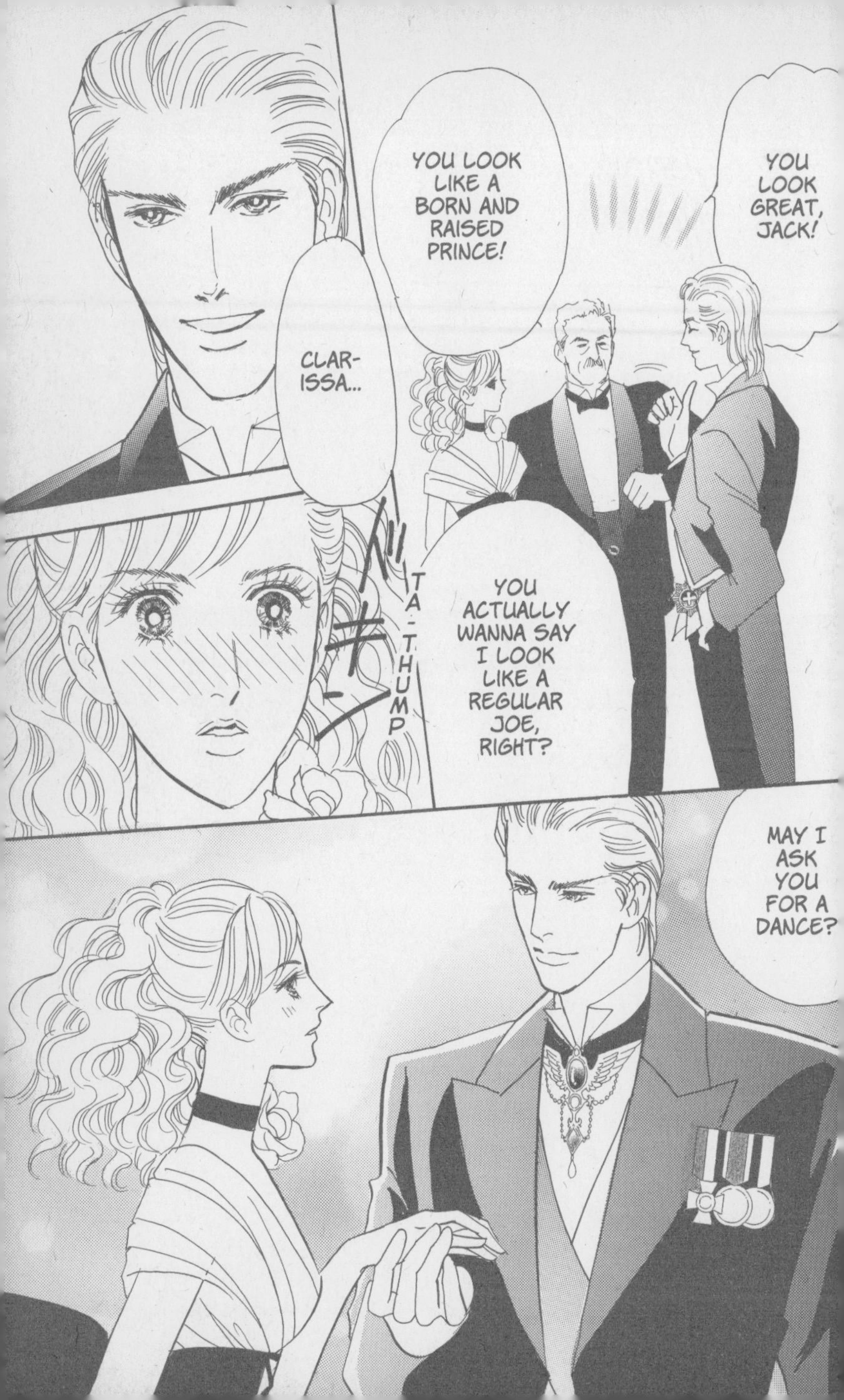
YOU LOOK GREAT, JACK!
YOU LOOK LIKE A BORN AND RAISED PRINCE!
YOU ACTUALLY WANNA SAY I LOOK LIKE A REGULAR JOE, RIGHT?
CLAR-ISSA...
TA-THUMP
MAY I ASK YOU FOR A DANCE?

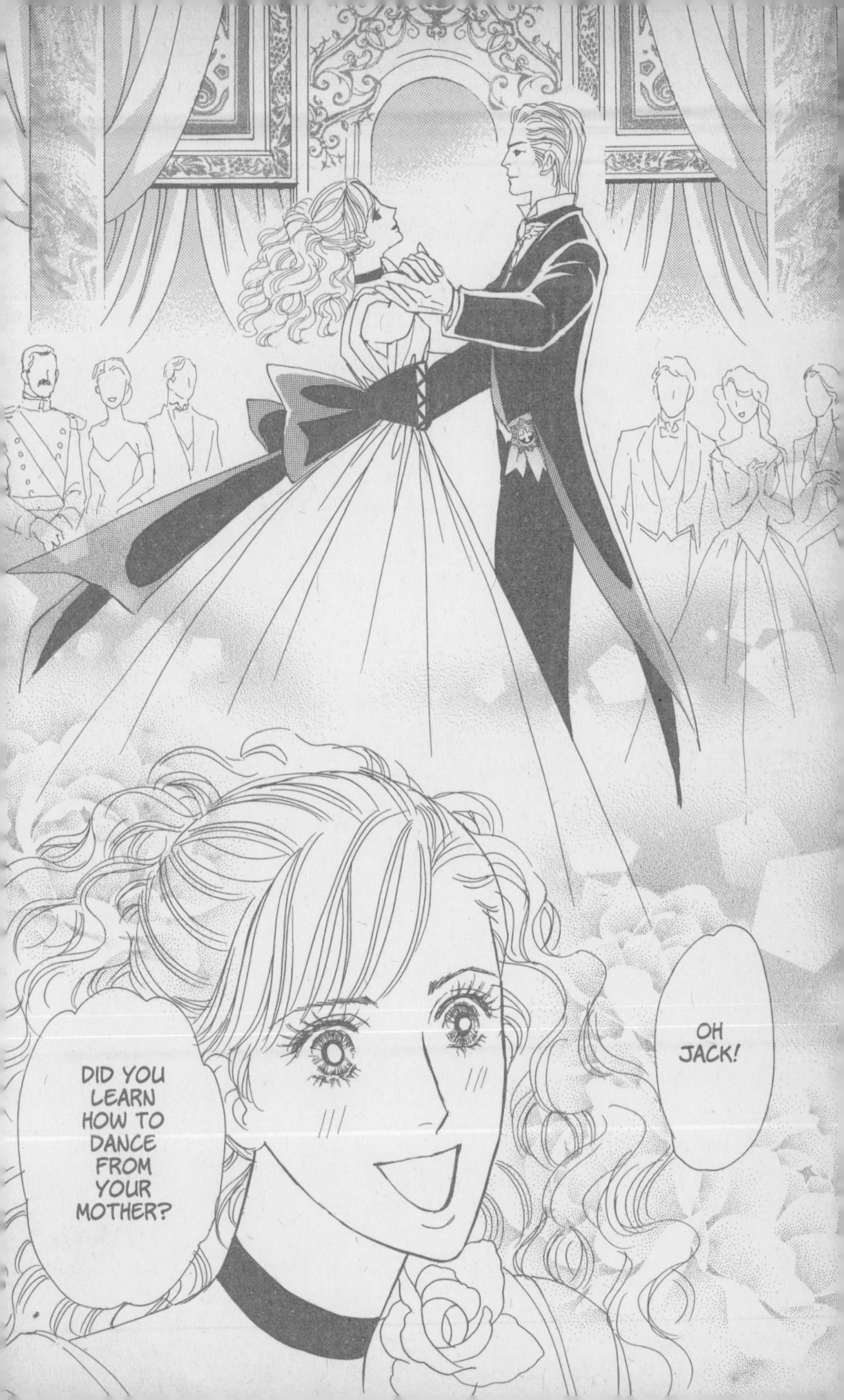
OH JACK!
DID YOU LEARN HOW TO DANCE FROM YOUR MOTHER?

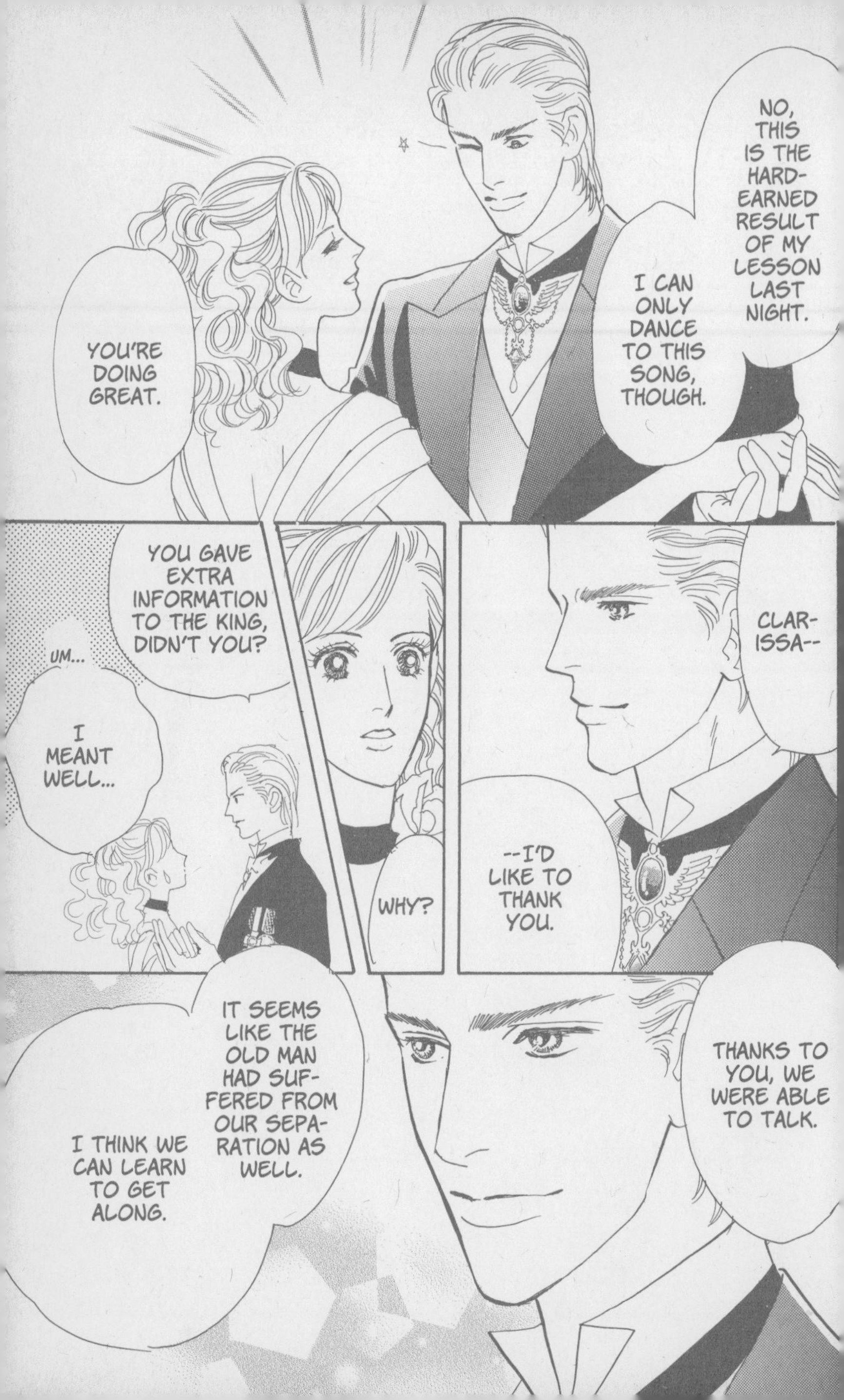
NO, THIS IS THE HARD-EARNED RESULT OF MY LESSON LAST NIGHT.
I CAN ONLY DANCE TO THIS SONG, THOUGH.
YOU'RE DOING GREAT.
CLAR-ISSA--
--I'D LIKE TO THANK YOU.
WHY?
YOU GAVE EXTRA INFORMATION TO THE KING, DIDN'T YOU?
UM...
I MEANT WELL...
THANKS TO YOU, WE WERE ABLE TO TALK.
IT SEEMS LIKE THE OLD MAN HAD SUF-FERED FROM OUR SEPA-RATION AS WELL.
I THINK WE CAN LEARN TO GET ALONG.

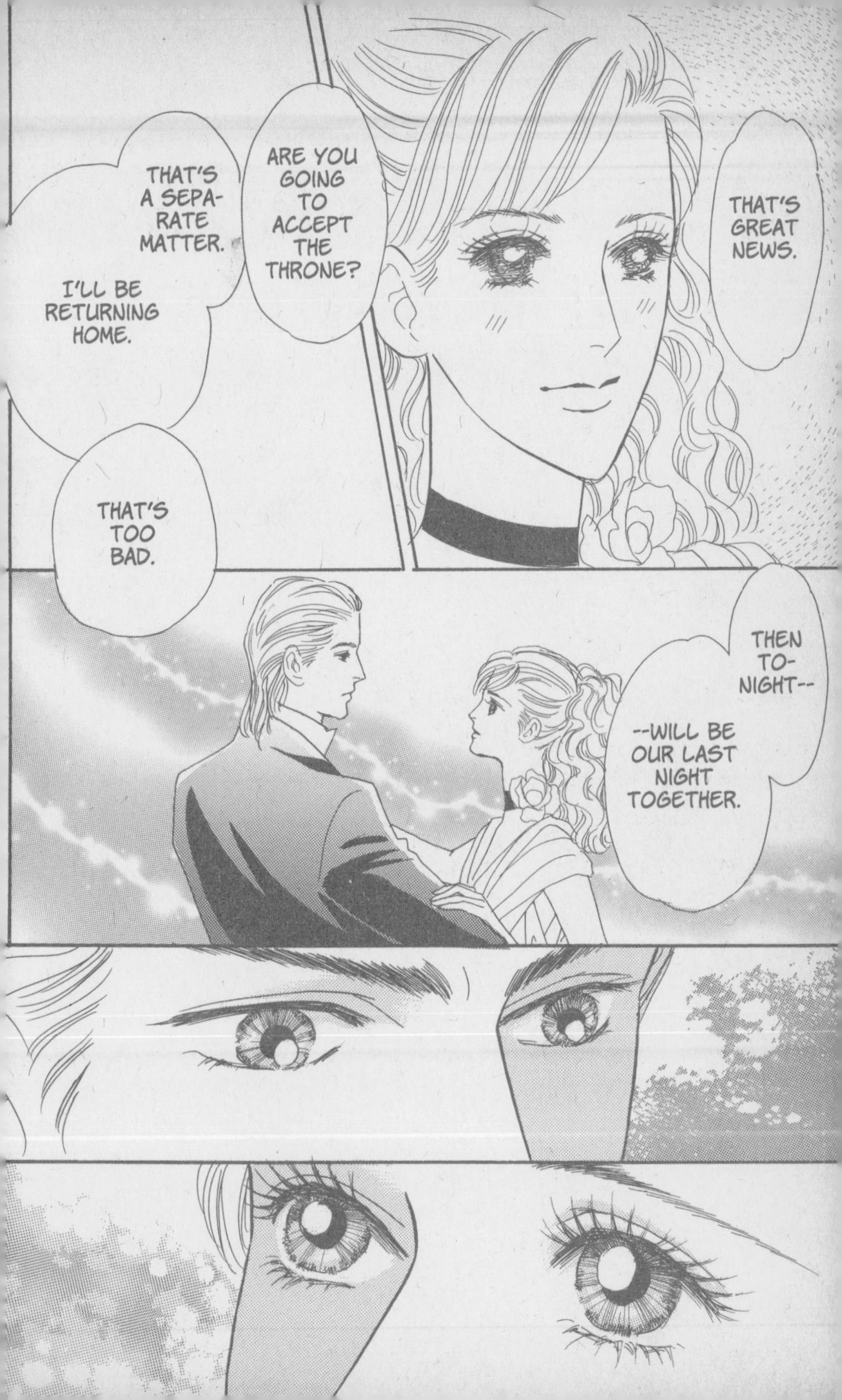

THAT'S GREAT NEWS.
ARE YOU GOING TO ACCEPT THE THRONE?
THAT'S A SEPA-RATE MATTER.
I'LL BE RETURNING HOME.
THAT'S TOO BAD.
THEN TO-NIGHT--
--WILL BE OUR LAST NIGHT TOGETHER.

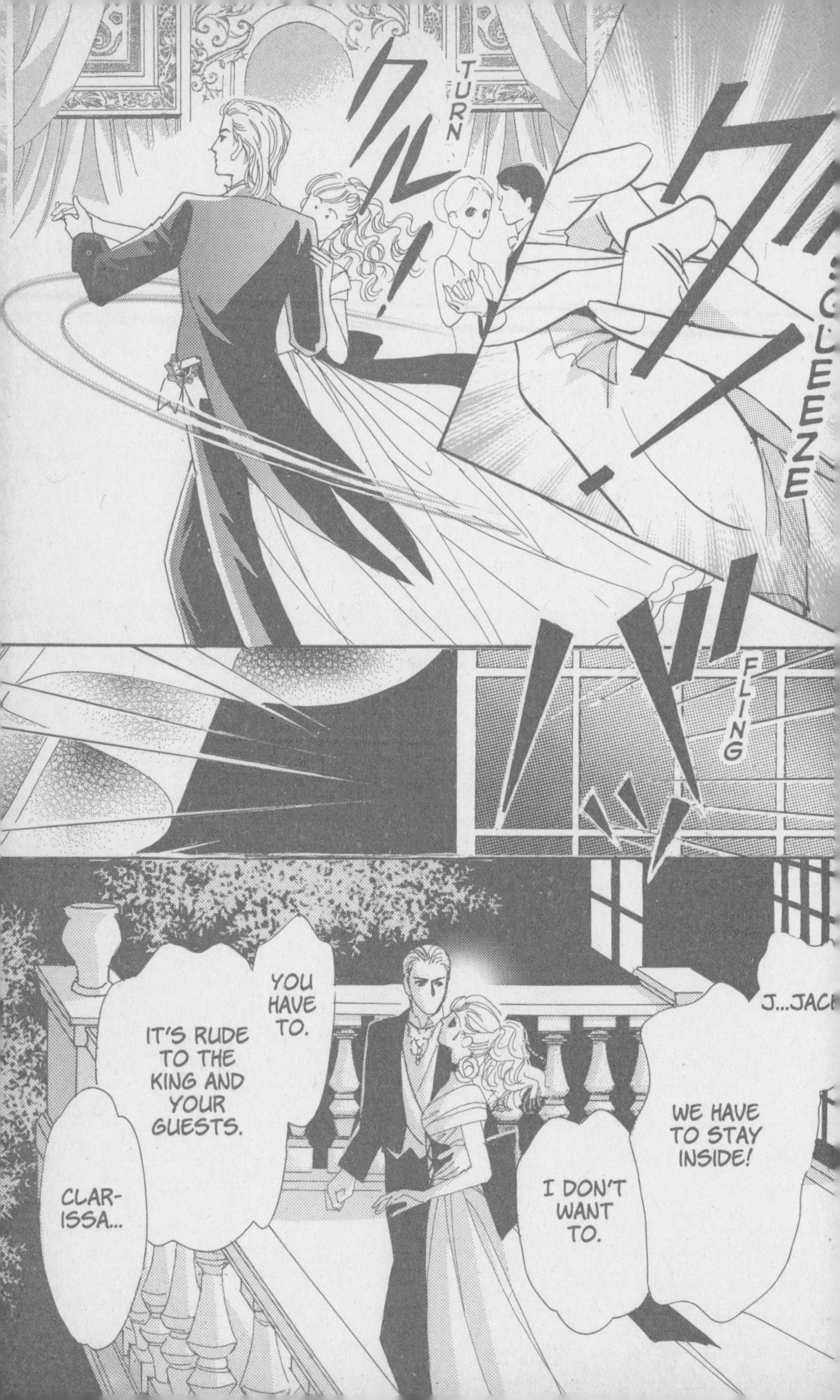
SQUEEZE
TURN
FLING
J...JAC
WE HAVE TO STAY INSIDE!
I DON'T WANT TO.
YOU HAVE TO.
IT'S RUDE TO THE KING AND YOUR GUESTS.
CLAR-ISSA...

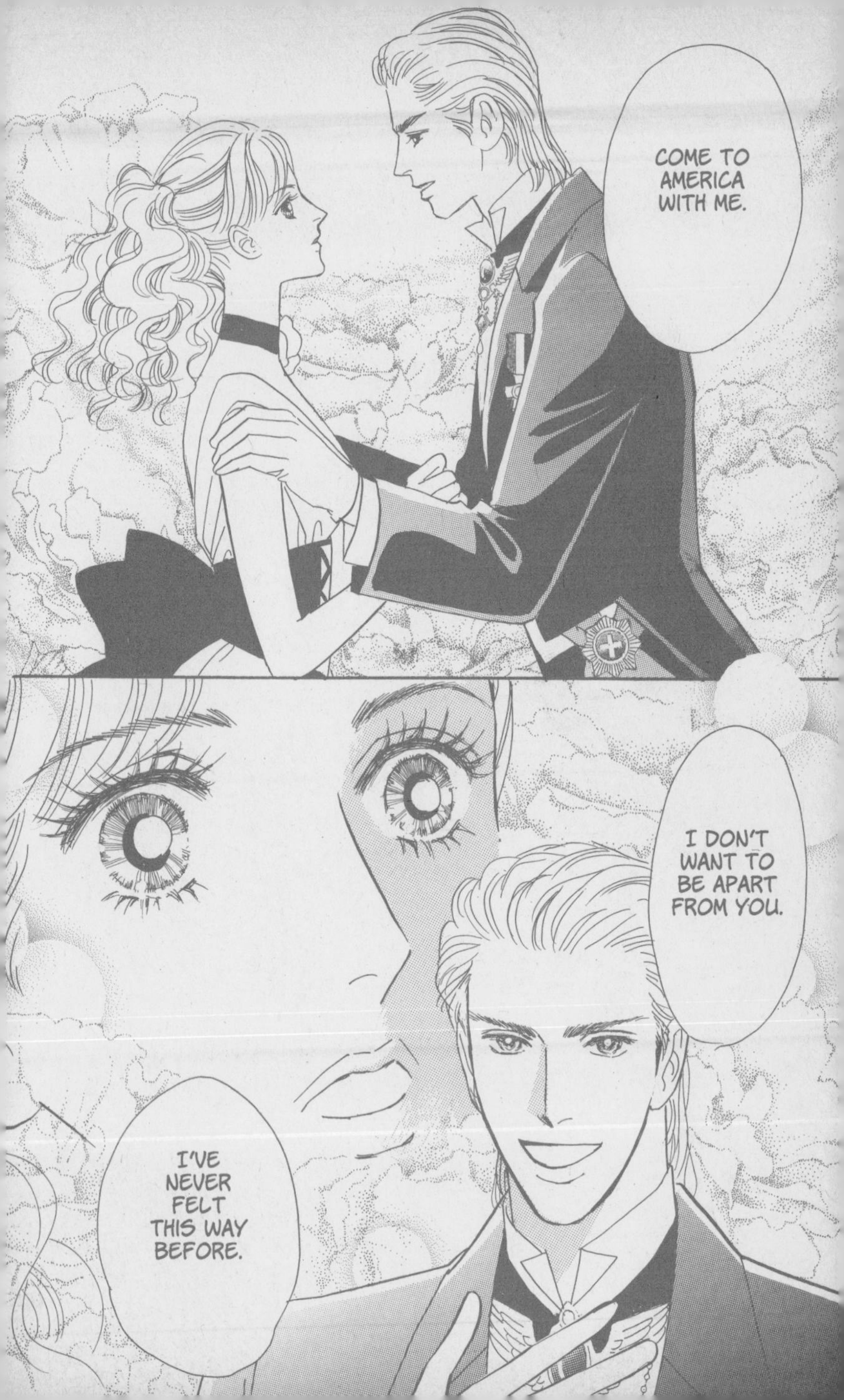
COME TO AMERICA WITH ME.
I DON'T WANT TO BE APART FROM YOU.
I'VE NEVER FELT THIS WAY BEFORE.

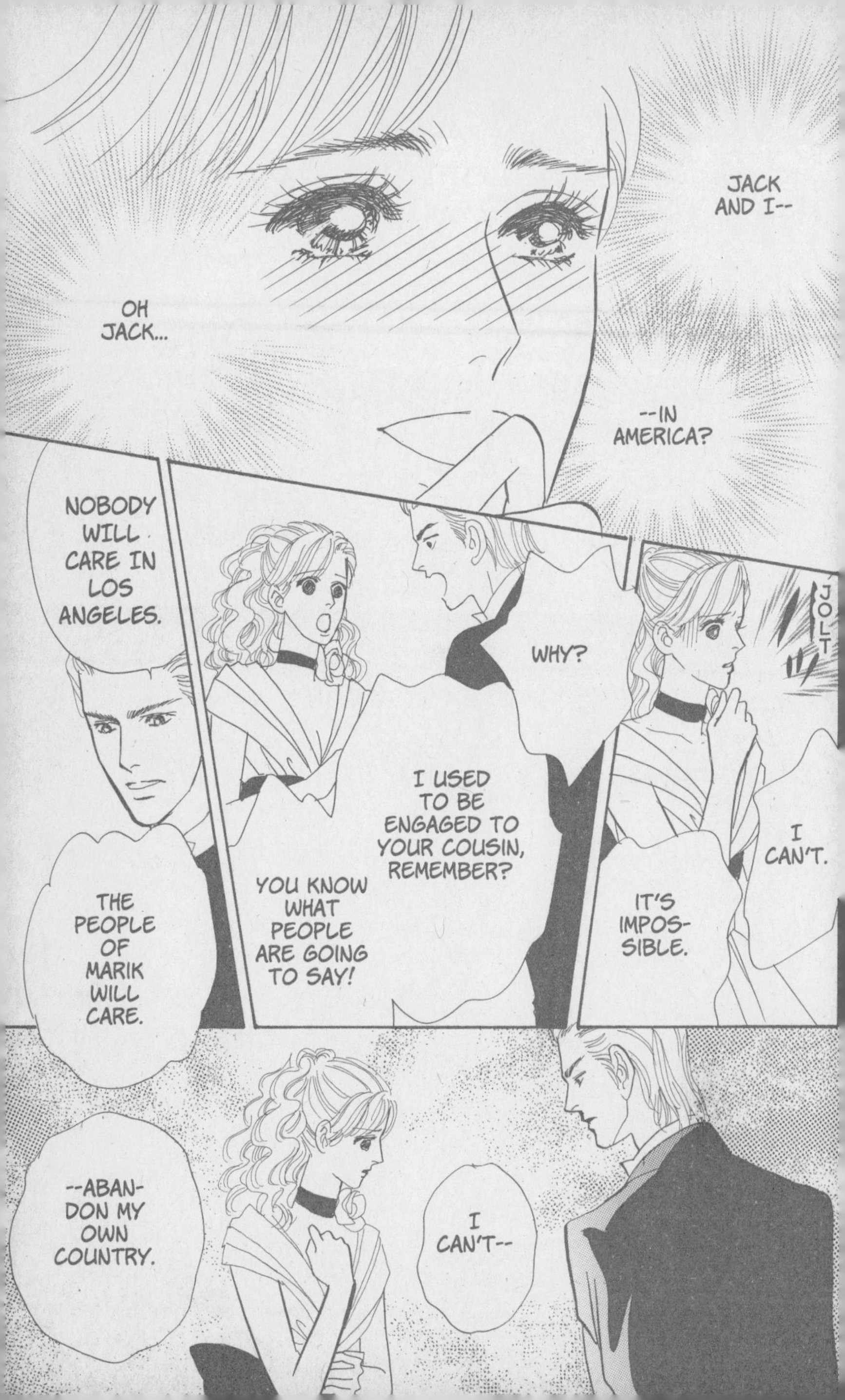
JACK AND I--
--IN AMERICA?
OH JACK...
JOLT
I CAN'T.
IT'S IMPOS-SIBLE.
WHY?
I USED TO BE ENGAGED TO YOUR COUSIN, REMEMBER?
YOU KNOW WHAT PEOPLE ARE GOING TO SAY!
NOBODY WILL CARE IN LOS ANGELES.
THE PEOPLE OF MARIK WILL CARE.
I CAN'T--
--ABAN-DON MY OWN COUNTRY.

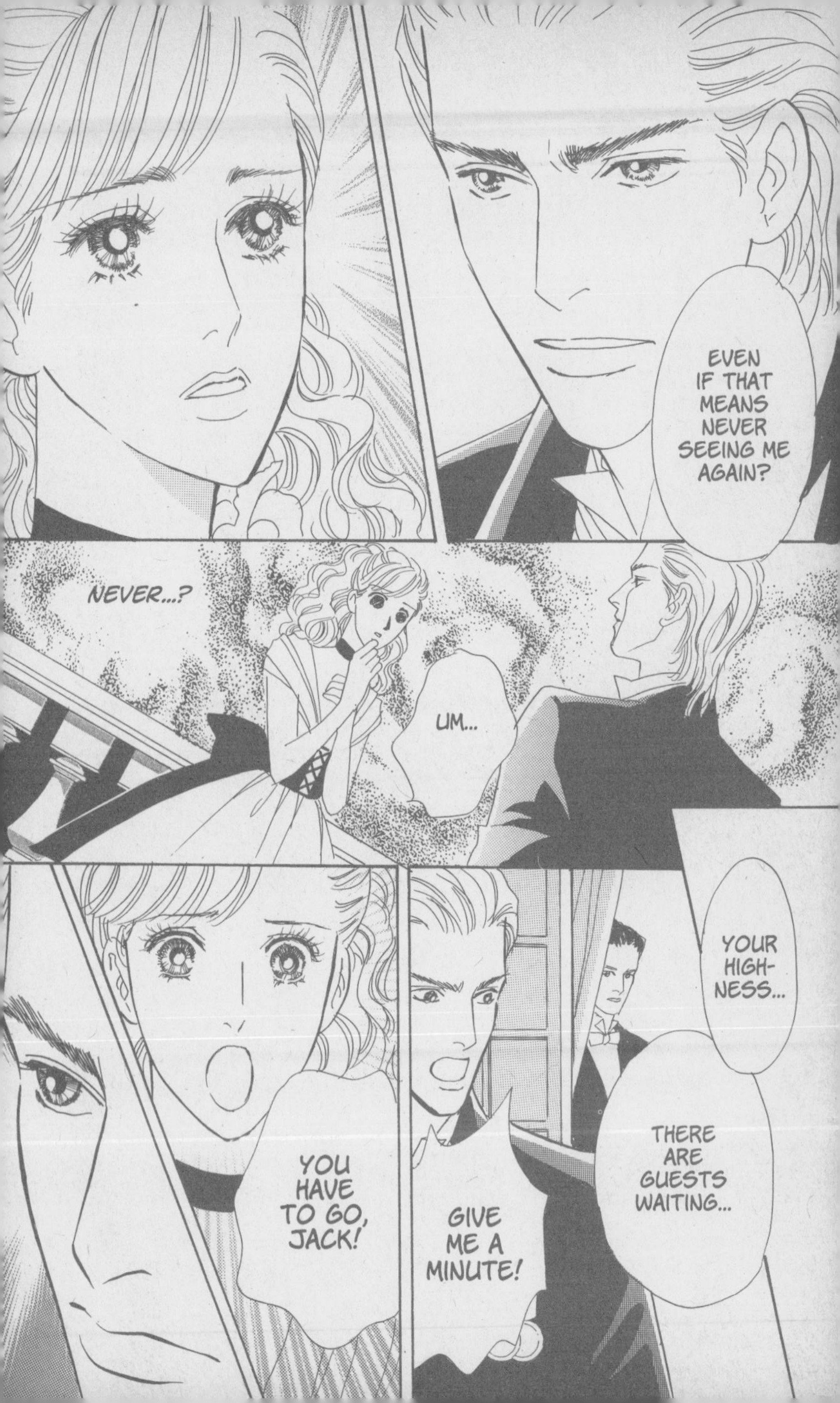
EVEN IF THAT MEANS NEVER SEEING ME AGAIN?
NEVER...?
UM...
YOUR HIGHNESS...
THERE ARE GUESTS WAITING...
GIVE ME A MINUTE!
YOU HAVE TO GO, JACK!

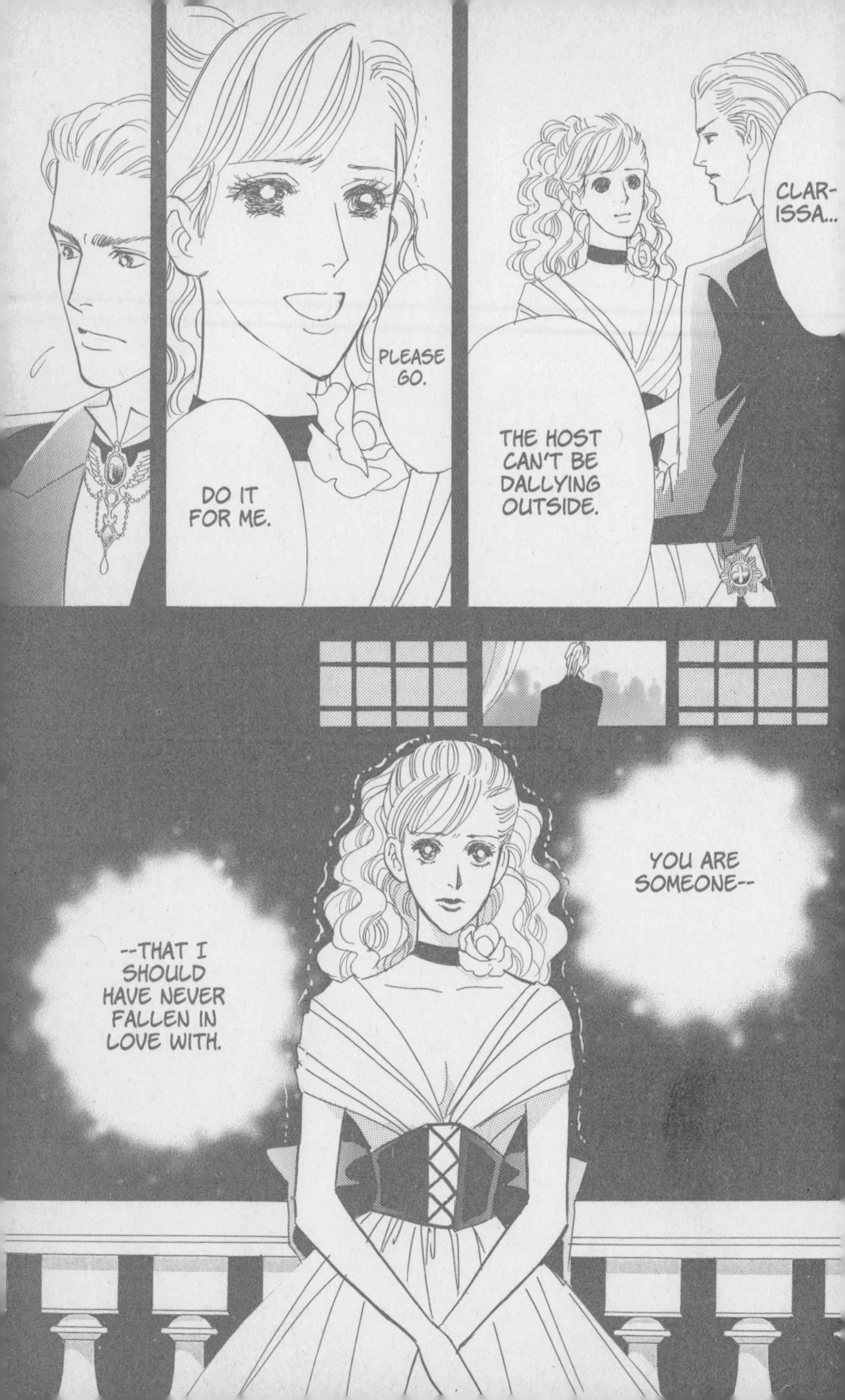
CLAR-ISSA...
THE HOST CAN'T BE DALLYING OUTSIDE.
PLEASE GO.
DO IT FOR ME.
YOU ARE SOMEONE--
--THAT I SHOULD HAVE NEVER FALLEN IN LOVE WITH.

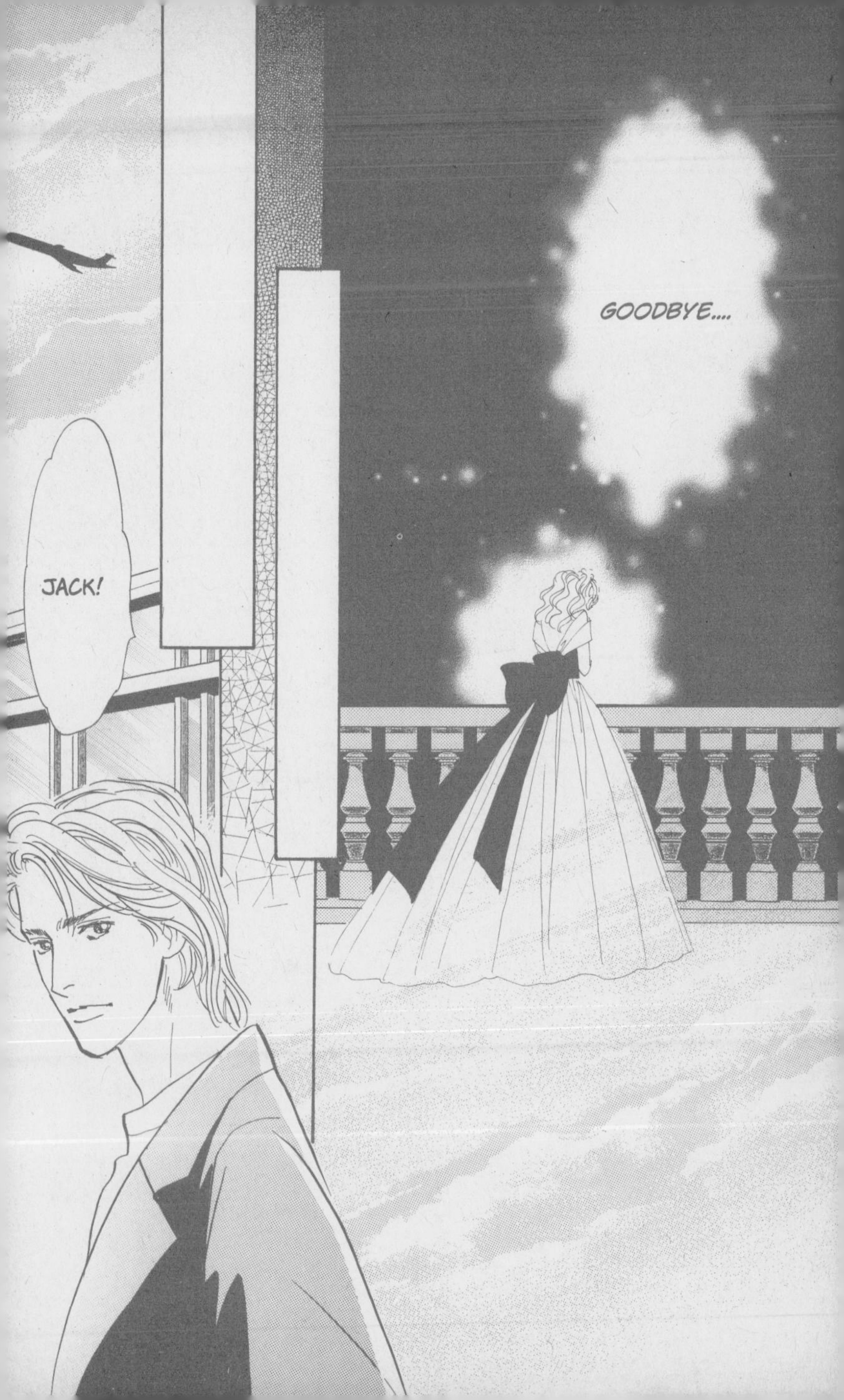
GOODBYE....
JACK!

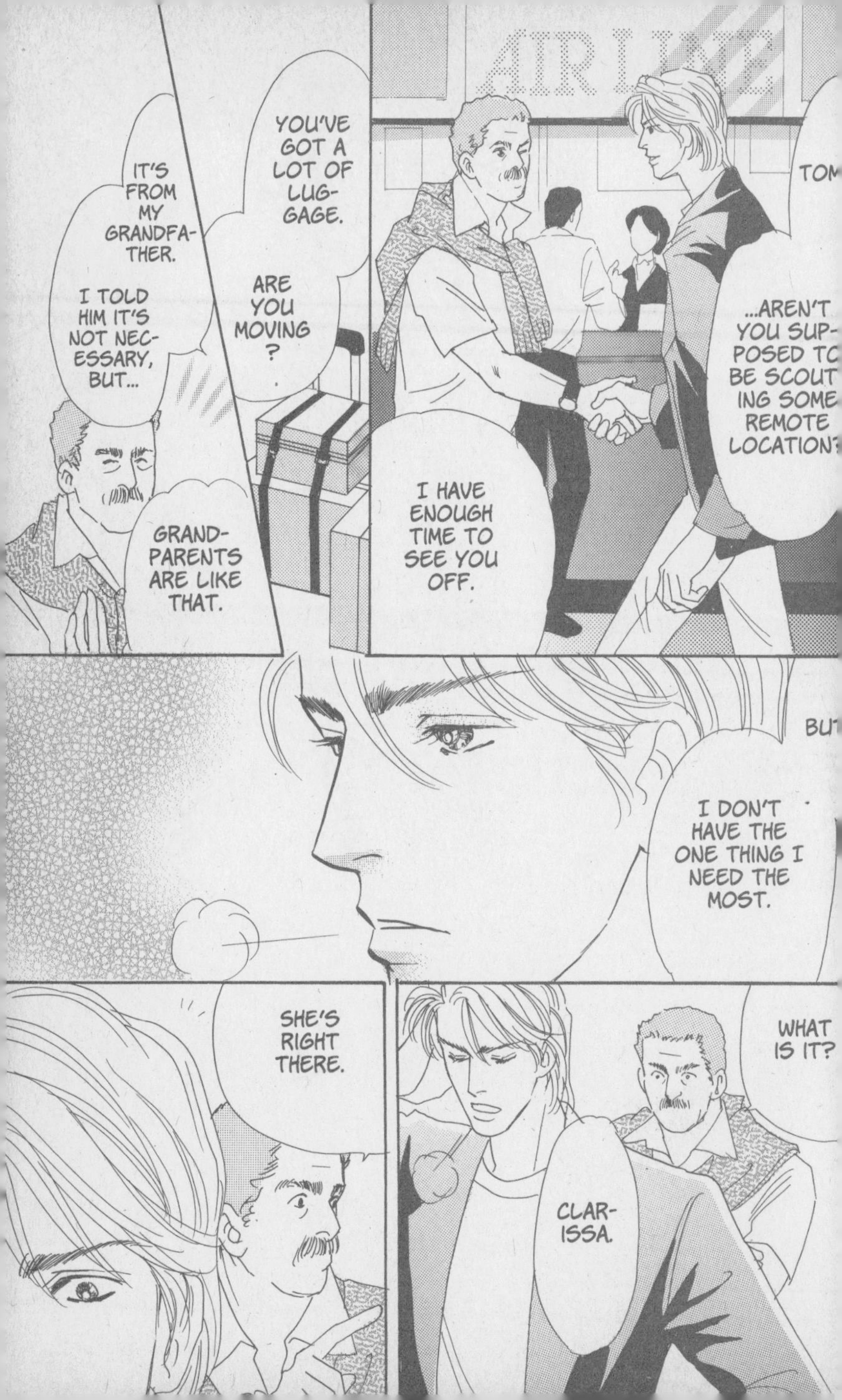
TOM
...AREN'T YOU SUPPOSED TO BE SCOUTING SOME REMOTE LOCATION?
I HAVE ENOUGH TIME TO SEE YOU OFF.
YOU'VE GOT A LOT OF LUGGAGE.
ARE YOU MOVING?
IT'S FROM MY GRANDFATHER.
I TOLD HIM IT'S NOT NECESSARY, BUT...
GRANDPARENTS ARE LIKE THAT.
BUT
I DON'T HAVE THE ONE THING I NEED THE MOST.
WHAT IS IT?
CLARISSA.
SHE'S RIGHT THERE.

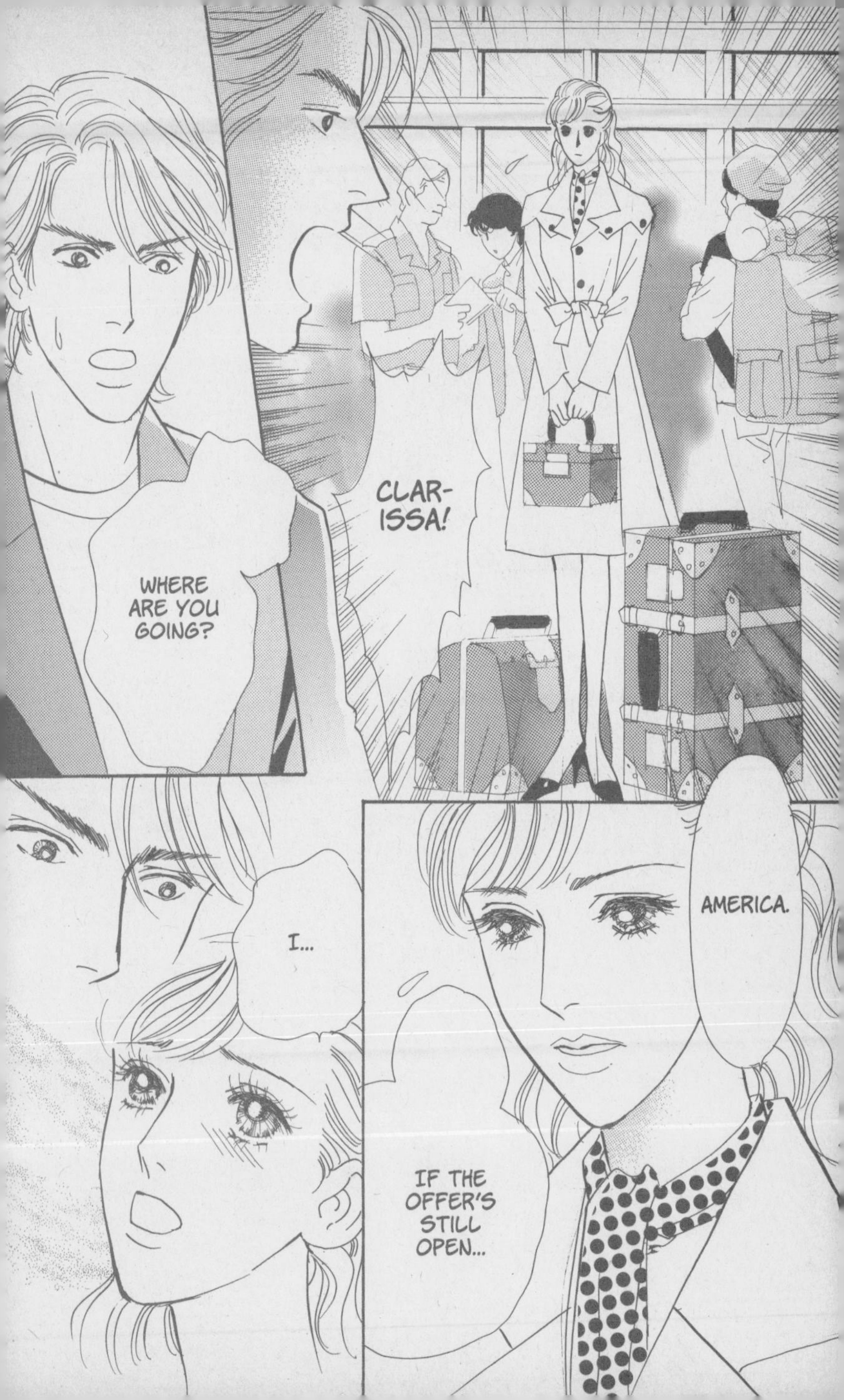
CLAR-ISSA!
WHERE ARE YOU GOING?
AMERICA.
IF THE OFFER'S STILL OPEN...
I...

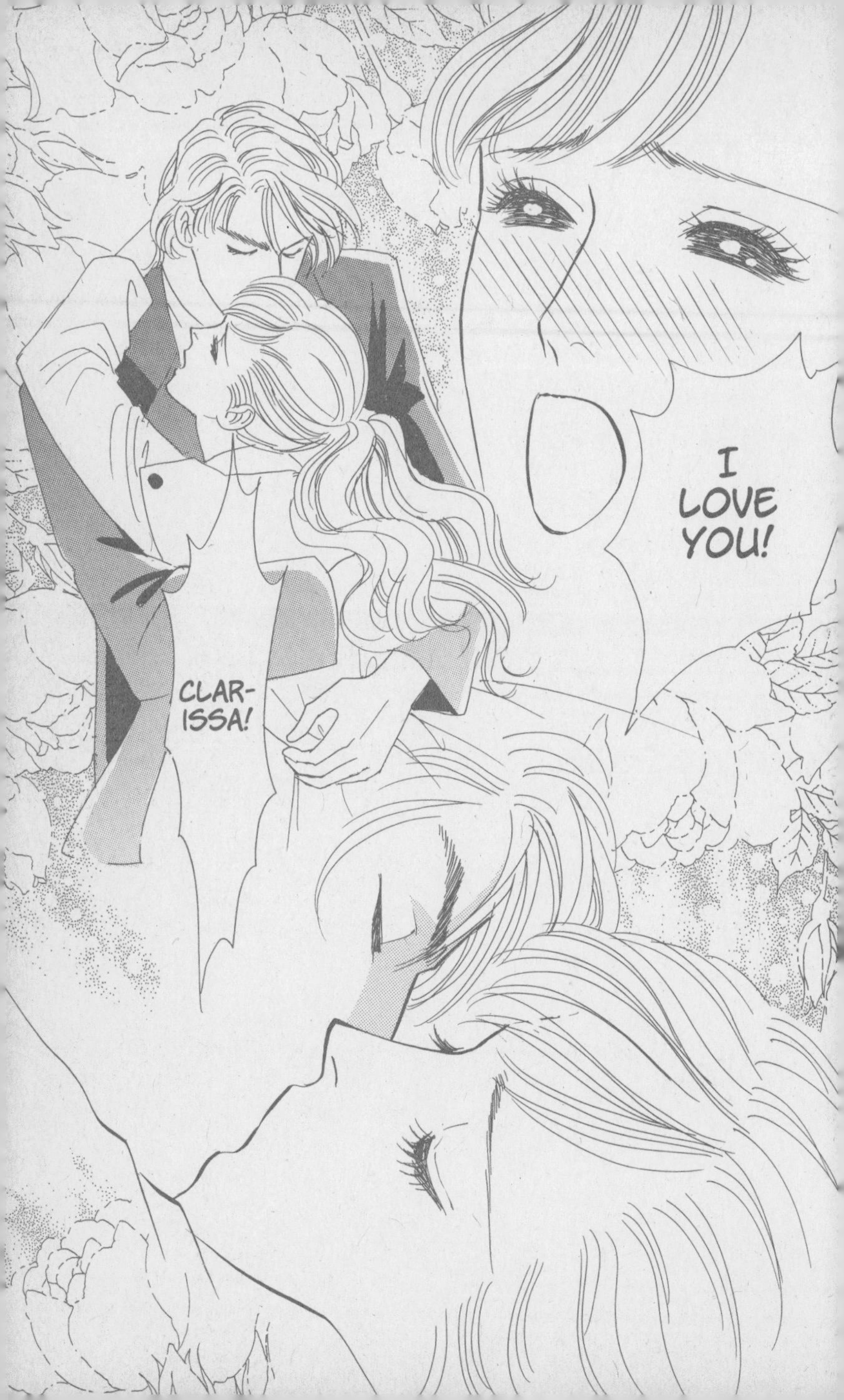
I LOVE YOU!
CLAR-ISSA!

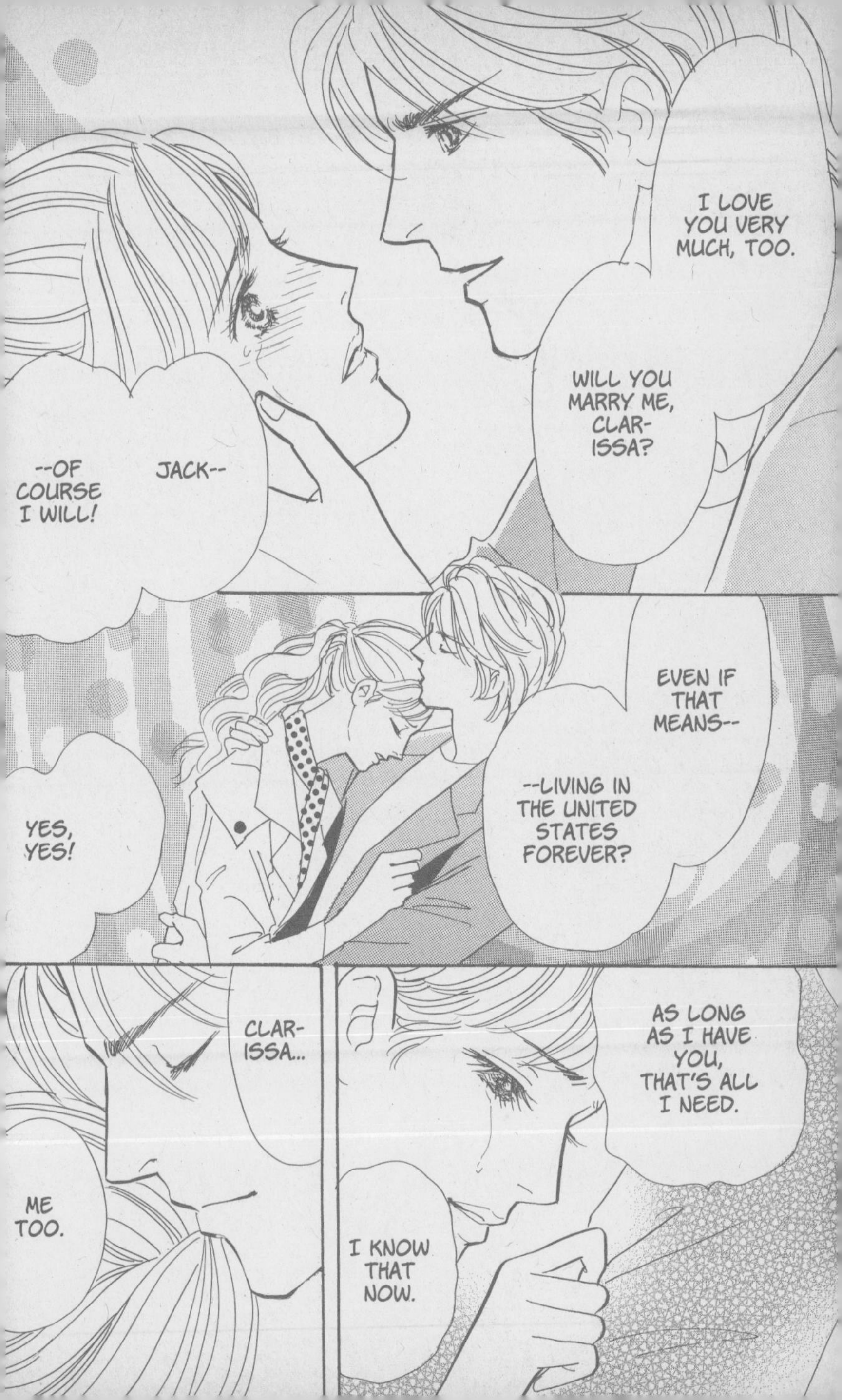
I LOVE YOU VERY MUCH, TOO.
WILL YOU MARRY ME, CLAR-ISSA?
JACK--
--OF COURSE I WILL!
EVEN IF THAT MEANS--
--LIVING IN THE UNITED STATES FOREVER?
YES, YES!
AS LONG AS I HAVE YOU, THAT'S ALL I NEED.
I KNOW THAT NOW.
CLAR-ISSA...
ME TOO.

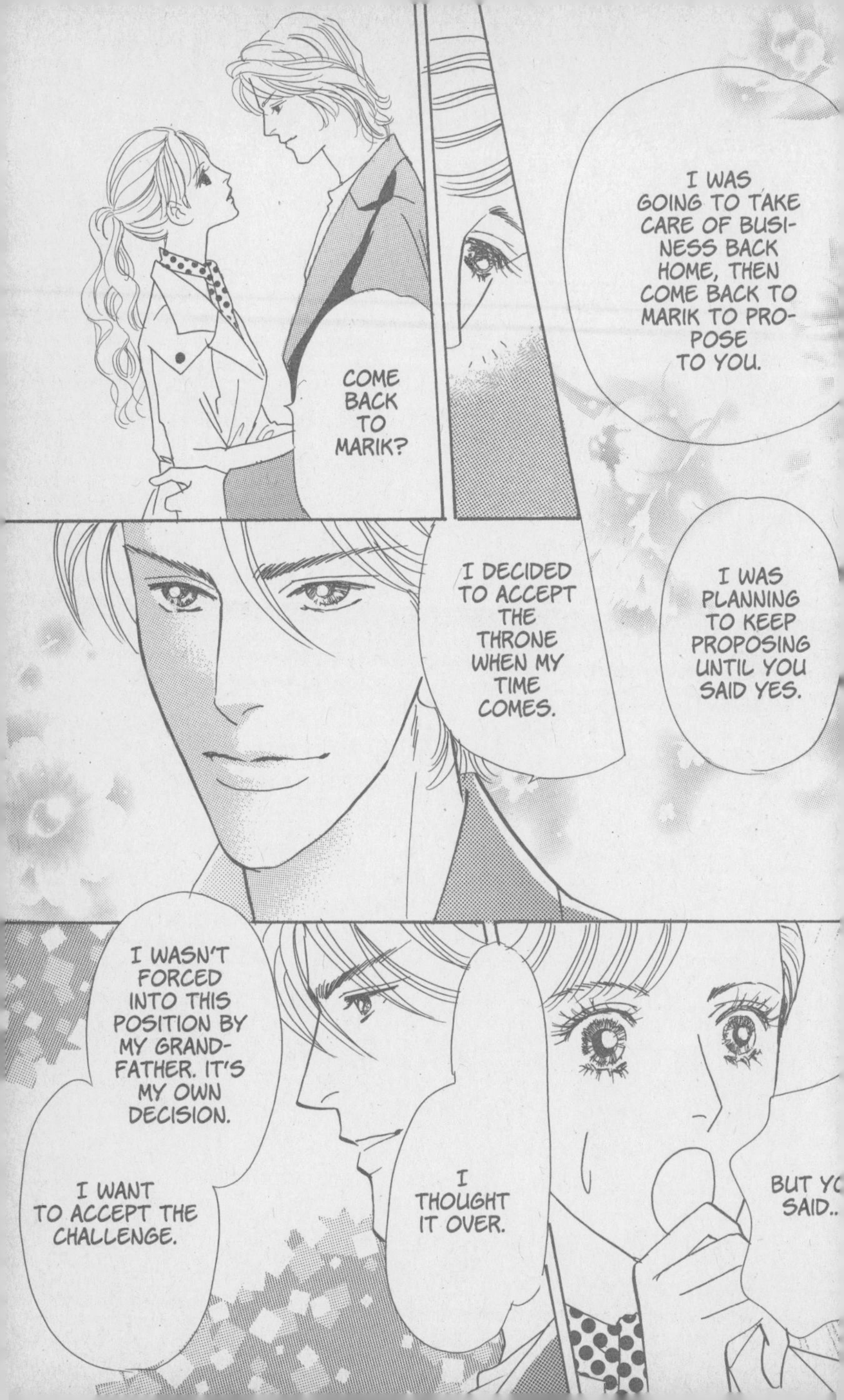
I WAS GOING TO TAKE CARE OF BUSI-NESS BACK HOME, THEN COME BACK TO MARIK TO PRO-POSE TO YOU.
COME BACK TO MARIK?
I WAS PLANNING TO KEEP PROPOSING UNTIL YOU SAID YES.
I DECIDED TO ACCEPT THE THRONE WHEN MY TIME COMES.
BUT YO SAID..
I THOUGHT IT OVER.
I WASN'T FORCED INTO THIS POSITION BY MY GRAND-FATHER. IT'S MY OWN DECISION.
I WANT TO ACCEPT THE CHALLENGE.

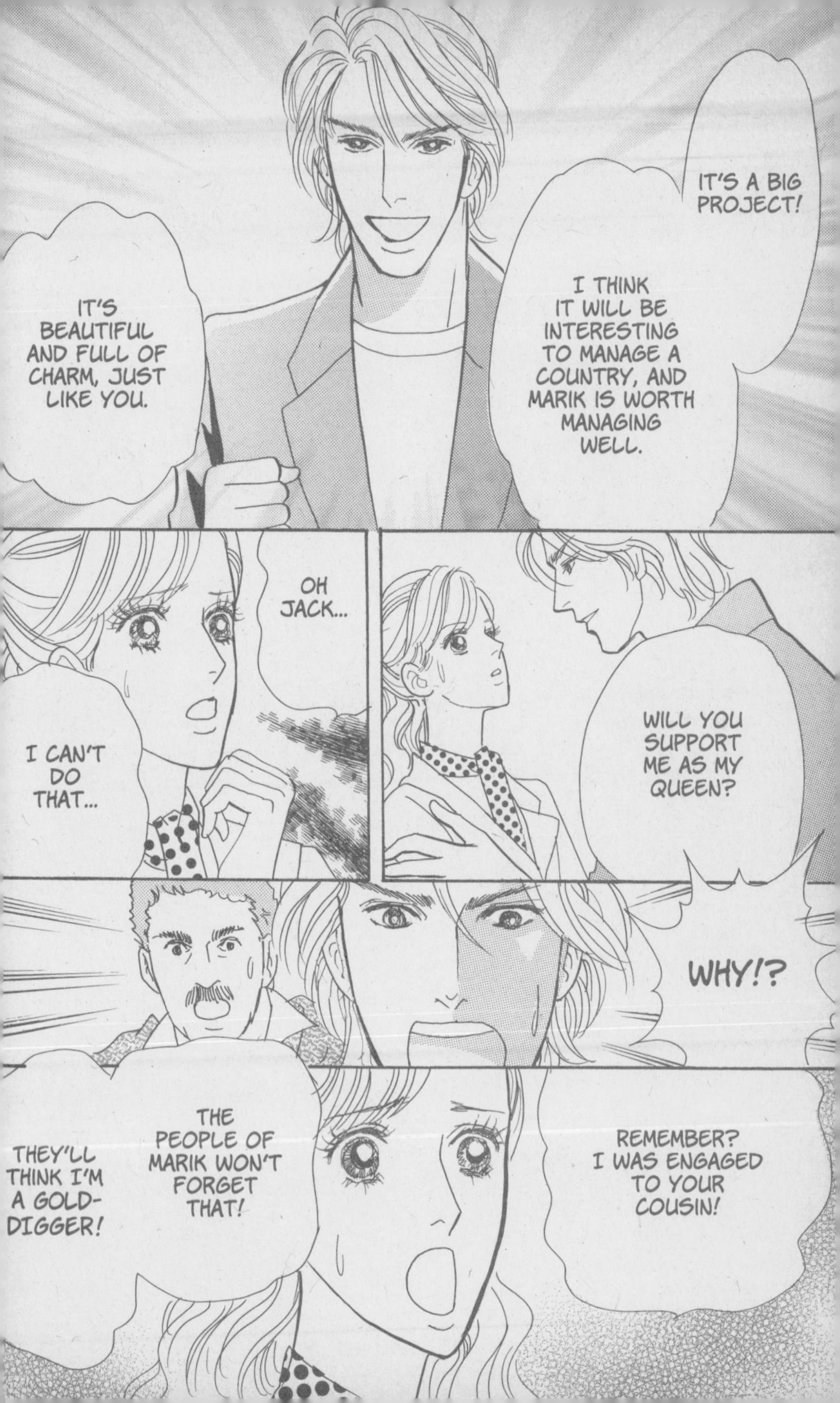
IT'S A BIG PROJECT!
I THINK IT WILL BE INTERESTING TO MANAGE A COUNTRY, AND MARIK IS WORTH MANAGING WELL.
IT'S BEAUTIFUL AND FULL OF CHARM, JUST LIKE YOU.
WILL YOU SUPPORT ME AS MY QUEEN?
OH JACK...
I CAN'T DO THAT...
WHY!?
REMEMBER? I WAS ENGAGED TO YOUR COUSIN!
THE PEOPLE OF MARIK WON'T FORGET THAT!
THEY'LL THINK I'M A GOLD-DIGGER!

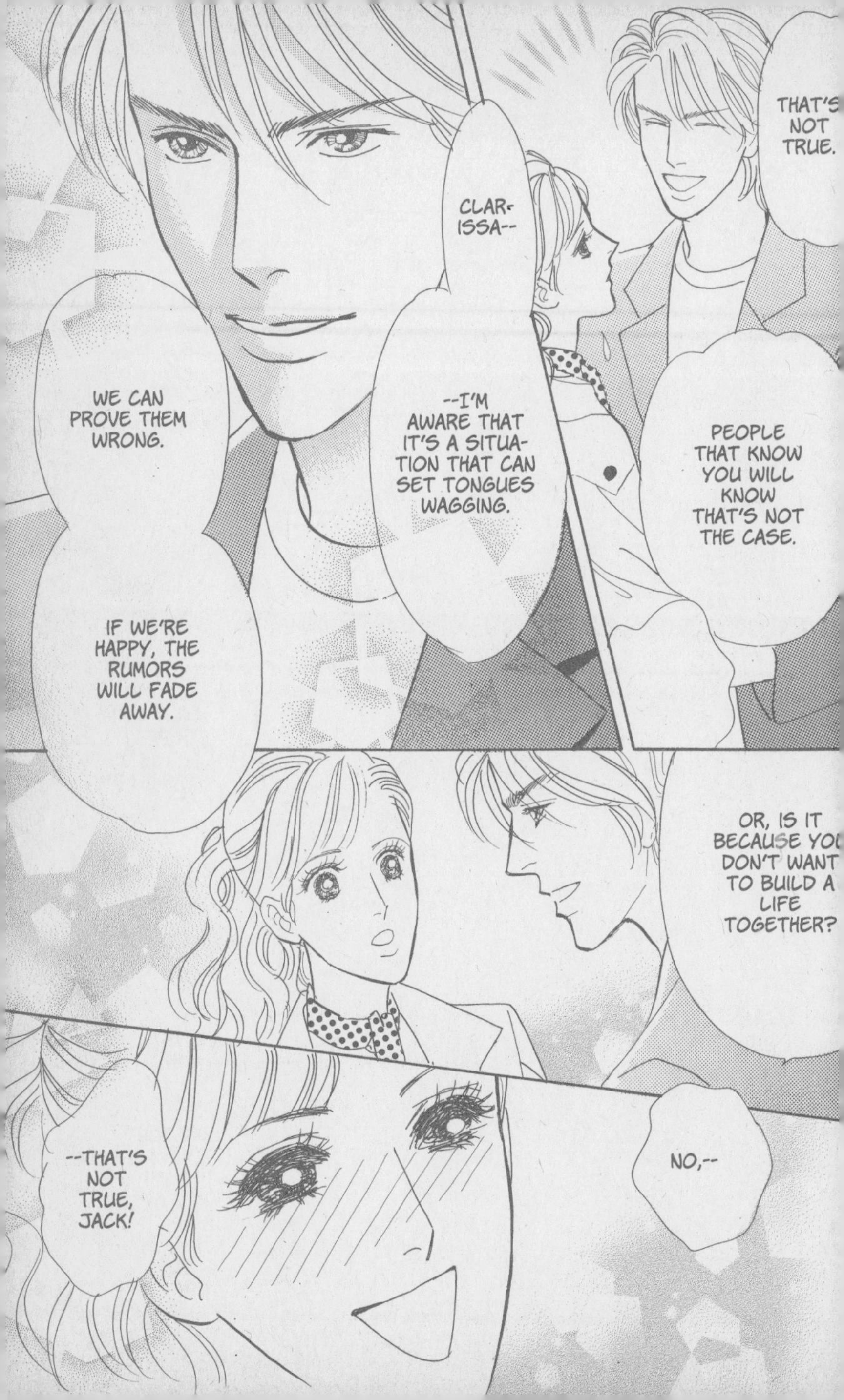
THAT'S NOT TRUE.
PEOPLE THAT KNOW YOU WILL KNOW THAT'S NOT THE CASE.
CLAR-ISSA--
--I'M AWARE THAT IT'S A SITUA-TION THAT CAN SET TONGUES WAGGING.
WE CAN PROVE THEM WRONG.
IF WE'RE HAPPY, THE RUMORS WILL FADE AWAY.
OR, IS IT BECAUSE YOU DON'T WANT TO BUILD A LIFE TOGETHER?
NO,--
--THAT'S NOT TRUE, JACK!

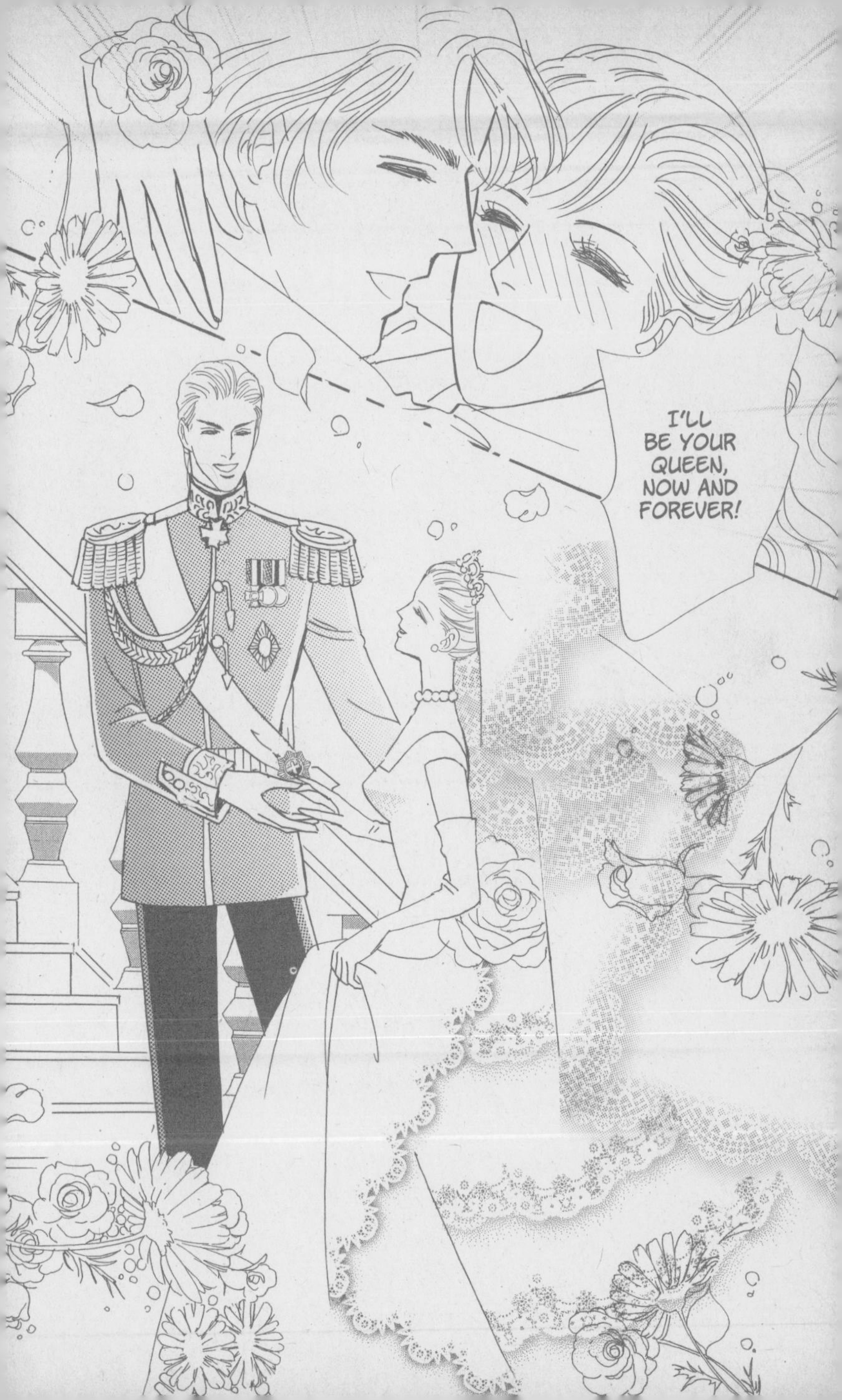
I'LL BE YOUR QUEEN, NOW AND FOREVER!

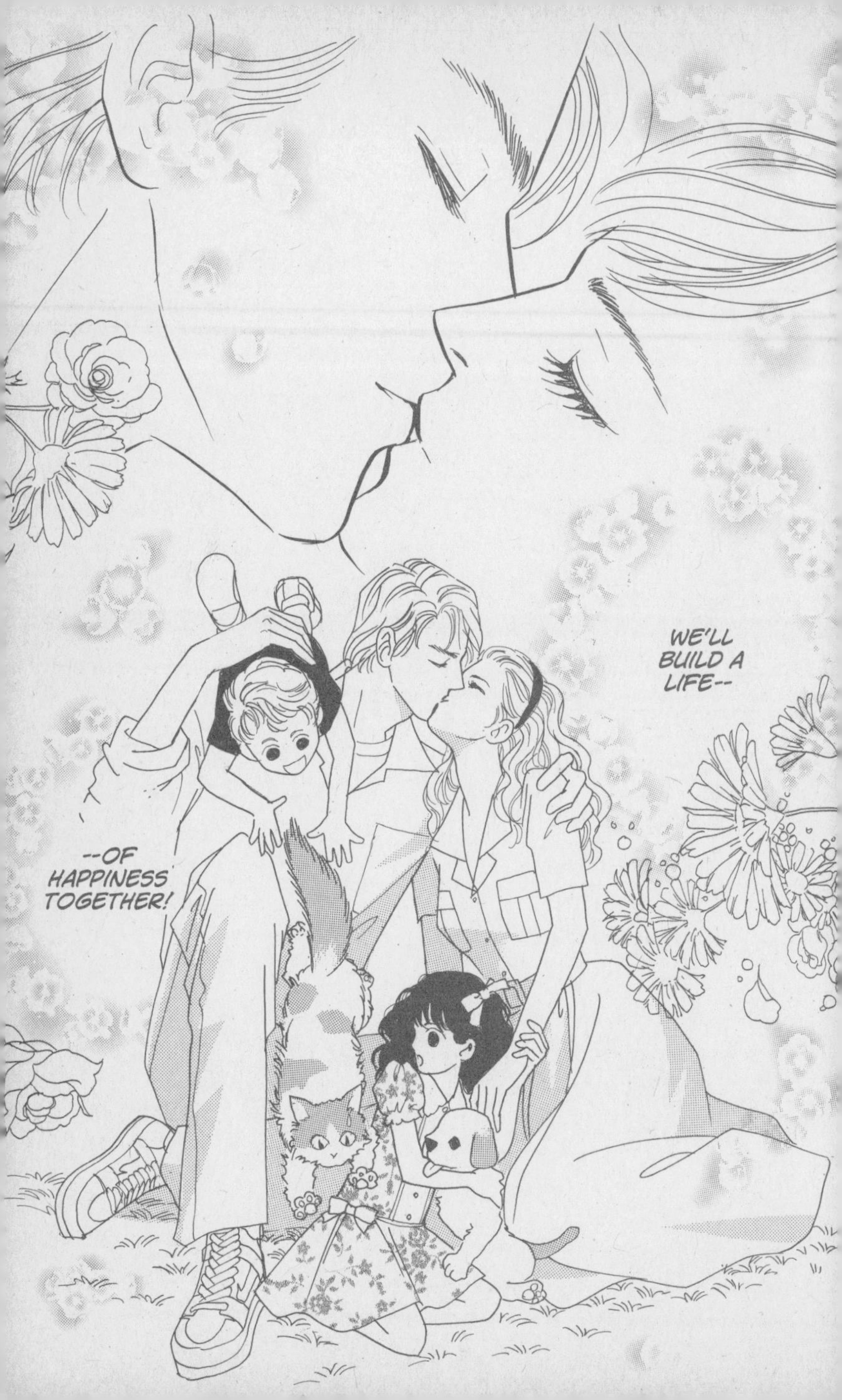
WE'LL BUILD A LIFE--
--OF HAPPINESS TOGETHER!

Now here's
a SNEAK PEEK at...

After years of living in her beautiful sister's shadow and losing countless boyfriends to her, Carrie Lockett cannot believe that hunky Shane Reynolds could really fall for her!

AVAILABLE THIS MONTH AT LEADING RETAILERS! GET IT NOW!

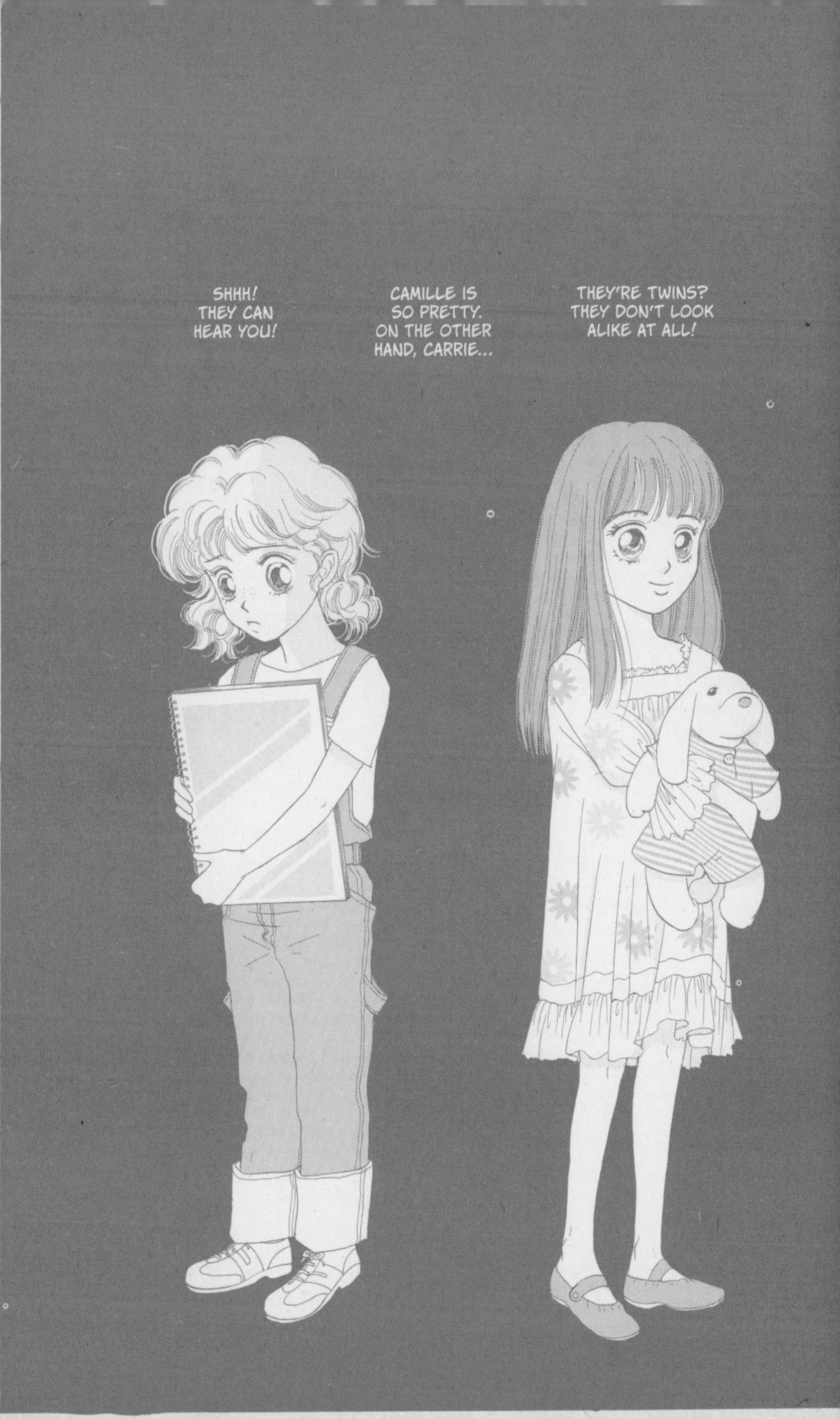
THEY'RE TWINS? THEY DON'T LOOK ALIKE AT ALL!
CAMILLE IS SO PRETTY. ON THE OTHER HAND, CARRIE...
SHHH! THEY CAN HEAR YOU!

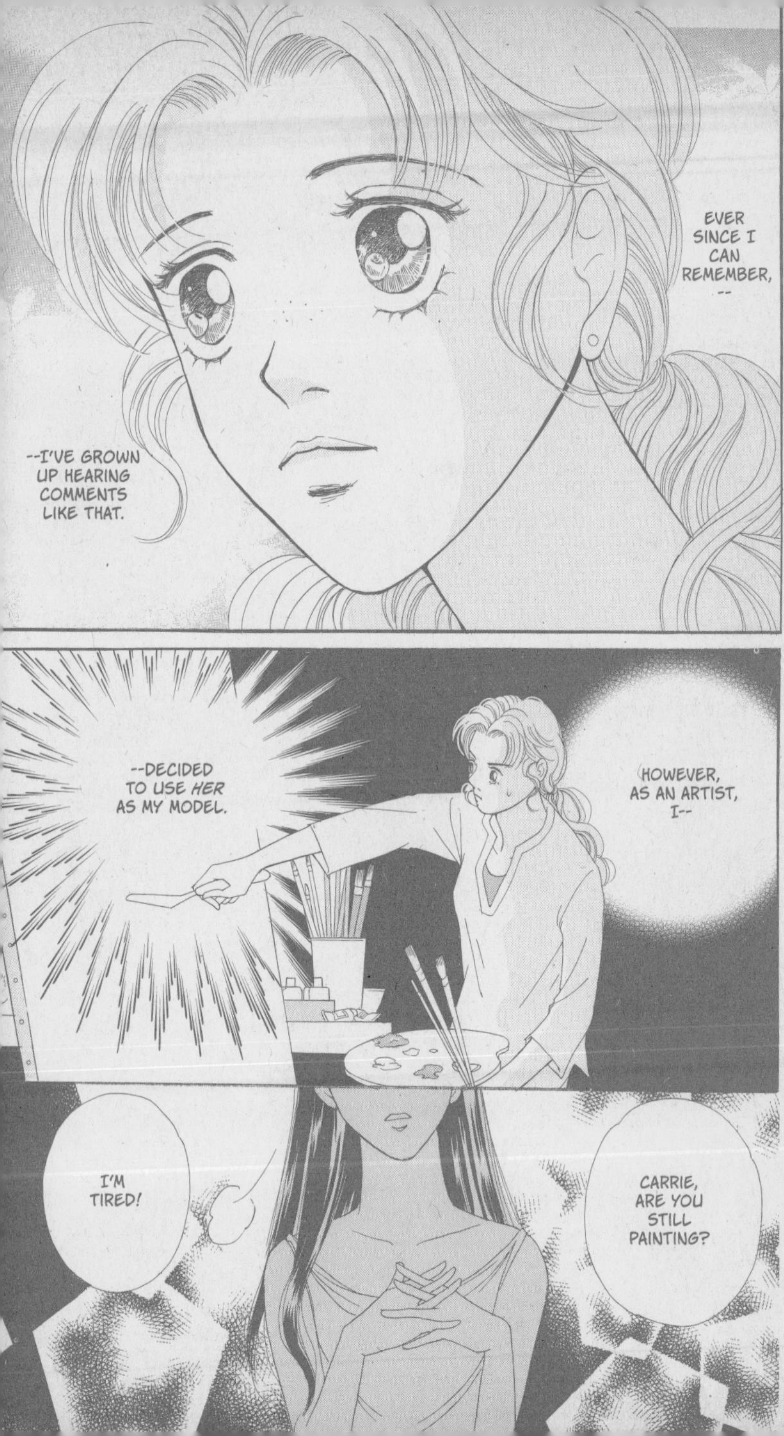
EVER SINCE I CAN REMEMBER, --
--I'VE GROWN UP HEARING COMMENTS LIKE THAT.
HOWEVER, AS AN ARTIST, I--
--DECIDED TO USE *HER* AS MY MODEL.
CARRIE, ARE YOU STILL PAINTING?
I'M TIRED!

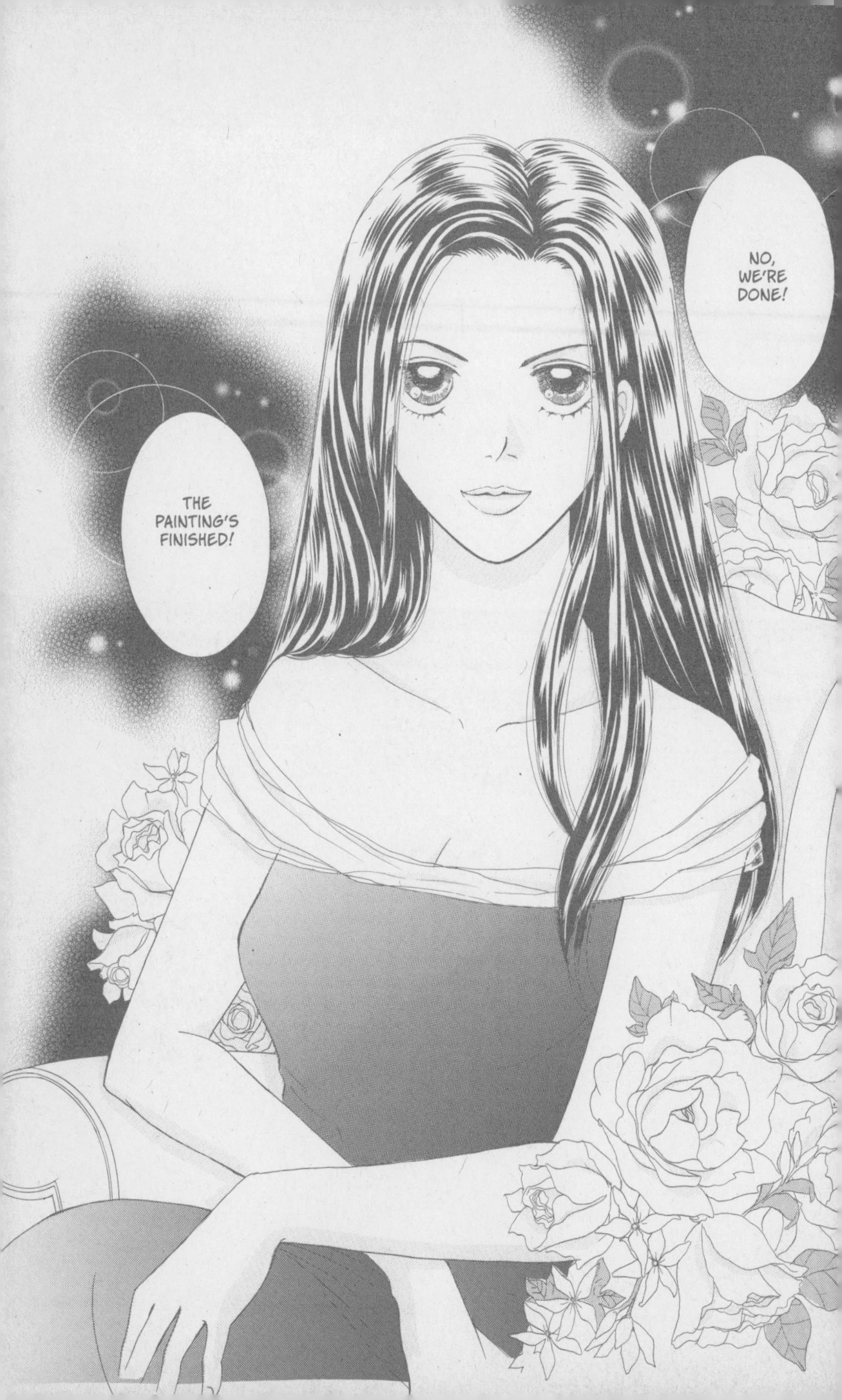
NO, WE'RE DONE!
THE PAINTING'S FINISHED!

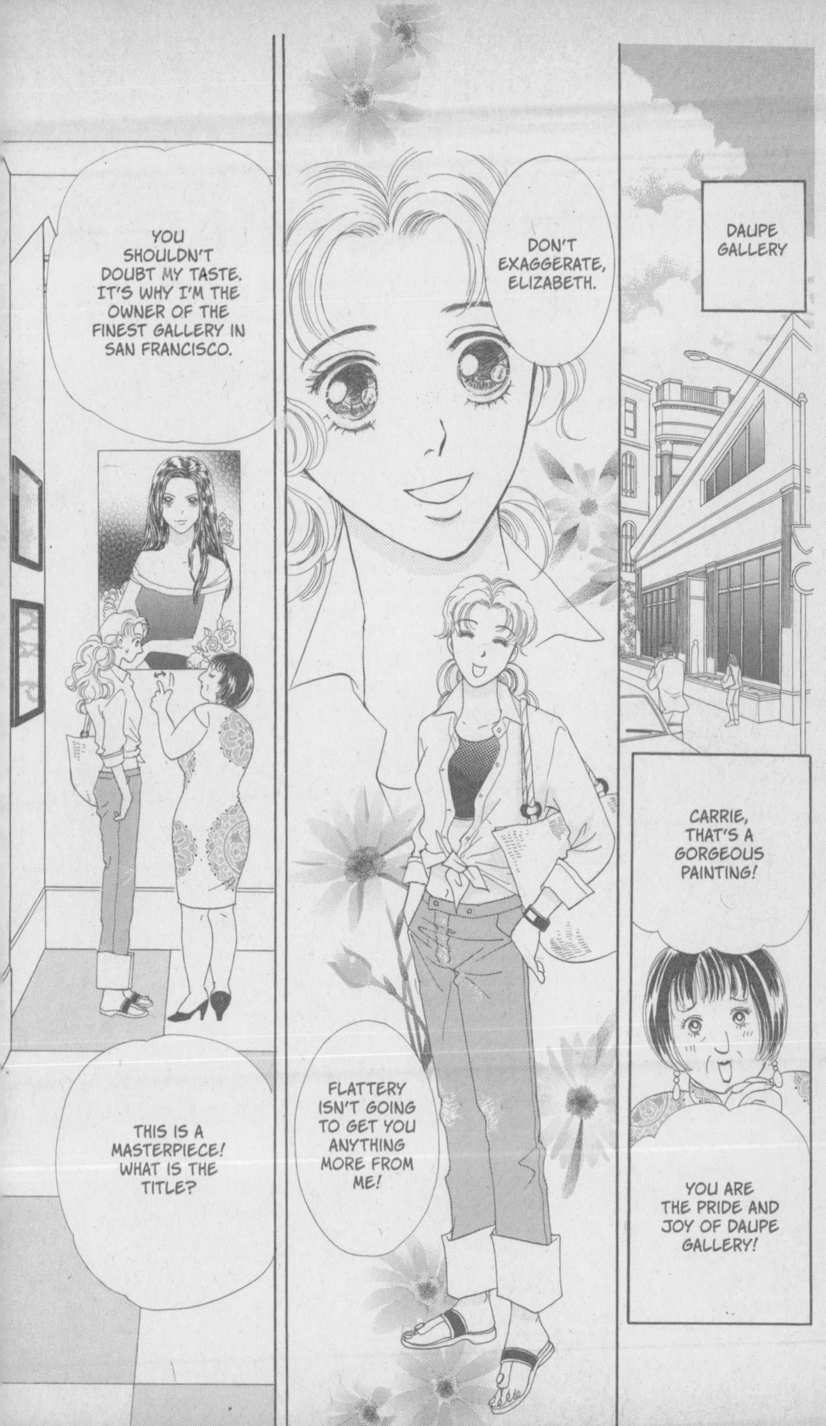
DAUPE GALLERY
CARRIE, THAT'S A GORGEOUS PAINTING!
YOU ARE THE PRIDE AND JOY OF DAUPE GALLERY!
DON'T EXAGGERATE, ELIZABETH.
FLATTERY ISN'T GOING TO GET YOU ANYTHING MORE FROM ME!
YOU SHOULDN'T DOUBT MY TASTE. IT'S WHY I'M THE OWNER OF THE FINEST GALLERY IN SAN FRANCISCO.
THIS IS A MASTERPIECE! WHAT IS THE TITLE?

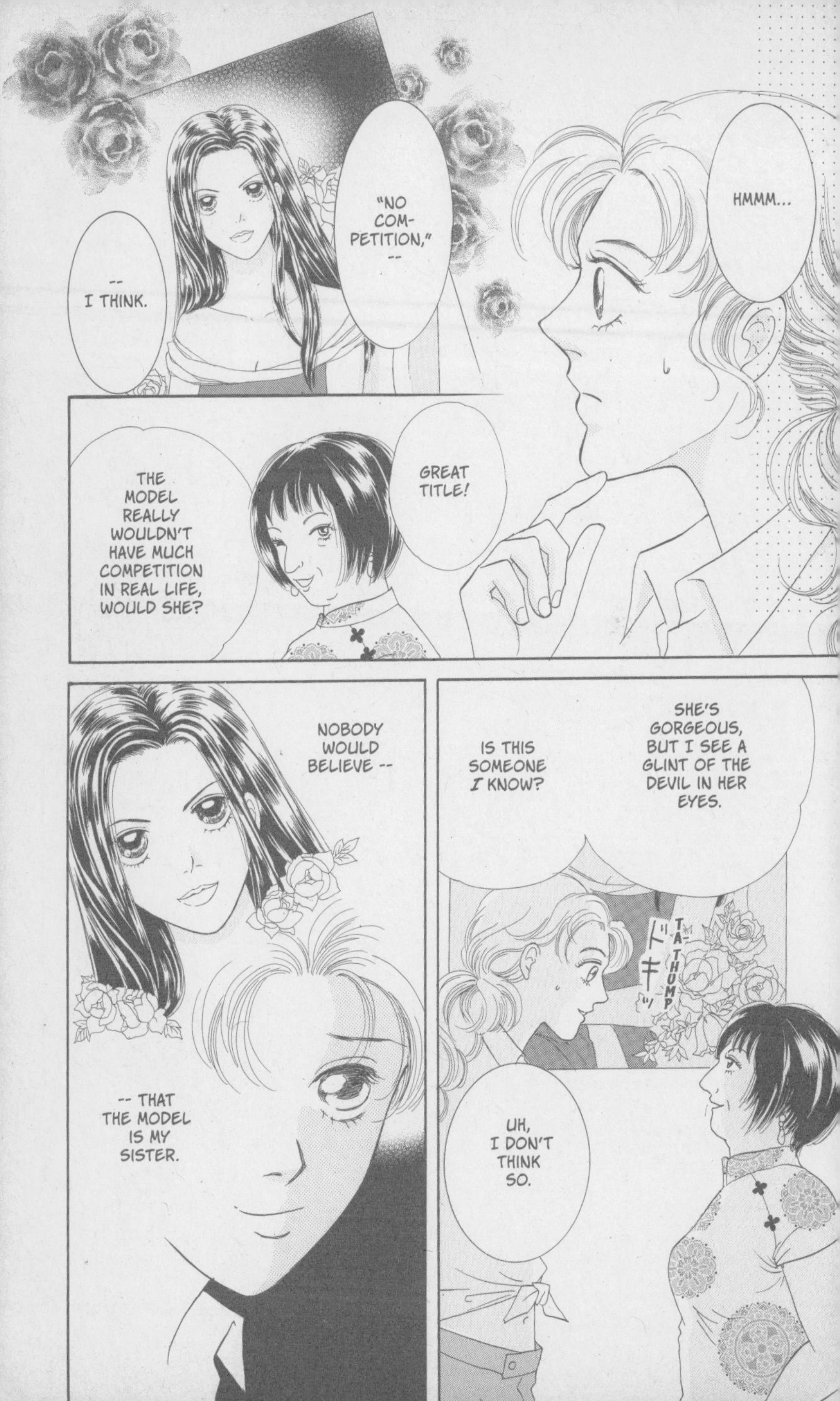
HMMM...
"NO COMPETITION," --
-- I THINK.
GREAT TITLE!
THE MODEL REALLY WOULDN'T HAVE MUCH COMPETITION IN REAL LIFE, WOULD SHE?
SHE'S GORGEOUS, BUT I SEE A GLINT OF THE DEVIL IN HER EYES.
IS THIS SOMEONE *I* KNOW?
TA-THUMP
UH, I DON'T THINK SO.
NOBODY WOULD BELIEVE --
-- THAT THE MODEL IS MY SISTER.

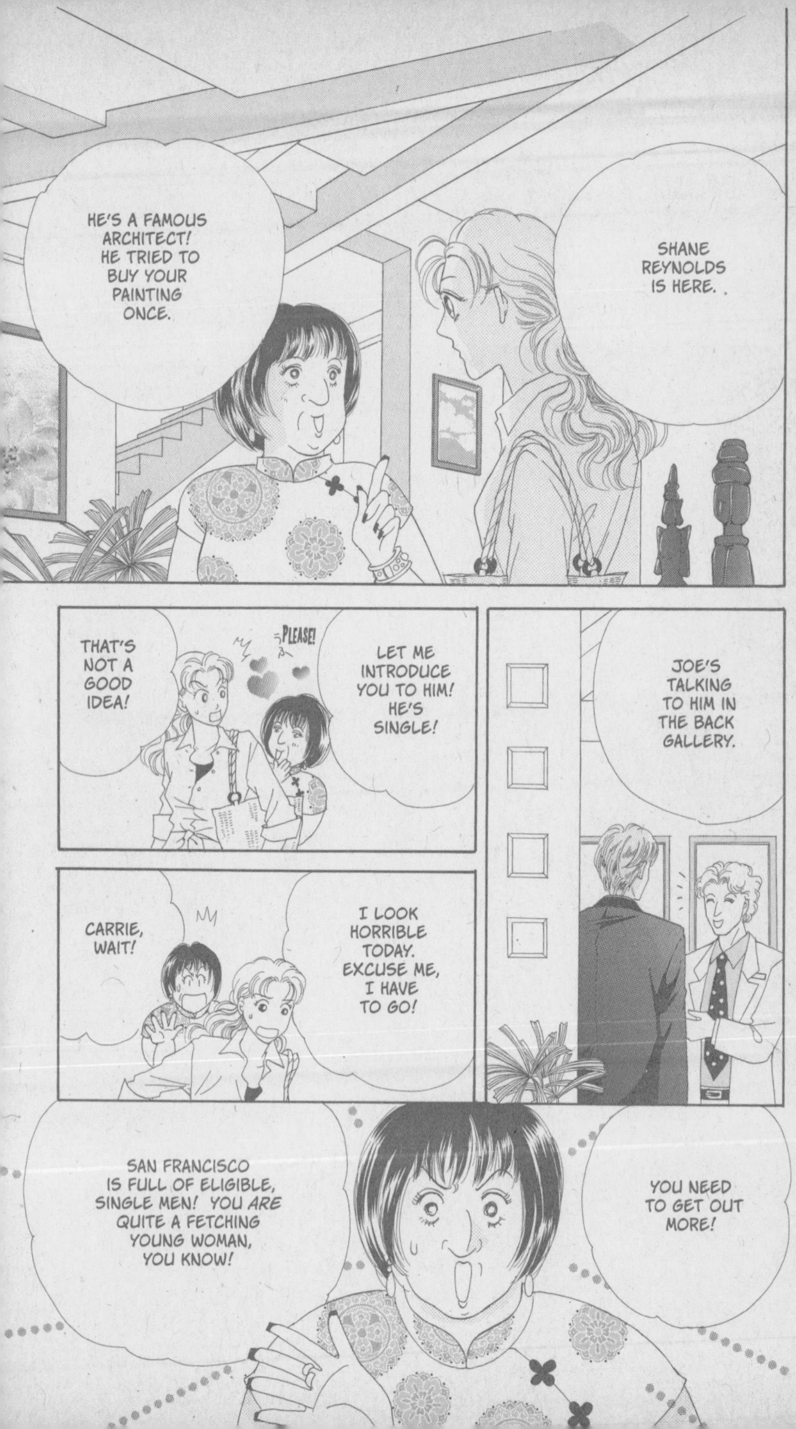
SHANE REYNOLDS IS HERE.
HE'S A FAMOUS ARCHITECT! HE TRIED TO BUY YOUR PAINTING ONCE.
JOE'S TALKING TO HIM IN THE BACK GALLERY.
LET ME INTRODUCE YOU TO HIM! HE'S SINGLE!
PLEASE!
THAT'S NOT A GOOD IDEA!
I LOOK HORRIBLE TODAY. EXCUSE ME, I HAVE TO GO!
CARRIE, WAIT!
YOU NEED TO GET OUT MORE!
SAN FRANCISCO IS FULL OF ELIGIBLE, SINGLE MEN! YOU ARE QUITE A FETCHING YOUNG WOMAN, YOU KNOW!

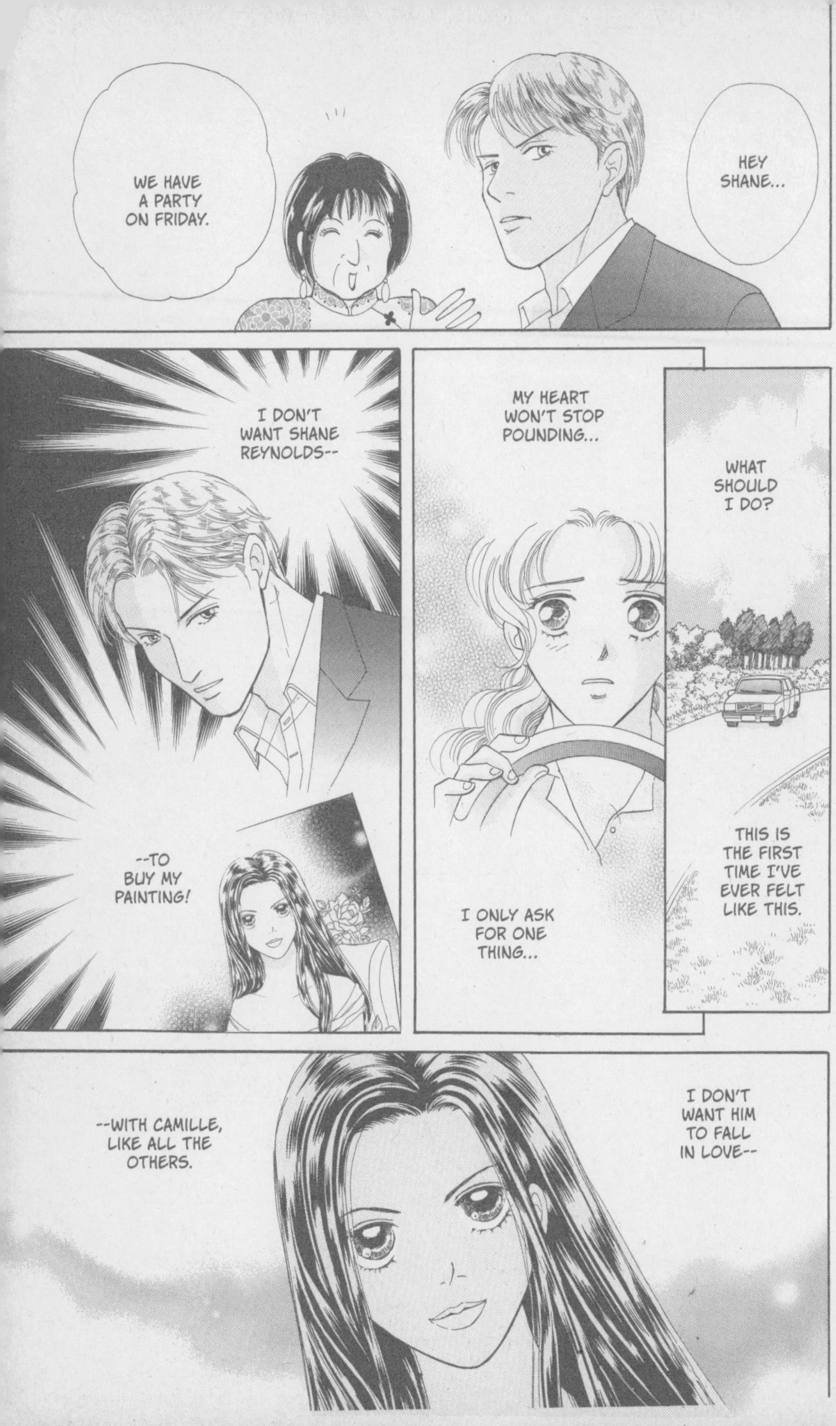
HEY SHANE...
WE HAVE A PARTY ON FRIDAY.
WHAT SHOULD I DO?
THIS IS THE FIRST TIME I'VE EVER FELT LIKE THIS.
MY HEART WON'T STOP POUNDING...
I ONLY ASK FOR ONE THING...
I DON'T WANT SHANE REYNOLDS--
--TO BUY MY PAINTING!
I DON'T WANT HIM TO FALL IN LOVE--
--WITH CAMILLE, LIKE ALL THE OTHERS.

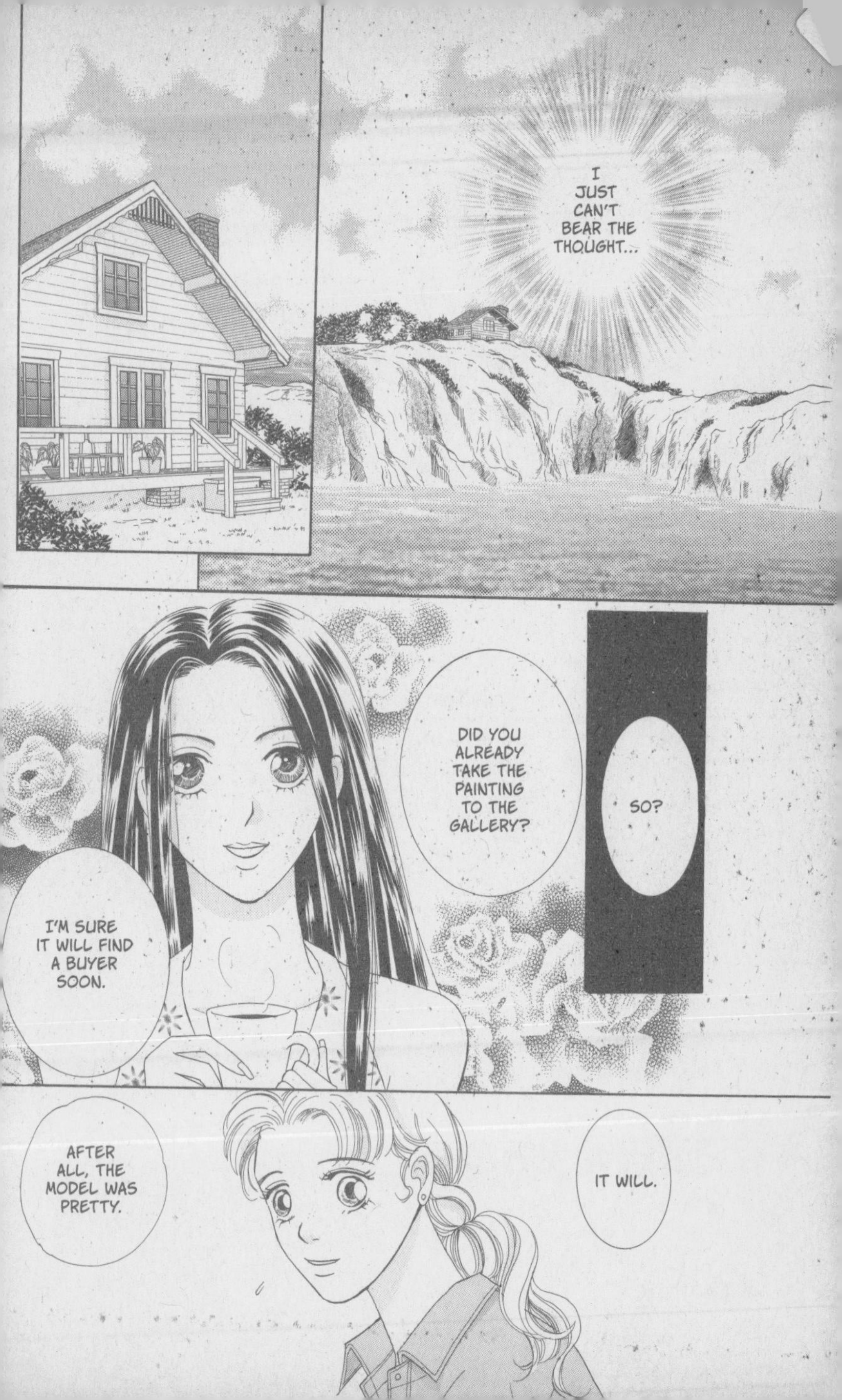
I JUST CAN'T BEAR THE THOUGHT...
SO?
DID YOU ALREADY TAKE THE PAINTING TO THE GALLERY?
I'M SURE IT WILL FIND A BUYER SOON.
IT WILL.
AFTER ALL, THE MODEL WAS PRETTY.

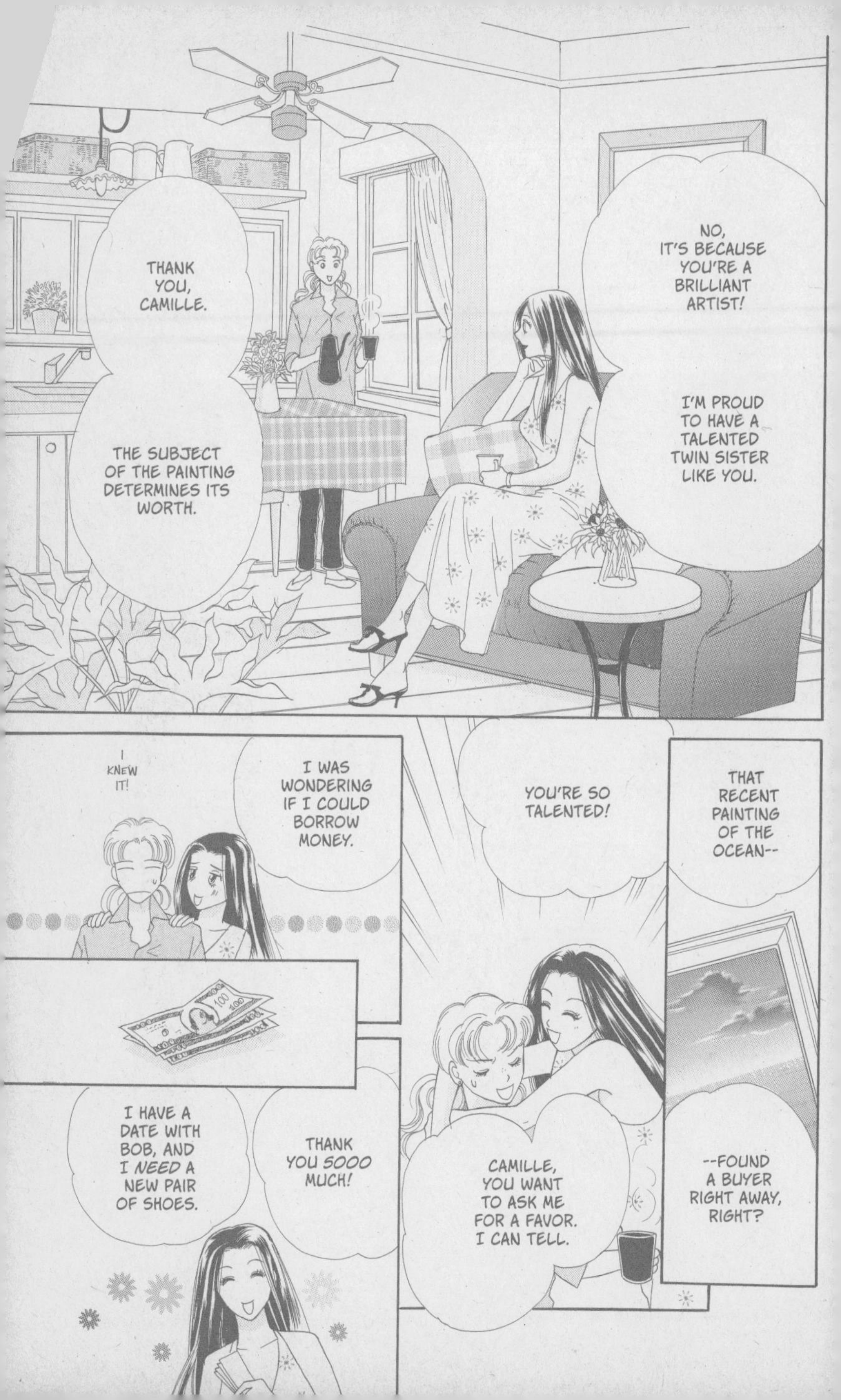

NO, IT'S BECAUSE YOU'RE A BRILLIANT ARTIST!
I'M PROUD TO HAVE A TALENTED TWIN SISTER LIKE YOU.
THANK YOU, CAMILLE.
THE SUBJECT OF THE PAINTING DETERMINES ITS WORTH.
THAT RECENT PAINTING OF THE OCEAN--
YOU'RE SO TALENTED!
--FOUND A BUYER RIGHT AWAY, RIGHT?
CAMILLE, YOU WANT TO ASK ME FOR A FAVOR. I CAN TELL.
I WAS WONDERING IF I COULD BORROW MONEY.
I KNEW IT!
THANK YOU SOOOO MUCH!
I HAVE A DATE WITH BOB, AND I *NEED* A NEW PAIR OF SHOES.

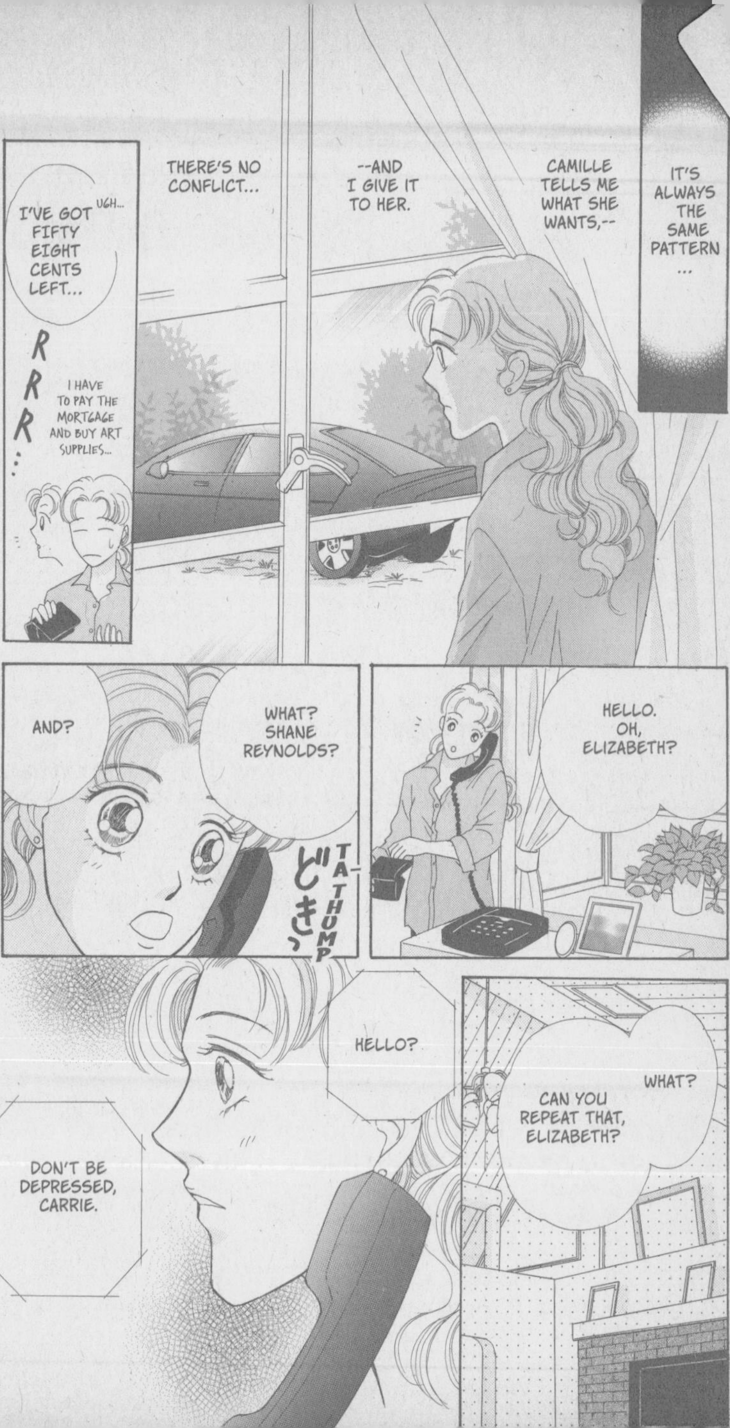
IT'S ALWAYS THE SAME PATTERN...
CAMILLE TELLS ME WHAT SHE WANTS,--
--AND I GIVE IT TO HER.
THERE'S NO CONFLICT...
UGH...
I'VE GOT FIFTY EIGHT CENTS LEFT...
I HAVE TO PAY THE MORTGAGE AND BUY ART SUPPLIES...
RRR...
HELLO. OH, ELIZABETH?
WHAT? SHANE REYNOLDS?
TA-THUMP
どきっ
AND?
WHAT?
CAN YOU REPEAT THAT, ELIZABETH?
HELLO?
DON'T BE DEPRESSED, CARRIE.

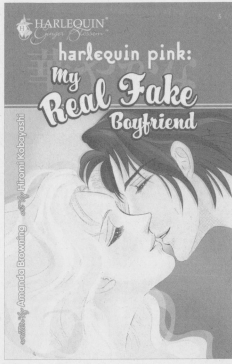

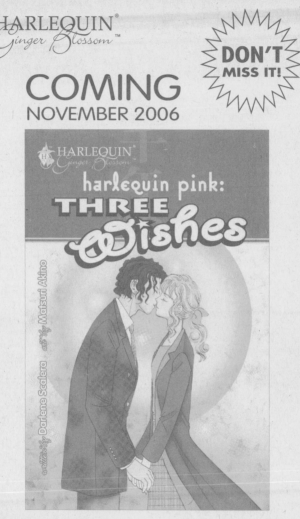

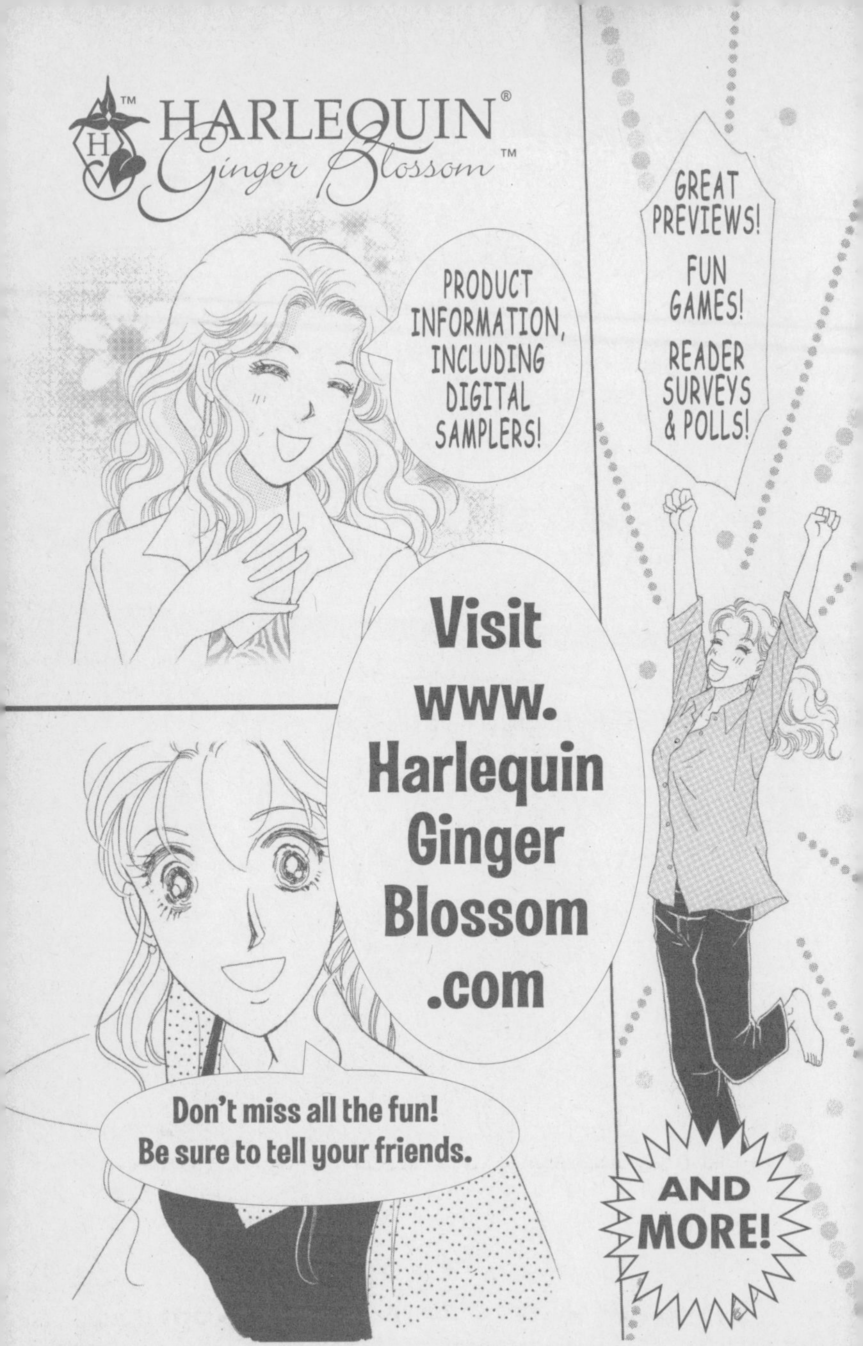
HARLEQUIN® Ginger Blossom™
GREAT PREVIEWS!
FUN GAMES!
READER SURVEYS & POLLS!
AND MORE!
PRODUCT INFORMATION, INCLUDING DIGITAL SAMPLERS!
Visit www.HarlequinGingerBlossom.com
Don't miss all the fun! Be sure to tell your friends.

STOP!

You are at the back of the book. You will need to turn the book over to find the START.

Manga books, like the Harlequin® Ginger Blossom™ book you are holding, started in Japan where books are read from right to left. To make this manga more fun, we've kept the original format. In case you haven't read a manga before, we've made the diagram below to show you how. Once you get started, you'll find it's fun and easy to read this way.

1
HMMM...
2
"NO COMPETITION." --
3
-- I THINK.
4
GREAT TITLE!
5
THE MODEL REALLY WOULDN'T HAVE MUCH COMPETITION IN REAL LIFE, WOULD SHE?
6
SHE'S GORGEOUS, BUT I SEE A GLINT OF THE DEVIL IN HER EYES.
7
IS THIS SOMEONE I KNOW?
8
UH, I DON'T THINK SO.
9
NOBODY WOULD BELIEVE --
10
-- THAT THE MODEL IS MY SISTER.

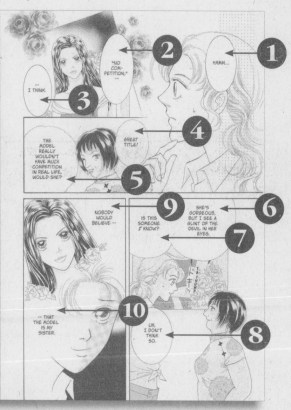